KU-303-438

TRACKERS

Also by Deon Meyer

Dead Before Dying
Dead at Daybreak
Heart of the Hunter
Devil's Peak
Blood Safari
Thirteen Hours

DEON MEYER

TRACKERS

Translated from Afrikaans
by K. L. Seegers

HODDER &
STOUGHTON

First published in Great Britain in 2011 by Hodder & Stoughton
An Hachette UK company

Originally published in Afrikaans in 2010 as *Spoor* by Human & Rousseau

1

A CIP catalogue record for this title is available from the British Library.

Hardback ISBN 978 1 444 72365 6
Trade Paperback ISBN 978 1 444 72366 3

Typeset in Plantin Light by Hewer Text UK Ltd, Edinburgh

Printed and bound by Clays Ltd, St Ives plc

Hodder & Stoughton policy is to use papers that are natural, renewable and recyclable products and made from wood grown in sustainable forests. The logging and manufacturing processes are expected to conform to the environmental regulations of the country of origin.

Hodder & Stoughton Ltd
338 Euston Road
London NW1 3BH

www.hodder.co.uk

In memory of Madeleine van Biljon (1929 – 2010)

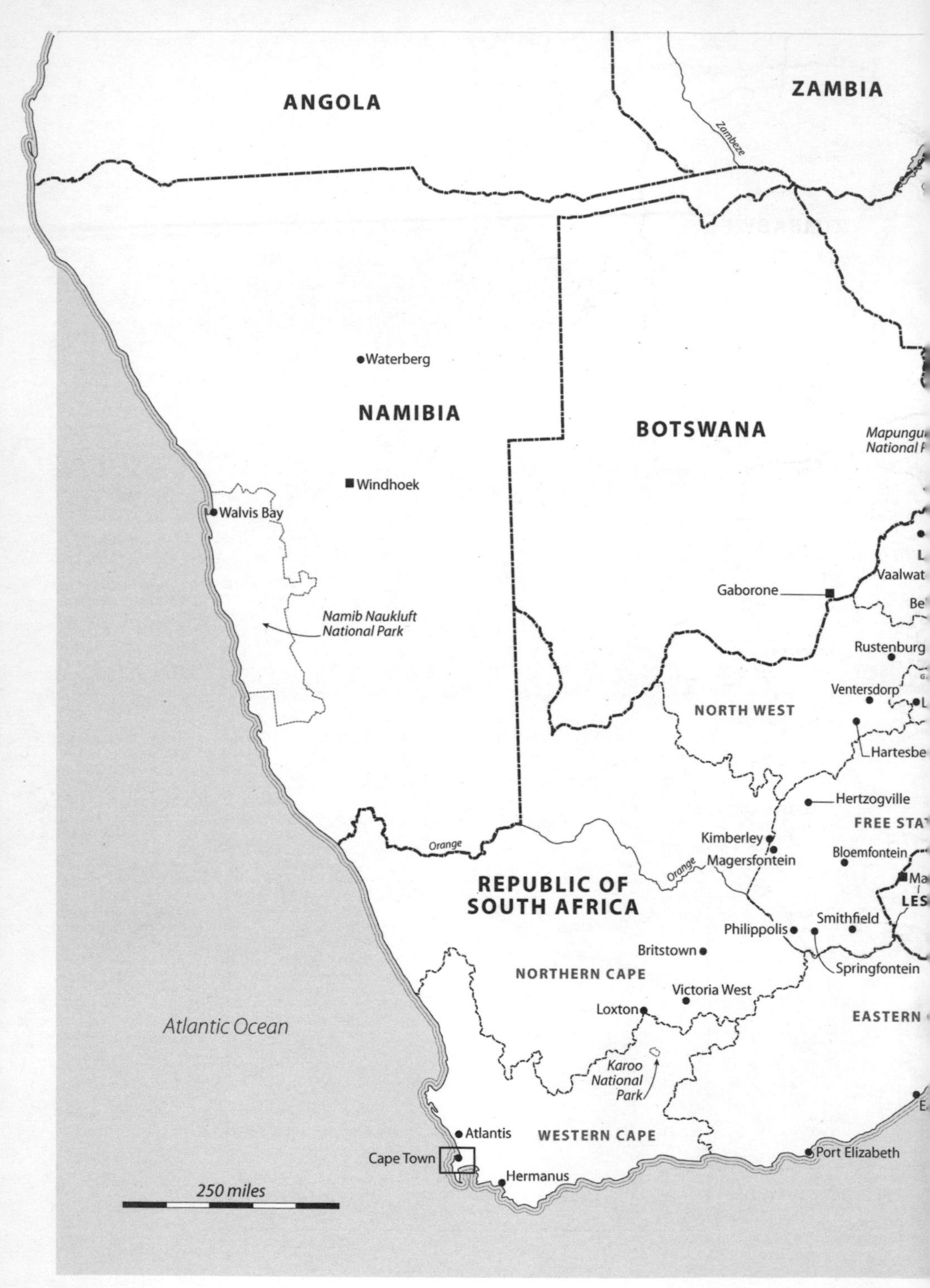
ANGOLA
ZAMBIA
Zambeze
Waterberg
NAMIBIA
BOTSWANA
Windhoek
Walvis Bay
Namib Naukluft National Park
Gaborone
Rustenburg
Ventersdorp
NORTH WEST
Hertzogville
Kimberley
Magersfontein
Bloemfontein
Orange
REPUBLIC OF SOUTH AFRICA
Philippolis
Smithfield
Springfontein
Britstown
NORTHERN CAPE
Victoria West
Loxton
Atlantic Ocean
Karoo National Park
Atlantis
WESTERN CAPE
Cape Town
Hermanus
Port Elizabeth
250 miles

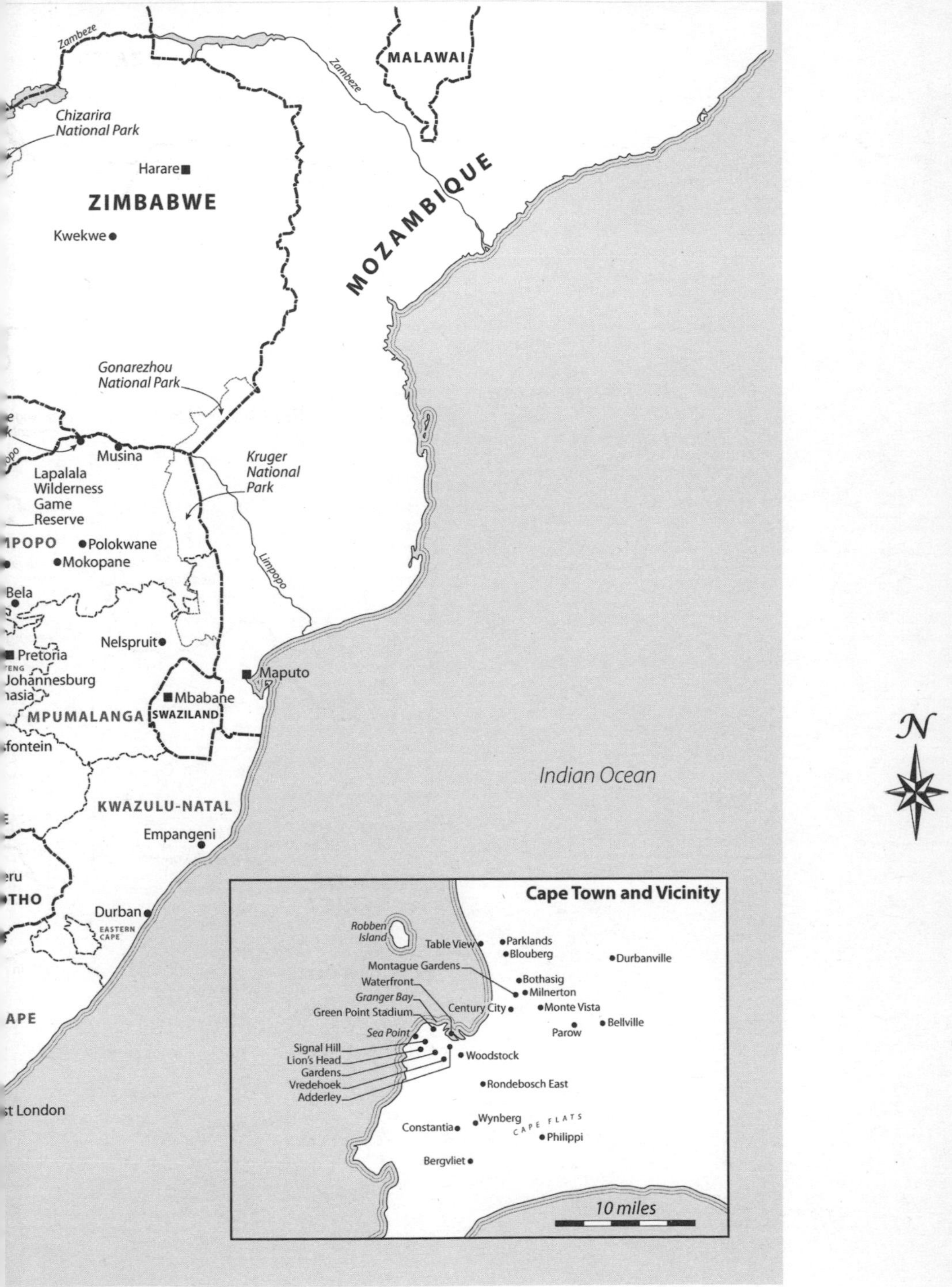

Zambeze
MALAWAI
Zambeze
Chizarira
National Park
Harare
ZIMBABWE
MOZAMBIQUE
Kwekwe
Gonarezhou
National Park
Musina
Kruger
National
Park
Lapalala
Wilderness
Game
Reserve
IPOPO
Polokwane
Mokopane
Limpopo
Bela
Nelspruit
Pretoria
Johannesburg
Maputo
Mbabane
MPUMALANGA
SWAZILAND
fontein
Indian Ocean
KWAZULU-NATAL
Empangeni
THO
Durban
EASTERN
CAPE
APE
st London

Cape Town and Vicinity

Robben
Island
Table View
Parklands
Blouberg
Durbanville
Montague Gardens
Bothasig
Milnerton
Waterfront
Granger Bay
Century City
Monte Vista
Green Point Stadium
Bellville
Parow
Sea Point
Signal Hill
Lion's Head
Gardens
Vredehoek
Adderley
Woodstock
Rondebosch East
Wynberg
Constantia
CAPE FLATS
Philippi
Bergvliet
10 miles

BOOK I: MILLA
(Conspiracy)

July to September 2009

. . . some days leave no tracks.
They pass as though they never existed, immediately forgotten in the haze of my routine. Other days' tracks are visible for a week or so, until the winds of memory cover them in the pale sand of new experiences.

Photostatic record: Diary of Milla Strachan,
27 September 2009

The US Department of the Treasury today moved to designate two South African individuals, Farhad Ahmed Dockrat and Junaid Ismail Dockrat, and a related entity for financing and facilitating al-Qaeda, pursuant to Executive Order 13224. This action freezes any assets the designees have under US jurisdiction and prohibits transactions between US persons and the designees.

Press release, US Department of Treasury, 26 January 2007
(Verbatim)

I

31 July 2009. Friday.

Ismail Mohammed runs down the steep slope of Heiliger Lane. The coat-tails of his white jalabiya robe with its trendy open mandarin collar flick up high with every stride. His arms wave wildly, in mortal fear, and for balance. The crocheted kufi falls off his head onto the cobbles at the crossroad, as he fixes his eyes on the relative safety of the city below.

Behind him the door of the one-storey building next to the Bo-Kaap's Schotschekloof mosque bursts open for the second time. Six men, also in traditional Islamic garb, rush out onto the street all looking immediately, instinctively downhill. One has a pistol in his hand. Hurriedly, he takes aim at the figure of Ismail Mohammed, already sixty metres away, and fires off two wild shots, before the last, older man knocks his arm up, bellowing: 'No! Go. Catch him.'

The three younger men set off after Ismail. The grizzled heads stand watching, eyes anxious at the lead they have to make up.

'You should have let him shoot, Sheikh,' says one.

'No, Shaheed. He was eavesdropping.'

'Exactly. And then he ran. That says enough.'

'It doesn't tell us who he's working for.'

'Him? Ismail? You surely don't think . . .'

'You never can tell.'

'No. He's too . . . clumsy. For the locals maybe. NIA.'

'I hope you are right.' The Sheikh watches the pursuers sprinting across the Chiappini Street crossing, weighing up the implications. A siren sounds up from below in Buitengracht.

'Come,' he says calmly. 'Everything has changed.'

He walks ahead, quickly, to the Volvo.

From the belly of the city another siren begins to wail.

She knew the significance of the footsteps, five o' clock on a Friday afternoon, so hurried and purposeful. She felt the paralysis of prescience, the burden. With great effort she raised up her defences against it.

Barend came in, a whirlwind of shampoo and too much deodorant. She didn't look at him, knowing he would be freshly turned out for the evening, his hair a new, dubious experiment. He sat down at the breakfast counter. 'So, how are you, Ma? What's cooking?' So jovial.

'Dinner,' said Milla, resigned.

'Oh. I'm not eating here.'

She knew that. Christo probably wouldn't either.

'Ma, you're not going to use your car tonight, are you.' In the tone of voice he had perfected, that astonishing blend of pre-emptive hurt and barely disguised blame.

'Where do you want to go?'

'To the city. Jacques is coming. He's got his licence.'

'Where in the city?'

'We haven't decided yet.'

'Barend, I have to know.' As gently as possible.

'*Ja*, Ma, I'll let you know later.' The first hint of annoyance breaking through.

'What time will you be home?'

'Ma, I'm eighteen. Pa was in the army when he was this old.'

'The army had rules.'

He sighed, irritated. 'OK, OK. So . . . we'll leave at twelve.'

'That's what you said last week. You only got in after two. You're in Matric, the final exams . . .'

'*Jissis*, Ma, why do you always go on about it? You don't want me to have any fun.'

'I want you to have fun. But within certain limits.'

He gave a derisory laugh, the one that meant he was a fool to put up with this. She forced herself not to react.

'I told you. We will leave at twelve.'

'Please don't drink.'

'Why do you worry about that?'

She wanted to say, I worry about the half-bottle of brandy I found in your cupboard, clumsily hidden behind your underpants, along with the pack of Marlboro's. 'It's my job to worry. You're my child.'

Silence, as if he accepted that. Relief washed over her. That was all he wanted. They had got this far without a skirmish. Then she heard the tap-tap of his jerking leg against the counter, saw how he lifted the lid off the sugar bowl and rolled it between his fingers. She knew he wasn't finished. He wanted money too.

'Ma, I can't let Jacques and them pay for me.'

He was so clever with his choice of words, with the sequence of favours asked, with his strategy and onslaught of accusation and blame. He spun his web with adult skill, she thought. He set his snares, and she stepped into them so easily in her eternal urge to avoid conflict. The humiliation could be heard in her voice. 'Is your pocket money finished?'

'Do you want me to be a parasite?'

The *you* and the aggression were the trigger, she saw the familiar battlefield ahead. Just give him the money, give him the purse and say take it. Everything. Just what he wanted.

She took a deep breath. 'I want you to manage on your pocket money. Eight hundred rand a month is . . .'

'Do you know how much Jacques gets?'

'It doesn't matter, Barend. If you want more you should . . .'

'Do you want me to lose all my friends? You don't want me to be fucking happy.' The swearword shook her, along with the clatter of the sugar bowl lid that he threw against the cupboard.

'Barend,' she said, shocked. He had exploded before, thrown his hands in the air, stormed out. He had used *Jesus* and *God*, he had mumbled the unmentionable, cowardly and just out of hearing. But not this time. Now his whole torso leaned over the counter, now his face was filled with disgust for her. 'You make me sick,' he said.

She cringed, experiencing the attack physically, so that she had to reach for support, stretch out her hand to the cupboard. She did not want to cry, but the tears came anyway, there in front of the stove with a wooden spoon in her hand and the odour of hot olive oil in her nose. She repeated her son's name, softly and soothingly.

With venom, with disgust, with the intent to cause bodily harm, with his father's voice and inflection and abuse of power, Barend slumped back on the stool and said, 'Jesus, you are pathetic. No wonder your husband fucks around.'

* * *

The member of the oversight committee, glass in hand, beckoned to Janina Mentz. She stood still and waited for him to navigate a path to her. 'Madam Director,' he greeted her. Then he leaned over conspiratorially, his mouth close to her ear: 'Did you hear?'

They were in the middle of a banqueting hall, surrounded by four hundred people. She shook her head, expecting the usual, the latest minor scandal of the week.

'The Minister is considering an amalgamation.'

'Which Minister?'

'*Your* Minister.'

'An amalgamation?'

'A superstructure. You, the National Intelligence Agency, the Secret Service, everyone. A consolidation, a union. Complete integration.'

She looked at him, at his full-moon face, shiny with the glow of alcohol, looking for signs of humour. She found none.

'Come on,' she said. How sober was he?

'That's the rumour. The word on the street.'

'How many glasses have you had?' Light-hearted.

'Janina, I am deadly serious.'

She knew he was informed, had always been reliable. She hid her concern out of habit. 'And does the rumour say when?'

'The announcement will come. Three, four weeks. But that's not the big news.'

'Oh.'

'The President wants Mo. As chief.'

She frowned at him.

'Mo Shaik,' he said.

She laughed, short and sceptical.

'Word on the street,' he said solemnly.

She smiled, wanted to ask about his source, but her cellphone rang inside her small black handbag. 'Excuse me,' she said, unclipping the handbag and taking out her phone. It was the Advocate, she saw.

'Tau?' she answered.

'Ismail Mohammed is in from the cold.'

Milla lay on her side in the dark, knees tucked up to her chest. Beyond weeping she made reluctant, painful discoveries. It seemed as though the grey glass, the tinted window between her and reality, was shattered, so that she saw her existence brilliantly exposed, and she could not look away.

When she could no longer stand it, she took refuge in questions, in retracing. How had she come to this? How had she lost consciousness, sunk so deep? When? How had this lie, this fantasy life, overtaken her? Every answer brought greater fear of the inevitable, the absolute knowledge of what she must do. And for that she did not have the courage. Not even the words. She, who had always had words, in her head, in her diary, for everything.

She lay like that until Christo came home, at half past twelve that night. He didn't try to be quiet. His unsteady footsteps were muffled on the carpet, he switched on the bathroom light, then came back and sat down heavily on the bed.

She lay motionless, with her back to him, her eyes closed, listening to him pulling off his shoes, tossing them aside, getting up to go to the bathroom, urinating, farting.

Shower, please. Wash your sins away.

Running water in the basin. Then the light went off, he came to bed, climbed in. Grunted, tired, content.

Just before he pulled the blankets over himself, she smelled him. The alcohol. Cigarette smoke, sweat. And the other, more primitive smell.

That's when she found the courage.

2

1 August 2009. Saturday.

Transcription: *Debriefing of Ismail Mohammed by A.J.M. Williams. Safe House, Gardens, Cape Town*
Date and Time: *1 August 2009, 17.52*

M: I want to enter the program, Williams. Like in now.
W: I understand, Ismail, but . . .
M: No 'buts'. Those fuckers wanted to shoot me. They won't stop at trying.

W: Relax, Ismail. Once we've debriefed you . . .

M: How long is that going to take?

W: The sooner you calm down and talk to me, the sooner it will be done.

M: And then you'll put me in witness protection?

W: You know we look after our people. Let's start at the beginning, Ismail. How did it happen?

M: I heard them talking . . .

W: No, how did they find out you were working for us?

M: I don't know.

W: You must have some sort of idea.

M: I . . . Maybe they followed me . . .

W: To the drop?

M: Maybe. I was careful. With everything. For the drop I did three switch backs, got on other trains twice, but . . .

W: But what?

M: No, I . . . you know . . . After the drop . . . I thought . . . I dunno . . . Maybe I saw someone. But afterwards . . .

W: One of them?

M: Could be. Maybe.

W: Why did they suspect you?

M: What do you mean?

W: Let's suppose they followed you. They must have had a reason. You must have done something. Asked too many questions? Wrong place at the wrong time?

M: It's your fault. If I could have reported via the cellphone, I would have been there still.

W: Cellphones are dangerous, Ismail, you know that.

M: They can't tap every phone in the Cape.

W: No, Ismail, only those that matter. What have the cellphones to do with this?

M: Every time I had to report, I had to leave. For the drop.

W: What happened after the drop?

M: My last drop was Monday, Tuesday, the shit started, there was a discreet silence between them. At first I thought it was some other tension. Maybe over the shipment. Then yesterday I saw, no, it was only when I was around that they got like that. Subtle, you know, very subtle, they tried to hide it, but it was there. Then I began to worry, I thought, better keep my ears open, something's wrong. And then this morning, Suleiman sat in council and said I must wait in the kitchen with Rayan . . .

W: Suleiman Dolly. The 'Sheikh'.

M: Yes.

W: And Rayan . . . ?

M: Baboo Rayan. A dogsbody, a driver. Just like me. We worked together. Anyway, Rayan never said a word to me, which is really strange. And then they called Rayan in too, for the very first time, I mean, he's a dogsbody like me, we don't get called in. So I thought, let me listen at the door, because this means trouble. So I went down the passage and stood there and heard the Sheikh . . . Suleiman . . . when he said, 'We can't take any risks, the stakes are too high.'

W: The stakes are too high.

M: That's right. Then the Sheikh said to Rayan: 'Tell the council how Ismail disappears'.

W: Go on.

M: There's no going on. That's when they caught me.

W: How?

M: The Imam caught me at the door. He was supposed to be inside. They were all supposed to be inside.

W: So you ran.

M: I ran, yes, and the fuckers shot at me, I'm telling you, these people are ruthless. Intense.

W: OK. Let's go back to Monday. At the drop you talked about 'lots of sudden activity' . . .

M: The last two weeks, yes. Something's brewing.

W: Why do you say that?

M: The Committee used to meet once a week, for months. Now suddenly, it's three, four times. What does that tell you?

W: But you don't know why.

M: Must be the shipment.

W: Tell me again about the phone call. Suleiman and Macki.

M: Last Friday. Macki phoned the Sheikh. The Sheikh stood up and went into the passage so that I couldn't hear everything.

W: How did you know it was Macki?

M: Because the Sheikh said, 'Hello, Sayyid'.

W: Sayyid Khalid bin Alawi Macki?

M: That's him. The Sheikh asked Macki as he was walking away, 'Any news on the shipment?' And then he said, 'September', like he was confirming it.

W: Is that all?

M: That's all I heard of their conversation. Then the Sheikh came back and told the others, 'Bad news'.

W: Bad news. Do you know what that means?

M: How would I know? It could be because the shipment is small. Or the timing is wrong. It could be anything.

W: And then?

M: Then they left, the Sheikh and the two Supreme Committee members. They went off to the basement. Then you must know, it's top secret.

W: Would you say the shipment is coming in September? Is that the conclusion you came to?

M: Best guess.

W: Is that a 'yes'?

M: That is what I think.

W: And the shipment. Have you any idea what it is?

M: You know, if it is Macki, it's diamonds.

W: What does the Committee want with diamonds, Ismail?

M: Only the Supreme Committee knows that.

W: And no one else talked about it?

M: Of course they talked about it, on the lower levels. But that is dicey intel, you know that.

W: Where there's smoke . . . What did the lower levels say?

M: They said it was weapons. For local action.

W: What do you mean?

M: That was the rumour. They wanted to bring in weapons. For an attack, here. For the first time. But I don't believe that.

W: A Muslim attack? In South Africa?

M: *Ja*. Here. Cape Town. The fairest Cape.

3

2 August 2009. Sunday.

On the sixth floor of the Wale Street Chambers, in the director's office of the PIA, the Presidential Intelligence Agency, Janina Mentz studied the transcript with focused attention. When she had finished, she took off her glasses and placed them on the desk. She raised her hands to rub her eyes.

She hadn't slept well, the news of the previous evening gnawed at her, the amalgamation rumour. Strange enough to be true. Or partially true.

And what would become of her?

She was seen as an Mbeki appointment. The former president had created the PIA. Although Mentz had not picked sides in the leadership struggle, although she and her people did excellent work, the stigma clung. On top of that she was new, only three months as director, no proven record with which to negotiate for a new position. And she was white.

How much of the rumour was true? Mo Shaik as head of the superstructure? Mo, brother of Shabir, the convicted, corrupt Shabir, former friend of the new president.

Anything was possible.

So many years of service. So much struggling and striving, so much hard work to get here. Only to lose it all?

No.

Janina Mentz lowered her hands and put on her glasses.

She reached for the Ismail Mohammed interview again. What she, what the PIA needed to survive, was an Exceptional Alarm. A Big Threat, a Sensitive Issue. And here it was, sent by the gods. Her responsibility was to exploit it.

She turned to her computer and searched for the historical reports in the database.

Report: *South African Muslim Extremism revisited*
Date: *14 February 2007*
Compiled by: *Velma du Plessis and Donald MacFarland*

1. Qibla in a new guise

Qibla was established in 1980 by radical Imam Achmed Cassiem to promote the establishment of an Islamic state in South Africa, using the Iranian revolution as its model. During the 1980s, Qibla sent members to Libya for military training, and in the 1990s, operatives trained in Pakistan and fought alongside Hezbollah in South Lebanon. After 9/11, it also recruited fighters to send to Afghanistan.

Because of the clampdown on related organisation People Against Gangsterism and Drugs (PAGAD) between 1998 and 2000, and the arrest of over one hundred Qibla supporters for violent offenses, including murder, Qibla all but disappeared.

In its place, a new, and far more secretive organisation was created. It is called The Supreme Committee.

3 August 2009. Monday.

Milla Strachan pulled the key out of the lock, pushed the front door open, but did not immediately enter. She stood a while, her body motionless, her dark eyes unfocused for a moment. Beyond the open door the rooms of the apartment were empty. No curtains, no furniture, just a worn wall-to-wall carpet of washed-out beige.

Still she hesitated at the door, as though some great force held her back, as though she were waiting for something.

Then in one swift movement she bent down, picked up the large travel cases on either side of her and stepped through the door.

She put the luggage down in the bedroom, conscious of the depressing emptiness. When she had been here on Saturday, the former tenant's furniture had filled it still, stacks of cardboard boxes for the hasty trip to Germany, called back on short notice to an aid organisation's head office. 'I am so grateful that someone saw the advertisement, this is such a crisis. You won't be sorry, look at the view,' the woman had said and pointed at the window. It looked out on Davenport Street in Vredehoek – and a thin slice of the city and the sea, framed by the blocks of flats opposite.

Milla had said she wanted the flat, she would sign the lease agreement.

'Where are you from?' the woman asked.

'Another world,' Milla answered quietly.

* * *

The three of them sat around the round table in Mentz's office, each noticeably different. The director had a strong face, despite the large, wide mouth, lipstick free. The severe steel-rimmed spectacles, hair tied back, conservative outfit, loose, grey and white, as if she wanted to hide her femininity. Faint, old traces of acne down her jaw disguised with foundation, slender fingers without rings, nails unpainted. Her expression was mostly inscrutable.

Advocate Tau Masilo, Deputy Director: Operational and Strategy. Forty-three, flat-bellied, colourful braces, matching tie, just a touch of flamboyance. The facial features strong, with gravitas, intense eyes, hair short and neat. Masilo's staff referred to him as 'Nobody' – from the phrase 'nobody's perfect'. Because in their eyes, Tau Masilo, phlegmatic and accomplished, was perfect. He was SeSotho, but he spoke five other South African languages effortlessly. Mentz had handpicked him.

And then, Rajkumar, Deputy Director: Information Systems. The Indian with his long black hair down to his tailbone. Mentz had inherited him.

Rajkumar's saving grace was his phenomenal intellect and his insight into electronics and digital communication, because he was fat to an extreme degree, over-sensitive, and socially inept. He sat with his forearms on the table, pudgy fingers intertwined, staring intently at his hands as if he were totally captivated by them.

Mentz got up slowly. 'Any other evidence?'

Rajkumar, ever ready and keen: 'The Supreme Committee's email traffic – there is a definite escalation. I think Ismail is right, they're cooking up something. But I have my doubts about the target . . .'

'Tau?'

'What bothers me are the reports from Zim. Macki is no longer a player – he and Mugabe can't stand each other.'

'Possibly not. Perhaps directly from Oman, perhaps from another source. Angola is a possibility.'

'And the fact that they are planning something in the Cape?' Mentz asked.

'I agree with Raj. Firstly: local terror would make their partners very unhappy. Hamas and Hezbollah are very grateful for our government's sympathy and support. Secondly: how do they benefit? What is the purpose? I can't see anything logical they can achieve through that. Thirdly: what would the motive be? Now?'

'Afghanistan,' said the Advocate. 'That's the new flashpoint. The mujahideen need more weapons and supplies, but how can they obtain them? Pakistan is working closely with the USA , blocking all the holes. NATO is keeping an eagle eye on traffic out of the Middle East. Thanks to the pirates, Somalia is no longer an option.'

'Price of opium is down too,' said Rajkumar. 'Taliban cash flow is not what it used to be.'

'So where do you send your supplies from?' asked Masilo and answered his own question: 'From here.'

'How?'

'I don't know. By ship?'

'Why not?' asked Rajkumar. 'Afghanistan has no coastline, but Iran has.'

'Then why not ship the arms from Indonesia. Lots of angry Muslims there.'

'Good point. Perhaps because that is what the US will be thinking too. They have a big naval presence . . .'

They looked towards Mentz. She nodded, pushed the papers into a neat pile in front of her. 'And yet, according to Ismail they are talking about a local attack . . .'

'On the lower levels.'

'You know how information filters down from the top, Raj.' She looked at Masilo. 'How easy is it going to be for us to replace Ismail Mohammed?'

'Not easy. Ismail's escape . . . it made them jittery. They don't meet in Schotschekloof any more, we still have to ascertain where their new hide-out is. If there is one.'

'That's a priority, Tau. Track them down. I want Ismail replaced.'

'That will take time.'

'You have less than a month.'

He shook his head. 'Ma'am, they weren't a priority for three or four years. It's a closed circle, Ismail was inside already.'

'There must be someone inside that we can . . . reach.'

'I'll prepare a list.'

'Raj, why can't you read their email?'

'They're using an encryption we've never seen before. It might be a variant of 128 bit, but the bottom line is, we can't crack it. We will continue to sniff every package. Sooner or later, they will make a mistake and forget to encrypt. It happens. Eventually.'

She thought for a while before she spoke: 'There is something brewing here, gentlemen. All the signs are there. The email traffic, the sudden action against Ismail, the rumours, the so-called shipment, after two years of quiet. I want to know what it is. If you need more people or resources, talk to me. Tau, double our surveillance. I want someone in Ismail's place, I want weekly progress reports, I want focus and commitment. Thank you for coming in early.'

She went to fetch two more suitcases, then the sleeping bag and the air mattress out of the white Renault Clio she had parked in the street. Outside she felt self-conscious. What did the people here think? A forty-year-old woman moving in alone. That vague anxiety in her, undefined, lurking there like a slumbering reptile just below the surface of the water.

She unpacked her clothes into the built-in cupboards of cheap white melamine. In the bathroom the little white cabinet above the basin was too small for all her things. When she pushed the door closed, it caught her in the mirror – almost a stranger. Black hair, between long and short, not well styled. Not dyed, the grey hairs visible. The sallow Mediterranean skin, wrinkles at the corners of the eyes, two creases at the corners of the mouth. No make-up, lifeless, tired. An awakening, God, Milla, no wonder – you let yourself go, what man would stay with you?

She turned around swiftly, went to inflate the mattress.

In the bedroom she sat on the floor and unrolled it, putting the valve between her lips. Words ran through her, as always, too many.

Some of those words she would write in her diary: *I am here because the woman in the mirror failed in a small way, day after day. Like holding a rope in my hands, the invisible weight on the other side of the cliff just heavy enough to slide down little by little, until the end slipped through my fingers. The cause, I know now, lay just here under my skin. In the texture of my tissue, in the twisting of my DNA. Simply made this way. Unfit. Unfit despite my best efforts and all my good intentions. Unfit* because *of my attempts and intentions. An inherent, inescapable, deep-rooted, total, frustrating, miserable unsuitability: I cannot be a wife to that man. I cannot be a mother to that child. And the strong possibility that I can't be a wife to anyone, that I am generally, simply unsuited to be a wife and a mother.*

From her handbag, her cellphone began to ring. She closed the mattress valve carefully, deliberately. She guessed it was Christo. Her ex-husband. For all practical purposes.

The envelope had reached him.

She took the cellphone out of her handbag and checked the screen. It was Christo's number at work.

He would be sitting in his office with her letter in front of him. And the documents from the attorney, drawn up in a hurry on Saturday afternoon. Christo would have the door closed, that angry expression on his face, that you-fucking-miserable-stupid-woman version. The swearwords would be damming up. If she answered his call he would open the sluice gates with: '*Jissis*, Milla.'

She stared at the screen, her heart thumping, hands trembling. She lowered the phone back into her bag. The screen glowed inside with an unholy light.

Eventually the ring went over to voicemail, the light dimmed. She knew he would leave a message. Cursing.

She turned away from the handbag and made a decision: she would change her number. Before she sat down beside the mattress again, the phone beeped to say she had a message.

5 August 2009. Wednesday.

They came to deliver the Ardo fridge late that afternoon. When they had left, Milla stood listening to its reassuring hum. She inspected its chunky shape and thought, here is something to hold on to. The first, solid shield against going back, against being swallowed up, against the fear of a formless future. This was a new unease she felt, the anxiety over money. A bed, a couch, table, chairs, desk, curtains, everything was ordered, a small fortune.

Her nest egg, her modest inheritance, had shrunk quite considerably.

She would have to find work. Urgently. For the money. But also for the liberation of it.

4

6 August 2009. Thursday.

She drove back to Durbanville at ten in the morning, when there would be no one home. She wanted to put the sleeping bag and inflatable mattress back in the garage; they belonged to Christo, and she would leave her keys there for the last time.

Herta Erna Street.

Christo had laughed at her when she said she refused to live in a street with that name.

He worked with figures, he never understood her relationship with words. Never understood that words were dynamic, they had rhythm and feeling. That the way her mouth and tongue shaped them was not separate from meaning, emotion and sound.

The Lombaards of Herta Erna Street. She had shuddered when they moved in.

She waited impatiently for the gate, as it slowly rolled aside. Behind it lay the big double storey. 'Developer's Delight', was how an architect had described this building style in some magazine. Or 'Transvaal Tuscan'. At best, 'Modern Suburban'.

They had come to look at it together back then. Two months of searching in this area, because Christo was determined to live here. His only reason: 'We can afford it'. Which really meant 'We are too rich for Stellenberg now.'

One Durbanville house after the next. She weighed them and found them wanting. Luxurious, cold houses without character. Not one of them had bookshelves. That was what struck her most, all these rich white people, but not a book in the house. But every single one had a bar. Elaborate, expensive wooden monstrosities, anything from converted railway sleepers to light polished Swedish wood, the hidden lighting often done with great care, skill and expense. Flick the switch and it would come to life, expand, reveal itself to you: a holy place, a cathedral to St Booze.

Until they had seen this house and Christo said: 'This is the one I want'. Because it looked expensive. She had objected, to everything, even the name of the street. He laughed it off and signed the offer to purchase.

Milla drove in, up to the triple garage doors. One for Christo's Audi Q7. One had been for her Renault. One for Christo's toys.

She pressed the remote for the garage door. It opened. She took the neatly rolled mattress and sleeping bag, climbed out of the car and walked in.

The Q7's spot was empty.

Relief.

She hurried to the back where Christo's stuff was stored so neatly. She put the bedding away in its place. Stood still, aware of the door on the left, the one that led into the house. She knew she must not go through it. She would smell Barend. She would see how they were living now. Here she would feel the gravity of her life pulling at her.

The sound of barking dogs down the street.

Depression laid a hand on her shoulder.

The dogs barked incessantly during the day in this neighbourhood. 'Dogville'. It was her name for Durbanville when she dared once more to complain about her lot to Christo.

'*Jissis*, Milla, does nothing satisfy you?'

She left the garage and hurried to her car.

At the Palm Grove Mall in Durbanville town centre she slipped into the first available car park, meaning to buy something for lunch at Woolworths. When she got out, she saw the sign for the Arthur Murray dance studio. She glanced at it for a moment, she had forgotten it was here, more evidence of the daze that she had been living in.

At the entrance to the supermarket she smelled the flowers and looked at them, their colours so bright. It was like seeing them for the first time. She thought about the words in her diary last night. *How can I regain who I was, BC? Before Christo.*

Back at the Renault she looked at the signboard again.

Dance. Christo wouldn't dance. Not even at university. Why had she so meekly accepted his choices, his preferences? She had got so much pleasure from dancing in those days, before it all changed.

She unlocked her car, got in, put the flowers and the plastic shopping bag with her lunch ingredients on the passenger seat.

She was free of Christo.

She got out again, locked the door and went in search of the studio.

On the dance floor in the bright light streaming through the windows were a man and a woman. Young. He was wearing black trousers, white shirt, black waistcoat. She had on a short wine-red dress, her legs long and lovely. A tango played through the speakers, they glided over the wooden floor, with effortless skill.

Milla stared, enchanted by the beauty, the flow, the perfect timing, their visible pleasure, and was filled with a sudden longing – to be able to do something like that, so well. One beautiful thing you could lose yourself in, where you could feel, and give and live.

If only she could dance like that. So free.

Finally she approached the desk in front. A woman looked up and smiled.

'I want to learn,' said Milla.

7 August 2009. Friday.

Her hair was cut and dyed. She had chosen her outfit with care. Her goal was informal professionalism, casual elegance with boots, slacks, black sweater and red scarf. Now, as she waited for The Friend in the Media 24 coffee shop she was uncertain – was her make-up too light, the scarf overdone, did she look too formal, like someone trying too hard?

But when The Friend appeared she said 'Milla! You look wonderful!'

'Do you think so?'

'You *know* you're beautiful.'

But she didn't know.

The Friend had studied with her, seventeen years ago, and made her career in journalism. The Friend, finely featured, was currently deputy editor of a well known women's magazine, and frequently spoke in accents and exclamation marks.

'How are things *going* with you?'

'Fine.' And then with some trepidation, 'I want to work.'

'Write your book? At last!'

'I'm thinking of a job in journalism . . .'

'No! Milla! What for? Trouble?'

She knew she couldn't talk about everything yet. So she just shrugged and said, 'Barend doesn't need me at home any more.'

'Milla! Not a good idea. You are the wrong colour. You have no experience, no CV, your honours degree won't help, not at our age. You will be competing with hordes of ambitious, highly qualified young people who are prepared to work for nothing. They know Digital Media, Milla, they live in it. And the economy! The media is fighting to survive! Have you any idea how many magazines they are shutting down? Jobs frozen, cuts. You couldn't have picked a worse time. Tell Christo you want to open a boutique. A coffee shop. Journalism? Forget it!'

9 August 2009. Sunday.

She sat in the sitting room on her new sofa. The Careers section of the *Sunday Times* was on the coffee table in front of her. Her eyes anxiously scanned the media adverts, companies searching for an eCommerce Operations Manager, a WordPress/PHP Developer, Web Developer and a Web Editor (*Internet/Mobile experience ess*).

The anxiety was growing, the doubt, she wasn't going to make it, wasn't going to survive. The Friend was right. On Friday afternoon an employment agency consultant had told Milla the same, hidden behind political correctness and corporate euphemism. She had no chance.

She couldn't accept it. At first she had called the magazines, directly, one after the other. She worked down her list of preferences to the dailies, Afrikaans and English. After that, reluctantly, the local, weekly tabloids, and finally, in desperation, tried to track down the publishers of company magazines.

Without success. The same message: No vacancies. But send your CV.

Right at the bottom of one of the inside pages she spotted a small block advert:

> Journalist. Permanent position in Cape Town. Relevant experience preferred. Excellent research and writing skills required. Must relish team work. Tertiary qualification essential. Market related salary. Please call Mrs Nkosi. Apply before 31/08/09.

It was the 'preferred' that gave her a modicum of courage, made her sit up straight, fold the newspaper so that the ad was clearly visible, and pick up the cup of rooibos tea.

5

11 August 2009. Tuesday.

At 12.55 the *bergie* tramp pushed a shopping trolley down Coronation Street with his left hand, past the row of cars in front of the mosque. He swayed drunkenly. In his right hand he held a bottle wrapped in a brown paper bag.

The street was abandoned, the owners of the cars inside the mosque for the Dhuhr prayers.

Beside a white 1998 Hyundai Elantra the *bergie* stumbled and fell. He held the bottle aloft, desperate to avoid breaking it. He lay a moment, dazed. He tried to get up, but did not succeed. He shifted around, so that his head was under the car, just beside the rear wheel, as if he were looking for shade. Then he pulled the bottle under the car to take a drink, and his hands were no longer in sight. He lay like that for a while, fiddling, before he slowly scuffled out again.

He put the bottle down on the tarmac, put one hand on the edge of the mudguard and tried to stand. He struggled, so that he had to take hold of the vehicle again, then pulled himself upright with great effort.

He brushed imaginary dust off his ragged clothes, picked up his bottle and, still unsteady on his feet, reached for the trolley and began meandering along again.

In the electronics room of the Presidential Intelligence Agency, Rahjev Rajkumar sat with a computer operator, while Quinn, the Chief of

Staff: Operations, stood beside them. All three stared at the computer screen that displayed a street map of Cape Town.

Quinn glanced at his wristwatch and then back at the screen.

A sudden electronic blip broke the silence. A tiny red triangle appeared on the screen.

'Zoom in,' Rajkumar said.

The operator clicked on the magnifying glass icon, then on the triangle, twice, three times, until the name of the street was clear: Coronation.

'I think we're in play,' said Rajkumar.

'I'll wait for Terry's report,' said Quinn. 'But so far, so good.'

Quinn, Chief of Staff: Operations, reported directly to Advocate Tau Masilo, the Deputy-Director: Operational and Strategy. In the late afternoon in his superior's office, Quinn told Masilo the GPS transmitter was successfully attached to Baboo Rayan's white Hyundai Elantra. The monitoring showed that the car had been parked in front of a new address for over an hour. 15 Chamberlain Street, in Upper Woodstock.

'Let's do a drive-by,' said Masilo.

'The pharmacy motorcycle?'

'That should do.'

'I'm on it.'

Photostatic record: *Diary of Milla Strachan*
Date of entry: *11 August 2009*

The Swing. One-Two-Three, One-Two-Three. Backstep.
The Foxtrot. Slow. Slow. Quick, quick.
The Waltz. One. Two. Three.
The Tango. Slow . . . Slow . . . Slow . . . Quick, quick. The Morse Code of dance. 'School figures', Arthur Murray called them, baby steps I have to practise. How different from the woman I had seen dancing last Thursday. But still, there was something comforting about it: if you want to get there, you must begin here. At the bottom. One step at a time. Strange how somehow it relieved the anxiety, the insecurity.

14 August 2009. Friday.

In her office, at the round table, Janina Mentz told Rajkumar and Masilo about the President's alleged vision of a single intelligence service. Masilo did not react. Rajkumar obsessively examined a piece of skin beside his thumbnail.

'Our careers are on the line,' she said.

Rajkumar began to chew the skin.

'Are we the only players in the Supreme Committee developments?' she asked.

'Of course,' said Tau Masilo.

'Then we must exploit it.'

'So you're saying . . .'

'Yes, Raj, I'm saying this is our ace in the hole. Our last resort. Unless you know of something else where we have exclusivity . . .'

'No . . .'

'Then we had better make it work for us, or we will be running the back-office of the new super-duper intelligence conglomerate the President is planning, wondering why we didn't work a little harder and a little faster when we had the chance.'

'But what if we're right? What if it isn't local action, just al-Qaeda in a last gasp attempt to send a few AK's to Afghanistan.'

'Then we will have to find a way to make that little fact work in our favour, Raj.'

Milla Strachan was reading when her cellphone rang at half past three in the afternoon.

UNKNOWN CALLER.

'Hello?'

'Is that Milla Strachan?'

'Yes.'

'I am Mrs Nkosi. From the agency. I have good news. We would like you to come for a job interview.'

'Oh . . .' She was relieved and surprised and thankful.

'You are still interested?'

'Yes.'

'Could you come next week?'

'Yes. Yes, I can.'

'Wednesday?'

'Wednesday would be good.' She'd nearly said 'great', had to steel herself not to sound too grateful or too eager.

'Wonderful. Twelve o'clock?'

6

18 August 2009. Tuesday.

Advocate Tau Masilo opened a file on his lap, took out a photo and placed it on the desk in front of Mentz. 'Late yesterday afternoon, taken by the pharmacy motorbike at 15 Chamberlain Street in Woodstock . . .'

The photo showed the Sheikh, Suleiman Dolly, Chairman of the Supreme Committee, walking around the front of a car.

'There's a strong possibility that this is their new meeting place,' he said.

She studied the pictures. 'They chose well.'

'They did. That says something. Look at that photo. Dolly isn't driving his Volvo any more, which means he is being very careful all of a sudden. This is the new meeting place, with live-in security, because we saw Baboo has moved into one side of the semi-detached. There's the choice of the house itself. Middle-class neighbourhood, most of the residents are at work during the day. Few inquisitive eyes, quiet streets. Strange vehicles will be spotted quickly. Double storey, from that highest window you can watch most of the street.'

'A great deal of trouble,' said Mentz.

'A great deal. There must be a reason for it.'

'What do you have in mind?'

'Our only option is to put someone in one of the four houses across the street. We are studying the title deeds. The ideal would be if one of them was let . . .'

'Is it going to help, Tau?'

'What do you mean?'

'Is it going to help to get someone into one of those houses? A few more photos of them coming and going. That gives us nothing new. We need to know what they are talking about.'

'Ma'am, we are planning a great deal more than a camera.'

'Oh?'

'We are going to erect cellphone antennae, parabolic microphones . . .'

Mentz made a dismissive gesture.

Masilo wasn't put off his stride. 'Look at this, for example, here on the front wall. If we can replace one of these screws with an electro-acoustic microphone . . .'

'If?'

'Ma'am, you know we have to do surveillance first.'

'Tau, sometimes I get the impression that we are just playing. With all this technology, with the idea of espionage. It's all so filmic, so much fun and excitement. But when it comes to results, we fall short.'

'I object . . .'

'You can object all you want, but where are the results? We had Ismail Mohammed inside, we tried to tap them with technology that I don't completely understand, and here we are. In the dark.'

'Not entirely.'

Janina Mentz pulled a face and shook her head. 'Bring me results, Tau.'

He smiled at her. 'We will.'

19 August 2009. Wednesday.

'Would you describe yourself as ambitious?' asked the maternal, middle-aged Mrs Nkosi.

Milla thought before she answered, because she suspected it was a trick question. 'I believe if you work hard, if you fulfil your responsibilities faithfully and to the best of your ability, you can be successful.'

Mrs Nkosi said 'uh-huh' again happily and wrote something on her papers. Then she looked up. 'Tell me a bit about yourself. Your background.'

Milla had expected that, and prepared for it. 'I was born in Wellington, I grew up and finished school there. My mother was a housewife . . .'

'A home maker,' said Mrs Nkosi, as if it were the most noble of professions.

'Yes,' said Milla. 'And my father was a businessman, I suppose you could say . . .'

Operation Shawwal
Transcription: *Audio surveillance, M. Strachan. No 14 Daven Court, Davenport Street, Vredehoek*
Date and Time: *7 October 2009. 23.09*

MS: They were Afrikaner hippies, my mom and dad. Very eccentric, very different from the other children's parents. I still don't know whether . . . what effect it had on me. There was a time when I was so ashamed of them . . . I mean, my mom was . . . Sometimes she walked around the house in the nude when we were alone. My dad smoked dope now and then. In our sitting room. He worked from home. The garage was his workshop. He fixed cash registers, at first. Then computers . . . He was . . . not just eccentric, he was clever. He read widely, science, history, philosophy . . . He was a great fan of Bertrand Russell, he considered himself a relatively political pacifist, his favourite quotation was 'free intellect is the chief engine of human progress' . . .

'I got married the year I completed my honours in journalism. Also pregnant. Then home maker . . .' she let the designation hang between them with a bashful smile, because it was Mrs Nkosi's. '. . . for seventeen years. And now I am on my own again. I must add, that I am not officially Strachan yet. It is my maiden name, but the divorce is not through . . .'

'Good for you,' said Mrs Nkosi. 'How long have you been on your own?'

'Oh a few months already.' A lie, born of necessity.

'Good,' said Mrs Nkosi. Milla had no idea why. The entire experience had a certain surreal feeling. The employment agency was a disappointment. On the fifth floor of a charmless building in Wale Street, the letters on the door were small and unimaginative. *Perfect Placement Employment Brokers.* The furniture and decor were without character, vaguely depressing. Which magazine was the position for, she wondered. A small industrial publication? A new, free suburban newspaper?

They chatted for over an hour and a half, wandered off in slightly apologetic exploration of her background, her personality, her opinions and ideology, every answer rewarded with a 'good', a fascinated 'uh-huh' and the occasional 'wonderful', as though it were perfect and exactly right.

Eventually: 'Is there anything that you would like to ask me?'

'I would like to know to which publication I am applying?'

'To be honest, it isn't a publication as such. In the first place my client needs journalists for their skill in the processing of information. And good writing, of course.' Mrs Nkosi consulted her notes. 'The successful candidate will be responsible for the assimilation and structuring of facts, and the writing of concise, clear and readable reports for senior management. The reports play a cardinal role in the decision-making process of the institution.'

'Oh.' Her disappointment was visible.

'It's an important job,' said Mrs Nkosi.

Milla nodded, lost in thought.

'You will earn exactly the same as someone in the media. Perhaps a little more.'

'What institution is it?'

'I am not authorised to reveal that now.'

7

Photostatic record: *Diary of Milla Strachan*
Date of entry: *20 August 2009*

The first six dance classes completed, the introductory cycle, and official transfer to Mr Soderstrom, my new, long-term instructor. I don't know what his first name is, that is Arthur Murray convention, the old-fashioned forms of address, 'Mr' and 'Mrs' and 'Miss', all gallantry and dignity. Mr Soderstrom is lean and such an incredibly good dancer. I asked him, after a session of sweat and struggle, did he think I could ever get there. 'Oh, yes,' he beamed. 'You *will* dance!'

I guess he says that to all his students.

Sat in front of the computer for three hours, trying to write my book. Nothing. Are there school figures for writing, an attempt at a novel reduced to one-two-three-backstep for amateurs? My thoughts drifted off to unfamiliar places. The nature of freedom, its relativity. Freedom, bound by conscience, by longing, guilt and dependence and money and stimulation and structure and talent and goals. And courage. I had lost mine, somewhere in the northern suburbs, years ago.

24 August 2009. Monday.

Milla was in the Pick 'n' Pay in the Gardens centre when Kemp, her attorney called.

'Two things. There is a letter here from your son. To you. And Christo phoned, very angry. He said people came to see him, at work. About your background check.'

'My background check?' Completely at a loss.

'Apparently you applied for a job somewhere.'

She battled to put two and two together.

'Did you?' asked Kemp.

'Yes . . .'

'He said they were asking questions about your political background.'

'My political background?'

'May I ask where you applied for work?'

'I . . . the . . . employment agency couldn't tell me much. It's a journalism job . . . What did Christo tell them?'

'His exact words?'

'Yes.'

'That you are a bloody communist, just like your father. And as crazy as your mother. Apparently he was very upset, it was a big embarrassment for him, he said you ought to have warned him . . .'

'How could I . . . ?' She heard the tone of another incoming call. 'Gus, I have to go . . .'

'I'll send our messenger to deliver the letter to you.'

'Thanks, Gus.'

He said goodbye and she checked her screen. UNKNOWN CALLER.

'Hello?'

'Hello, Milla, this is Mrs Nkosi . . .'

Milla wanted to ask about the checks, she wanted to protest politely, but before she could react: 'I have very good news for you. You are on the short-list. Can you come in tomorrow for another interview?'

It was so unexpected that Milla asked: 'Tomorrow?'

'If that's convenient.'

'Of course.' She confirmed a time, and said goodbye. She stood behind her trolley in the middle of the shopping centre aisle, trying to absorb it all. Apparently Christo's comment about her father, the communist, hadn't done too much harm.

Then Milla turned and walked back into Pick 'n' Pay and bought herself a pack of cigarettes and a Bic lighter. For the first time in eighteen years.

In the Presidential Intelligence Agency Operations room, the big screen displayed a photo of the man in a suit getting out of a car. He was coloured, dressed in a tasteful dark suit, white shirt and grey tie. He carried a black briefcase over his shoulder. It was a grainy image with little depth, and gave the impression of a telephoto lens.

Janina Mentz and Advocate Tau Masilo sat and studied it. Beside them stood Masilo's right-hand man, Quinn, the Chief of Staff: Operations. He pointed at the screen.

'That is one of the members of the Supreme Committee, Shaheed Latif Osman,' said Quinn. 'You don't often see him in a suit, more usually in traditional Muslim dress. The photo was taken on Sunday, at about half past twelve, at a five-star guest house in Morningside, Johannesburg. Osman booked in under the name of Abdul Gallie. Here he is on his way back to the airport. Twenty minutes earlier this man . . .' Quinn clicked the mouse of the laptop and another photo appeared. '. . . also left the location.' A big black man, smart in a dark blue jacket and grey trousers, getting into the passenger seat of a black BMW X5 in front of the guest house.

'This morning we identified him through the vehicle number plate. His name is Julius Nhlakanipho Shabangu. He goes by the alias 'Inkunzi', which means 'bull' in Zulu. The greatest source of information on him is in the SAPS Criminal Intelligence database, connecting him with organised crime in the Gauteng area. He has a criminal record, two jail terms for armed robbery. He is under suspicion of being the brains behind a car hijacking network and various cash-in-transit robberies over the past four years. There is more information in the former Scorpions' files, but that will take a while to access.'

'According to one of the kitchen staff, Shabangu and Osman met in the library, behind closed doors,' said the Advocate.

Quinn confirmed this with a finger pointed at the screen: 'Shabangu arrived at the guest house at ten in the morning. His chauffeur waited outside. Two hours later he emerged, and shortly after that, Osman came out. Osman had not left the guest house since the previous evening.'

'Interesting,' said Janina Mentz.

'We have no previous record of a meeting between these two. Osman frequently travels to Johannesburg, but normally to mosques in Lenasia, Mayfair and Laudium. Shabangu was never seen at any of those places,' said Quinn.

'A new partnership.' Janina Mentz was pleased. This was progress.

'Strange bedfellows,' said Tau Masilo.

'I presume we are going to keep an eye on Shabangu.'

'Indeed.'

She wanted to light a cigarette before opening the letter. She realised she didn't have an ashtray. She went to the kitchen to fetch a saucer, lit the cigarette and inhaled deeply. And coughed.

She smoked the whole cigarette, staring at the letter on the coffee table. She picked it up reluctantly and tore it open.

Dear Ma

I'm very sorry, Ma. I was rude and I didn't behave right. I didn't appresiate you, only when it was too late. Ma, I have learned my lesson, I promise you. If you can forgive me, I will make it up to you. I swear, Ma. Pa says if you can just talk, we can make it all right again. Please, Ma, I miss you and need you in my life. I don't know what to say to my friends.

Call me, Ma

Barend

His handwriting was usually untidy, sometimes illegible. She didn't know where he had found this paper, thin, expensive, she could see here he had written with a great deal of care. Despite the spelling mistake.

Milla pushed it away across the coffee table, because the guilt and the longing burned right through her.

Late that night she lay in her bed, staring at the ceiling in remorse, building containing walls against the guilt by composing an answer to Barend in her head.

Let me tell you the whole truth: it won't help for me to have a talk with your father, because I don't love him any more. And to my shame, I don't know if I ever loved him. I don't hate him either, I moved on from that a long time ago. I feel nothing for him.

I love you, because you are my child.

But love is like a message. It only exists if there is someone to receive it. You have to admit that you haven't been receiving for a long time now. You, Barend, begging and pleading and full of remorse now, where was that when I sat down with you time after time in love and tenderness and asked, please, just talk civilly to me, because the way a man talks to a woman defines him? You are bigger and stronger than I am; physically I am afraid of you. I don't want to list your sins, because I can already see your face if you had to read them, those meaningless, suburban, domestic sins of the teenager: your pigsty of a room, your dirty washing always on the floor of the bathroom despite my pleas. Your dullness, your selfishness, your superiority, as though I were trash, to be endured only with effort. Your general lack of consideration, your self-centred existence, your endless requests for more money, more possessions, more favours. Your reaction when I say no, the explosions, the swearing. Your accusations, so bitterly unfair, your manipulation, your lies. You are a bully and a fraud and I love you despite all of it, but it doesn't mean I have to live with it for ever.

She composed that in her head, knowing that it would never be put down on paper.

Tomorrow morning she would write Barend an actual letter. She would say that she was not going to phone him just yet. He was to give her time to find her feet, please. But they could correspond and she would always reply to his letters.

That she had forgiven him already. That she loved him endlessly.

8

25 August 2009. Tuesday.

In the same vaguely depressing, characterless interview room, this time with four people: the cheerful Mrs Nkosi, a black man who just introduced himself as 'Ben', and at the back against the wall, two unidentified spectators, a very fat Indian, and a white woman in her fifties.

'I must say the background check was a bit of a surprise,' Milla cautiously addressed herself to the good nature of Mrs Nkosi.

'Understood,' said Ben, who reminded Milla of Shakespeare, one of Julius Caesar's 'lean and hungry men'. 'Unavoidable. Giving notice would defeat the purpose. Undermine the credence.' His sentences marched out like soldiers.

'But the good news is that you made the short-list,' Mrs Nkosi said. 'The job is just as I described it to you. And now we can tell you a little more.'

'It's for a government agency. A very important one. Are you willing to work for the government?' Ben asked.

'Yes, I . . . May I ask, which other people you spoke to? About me?'

'Usually, we take a look at your body of work as a journalist. Talk to previous employers and colleagues. Your case was different. Spoke to your ex-husband. A former schoolteacher. Former lecturer. You passed. Flying colours.'

She was dying to ask which teacher, Wellington had all those conservative *Broederbonders* . . .

'Now. The job. For a State Department. Secrecy is essential. The major factor here: you won't be able to talk about your work. The real work. You will have to lie. To your friends. Your family. All the time. It can be a strain.'

'In the beginning, really just in the beginning,' said Mrs Nkosi soothingly. 'You get used to it.'

'Of course, you will be trained. To manage. But, perhaps this is not what you had in mind at all.'

'It's . . . I had no idea . . .'

'We understand, it is sudden, it's unexpected. Don't worry, you'll have plenty of time to think it over. But if you feel right now that it is something that you absolutely don't want to do . . .'

'No,' said Milla Strachan. 'I . . . It sounds . . . exciting.'

27 August 2009. Thursday.

Rajhev Rajkumar knew Janina Mentz well. He knew how to win her favour.

'About the Report Squad appointment . . .'

'Yes?'

'This one, I think, was the strongest candidate,' he said and tapped a fingernail on a folder.

'Why?'

'She's intelligent, little bit flustered, but Ben can be difficult. She's politically almost neutral, with a liberal background. Living on her own. And, of course, she can start on the first, which is a bonus.'

'She has no real applicable experience.'

'None of them had. As you know, it's a blessing in disguise. No bad habits, no media ideology.'

'Mmm . . .'

Rajkumar waited patiently, because he knew Mentz had read the full transcripts, he knew which paragraphs would make the breakthrough.

Personnel Interview: *Vacant position – Report Squad*
Transcription: *M. Strachan, interviewed by B.B and J.N.*
Date and Time: *25 August 2009. 10.30*

BB: Will you receive alimony?

MS: No.

BB: Why not? Surely, you deserve it. And your husband is a wealthy man.

MS: Taking money from him would be an acknowledgement of dependence. And submissiveness. Weakness. I am not weak.

'Yes,' Janina Mentz said at last. 'Appoint her.'

1 September 2009. Tuesday.

Fourteen chairs in the training room, a lectern in front, but she and the induction official sat side by side. His voice droned on, his face frowning and serious. 'Your primary cover is what you tell your family, and your friends. In your case, your primary cover is *News This Week*. It is a publication that actually exists, it is produced by the government's Department of Communication, distributed to ministers and directors general and their staff. So you tell people that you work there, that you scan the print and electronic media daily for grassroots level news from Limpopo and Mpumalanga, your area of focus. And that you write a weekly page on this in the newsletter. You should know, the Government really cares, they actually want to know these things. And you should also study the actual newsletter every week, so that you know the contents. Now, it is essential for a cover to have aspirational aspects, so you can also tell people that you hope to handle one of the bigger areas one day, like the Western Cape, and perhaps become the assistant editor in a few years.'

Milla wondered why she couldn't aim a bit higher, fictitiously speaking, at the editor's job itself.

Just before lunch she met her new boss, Mrs Killian, the manager of the 'Report Squad' as her induction official called it. Milla recognised her, she was the one sitting quietly against the wall at the last interview, the kind-looking one, everyone's grandma. There was only time for a brief handshake with her other colleagues – the spectacular Jessica, wild red hair and a magnificent bosom, and two bald old men whose names ran by her too quickly.

She realised she was dressed too smartly, because Jessica was simply wearing an old, outsize jersey and jeans, while one of the old guys had on a cravat, with a checked sleeveless pullover.

2 September 2009. Wednesday.

Janina Mentz stared at the article in *Die Burger* for a long time. It was titled '*Nuwe vrae duik op oor wapens*': New questions about arms emerge.

With a small smile she took a pair of scissors from her desk drawer and cut out the article.

Before she filed it in a new folder, she read it through again. Especially the fifth paragraph with the quote from David Maynier, Member of Parliament for the Democratic Alliance. 'What is happening, is wrong. We are about to supply flying suits for pilots to President Mahmoud Ahmadinejad of Iran, we have already sold grenade launchers and missiles that could be used to launch nuclear weapons to Colonel Muammar Gaddafi of Libya, as well as guns to President Hugo Chavez of Venezuela. The government should explain why they are selling weapons to a string of pariah states – and illegally to boot.'

At around 10.14 on the Wednesday morning of the second of September, the red Toyota Corolla with an Eastern Cape registration number stopped in front of 16A Chamberlain Street. The house was one of six single-storey semi-detached houses, each painted a different bright colour. Number 16A was an indescribable pinky-purple, with red-painted tops on the two pillars of the equally red garden gate. A coloured man and woman in their thirties took their time getting out of the car, stretching, as if the journey had been long and wearying, before approaching the little gate and entering. The young man took keys out of his pocket and opened the front door. Both disappeared into the house, which had stood empty since the previous day.

About a quarter of an hour later a lorry stopped in front of the house. The lettering on the sides read *Afriworld Removals, Port Elizabeth.*

The coloured couple came out of the front door, greeted the driver and pointed at the house.

Diagonally opposite, Baboo Rayan, dogsbody of the Supreme Committee, kept an eye on proceedings from the top window of number 15 – the opening of the lorry doors, the transfer of simple, middle-class furniture.

During the late-afternoon meeting, Advocate Tau Masilo reported that the two operatives were successfully installed opposite the house of the Supreme Committee. (Masilo had banned the word 'agent' from the PIA lexicon. 'We are not selling insurance.' His standpoint was not negotiable. 'The operatives will maintain a very low profile for the next week or two, ma'am. Tomorrow the man will begin work at a spare parts company in Victoria Street. For now the woman will play the apparent housewife and start photo-surveillance of 15 Chamberlain Street. We hid the voice and cellphone monitoring equipment in the furniture. He will set it up tonight and we should be operational by tomorrow. Then it just leaves the insertion of the electro-acoustic microphone, but we will only do that once we are absolutely certain of their movements . . .'

'Good work, Tau.'

'Thank you, ma'am.'

She looked to Rajkumar. She knew the Indian had good news. Since the start of the meeting he had had that self-satisfied smile on his face. 'Raj?'

'Julius Shabangu, our crime kingpin in Jo'burg. We have very interesting insights . . .'

Mentz lifted her eyebrows.

'We've had two vehicles, disguised as private security patrols from the Eagle Eye company, in Shabangu's neighbourhood for the past week,' Rajkumar paused for Janina Mentz to appreciate the wit and irony.

She just nodded.

'Anyway, they've been monitoring cellphone traffic. We've been processing a lot of data, and the good news is, we have two cell numbers that probably belong to him or his people . . .'

'Probably?'

'Madam, we have more than twenty houses in the block, and a lot of cellular traffic. But the calls in question correspond to the times Shabangu and his staff have been at home. We have now isolated them, and will eavesdrop as from tonight. But here's the interesting thing. They've been talking to Harare. Two calls, from two different cellular phones, to the same number in Zim.'

'My, my,' said the Advocate.

'But we don't know who the Harare number belongs to,' said Mentz.

'We don't have access to infrastructure in Zim. But we will now start listening to any future calls from those numbers . . .'

Mentz gave him a full-blown smile. 'Raj, that is good work.'

'I know,' the Indian said.

Photostatic record: *Diary of Milla Strachan*
Date of entry: *2 September 2009*
Exhausted. What a day. Nine hours of training – Computer Literacy, Internet Skills, Search Procedures, Report Writing, Writing Style, everything in one room in front of one computer, with four different, equally soul-destroying instructors.

Photostatic record: *Diary of Milla Strachan*
Date of entry: *3 September 2009*
Highlight of the day: for the first time I saw the words 'Spy the Beloved Country'. The words marched slowly across the computer screen of Oom Theunie, my bald colleague. His screen saver.
He smelled of pipe smoke, like my father.

9

4 September 2009. Friday.

They sat in the Bizerca Bistro, the elegant black Advocate Tau Masilo, and the crushproof white woman, Janina Mentz, heads together like lovers. They were an island of solemnity in the light-hearted lunch hour.

Masilo's voice was quiet. 'My source says our Minister's recommendation is that we be left in peace in the amalgamation, but there are other cabinet members who differ.'

'Who?'

'The Minister of Defence, apparently, and the Minister of Home Affairs.'

Senior cabinet members, Mentz realised. She digested the information before asking, 'Who else supports us?'

'The Deputy President.'

'Is that all?'

'You must understand, the information is second-hand, and I suspect much of it is speculation. But the important thing is, the President is not yet certain that we are included.'

They ate in silence. Masilo enjoyed his food with visible pleasure.

Eventually he put his knife and fork down. 'No wonder the Minister of Finance eats here too. Ma'am, may I make a suggestion?' he asked.

'Of course, Tau.'

'Now is the time to make a fuss. To convince the President . . .'

'How?'

'With what we have. I know, I know, seen objectively, it's not much. But a short report, cleverly written . . .'

'It's dangerous.'

'Why would that be?'

'Tau, how much credibility will we lose if the Muslim affair is completely off-target?'

'Will it matter, in a month or two?'

'We simply don't have enough yet,' with disguised regret.

'I don't know if we can wait much longer, ma'am. It's a window of opportunity, and it won't stay open for long. The President could make his decision any day now . . .'

Janina Mentz adjusted her spectacles. Unconvinced.

Masilo's cellphone rang. He answered and listened. Spoke into the instrument: 'From where?' Then again: 'I'll be there now.'

He put the phone away. 'That was Quinn. I think the cellular taps in Gauteng have borne fruit.'

Quinn, the Chief of Staff: Operations, in a black turtleneck sweater and khaki chinos, caressed the facts with his quiet voice: 'Inkunzi Shabangu and his people are clever, as befits members of organised crime. Every week they replace their cellphone SIM cards. It takes Raj and his people three or four days to isolate the new numbers, because we can monitor Shabangu's house, that is our one constant site. That leaves only three days of surveillance before we have to start all over again. Incidentally they never use the same SIM card twice, and we suspect every new number is SMSed to important contacts on Sunday evenings. This was recorded this morning. One voice is Shabangu himself. The call came from Harare, it is a typical Zim accent . . .'

Quinn clicked on the mouse. The sound was excellent on the impressive system.

'Hello.'

'*Mhoroi*, Inkunzi, how are you?'

'I am very well, my friend, and how are you?'

'Not so well, Inkunzi, times are tough over here.'

'I know, my friend, I know, the newspapers are full of it.'

'What can you do . . . ?'

'So, my friend, *ndeipi*?'

'The news is that you were right, Inkunzi. Chitepo is working on a new route, and it will go through South Africa.'

Quinn paused the recording for a moment. 'Most likely that's Johnson Chitepo, head of Zimbabwe's Joint Operations Command, and Mugabe's right-hand man. But listen to this . . .' and he reactivated the recording.

'And you are sure?' said the voice of Julius Shabangu over the speakers.

'Almost sure. Ninety-nine per cent. But it looks like he is keeping Comrade Bob in the dark.'

'Chitepo?'

'*Yebo*.'

'He's stealing from Mugabe now?'

'He is looking after himself.'

'OK. So when is it going to happen?'

'Soon, I think. But we will try to find out more.'

'And the route? How does it work?'

'All I know is, he's working with a South African. Somcone in nature conservation. So it could be through Kruger, you know, the transfrontier park. They are connected now, Gonarezhou and Kruger. That is what we think, they will take it through there.'

'OK. My friend this is very good. But we need the details.'

'I know, Inkunzi. I will keep listening.'

'*Tatenda*, my friend. *Fambai zvakanaka*.'

'*Fambai zvakanaka*, Inkunzi.'

Quinn paused the recording again. 'That just means "go well" in Shona. The conversation is quite typical, they keep it short, just like the following one. This is Shabangu phoning, the number he called is a house here in Cape Town, in Rondebosch East, which we'll naturally monitor from now on. The house belongs to one Abdullah Hendricks. Up till now he has not been on our radar at all.' He clicked on a new electronic folder.

'Hendricks.'

Inkunzi's voice, deep and authoritarian: 'I have a message for Inkabi.'

'Inka . . . ? Yes, Inkabi. What is the message?'

'Tell him he was right. Our friend in Zimbabwe is back in the export business, but he has new partners, and he wants to export to South Africa. Tell him this is ninety-nine per cent sure, but that is all we know. We will try to get more.'

'I will tell him.'

'OK, my friend. That's all.'

'*Khuda hafiz.*'

'OK.'

The electronic noise of a call being terminated. Quinn turned away from the screen and looked at Mentz and Masilo. '"Inkabi" is the Zulu word for "ox", "*os*" as in Osman, which of course, refers to the Supreme Committee member Shaheed Latif Osman. Most likely that is the code Shabangu and Osman agreed on during their meeting. Obviously, Shabangu has a sense of humour.'

Only Masilo smiled.

'Hendricks might be Supreme Committee too, or on the fringes. He's new to us. You can also pick up that he was taken a little by surprise. He didn't recognise the code immediately. We believe this is the first call from Shabangu to this number, the first time that he has used the code to report to Osman since they met in Johannesburg,' said Quinn.

'What does "*khuda hafiz*" mean?' Mentz asked.

'It's a Muslim greeting. Something like "may God protect you". As we could hear, Shabangu didn't know either.'

'Have we no idea who Inkunzi Shabangu's contact in Harare is?'

'No, ma'am. But we do know quite a few other things. We know why Osman went to see Shabangu.'

'Share your insights,' said Janina Mentz.

'It is still an incomplete picture . . .'

'That I know, Quinn. And it's quite a muddled picture to me.'

'Take it from the top,' said Masilo. 'It is very important that we all understand exactly what's going on here.'

Quinn nodded, thought a moment before he came and sat down opposite them.

'Very well,' he said. 'Picture it as a drama, with two main actors and two supporting roles. Main character number one is Johnson Chitepo. He is Zimbabwe's Chief of Joint Operations Command, he was Mugabe's right-hand man, the man who negotiated the deal to acquire the diamond mine concessions in the Congo. He was also the one who sold the diamonds in the carefree years so that he and Comrade Bob could put money aside. Huge amounts of money. But that was then. Things are appreciably different now. Mugabe and Chitepo are slowly but surely losing their grip on power in Zim. Their diamond sales are curtailed by sanctions and international agreements, their bank accounts are frozen, for all practical purposes that money is lost. Chitepo's burning desire right now is to quickly build up a new nest egg. Before the end arrives, and the end will arrive, it's only a matter of time. He's sitting with at least a hundred million dollars' worth of diamonds. Multiply that by seven, it's a lot of rands . . . And he can't sell them directly. But now he seems to have found new partners. Someone in nature conservation, someone who can smuggle them out via the greater Kruger Park. Does that make sense?'

Mentz nodded.

'Our second lead actor is Sayyid Khalid bin Alawi Macki. He was the one who formerly helped Chitepo with the diamond sales, he was the one who converted the Congo diamonds into cash, laundered the money and deposited it in the Swiss bank accounts of Mugabe and his cronies. But once his channels were choked off, the big friendship between him and Chitepo soured. Before I go on, there are a lot of things we must keep in mind when it comes to Macki. One: his core business is money laundering, and he operates all over Africa. We know he does it for the pirates in Somalia, for the fraud and drug networks in Nigeria, and the car-theft syndicates in Mozambique. Two: the international economic crisis hit him hard. He lost huge investments in Dubai, his turnover is generally over sixty per cent down, he is battling at the moment. Three: he is a militant Muslim from Oman, currently the new and greatest growth point for al-Qaeda. And four: Macki has a soft spot for al-Qaeda. His success, his wealth and his support have given him prominence in those circles. Prominence that he badly wants to regain.'

Quinn gave Mentz a chance to take it all in.

'The main intrigue of our drama is Chitepo's desire to sell diamonds, and Macki's view that the little stones belong to him, or that he has at least a fifty per cent share in them, according to the original agreement. Somehow or other, Macki heard of Chitepo's plans, and he is determined to intercept the booty. The so-called "shipment". His problem is that he no longer has friends in Zimbabwe, and he is sitting in Oman. So, what can he do? His only recourse is to talk to his contacts closest to the action, his Muslim brothers.'

'The Supreme Committee,' said Janina Mentz.

'Here in the fairest Cape,' said Advocate Tau Masilo.

'Exactly,' said Quinn. 'That is why Macki called the first supporting actor on the stage. Suleiman Dolly, Chairman of the Supreme Committee.'

'The call that our mole, Ismail Mohammed overheard.'

'That's right. Macki knew Dolly and the Supreme Committee needed funds urgently for the project they are working on.'

'The local project, which according to Ismail Mohammed is the smuggling in of weapons.'

'And now, the entrance of our second supporting actor, Julius "Inkunzi" Shabangu. My gut feeling is that Macki recommended Shabangu. Remember, Macki is a money launderer. Through the Mozambican car syndicates he would be at least aware of Shabangu, but more likely he has done business with him directly already . . .'

'We also know,' said Tau Masilo, 'that Inkunzi Shabangu has a lot of Zimbabweans working for him in Gauteng. Car hijackers.'

'Exactly,' Quinn agreed. 'And according to the Scorpions' dossiers he is also suspected of supplying false passports to Zimbabweans and Nigerians. So he will have good contacts in Harare . . . In any case, when Macki talked to Suleiman Dolly, ten to one he recommended Inkunzi as a possible partner in the whole scheme. And Dolly sent one of his Supreme Committee members to consult with Inkunzi. Osman, in the guest house in Johannesburg. Inkunzi will be keen to keep Macki happy, but above all he is a businessman. He will take a percentage of every transaction. Osman's suggestion of a cooperation was entirely acceptable to him.'

'Mmm,' said Janina Mentz.

'Inkunzi and his strange new associate, the Supreme Committee, want to intercept Chitepo's new parcel of diamonds,' Tau Masilo said.

'The shipment,' said Quinn.

'And Inkunzi has to find out which route it will take. Which South Africans are involved.'

Both men looked at the Director. She pushed up her spectacles and stood up.

'I think this will make a very interesting report,' said Tau Masilo. 'For the President.'

Mentz took her time. The men waited in suspense.

'You are making one cardinal error,' said Mentz. 'Allocating roles. The report will be a failure if you present Chitepo and Macki as lead actors.'

Advocate Tau Masilo was quick to understand. 'For our purposes the main role will be played by the Supreme Committee and their weapons deal.'

10

7 September 2009. Monday.

Milla was dressed in her black dress and boots, with the short blue denim jacket. She felt comfortable, as though she were developing a style, the working woman adapted to the informality of the Report Squad. She sat behind her computer at a quarter to nine, reading her first *News This Week*, the titbits from Limpopo and Mpumalanga. There was an air of expectation in the office. Theunie, one of the two bald men who were both very comfortable with the respectful Afrikaans address form of 'Oom', had said there was Something Big brewing, because Bigfoot had summoned Mother, a definite omen.

Oom Theunie and his nicknames. 'Mother' was Mrs Killian, 'Bigfoot' referred to Rajkumar, the fat Indian, whom he also called 'AS', short for 'Abominable Snowman', or 'The Incredible Bulk', or sometimes just 'The Bulk'.

Milla he called 'Carmen', Jessica, 'Freia' (or 'The Goddess' when referring to her in the third person), Don MacFarland, the other old man in the team, was 'Mac' of 'Mac the Wife'.

'Why "Mac the Wife"?' she had asked.

Don answered her himself. 'Because I'm gay, my dear.'

At a quarter to nine Mrs Killian hurried in and called them together with a bundle of thin folders in her hand.

'The Bulk has spoken,' said Oom Theunie.

'Theunie, you are going to write the executive summary, the rest of you will be doing addenda.' She handed Milla a folder. 'Your subject is Johnson Chitepo, see if you can find something more recent on the Internet, and let Theunie explain how the format works. Jess, you will be doing Sayyid Khalid bin Alawi Macki . . .'

'Who?'

'It's all in here, but it's badly dated. Interesting man. Don, I'm giving you the important stuff.'

'Of course you are.'

'Qibla, the Supreme Committee, al-Qaeda, and a brand new subject. A Mr Julius Nhlakanipho Shabangu, aka "The Bull".'

'Because he has such a big horn?'

She didn't laugh. 'It's big and it's urgent. Let's get going.'

On her couch, the adrenaline of the day still coursing through her, the pleasure of camaraderie and the learning curve and fraternal witticisms still warming her, with sudden impulsiveness, she phoned her son.

'Hello?' he said, teenage suspicion at a number he didn't recognise.

'Barend, it's me.'

'Ma?' Dumbfounded.

'I just wanted to hear your voice.'

'Where are you, Ma?'

'I'm at my new house. How are you?'

'Ma . . . *Jissis*, Ma . . .'

'Barend . . .' Sorry she had phoned. Realising that her euphoria was hers alone.

'You've got a house, Ma?'

'Just a little flat. Could we just talk?'

Her son hesitated before he answered, a tentative 'OK.'

'How are you?'

'Ma . . . Do you really want to know?'

'Yes, Barend, I really want to know. You know I love you very much.'

'Then why did you run away?'

Run away. 'Did you get my letters?'

'Are we really *that* bad, Ma?'

Something in the words and the way he said them made her think they came from Christo's mouth. Suddenly she didn't want to talk any more, but she had no choice now. She sat up straight and concentrated. 'I tried to explain this clearly for you, that it's not you . . .'

'Ma . . .'

'Just listen. Please. I had to get away, precisely because I love you, Barend, I don't know if you can understand that.'

He said nothing.

'Can I tell you something? I have a job, I had an amazing day today, I felt I meant something . . .'

'You could have stayed and still got a job. Why did you have to run away?'

She was about to fall into the old rut, but stopped herself in time. 'How is your school work?'

'How do you think? We have a maid now, I have to come home to a bloody black . . .'

'Barend!'

He mumbled something.

'Where did you learn that?' But she knew where. Christo, the covert racist, bemoaning his lot in front of his son: 'Now we have to come home to a bloody black. Thanks to your mother.' Without wondering for one second whether he shared the blame for it.

'Ma, what do you care?'

Milla reached for her cigarettes. She must keep her cool. 'I had hoped we could talk. Without blame. I thought if we talked often, we could try to rebuild our relationship.'

'So *I* drove you away.'

'Barend, our relationship was totally wrecked. I am prepared to try and fix it. If you are.'

'Will you come home?'

'Maybe we shouldn't talk about the future. Let's take it day by day. Let's just try to fix it first. What do you think?'

He was silent for a long time. 'OK.'

11

8 September 2009. Tuesday.

In Rajkumar's office Janina Mentz put the Report Squad's work down in front of the fat Indian and said, 'It's not good enough.'

And then she told him what changes she wanted, more emphasis to be laid on possible weapons transactions. She did not enlighten Raj as to the source of her inspiration. Only an hour before she had read the latest article in *Die Burger* describing the parliamentary storm that had erupted over the DA MP's allegations that the ANC government had been selling weapons to so-called pariah states. 'National security has been jeopardised. Maynier could be criminally charged,' a member of the ruling party had said.

Janina Mentz was delighted at this turn of events, the whole question of arms deals brought back into the spotlight. She knew that was the last thing the President wanted, given the stigma that clung to Mo Shaik, likely candidate to head the new intelligence superstructure, even if only by association with his convicted brother.

If she handled it right, this offered her leverage.

9 September 2009. Wednesday.

D-Day for Operation EAM.

Quinn sat at three monitors wearing a communications headset. He was alone; they wanted no witnesses if this went awry. He was tense, this operation had been his idea and it was risky. A small error could be glossed over, managed as a temporary setback. But if things went badly pear-shaped, the whole Supreme Committee project would be down the tubes.

The goal was to plant an electro-acoustic microphone (EAM) in the wall of 15 Chamberlain Street. Also known as a concrete microphone, the device was sometimes used by plumbers to detect water leaks in walls.

He had come up with the plan himself a week ago, to use an existing structure to plant the microphone deep within the brick and cement of No 15's front wall – the TV satellite dish, which a former owner had bolted to the exterior wall just to the left of the front door.

Step two was the preparation. The PIA's technical division, led by an enthusiastic Rajkumar, had made an identical replica of the dish and supporting arm, based on photos taken through the window of the house opposite. One of the four bolts now housed the microphone. A radio transmitter and battery were built into the pipe of the support arm. The radio receiver was already installed in the surveillance house at 16A Chamberlain.

Step three would begin now. This was the risky part. They must replace the original dish with a new one. They had nine minutes in which to do this.

Nine minutes, that was how long Baboo Rayan, Supreme Committee dogsbody and watchman, left the premises every morning to buy milk and a newspaper at a café in Victoria Street. Sometimes it was longer, depending on the traffic in Mountain Street, but it was never less than nine minutes.

On the monitors in front of him were three different images. The middle one came from number 16A, a video feed showing the Supreme Committee house across the street, where Baboo Rayan's white Hyundai Elantra was parked. The second monitor, to the left, was from inside the panel van around the corner and showed the driver's view of the street. The third, on the right, showed the front of the café where Rayan did his shopping every morning without fail.

There was no video in the old, beat-up bakkie on the corner of Chamberlain and Mountain Street. It was Quinn's crisis management, his plan B – a way to block off the street and delay Rayan. He did not want to use it, because it could easily create suspicion among the extremists, who had been hyper-suspicious and extra cautious over the past weeks. About everything.

On the centre screen the front door of 15 Chamberlain opened and Rayan appeared.

'Stand by,' said Quinn into the small microphone in front of his mouth.

He watched Rayan stop on the pavement and look up and down the street, as he always did. Then he unlocked the door of the Elantra and got in. He adjusted the car radio first. He started the car and shifted gears.

Rayan began to drive.

Quinn pressed the button of the stopwatch. 'OK, Handyman, it's a go,' Quinn said.

The panel van began to move, the one with the fictitious TV installation company logo on its sides.

Rayan's Elantra disappeared from the centre screen.

Quinn checked the image on the left. The panel van turned into Chamberlain Street. Rayan's car approached from the front. Rayan ignored the van and drove past it.

'Let's speed it up.'

Central monitor. 15 Chamberlain. He waited for the panel van to appear. Seconds ticked away.

'T minus eight,' Quinn read the time from the stopwatch.

The panel van made a U-turn and parked so that the video camera faced down the street and the front door and satellite dish were visible from number 16A.

The technician and his assistant jumped out and jogged around to the rear doors.

'Take it easy. Don't rush. Act normal.'

They moved a little more calmly. Opened the rear doors, removed the first ladder and the toolbox.

Nervously Quinn checked the video footage of the café, although it was far too early for Rayan to be there.

His team carried the ladder and toolbox to the gate of number 15. One of them opened it. They began unfolding the ladder, as the dish was set up high. Leaned the ladder against the wall. The technician climbed up and carefully examined the bolts, called down to his colleague below, 'Thirteen socket.'

Rayan had not yet reached the café.

The technician loosened the TV cable and began unscrewing the bolts, while his assistant walked back to the van to fetch the new dish and foot piece.

'T minus seven.'

Rayan's Elantra stopped in front of the café.

'He's a little ahead of schedule, let's focus,' said Quinn.

‘Bolts are rusty,’ said the technician on the ladder. ‘Pass me the Q20.’

Quinn said nothing. Just watched. The assistant was on his way back to the panel van to fetch the second ladder. All according to plan.

Rayan got out and walked into the café.

Please let there be other customers, Quinn thought.

‘Bolts are a bit of a problem,’ said the technician.

‘What?’

‘Rust. Can’t move two of them.’

Rayan had disappeared into the café. Quinn checked the stopwatch. ‘You have one minute to make the abort call.’

‘Roger.’ Quinn saw the technician spray more Q20 on the bolt. The assistant put the second ladder next to the first.

The technician struggled to loosen the bolt. Strained at it.

Seconds ticked away.

The technician sprayed and tried again. The bolt wouldn’t budge. Sprayed again, all the bolts. For a long time. Coupled the socket spanner to the bolt, wrenched at it, determined.

Progress too slow.

‘T minus six.’

Still he struggled with the bolts. Quinn’s palms were sweating. Rayan was still in the café.

‘Damn,’ said the technician.

‘Thirty seconds to make the call.’

He watched the man wrestle with the equipment. One bolt loosened. ‘One down.’ He removed it, hurriedly.

Rayan was still in the café.

Maybe he should put the team in the bakkie on standby, Quinn thought. There was more rust than they had bargained on.

Not yet. Keep that for a last resort.

‘Two down.’

‘Too slow.’

‘Hang on, I’ll get them . . .’

‘T minus five approaching. This is the point of no return. What’s your call?’

He heard the technician grunt with effort. ‘Three down, it’s a go.’

‘Roger. Speed it up.’

Rayan emerged from the café, plastic bag with milk hanging from his forearm, the newspaper in his hands, his eyes scanning the headlines.

Take your time, Baboo.

'Four down. It's out.'

Quinn saw the old dish handed down to the assistant. He put it on the ground and climbed up the second ladder with the new one. He got to the top and took the new screws carefully out of his pocket, passed them one by one to the technician. During the dress rehearsal they had dropped the screws twice, losing precious seconds.

Baboo Rayan reached the Elantra. He lowered the newspaper. Looked across the street, momentarily straight into the TV camera lens. He's a fool, thought Quinn, a moron going through the motions of observation, but seeing nothing. They had had a GPS transmitter on his car for a month, they had been observing him for nearly two weeks, right under his nose, and he was blissfully unaware. He looked, but saw nothing.

Rayan took out his keys and unlocked the door of the Elantra. He tossed the newspaper on the passenger seat and took the plastic bag off his arm . . .'

'T minus four.' Behind schedule.

Rayan got into his car.

The assistant pressed the new foot piece against the wall. The technician pushed the first bolt in.

Rayan fiddled with the radio again.

The technician put in two more screws, one after the other. The fourth was the microphone, he had to work carefully, there were thin wires to be connected.

Began tightening the three screws.

The assistant let go and climbed down the ladder and folded it.

Rayan's Elantra began to move.

The assistant took the ladder back to the panel van.

'Microphone going in.'

The assistant came back for the old dish.

'T minus three.'

'Microphone in. Connecting now.'

The assistant packed the old dish away and came back for the toolbox. The technician was having trouble with the delicate wiring.

'Dammit,' he said.

'Connect the TV cable now. We can connect the microphone tomorrow.'

'I'll make it.'

'Do it.'

'Roger.'

The technician connected the TV cable.

The assistant came and stood at the foot of the first ladder, ready to take it.

'TV connected.'

Quinn checked the stopwatch. Rayan was at least a minute away from the corner.

'You have thirty seconds.' He decided to put the intercept team in the bakkie on standby. 'Intercept team, start your engine.'

'Roger.'

The technician was back to working on connecting the microphone wires.

'Twenty seconds.'

Quinn looked at the left-hand monitor. He would be able to see the Elantra come around the corner.

'Ten seconds.'

'Damn, damn, damn.'

'Nine, eight, seven, interceptor team, stand by . . .'

'Roger.'

'Connected,' the technician said with great relief.

'Get the fuck out of there,' Quinn couldn't keep the tension out of his voice.

The technician slid down the ladder. The assistant grabbed the ladder. They ran to the panel van. Pushed the ladder in and slammed the door. Went around to the cab.

'Close the gate,' said Quinn sharply. The technician ran.

'Don't run!'

Walked. Closed the little gate. Walked back to the panel van, got in.

They were out of time.

The van drove off.

Ten seconds later Rayan turned the corner.

Quinn gulped and leaned back in his chair. He wiped his palms on his trousers.

'Intercept team, stand down. Gentlemen, that was magnificent. Please test the microphone.'

The voice of the female operator in number 16A was heard for the first time. 'Microphone is a go.'

'Well done,' said Quinn. 'Very well done.'

He switched off his headset microphone. So that he could exhale loudly.

12

Photostatic record: *Diary of Milla Strachan*
Date of entry: *9 September 2009*

Jessica invited me to dinner. She is such an enigma, with her looks she could have been a model.

Highlight of the day: the tango. I struggled with it. Then Mr Soderstrom said the tango is four legs, two bodies, one heart. 'Most dances,' he quoted someone, 'are for people who are falling in love. The tango is a dance for those who have survived it, and are still a little angry about having their hearts so badly treated.'

Then I understood.

10 September 2009. Thursday.

They stood staring at the TV screen with grim faces. Rajkumar was the only one sitting. Quinn and Masilo stood.

They watched the video footage of the members of the Supreme Committee arriving within minutes of each other – Suleiman Dolly the last one – and entering the front door of 15 Chamberlain Street.

Via the EAM in the satellite dish support they heard the men talking. The sound was hollow and fuzzy. Rajkumar's team would use programming to refine it later. But it was still good enough to hear the extremists greeting each other, light-heartedly enquiring about each other's health inside the house.

'Come. The agenda this morning is short.' It was probably Suleiman Dolly's voice coming over the system, and the three observers pricked up their ears. Hope burgeoned.

'That's understandable, Sheikh,' said another Committee member.

'Why haven't we had any news yet? We've run out of time,' said another.

'We must just have faith,' said Dolly.

'*Allahu Akbar*.'

'Come, let us go,' said Dolly.

Quinn looked at Masilo.

'Does that mean what I think it means?' asked Rajkumar.

'Hang on,' said Masilo.

Over the loudspeakers came the sound of feet shuffling.

'They are moving,' said Raj and looked at the blueprints of number 15, which were spread out in front of the big TV screen. The question was, where to? And how well the EAM would work.

The loudspeakers fell silent

'Shit,' said Raj. 'They're going down to the basement.'

Quinn adjusted the volume. There was a hissing, very faint echoes of a man's voice, but indecipherable.

'Would you be able to filter that?' asked Quinn.

Rajkumar shook his head, very disappointed. 'Probably not.'

They stood and listened to the speakers, till the last shred of hope evaporated.

'Come on, Raj,' said Masilo, encouragingly. 'We all knew the chances were going to be slim. They are not stupid.'

'I know. But fuck knows, we need a break. I mean, we deserve it. Just a bit of luck.'

'All things come to those who wait,' said Tau Masilo.

Rajkumar completed the saying in his usual, pessimistic manner. 'They come, but often come too late.'

11 September 2009. Friday.

Janina Mentz was on her way to the office of the Minister of Safety and Security, three blocks away, for their eleven o'clock appointment.

She walked erect, full of confidence, in the rain. She had prepared well. In her briefcase was The Report. But that was just the final planting of the seed. First she had to do the spadework, the much more important preparation of the seedbed. She had planned the process, visualised it: the Minister, a jovial man with shaven head and an easy smile, would receive her cordially and ask her to take tea with him. She would accept with thanks. She would sit down, take her time opening the combination locks of the briefcase, take out the file, but keep it on her lap.

He would ask how things were with her, and the Agency. She would say things were going particularly well, thank you, Mr Minister. And thank you for making time on such short notice, but I wanted to bring this to your attention as quickly as possible. Especially in the light of recent events.

She would wait for his reaction, for the raising of an eyebrow and freezing of his smile. Then she would say, choosing her words carefully, that it was a sensitive issue. Too . . . awkward to discuss at the weekly Security Meeting.

She would let that sink in. The Minister was a clever man. He would draw the necessary conclusions. Perhaps she would help things along a little by emphasising that only the PIA had access to this information (with a nod in the direction of the file). That it was consequently safe.

And then she would tell the Minister that it had to do with arms dealing.

She would depend on the baggage connected to the last term, baggage that the ruling party and the candidate for the new intelligence superstructure could not shake off. And on the latest controversy, so timeously unleashed by the Opposition. That ought to make the Minister's heart rate speed up. Janina Mentz was depending on it.

Again she would delay, before she made the next, complex revelation.

Sir, there are Muslim extremists involved. And all indications that they are planning an act of terrorism in Cape Town. Using imported weapons . . .

That would give him something to ruminate over.

We are going to focus all possible resources on this, because we are so aware of what a difficult position this could place the President.

The Minister would understand what the 'difficult position' meant. Given the arms sales to Iran and Libya.

And then she would slowly raise the file from her lap and place it solemnly on his desk. As if she bore a great weight.

Should you want to discuss this case in any way once you have studied the detail, I am at your service twenty-four hours a day.

Before the Parliament Street crossing Janina Mentz lifted her briefcase to look at her wristwatch. A little too early. She slowed her pace, holding the umbrella tightly while the cold front raged around her.

13

12 September 2009. Saturday.

'You *do* realise, we are all rejects,' said Jessica the Goddess as she poured more red wine, her words fuzzy from the alcohol. 'All those questions you answered during the interviews, all the psycho-babble like "are you an ambitious person?", it's all bullshit. All they wanted to know was, are you a reject. They like that. A lost cause, an outsider. Damaged goods, well isolated.'

Milla was hardly sober either. Her nod was a bit too effusive.

'I mean, look at us. The rest of the Agency is a model of affirmative action, a perfect reflection of the Rainbow Nation, but we are all white, all over forty, and all fucked up. Theunie was fired from a daily in Jo'burg because he plagiarised a column. Twice. That's why his third wife divorced him. Mac used to be the arts editor at a Johannesburg daily, until they caught him with the mail boy. In the mail room. And you're the runaway housewife. And then there's me. Want one?' and she held out the pack of long thin cigarettes to Milla.

'Thank you.'

Jessica lit her cigarette first, concentrating. Then she raised her glass in a toast. 'To the Scandal Squad.'

Milla did the same, clinking her glass against Jessica's. 'You had a scandal?'

'Oh, yes.'

It was the wine that gave Milla the courage. 'What did you do?'

'You haven't heard?'

'No.'

'Strange.' The Goddess smiled through her perfect teeth. 'Mine being the more interesting, I would have thought Mac would have at least hinted . . .'

'Oh, no,' said Milla.

'Well, then, let me share,' said Jessica, and drew deeply on her cigarette. 'I was the parliamentary correspondent for the *Times*. And then I went and fucked a very senior government official . . . Don't ask, because I won't tell. Had an affair, for two years. Until his wife walked in on us. Big scene. Hysterics, lots of throwing of small household objects, the most charming death threats. She had me fired. He organised the Agency job. Was a great fuck he was. Speaking of which, when last did you?'

'Me?'

'You.'

'Have a great fuck?' The word surprised Milla as if she didn't know it still inhabited her somewhere.

'Yes.'

'I don't know . . .'

'How can you not know?'

'I don't think I've ever had a really great fuck.'

'Never?'

'OK, maybe not never . . . the first time was pretty good.'

'With your husband?'

'My ex-husband.'

'You've slept with one man?'

'Well, you know . . . I got pregnant, then we had to get married . . .'

'Jesus Christ.'

'I know . . .'

'Why didn't you have an affair, for God's sake?'

'It . . . Well . . . I don't think . . . I don't know . . .'

'Never lived dangerously?'

'No . . .'

'And now? You've been single for what, two months already . . .'

'I've . . .'

'You've been wasting time.'

'I suppose . . .'

'Want me to introduce you to someone?'

'No!'

She examined Milla speculatively. 'I love lost causes. We have a lot of work ahead of us.'

Milla laughed.

'I'll have to introduce you to the pleasures of the cougar.'

'The cougar?'

'I am, dear Milla, a self-confessed, unabashed . . . no, proud, cougar. A ravisher of younger men. Early twenties. Lean, mean, hungry, NSA.'

'NSA?'

'No strings attached. Perfect solution. Hard young bodies, stamina, so very enthusiastic. And a shared dislike of commitment. Love them and leave them.'

'Aaa . . .'

'I'm going to set you up . . .'

'No, Jess. No, no, no . . .'

Operation Shawwal
Transcription: *Audio surveillance, M. Strachan. No 14 Daven Court, Davenport Street, Vredehoek*
Date and Time: *7 October. 23.32*

MS: Christo was handsome. You know how it is, at that age, if a good-looking young man with confidence picks you out from all the rest, and your friends 'ooh' and 'aah'. I had issues with my self-image, I was just so – relieved that he showed interest in me. So . . . grateful . . . He was so . . . He seemed to be worldly wise, so easy with himself. I don't know if I was ever in love with him. Maybe I'm lying to myself . . . I was drunk that night. It was Rag Week. Everyone was drunk. That's no excuse, I would have slept with him some time or other, I was ready for it, I wanted to know what it felt like . . .

13 September 2009. Sunday.

It was after ten before Milla woke from her drunken slumber.

Fragments of the previous evening milled in her head. Jessica's sensual, drink-befuddled voice:

We are all rejects.

You're the runaway housewife.

You've slept with one man?

Never lived dangerously?

Lord, had she really taken part in that conversation?

She had, and more. She had told her story, late in the night, the whole truth, in drunken melancholy, and Jessica had held her hand and wept along with her. It was all coming back, and mortification descended on her in waves.

And the worry: how on earth had she got home? She couldn't remember.

She jumped up and looked out of the window and saw her Renault Clio parked there, a small relief, because suddenly the headache began to pound. She climbed back into bed, pulled the covers over her head. She had driven home in her drunken state, she could have caused an accident . . . She could have been locked up, how Christo would have enjoyed that. How could she do that to her son? 'Was that *your* drunken mother in the newspaper? The one who ran away?'

She couldn't do that sort of thing.

She lay there feeling guilty until she could stand it no longer, got up gingerly, put on her dressing gown and slippers, and shuffled off to the kitchen to get the coffee machine going.

And then thought, well, last night she had lived a little. Of all that she had lost, she had regained at least a little piece.

Transcription: *Audio surveillance, J.L. Shabangu (aka 'Inkunzi') and A. Hendricks, telephone conversation*
Date and Time: *13 September 2009. 20.32*

S: I have a message for Inkabi.
H: What is the message?
S: The export deal . . .

H: Yes.

S: The guy who wants to buy the goods, you know? He is in Cape Town. He is an Inkosi . . .

H: I don't understand Inkosi.

S: Inkosi is a big man. A chief. You know . . . of a . . . company. How can I say? We are in the same business, this buyer and I . . . But his business is in Cape Town . . .

H: OK.

S: We have heard that his name is Tweety the Bird.

H: Tweety the Bird.

S: That is what we have heard. So we think you can help to find him.

H: OK.

S: And we think the goods are going to travel at the end of the month. Any time from the 24th.

H: Do you know more about the transport and the route?

S: We think it will be by truck, but the route is not certain. That is why you must find this Tweety the Bird. He will know the route. You must make him tell us.

H: OK.

S: I will give you a number. The number will change next Sunday, and then I will call you again.

H: What is the number?

14

14 September 2009. Monday.

At 6.46 when Quinn was having breakfast with his wife and two teenage sons in their house in Nansen Street, Claremont, he received an SMS. He glanced at the screen of his cellphone, excused himself from the kitchen table, went into the bedroom and phoned Advocate Tau Masilo.

'Osman is at the airport, on his way to Walvis Bay,' he said when Masilo answered.

'What time does his flight leave?'

'Probably within the hour.'

'Then we better get cracking.'

'We only have one operator in Namibia. In Windhoek. I will phone him now and hear how soon he can be in Walvis Bay.'

'Thanks Quinn . . . Walvis Bay? What would the Supreme Committee do in Walvis Bay?'

'Why Walvis Bay?' Janina Mentz asked at 8.41 at the round table in her office.

'Import harbour. For the weapons.' Tau Masilo said.

'You're speculating.'

Masilo has prepared. 'Occam's Law. The simplest explanation is usually the right one. After the Ismail Mohammed debacle, the Supreme Committee will want minimum attention drawn to the Cape, they are warier than ever. They know it will be hard to land the weapons here, and if things go wrong, the focus will be on them. Give them credit. Walvis Bay is a clever move. Low security, cheaper bribes, good transport links via the Trans Kalahari corridor to Gauteng. And if some error slips in, there is little evidence of their involvement.'

Mentz considered that viewpoint and nodded. 'Could be. What do we do?'

'Osman's flight is via Windhoek, where he must change planes. We have only one operative there. He is already on his way to Walvis by road, and he ought to be there an hour before Osman.'

'What time is Osman arriving there?'

'One o'clock this afternoon.'

'How good is our man in Namibia?'

'His name is Reinhard Rohn. Thirty years' experience. An old fox. His reports are always thorough. Prompt.'

'Where do we find these people?' But then Mentz frowned. 'If only we had someone inside, Tau, we could have had three of our best teams waiting there for Osman.'

Masilo merely nodded, having little stomach for this argument. Then he changed the subject. 'We know who is supposed to buy Johnson Chitepo's shipment of diamonds.'

It took Mentz a moment to make the leap. 'Oh?'

'The role allocations in this drama keep getting more interesting. Inkunzi Shabangu called the Committee this weekend with the news.

The latest supporting player is apparently one Mr Willem "Tweetybird" de la Cruz, gang leader on the Cape Flats.'

'You're not serious.'

'Come on, Mac, we have work to do,' Mrs Killian said just after ten, and rolled her chair up to Milla's desk. She waited for MacFarland to ride his chair closer before she sat down and put the fat files down on the desktop.

'Milla, this is your first big one, and we must have something ready by tomorrow morning,' she said. 'But don't worry, Mac will be your safety net . . .'

Mrs Killian handed the first file to Milla.

'Criminal gangs in the Cape Flats. There is a lot of material here, the challenge is to reduce it to three or four pages. One on the background, but focus on the last decade, the rest is really irrelevant. And one on the current state of affairs, again just broad strokes, a brief overview. Remember, we want the top management to be informed, but we don't want to waste their time. And then one page on a particular syndicate: the Restless Ravens. Not more than a paragraph or two on their history, keep the focus on how they look now, what they are involved in. Which brings me to you, Mac. You will be looking at a Mr Willem de la Cruz, also known as "Tweetybird" or "Willy" . . .'

'My, my . . .'

'Not now, Mac. De la Cruz is the leader of the Restless Ravens, he's the one who most concerns us . . .'

'As he should. You know what they say, a tweetybird in the hand is worth . . .'

'Mac!'

'Come on, mother. Tweetybird. The Ravens. And Willy . . . Freudian, to say the least?'

At twenty-five past twelve, Quinn put his head into Masilo's office. 'Reinhard Rohn, our man in Namibia, just called. He is in the arrivals hall of Walvis Bay airport and waiting for Osman.'

'He knows he must be very discreet?'

'He knows.'

'How will he identify Osman?'

'I sent three photos to his cellphone.'

Masilo was content. 'Keep me up to speed.'

'I will . . .' Quinn hesitated. 'Advocate, this thing with Tweetybird de la Cruz . . .'

'Yes?'

'If the Supreme Committee . . . This whole thing can spark a war on the Cape Flats. If Suleiman Dolly starts whispering to their fellow Muslims at PAGAD. The People against Drugs and Gangsterism might get very excited . . .'

'I don't think Dolly will be that stupid. He wants the diamonds, and if he foments trouble, the smugglers may look for another buyer.'

Quinn shook his head. 'I hope you're right.'

Fourteen kilometres east of Walvis Bay – and only two kilometres from the border of the Namib Naukluft National Park – lay the Walvis Bay airport, a tiny oasis in the flat and endless stretches of the Namib Desert.

The modern airport building, with its grey steel roof and salmon-coloured walls, stood among palm trees and small patches of green lawn. For Reinhard Rohn, Presidential Intelligence Agency operative, the greatest advantage and disadvantage was the fact that the building was relatively small and the airport reasonably quiet. Departures and Arrivals were alongside each other, and easy to watch. But someone trying to be discreet there had little place to hide.

Rohn was a fifty-one-year-old veteran. Therefore he stood at the windows looking out over the runway to make sure he identified Osman when he disembarked from the plane, and on the way to the building. Rohn memorised his face, the colour of the tailored suit (light brown), the open-collared shirt (light blue) and the small black travelling case that Osman dragged along on wheels.

Then he walked out of the building, across the grey-paved path and the sandy parking area to where his white Toyota bakkie was parked. He got in and wound the windows down, took the small pair of binoculars out of the cubbyhole, focused them on the entrance, and waited.

Seven minutes later he saw Osman emerge, saw that the coloured man had no other luggage, just the travel case.

He watched him as he walked to the Avis parking lot, until he was out of sight.

Rohn switched the bakkie on and turned it around, so that he could watch the correct access road.

15

At nine minutes past four in the afternoon Quinn reported to his boss that Rohn's tailing of Shaheed Latif Osman in Walvis Bay had proceeded perfectly.

'Osman took an Avis car straight to the harbour, where he parked in front of the offices of Consolidated Fisheries, in the area of the fishing fleet. He went in to the company's building at 13.35 and only emerged two hours later, at 15.30. After that he went to the Protea Hotel in Sam Nujoma Avenue, where he booked in. Rohn also took a room and kept an eye on proceedings there. We are researching Consolidated Fisheries, and Raj's people will have a report ready tomorrow morning.'

At twenty past four Mother Killian summoned Jessica the Goddess to give her the new task. When Jessica walked back to her work station ten minutes later, spitting ('A fucking fishing company in a fucking boondocks harbour town . . .'), she broke Milla's intense concentration, so that she raised her head from the bulky research on street gangs and said to Donald MacFarland, 'Mac, there's stuff in here that does not reflect well on the government.'

'So?'

'So, do I include it?'

'Of course. Spy the Beloved Country, even if it hurts.'

'OK.'

Report: *Criminal Gangs of the Cape Flats*
Date: *14 September 2009*
Compiled by: *Milla Strachan and Donald MacFarland*

Background

In the last decade of the Apartheid-era, gang-related activities in the former Cape Province were limited mostly to the former coloured group areas, especially in the lower socio-economic neighbourhoods of the Cape Flats.

The type and extent of their crimes was relatively limited, mainly as a result of international isolation, limitation by the Group Areas Act, and an effective, experienced police force with extensive powers, including detention without trial and dubious interrogation methods.

This situation began to change subtly in the early nineties, when the former SA Police Force was used more and more for suppression of political unrest. Street gangs could relax, accelerate their recruitment and systematically expand their activities, which up till then were small-scale and limited.

It was in fact the transition to a democratic government in 1994, and the major changes in the following six years, that gave organised crime the opportunity to move from a cottage industry to international players.

The following factors apply:

Post 1994: Opening of borders and international influx

Dispensing with strict border control, and South Africa's re-entry to international trade resulted in an influx of foreign tourists, currency and investment, which included the most notorious players in trans-national organised crime. It was primarily the syndicates from Nigeria, Russia, China, Italy and Colombia who saw the opportunities, and who rapidly established themselves, mainly in Johannesburg, Durban and Cape Town.

It is estimated that more than 100,000 Nigerian nationals illegally entered South Africa in that period, and settled here.

Existing infrastructure

Despite the country's isolation, the South Africa of 1994 possessed excellent infrastructure – a highly efficient banking service, excellent telecommunications networks, and extensive road-, rail-, and air-links.

Crime syndicates benefited just as much from these as the foreign investors and legal new businesses.

In addition, there was already a basic framework of organised crime in place, in the form of the gangs of the Cape Peninsula. Heroin and cocaine in particular began flooding into the country, and found an existing basic handling and distribution network, however unsophisticated.

The smuggling of, and trade in, other drugs, arms, ivory, wood, precious stones, abalone and humans, increased gradually.

A weakened police force and modern legislation

In the midst of the influx of trans-national crime syndicates, from 1994 to 1998 the former SAP transformed into the new South African Police

Services (SAPS). Ironically, the consequences of this process would be considered one of the key factors in the rise of organised crime in the Western Cape in particular.

Affirmative Action, a high percentage of resignations and retirements of senior officers, retraining and redeployment, alteration of structures and transfers not only led to massive loss of experience within police ranks, but also seriously harmed trust between members and general morale within the Service. Infighting, frustration, obstruction and politicisation contributed to the SAPS taking its eye off the ball of organised crime.

Legislation on criminal procedure, founded on modern, humanitarian, and internationally acceptable human rights principles, also followed during this period, forcing law enforcers to respect the rights of suspects, change arrest protocols and interrogation techniques considerably (including a total shift from the so-called confession formula – read physical intimidation – of the Apartheid-era).

To a large degree, crime intelligence collapsed as a result of this, and had to be rebuilt from the ground up.

The result was a window of opportunity for organised crime, which was utilised fully.

PAGAD, CORE and POCA

With the police paralysed, civilian resistance to crime in the coloured areas exploded. The most famous of these was PAGAD (People against Gangsterism and Drugs), the Muslim pressure group that initiated vigilantism against gang bosses in the Cape Flats in 1996.

Marches on drug houses, shooting incidents, assaults and elimination of leaders seriously interfered with existing gangs, destroyed command structures, and dramatically limited criminal activities.

It was an evolutionary process for gang leaders – only the strongest survived. The remaining syndicate bosses reacted by forming the Community Outreach Forum, or CORE. The name was deliberately cynical, and had nothing to do with the community whatsoever. It was a consolidation and regrouping, and, for the first time in their history, organised crime bosses agreed to cooperate. They set up a small, effective executive committee, which, within months, had streamlined money laundering, smuggling and international cooperation and taken them to new heights of professionalism and secrecy.

The other consequence of PAGAD's behaviour was that the senior management of the gangs moved out of the coloured community and into traditional white neighbourhoods – and expanded their activities to these areas as well. The sale, especially of cocaine and marijuana, among others, found a new market.

A final factor was the parliamentary acceptance of the POCA (Prevention of Organised Crime Act), wide-reaching legislation that also gave the State the power to confiscate the assets of gang leaders and their confederates.

The Restless Ravens

The Restless Ravens were a relatively small, but very effective street gang that in the early nineties mainly operated in Manenberg, Bonteheuwel, Bishop Lavis, Heideveld, Surrey and Primrose Park.

Their leader was the ruthless, ambitious and highly intelligent Willem (Willy) 'Tweetybird' de la Cruz (53), who had by then already served two terms in jail, for assault (1978–1981), and robbery (1983–1988). He owed his nickname to his hobby, the breeding of budgies, but also from the ritual of placing a living bird in the mouth of traitors after he had killed them.

De la Cruz and the Restless Ravens profited largely from the chaos that PAGAD caused in 1996. Particularly because they were small and therefore seen as less of a threat, PAGAD generally left them in peace. Not only did the Restless Ravens survive this period, but as a result of the vigilantism, they acquired new recruits and new territories.

De la Cruz was also one of the founding members of CORE, and with his good negotiation and networking skills he played a key role in the alliance. He also recognised, from an early stage, the threat of the POCA laws and the application of them through the special investigation unit, the Scorpions.

His fear that authorities would seize his considerable financial and property assets led him to make two important appointments – each one a confidant whom he had met in prison.

The first was an accountant, the former bookkeeper Moegamat Perkins, (49, sentence for fraud served out from 1982–1988), who had to ensure that the assets of the Ravens were, firstly, not in the name of de la Cruz, and secondly, structured so that confiscation was well-nigh impossible.

The second appointment was that of a 'general', a strongman who could assert the Ravens' authority through murder, assault and intimidation, but also a counterweight to ensure that the influence of the accountant, Perkins, was limited. His choice fell on Terrence Richard Baadjies (50, 'Terry',

'Terror', 'The Terrorist' – sentenced to a young offenders' institution at age 15 for murder, later serving jail time for dealing in forbidden substances, assault with intent, and manslaughter).

Both appointments were master strokes. When the Scorpions, and especially the SAPS Unit for Organised Crime, seized nearly R200 million in gang assets in the Cape Peninsula in the period 2000 to 2006, the Restless Ravens were untouchable. With Terror and his soldiers always ready to take over disadvantaged syndicates' business through violent means, the Restless Ravens developed into one of the most successful criminal organisations during the same period. De la Cruz's prominence in CORE was also boosted.

Recruitment of young coloured men from the Cape Flats into the Ravens was also helped considerably by the socio-economic deterioration of that community since 1994. Some of the most important factors are:

The drug Tik (Methamphetamine, or 'Meth'): 91% of all Tik dependents are coloured – with an average age of 16.6 years.

18% of all coloured youths between the ages of 14 and 34 are in jail for crimes.

21.8% of coloured youths at age 16 are not at school.

48% of the coloured community are economically inactive, or unemployed. (Of a total of 2.7 million, 975,000 are economically inactive and 340,000 unemployed.)

In conclusion:

The success of the Restless Ravens (and their POCA evasion) has attracted just the sort of attention they wished to avoid. According to a recent report in *Die Burger* (28 August 2009) the new provincial DA government in the Western Cape has given instructions that a special prosecutor be appointed to investigate the activities of the gang – with an eye to charges of tax evasion.

16

15 September 2009. Tuesday.

Late that afternoon Mentz invited them in with a smile and a light-hearted, 'Sit down, gentlemen.' She told them the Minister had called her after lunch. He was keen to hear of any new developments. She was able to tell him about Walvis Bay. Then he said, Janina, the President and I have great appreciation for your work, but particularly for the manner in which you are handling this. Have a look at your budget. If you need more, talk to us, because this is a high priority for us. Something else I must mention: you may have heard the rumours of a new Intelligence Structure, I hear the corridors are full of it. Now, Janina, I would like to tell you now, provisionally your Agency is not part of the President's plans.

Janina Mentz leaned back in her chair and looked at the two men with great satisfaction.

Masilo pressed his thumbs under his braces and smiled slowly and broadly.

Rajkumar, loyal to his nature, pounced on the word 'provisionally'.

Mentz reassured him, but today without the habitual frown and suppressed irritation. 'That was exactly what we wanted, Raj, it was our primary goal, and we achieved it. Let's enjoy the moment. And let me thank you both for excellent work.' And then she added: 'I want you to convey my congratulations to the Report Squad. I thought their work yesterday was excellent. And let Mrs Killian take them to lunch somewhere nice. On my account.'

The men disguised their astonishment. They could not remember ever seeing Janina Mentz like this.

Mentz directed her smile at Masilo. 'And how is our man in Walvis Bay?'

The advocate reported that according to operator Reinhard Rohn, Osman had spent the night in the Protea Hotel and flown back to Cape Town the next day at 12.55. A team was waiting for him here and carefully followed him to the meeting house of the Supreme Committee in Chamberlain Street, where it is assumed he gave his report. In the meantime Quinn had given Rohn orders to stay in Walvis Bay and see what he could do to solve the riddle.

'And what do we know about Consolidated Fisheries, Raj?'

He handed her Jessica's concise report, and said that the Report Squad could find no evidence whatsoever that the company was involved in any form of illegal activity. 'They are part of the Erongo Group of companies, which is listed on their Stock Exchange. They own a fishing fleet of nine stern trawler vessels, a fish and tinning factory, and they exploit the Benguela region. There's nothing there.'

'But,' said Tau Masilo, ever the lawyer at work, 'listen to this for a second,' and he straightened a sheet of paper in front of him and read aloud: 'All vessels wishing to enter Walvis Bay Harbour, require the following information to be submitted seventy-two hours prior to the vessel's arrival, by email or fax: International Ship Security Certificate Number, Security Status of the vessel, Date of departure from last Port, et cetera . . .'

Masilo looked up at Mentz, 'All vessels,' he said and let that hang there for a moment before completing the sentence: 'with the *exception* of fishing vessels . . .'

'Damn,' said Rajkumar.

'I suggest, ma'am, that we deploy our three teams in Walvis Bay. That is where they plan to land the weapons. Without a shadow of a doubt . . .'

17 September 2009. Thursday.

The electro-acoustic microphone in the wall of 15 Chamberlain Street yielded dividends for the first time.

Just after eleven in the morning, Shaheed Latif Osman arrived and went inside while the female operative across the street recorded it in photographs, and on video. She was wearing her headset, but did not expect to hear much through the concrete microphone; usually the men spoke little in the front room.

But to her surprise she heard Osman's voice: 'All quiet?'

Transcription: *Audio surveillance, S.L. Osman and B. Rayan, 15 Chamberlain Street, Upper Woodstock*
Date and Time: *17 September 2009. 11.04*

SLO: All quiet?
BR: Dead quiet, Uncle.
SLO: Are you absolutely sure, Baboo?
BR: I am.
SLO: Garage cleaned out?
BR: Yes, Uncle. The car will fit in easily.
SLO: Very well. You wait in the garage. When I tell you, open the doors. Once the car is inside, close them again. Baadjies has a bag over his head, but he understands it has to be like that. You will lead him through here

and then downstairs. Then you come out again, the fewer faces he sees, the better. Understood, Baboo?

BR: Understood, Uncle.

The woman operative made sure the conversation had been recorded on the laptop before she phoned Quinn.

Quinn hurried to the monitoring room, where he quickly turned on the TV screens and channelled the live video and audio feeds. He was just in time to see Baboo Rayan push open the second brown wooden door of the garage at number fifteen, look around quickly to see if anyone was watching, and then walk back into the deep shadow inside the garage.

A white Chrysler Neon turned in the driveway and drove into the garage. Baboo Rayan quickly closed the doors.

Quinn listened to the audio feed.

It was quiet for twenty seconds. Then he heard Osman's voice. 'Slowly, Terry, you're going down the stairs now.'

An unfamiliar voice said 'OK.' There were shuffling noises, then it went quiet.

They stood on the roof of Wale Street Chambers so that Masilo could smoke a cigar, 'in celebration'.

Rajkumar was not in a festive mood. 'The Supreme Committee, consorting with a Cape Flats crime gang. Doesn't make sense.'

'Of course it does,' said Advocate Tau Masilo.

'What do you mean?' Rajkumar asked.

Masilo explained. The Supreme Committee had Inkunzi Shabangu on one side, who would try to intercept the diamonds, and now they were talking to Terror Baadjies of the Ravens, the eventual buyers of the diamonds. 'Because they want to cover all their bases. If Bull Shabangu does manage to hijack the stones, they buy it from him. If he doesn't, they do a deal with the Ravens.'

Rajkumar was not yet convinced. 'But at what price?'

'You have to understand the nature of the game. Diamond smugglers all have the same problem; how do they get the most bang for their buck, because international agreements and law enforcement are making it very difficult to sell the stuff these days. The big money is now in India, where more stones are being processed than in Holland. But to sell to the Indians, you need to work through three or four middlemen, each taking a cut. The Ravens will probably get forty cents on the rand if they sell through their channels. But the Supreme Committee has a trump card: Sayyid Khalid bin Alawi Macki. Remember, he is a money launderer, and he probably has a direct line to the Indians. So they can offer the Ravens fifty or sixty cents on the rand, and still get in excess of eighty cents in India. Keep in mind that we are talking about a shipment in the region of a R100 million. The Committee is looking at a worst-case scenario of at least R20 million clear profit. More, if Bull Shabangu intercepts, which still makes that first prize.'

'I did not mean the actual monetary cost,' said Rajkumar, resigned. 'What about the cost of doing business with a crime syndicate, a drug organisation? I mean, PAGAD will shit their pants. The whole extremist community will be up in arms.' He lifted both hands and swept his hair back over his shoulders. 'What I'm trying to say is: the stakes are very high. Which means the ultimate goal is very, very important. Big. Bigger than the terms we've been thinking. So big that they must be able to say the end justifies the means. If this is going to be an act of terrorism, it's going to be ugly. Which makes this really bad news.'

'Bad?' said Masilo. 'We'll stop this thing. And, you have to think like the Director, Raj. In terms of our future, I think it's *great* news.'

Jessica came to fetch Milla from her desk. 'Walk with me,' she whispered.

Milla followed her to the ladies' room. The Goddess took her lipstick out of her handbag and stood in front of the mirror to make repairs. 'A friend of a friend is coming down from Jo'burg this weekend. He's an articled clerk at this big law firm in Jo'burg, beautiful guy, would love to have company.'

'Oh?'

'He's twenty-four, and . . .'

'Twenty-four?'

The Goddess laughed at her and put away her lipstick. 'The perfect age. So much energy. Anyway, he's an articled clerk at this big law firm in Jo'burg, he's down here for the weekend. And he's beautiful . . .'

'Jess, I don't know . . .'

'Just let him take you to a club, have a few drinks, dance a little, have some fun. If he's not your type, you've had a great night. If he is, you fuck him blind.'

Milla blushed. 'I . . .'

'Oh, live a little, Milla.'

She suppressed her discomfort. 'I'll think about it.'

Mentz asked the one question they had not foreseen. 'Why Terrence Baadjies, the enforcer?'

'Ma'am?' Tau Masilo asked, to gain time.

'Why did Tweetybird de la Cruz send his general to the Supreme Committee? Why not Moegamat Perkins, the money man?'

He should have known she would study the report in detail. He was annoyed with himself, with Quinn and Rajkumar, that not one of them had thought of it.

'And more,' said Mentz, 'why would the Committee agree to negotiate with Baadjies? He is everything they despise, and he is, I understand, a very dangerous man.'

Masilo knew he couldn't fool her. 'I don't know,' he said.

'Then we must find out, Tau,' she said.

The frown was back.

She phoned Jessica at half-past nine that night.

'I can't,' she said. 'He's barely older than my son.'

'That's exactly why I never want children,' said the Goddess.

When Milla had rung off and lay back on her couch, she suspected Jessica knew the truth: it was lack of confidence. In herself.

17

18 September 2009. Friday.

For Suleiman Dolly, also known as the Sheikh, it was the day he would be informed of The Date.

His cellphone rang at 07.28. Sayyid Khalid bin Alawi Macki greeted him in the Muslim manner. He said, 'Sheikh, it has been confirmed. Twenty-three Shawwal 1430.'

Dolly's heart beat faster, and he repeated the words. 'Twenty-three Shawwal 1430. *Allahu Akbar.*'

Julius 'Inkunzi' Shabangu would be dead in twelve days, in a pool of blood in his bedroom. But for those twelve days he would remember 18 September as 'Black Friday', because that was the day the Muslims cheated him. And the day that dog Becker crossed his path.

Some time after nine, Abdullah Hendricks, spokesman for Osman, phoned. 'Sir, there have been developments.'

Inkunzi drove his BMW X5 in Sandton's peak traffic without a hands-free set for his cellphone, dividing his focus between the road and the call. So he wasn't alert to trouble initially. 'What developments?' he asked.

'Well, it seems that market forces are at work, if you know what I mean . . .'

'No, I don't know what you mean.'

'Supply and demand, these things are always changing. I have been asked by Inkabi to renegotiate with you.'

'Renegotiate?' Shabangu's complete concentration was now on the phone call and he smelled a rat.

'Yes, sir, unfortunately we are now only able to offer you thirty cents.'

'That's bullshit . . .'

'I am really sorry, but that is my instruction.'

'We had a deal, you tell Osman we had a deal.'

'Please, sir, no names . . .'

'This is bullshit. Why is Osman doing this?'

'Please, sir, we have to stick to the agreed protocols . . .'

'Fuck the protocols, what is Osman doing?'

'Well, to be honest, sir, we have reason to doubt your sources. About the route.'

'The route? I said from the beginning, it will take time, it's a process . . . Wait a minute . . . you bastards . . .'

'Excuse me?'

'You fucking bastards. It's Tweety the Bird, isn't it. You've done a deal with him. That's why you know about the route.'

'No, sir,' Hendricks remained calm, courteous. 'It's simply market forces, our buyer has made a lower offer, and we have to . . .'

'You are fucking screwing me . . .'

Hendricks tried to say something, but Shabangu shouted him down. 'I'm telling you now, I'm going to get the diamonds, and then we'll see what price you pay. I'll find out what fucking route they are going to use, and I'll hijack the whole fucking lot!'

'Please, sir, you are using your cellphone . . .'

'Fuck you,' Inkunzi shouted, and killed the call with a hand shaking in fury. He cursed for ten minutes solid, hitting the steering wheel, glaring at the traffic around him. Then he called both his lieutenants to discuss the Muslims' treachery, and then his chief informer in Harare.

'Why the fuck do I pay you?'

'Inkunzi?'

'Why the fuck do I pay you? You have the route all wrong, and I'm telling you now, if you don't get the right one in time, I'm going to cut out your fucking balls personally, do you understand me?'

By eleven, Inkunzi Shabangu was back in his luxury home, in a slightly better mood thanks to the assurances of his lieutenants, his informer and his other Zim contacts that they would pin down the route, come what may.

Then his cellphone rang again.

'Yes?'

'*Ouboet*, my name is Lukas Becker, and you accidentally stole my money. I'm not angry, *bro'*, but I want it back.'

The laconic style and slow rhythm of the voice was so strange and unexpected, the choice of '*ouboet*', meaning elder brother in Afrikaans, the suspected source – a white Afrikaner – that Shabangu burst out laughing.

And Becker said, 'I can work with a man who can laugh, *Ouboet*.'

A surveillance operator sent for Quinn shortly after the conversation between Shabangu and Hendricks, and he listened to the recording at the operator's computer, requested that it be placed in the shared folder on the server and transcribed, and went to Masilo's office to tell him.

The Becker conversation was sent to him later by email – two audio files attached. The operator wrote: *Thought you'd enjoy this. Pretty amazing.*

Quinn listened to it.

(Shabangu laughs uproariously.)

I can work with a man who can laugh, Ouboet.

Who the fuck are you?

Lukas Becker. Your guys hijacked my car yesterday. I rented it, Ouboet, *so you can keep it. But my money was in it. Now I'm asking you nicely: I want my money.*

Money? What money?

A lot of money. In pounds Sterling. Cash.

My guys? Why do you say they were my guys?

I've got one of them here with me. Says his name is Enoch Mangope, the one with the white eye. He says he works for you.

I don't know anyone like that.

Ouboet, *he didn't want to say anything at first, but when we stopped in front of the police station, he started talking. I don't think he's lying. Listen, let's keep this simple. I just want my money.*

I know nothing about your money.

I believe you, bro', *but your people will know. The money was in my rucksack, the rucksack was in the boot. You can keep the rucksack too, just give me my money.*

Or?

No, let's not talk about 'or' yet.

Here's one for you: or you can fuck off.

Ey, Ouboet, *that attitude will only make trouble.*

Trouble? Who the hell do you think you are?

Lukas Becker. I thought I told you that already.

(Shabangu laughs curtly.) You must be joking.

(Call terminated.)

End of the first audio file. Quinn grinned and activated the second.

Ouboet, *I understand how you feel, a white guy just calling you out of the blue, but I'm not joking. I just want to sort this thing out in a civilised manner. What do you say?*

(Shabangu laughs incredulously.) Do you know who I am?

I don't know you, bru, *but your man Enoch-One-Eye here says you're an* Inkosi. *A dangerous* oke.

That's right. I'm not your fokken bru *...*

That's just the way I talk ...

... and if you phone me again, you will find out just how dangerous I am.

I believe you are very dangerous, bru, *but I also believe you are a man who will understand. I worked hard for that money.*

I don't give a fuck.

Ay, Ouboet, *don't say that.*

What will you do? Come hit me?

I'm going to keep asking you nicely, Ouboet. *Until it won't help any more.*

(Shabangu laughs.) You're fucking crazy.

Not yet ...

Listen, get off my back. And tell Enoch he doesn't work for me any more.

18

Tau Masilo did not concern himself much with dates that lay in the past. His focus was mostly on the future. But he left a trace of 18 September in his appointment book.

Ever since Janina Mentz had caught him unawares with the question about Baadjies, it had bothered him. In the first place it was a matter of honour to the Advocate; to be prepared and informed, to consider every angle and perspective and understand, to give a well thought-out and even-handed opinion. That was why Mentz had appointed him in the first place.

He knew why he had been caught napping with the Baadjies affair – there was simply too much happening, too fast. But he didn't believe in apologies and excuses. It was afternoon before he had a chance really to think it through, after all the excitement of the recorded conversations and the interception of email. He read the Report Squad document on organised crime again, he looked at all the relevant transcriptions, he allowed himself to speculate. In his mostly illegible handwriting he scribbled quick keywords in the open spaces of this Friday's appointment book.

Using this process he systemically developed The Supposition.

That the Supreme Committee knew more about the inner working of the Ravens than the Presidential Intelligence Agency.

That it was not the decision of Tweetybird de la Cruz to send Terror Baadjies to negotiate with the Committee.

That it was all important, one way or the other.

That he would have to get to the bottom of it.

Janina Mentz and Rajhev Rajkumar would remember that day because of the email Raj's team intercepted.

Masilo was in Mentz's office informing her of the Shabangu-Hendricks conversation. The Indian steamed in holding a sheet of paper. 'You won't believe this, you just won't believe this . . .'

At first Mentz was just vexed. 'What, Raj?'

'One of these apes made a mistake. He forwarded an unencrypted mail with the date in it.'

'You're not serious,' said Masilo.

'Look at this,' Rajkumar slapped the email down between them. 'The original email came from the Supreme Committee, all secure and encrypted. And then one of the recipients had a brain freeze . . .'

Mentz slowly read through the very short email and looked up at the excited man in front of her desk. 'It's a date?'

'Twenty-three Shawwal 1430 is the Muslim calendar date for 12 October 2009.' Then, as though she were incapable of working it out herself, he added, 'That's less than a month away.'

'I know that, Raj. But what does it mean?'

'It's when the thing is going to happen.'

'Which thing?'

'You know, the transaction. The weapons.'

'According to Ismail Mohammed, that's happening in September.'

'Maybe they've changed . . . Shit. You think it might be the day of the attack? The act of terrorism?'

'We had better find out, don't you think?'

19 September 2009. Saturday.

Advocate Tau Masilo was at the office from nine o'clock, where it was Saturday-quiet. Only key personnel.

First he read the report from Reinhard Rohn, their man in Namibia. Nothing new. He was worried.

Then he reread his notes about the Restless Ravens from the previous day. He felt the same unease.

He looked at Rajkumar's report. Twenty-three Shawwal. 12 October 2009.

He pushed everything aside and moved his fingers over his laptop keyboard. He opened his web browser. He typed: *12 October 2009, Cape Town*

He scanned the list of possibilities. The sixth description attracted his attention. He clicked on it. It was a story from a local daily, and his heart went cold.

Cape Town. The American soccer team taking part in the World Cup 2010 will pay a brief visit to the new Green Point stadium in Cape Town.

Their arrival coincides with FIFA's inspection of building progress on the 12 October, when Mr Sepp Blatter, boss of FIFA, and a delegation of some sixty officials will supervise a sod-turning ceremony.

'Jesus,' said Tau Masilo.

He stared at the screen for a long time. Then he printed out the article. And phoned Janina Mentz.

BOOK 2: LEMMER
(The Black Swan)

September 2009

The art of tracking involves each and every sign of animal presence that can be found in nature, including ground spoor, vegetation spoor, scent, feeding signs, urine, faeces, saliva, pellets, territorial signs, paths and shelters, vocal and other auditory signs, visual signs, incidental signs, circumstantial signs and skeletal signs.

The Basics of Tracking: Spoor Identification. (From: The Art of Tracking, New Africa Books, December 31, 1995, Louis W Liebenberg)

19

Territorial boundaries may be scent-marked with urine, faeces or scent transferred to bushes from special scent organs.

The Basics of Tracking: Classification of signs

I don't go looking for trouble, it comes looking for me.

Eleven on a Saturday morning at the tail end of September. Emma le Roux and I, alone together in the Red Pomegranate. My world at this moment near perfect, complete. The lazy sounds of Loxton village, a wagtail chirping hello as it bobbed over the restaurant threshold, a sunbeam shining through the north window. I had finished my big breakfast with gusto; the filter coffee tasted rich and strong. Emma was still eating her fresh scones with jam and cream, slowly and with obvious pleasure. A pot of tea stood waiting. Her skin glowed and there was a blush to her cheeks, because only two hours earlier we had been entangled on the sheets of my bed. Now she was describing the book she was reading in a voice that was always deeper than her delicate figure suggested. On the perfect bow of her lip, a fleck of cream, like a snowflake.

It was all too good to be true, because I am Lemmer.

The gods must have woken, because a faint sound, deep, mechanical, grew louder, until Emma stopped talking and turned her head. Tannie Wilna, the heart and soul of the Red Pomegranate, came in from the kitchen wiping her hands on her skirt. 'Do you hear that too?'

We listened as the rolling thunder grew, the direction clearer. An invasion via the Carnarvon Road.

We all looked out on the wide traffic circle around the church. The village seemed to pause, people tumbled out of the general dealer, out of the farmers co-op. A group of coloured children came running from the direction of the church hall, their shouts drowned in the cacophony. They pointed excited fingers up the street.

A dramatic entry on the traffic circle, at nine o'clock: outlandish creatures of chunky chrome, steel and black. Long leather tassels fluttering from handlebars and saddlebags, four Harley Davidsons – the riders in shades and stupid helmets, garish bandanas pulled over their mouths and noses, arms and legs stretched to reach the pedals and handlebars. They disappeared behind the church, followed the curve around to the restaurant and pulled up in front of it. They shoved the back ends of the bikes towards us, neatly in line, the front wheels pointing to the street. A final revving of the engines, an ear-splitting racket, stands kicked out and the bandanas pulled down.

Merciful silence.

The number plates were tiny. I read them in order. NV ME. BOY'S TOY. LOUD, PROUD. And HELLRAZOR. All from the Cape.

NV ME climbed down from his throne, unbuckled his helmet, pulled off the fingerless leather gloves, then the tasselled leather jacket. He had steel grey hair, stylishly and expensively trimmed, and a boyish face full of confidence. The T-shirt somewhat tight.

He cast an imperious gaze across Loxton. 'Fucking one-horse town,' was his verdict, pronounced for all to hear.

The labourers from the shop sidled up, the children came running.

All four riders had their feet on solid ground, leather trousers, shiny black boots, adorned with silver baroque. All were on the fib-side of forty. Number two was big, maybe two metres tall, number three was short and small with a ratface. Number four was average, but sporty.

'Stand back! You can look, but no touching,' Steel Grey ordered the children.

They stared at him wide-eyed, but kept their distance.

The Knights of Harley trooped in, led by Steel Grey, followed by Ratface and Sporty. The Big Guy covered the rear. A pecking order.

'Good morning,' Tannie Wilna said, 'welcome to Loxton,' with the affectionate warmth she offered everybody.

They inspected her and her restaurant. 'Do you have any beer?' Steel Grey asked, unimpressed.

Emma turned back to me, shaking her head slightly and ate her scone.

'Unfortunately we are not licensed, but the bottle store is just across the way. I'll send Mietjie over quickly. Please, sit down . . .' and she held out her hand to the large table for six.

Steel Grey checked me over once. Ratface eyed Emma speculatively.

They sat down. The back of Sporty's T-shirt read '*If you can read this, the bitch fell off.*'

Tannie Wilna brought them menus. 'What beer do you prefer?'

'Black Label,' said Steel Grey. 'Cold.'

'Run over and fetch us four Black Labels from Zelda, please,' Tannie Wilna said to Mietjie. 'Ask her for the cold ones.'

'Make that twelve, Aunty,' said Steel Grey.

'Lots of drinking to do,' said the Big Guy.

'The Thirstland Trek,' said Ratface, court jester to the House of Harley. They all laughed. Hu-hu-hu. Comrades.

Mietjie went out on her errand. A moment's silence.

Outside four coloured people rode by on a donkey cart towards Beaufort, the hooves clip-clopping on the tar. Sporty watched them, and said, 'Back roads.' The others guffawed again, some in-joke. They began a conversation, voices louder than necessary so that we, the audience, could listen.

Emma gave me a small, nostalgic smile, acknowledging that our magic moment was over.

20

> Rabid animals are often characterised by unusual behaviour, which may include attacking humans.
>
> *The Basics of Tracking: Dangerous animals*

'Where were we?' she asked quietly.

'The Black Swan,' I said and sipped my coffee. It was the gripping book she had been telling me about.

'I was just about finished anyway.' Emma poured tea into her cup and picked up the last scone.

At the next table Steel Grey announced he was going to buy a Porsche Cayenne.

'Why?' Sporty asked, 'Your Q7, it's a year old.'

'Because I can.'

Hu-hu-hu.

Steel Grey was trying too hard to be the bold, tough vagabond, the

Hell's Angel clone. Clearly he was well-off, but the masquerade revealed some deep discontent. He probably had some high position in a large corporation, senior management, but the role of chief executive had eluded him, probably because his bosses saw the vicious dictator inside him. Best guess: Financial Services sector, Fund Manager. Risk, adrenaline, big bucks, megalomania, consuming ambition.

I considered the others. The Big Guy was the easiest to place; he was Steel Grey's corporate underling, his watchdog. The other two were more difficult, not colleagues, but kindred spirits. Steel Grey's clients, possibly. Played golf together, had long drinking-buddy lunches and the occasional sneaky visit to Teasers. All four were rich Afrikaners from Cape Town's northern suburbs, off on a flight of fancy in the school holidays, having parked the wife and children at the beach house in Hermanus. But the chasm between what they really were and the image they wanted to project was just too wide.

'You've got too many toys,' said Ratface.

'Toy makes the boy,' the Big Guy said and looked to Steel Grey for approval.

He got it: 'Fucking right.'

So they began talking about their possessions.

Mietjie arrived with the beer, and Tannie Wilna served them. 'Forget the glasses,' said the Big Guy.

They drank deeply from the bottles, with great satisfaction. Steel Grey banged his bottle down hard on the table, wiped his mouth. 'Mother's milk.'

Emma leaned over her tea towards me. 'Regression,' she whispered. 'Students again.'

More like complete arseholes, I thought.

'More beer,' Ratface shouted.

Tannie Wilna brought it.

As she passed us I asked for the bill.

'Aren't you going to have a double thick?' she asked, surprised. The Knights went suddenly silent, listening intently.

'Not today, thank you, Tannie,' I said quietly.

'Double thick,' giggled Ratface.

Hu-hu-hu. And they drink more beer.

'The scones were delicious,' Emma said to Tannie Wilna.

'Thank you, Emmatjie.'

Emma poured more tea into her cup.

'Emmatjie, come and sit with us,' said Sporty.

'Don't bother, she's double thin,' said Ratface.

'The closer the bone, the sweeter the meat,' said Sporty.

Hu-hu-hu.

'*He* looks a bit thi-i-i-ck,' said the Big Guy, looking at me and tapping his head.

Lemmer's first Loxton Law: No hand to be raised in anger in town. I stood up, walked over to the counter, and took out my wallet with my back to them.

'Why wasn't Jesus born in Loxton?' asked Ratface.

Tannie Wilna frowned.

'Because they couldn't find one wise man here,' said Steel Grey.

Hu-hu-hu.

'Couldn't find a virgin either,' said Big Guy.

Hu-hu-hu, an octave higher.

Tannie Wilna wrote out our bill. Slowly and carefully as ever.

'I don't know, Emmatjie looks like she could be a virgin still,' said Steel Grey.

I put my hand on the counter, let my head drop, breathed slowly. Inhale, exhale. I knew how their minds worked. They had checked me out, seen a grey, skinny country bumpkin and they had found courage in their numbers.

'Double-thin virg-in,' said Sporty.

'You're a poet, and you know it,' said the Big Guy.

'Emma, oh, Emma,' Ratface sang.

Hu-hu-hu.

'. . . go and tell your grandma, this uncle wants a baby with you.'

Raucous laughter at his version of the old Afrikaans song *Emma, ko' le ma'*.

I opened my wallet, fingers poised, ready to pay. I could see the tremor in my hands.

'Don't worry, Emma, I'll be gentle with you,' said Ratface.

'Or maybe not,' said Sporty.

Hu-hu-hu.

I heard Emma's chair scrape back. I knew the trouble had arrived.

'Come on, then,' said Emma. 'Just try.'

'*Hoooo . . .*' said Ratface, but with diminished bravado.

Emma's voice cut like a knife: 'I wonder what your wife would say if she could see you now. And your children . . .'

They had no smart alec reply to that.

'That will be ninety-five rand,' said Tannie Wilna in a whisper. For her sake we had to get out of here. Now.

'You are *so* pathetic,' said Emma.

Pregnant silence. I hastily put the money down on the counter and turned. Emma faced them all, her body taut with fury. 'Emma . . .' I said, because I had seen her in action before, seen her nine months ago poking a delicate finger into a burly policeman's chest, repeatedly and fearlessly.

I saw Steel Grey's face, the venom, and I knew what he said next would change everything. I was on my way to Emma when he said, 'Who the fuck do you think you are?'

I clung desperately to my last shred of self-control. My head screamed: Walk away.

'*You* are fucking pathetic, you scrawny little bitch,' Steel Grey hissed.

Rage washed all resolve away. I changed my direction, towards him.

21

> Spoor includes a wide range of signs, from obvious footprints, which provide detailed information on the identity and activities of an animal, to very subtle signs, which may indicate nothing more than that some disturbance had occurred.
>
> *The Basics of Tracking: Classification of signs*

'Hell, those are bloody beautiful bikes out there, you guys must be stinking rich,' a deep jovial voice emanated from the doorway. A large body swiftly stepped in front of me, a familiar face winked at me, diverted me. 'Lemmer, buddy, I've been looking all over town for you,' as though he knew me well.

I registered who he was, somewhere in the back of my mind.

Diederik Brand, local farmer. I walked around him, I wanted to start with Steel Grey and I wanted to hurt them. The Big Guy was rising to his feet.

Emma saw me and came to her senses. 'Lemmer, no,' she said.

Diederik put a broad, firm hand on my shoulder and spoke in a soothing voice: 'You don't want to do this to yourself.' He turned to their table. 'Gentlemen, tell me, what does one of those babies cost?' Steering me towards the exit at the same time.

Emma saw his plan, and she took my other arm, cool hand on my skin.

'Two hundred and twenty,' said Ratface in a voice squeaky with tension. 'Without the extras.'

Diederik and Emma had me at the door. My eyes were on Steel Grey, he saw something in them and looked away.

'Incredible,' said Diederik. 'Lovely machines,' and then we were outside and he said quietly, 'that's not what you want.'

Emma tugged hard on my arm. 'I shouldn't have lost my temper,' she said. 'I should have ignored them.'

'No,' I said and strained back towards the restaurant.

'Lemmer!' said Diederik Brand sharply. I looked at him, saw two dimples and a reassuring smile.

I stopped.

'Listen,' he said. 'How would you like to save the last two black rhino in Zimbabwe?' As if it were the most logical thing to ask, in the circumstances.

I only knew two facts about Diederik Brand. He farmed, in a big way, between the Sak River and the Nuweveld Mountains. When Loxton folk mentioned his name they said 'Ay, that Diederik,' and then they would laugh and shake their heads, as if he were some beloved but mischievous son.

I had seen him around, mostly just a hairy arm waving from a bakkie window as he drove by. Now he was sitting in my living room, on the new leather couch that was Emma's peace offering after rolling my trusty Isuzu on the bend in the gravel road just before Jakhalsdans.

We had driven here with him, both he and Emma gently convincing me that the Knights weren't worth the trouble. I was listening to

Brand, with a part of my mind still in the Red Pomegranate meting out punishment.

Diederik was a large man, in his fifties, broad shouldered, with the sun-beaten face of all Karoo farmers. Black and grey hair curled over his ears and the collar of the neat khaki shirt. He sported a military moustache and there were laugh lines around his mischievous eyes. His natural charm was of the engaging, self-deprecating sort. He leaned forward, elbows on knees, and told his fascinating tale skilfully and with great urgency. Emma hung on his every word.

'For two years we've been trying to get hold of black rhino, but it's not easy. It's practically impossible to get a permit – there is a hell of a waiting list, you have to be approved, have a big enough farm, the right habitat. You have to be prepared to get involved with the breeding programmes. The National Parks get preference. Last year Zambia got the only ten available, because since '98 they have been thought to be totally extinct there. The black rhino is expensive, we're talking half a million rand per head. So, one has to make a plan, because they were once native to this area, long ago. Now, because I've been asking all over, everyone in the industry knows I am looking for the animals. Three weeks ago a guy called me from Zimbabwe, someone from Zim Nature Conservation, squeezed out long ago by Mugabe's storm troopers, but still running private safaris in the Chete. Anyway, he called and he said they had found a bull and a cow, by chance, on the banks of the Sebungwe River, just south of Kariba. The animals were frightened, wild, very aggressive, you couldn't get near them. He said if we didn't save them, they would soon be shot for their horns anyway, but he didn't have the money for sedation and transport. If I would put up the money for expenses, they would smuggle the animals to the border, I would just have to pick them up there. That's not as easy as it sounds. Sebungwe is 700 km by road from the South African border and they would have to be careful with all the roadblocks and things. It's quite a sacrifice on their part, but for all of us it's about —'

He stopped suddenly, mid sentence, and glanced towards the window. Outside we could hear the high drone of an aeroplane, a single engine, growing louder. Diederik Brand nodded as though he had been expecting it.

Our sleepy little town. As busy as a termites' nest this Saturday morning.

'Mr Brand, can I offer you some coffee?' Emma took advantage of the pause. I sat there wondering what his story had to do with me.

'Diederik, call me Diederik. Emma, thanks, but no. Trouble is, we haven't got time.' He picked up the black file that he had put down on the wagon box coffee table when he came in, and flipped it open. He paged through the pile of documents. 'Now, the first thing I did was talk to our Minister's people. It's no good arriving at the border with the animals if they can't come in. Environmental Affairs are very sympathetic, I think they feel some guilt about Zim, if you understand what I mean, but it's a problem for them because we won't get a certificate of origin, no export permit from Zim, it's smuggling whichever way you look at it.'

He selected a document and placed it solemnly on the wagon box. 'Now, there are a couple of things that made the breakthrough. The first one is the gene pool. In South Africa it's tiny, our black rhino are almost all descendants of the Kwazulu and Kruger herds. So in that respect the Zim animals are priceless. I had to sign an agreement that gives Nature Conservation first option on the calves. The second thing is that I am remote. Only a handful of people will know that I am going to breed rhino, you among them, so please, keep it between us because the horns are selling at around $20,000 a kilogram here, that's more than $60,000 for one horn, almost half a million rand. The third thing is, I have the space, and my fences are electrified. Here . . .' and he tapped his large finger on the document '. . . is my permit.'

He took another sheet of paper out of the file. 'Here is a letter from the Director confirming that they are making an exception with the import permit, since it is an "emergency",' and he drew quotation marks with his thick index fingers.

'Diederik . . .' I said.

'Lemmer, I know what you are going to ask. What has all this to do with you? Let me tell you then. You know Lourens le Riche?'

'I know of him.'

'You know Nicola, the game farmer?'

'He is a friend.'

'Right now Lourens is in Musina with Nicola's game lorry. Tonight he is loading the rhino just east of Vhembe on the Zim border, and then he has to drive all the way here with a cargo that is worth a fortune, and I don't just mean in money terms. That's over 1,500 kilometres. If something goes wrong . . .' Brand looked at me meaningfully. It took me a while to get it.

'You want me to travel with him?'

'Please, Lemmer, buddy.' Like we were old friends. 'I will pay full price, just let me know your fee.'

I could read on Emma's face that she thought I should support this worthy cause.

'Diederik, it's not that simple . . .'

'Everything is official, Lemmer, you don't have to worry about that.'

'That's not the issue. I'm on contract. I can't do freelance work.'

'What do you mean?'

'I work for a company in Cape Town. Body Armour.'

'Yes, yes, your bodyguard job. You look after all those rich and famous . . .'

There are no secrets in the Bo-Karoo, only false impressions. 'They are mostly businessmen from overseas . . . ' I said.

'But you're off now?'

'Diederik, I have a contract with Body Armour. It says I can't do freelance work. Everything has to go through them.'

'They must take a commission.'

'That's right.'

'Lemmer, man . . . how will they know? You load tonight, the day after tomorrow you'll be back.'

How could I explain – without offending him – that my loyalty to Jeanette Louw, my boss, was not negotiable?

'I'm like you, Diederik, I prefer official sanction too.'

He looked at me thoughtfully.

'OK,' he said. 'Who is in charge there? What's his phone number?'

'How will that help? Musina is a day's drive from here.'

'That plane . . .' he pointed his thumb towards the airfield. 'It's Lotter. He's waiting for you.'

After a ten-minute conversation he passed the phone to me. 'She wants to talk to you.'

'Jeanette,' I said.

'Glad to hear you are recruiting clients yourself now . . .' She had the usual irony in her hoarse Gauloise voice, followed by the single barked 'Ha!' Which meant she was laughing.

I said nothing.

'I'll manage the admin, if you want the job.'

Did I want the job? This one was close to home. I had questions, as yet unformed, everything was moving too fast, too soon after the Knights. And then there was Lemmer's First Law: Don't get involved. And this was all about getting involved. With a local farmer, with Something Big.

Jeanette interpreted my silence correctly. 'Perhaps you know more than I do. It's your decision.' Then she added: 'It's in a good cause, Lemmer. He sounds like a *mensch*. And you know how it is, with the recession . . .'

I knew. Body Armour's turnover was down by fifty per cent, thanks to the international meltdown. It was two months since I'd earned a cent.

I looked at Emma's pleading eyes. Just like Jeanette, she was a Diederik disciple already. I thought of the young Lourens le Riche, hard-working student. What would the village say if I forsook him? I thought about the payment on the new Ford bakkie. And my roof. Oom Ben Bruwer's soft whistle as he climbed down out of the ceiling and told me the woodwork was rotten. I would have to put on a whole new roof.

I sighed. Deeply.

'I'm in,' I said.

22

> To be able to recognise signs, trackers must know what to look for and where to look for them. Someone who is not familiar with spoor may not recognise it, even when looking straight at the sign.
>
> *The Principles of Tracking: Recognition of signs*

Lotter looked like a middle-aged rock star. Balding, the hair he still had all gathered into a ponytail, with round spectacles on a gypsy face. He shook my hand with a friendly smile, took my black sports bag and walked over to the aircraft. It was incredibly small, a toy plane in white, red and blue, with a Perspex bubble dome over the cabin, two seats, and a slim joystick where you would have expected something more substantial. It looked like the sort referred to in news bulletins as a microlight, usually followed by the word 'crashed'.

Emma inspected it curiously, caught up in what she had just referred to as my 'fun adventure'.

Diederik Brand came to stand beside me. 'You don't have to worry, Lotter is an international champion.'

It wasn't how he flew that worried me, but what he flew. I held my tongue.

'This is just in case,' Brand said, and passed me a package wrapped in a grimy cloth.

I smelled gun oil, and started to unwrap it.

He put a hand over it. 'I would wait until you're in the air . . .' and he cast a significant look at Emma. 'I don't want to upset her.'

'Is there something I should know?'

'You know how it is on our roads,' he said.

I hesitated. My Glock 37, with ten .45 GAP rounds in the magazine, was in my sports bag. I didn't need anything else. But Diederik Brand had already turned away and walked towards the deathtrap. He clapped his hands, 'Come on, you must get moving.'

I checked my watch. Five to twelve.

Two hours ago my life had been a breeze.

I stood at the wing, ready to board. Emma came to me with a peculiar mix of emotions on her face – concern, pride, tenderness . . .

I wanted to kiss her. She embraced me unexpectedly and pressed her body against mine. She said something that was lost in the roar of the plane's engine.

'What?' I shouted.

Emma moved so her mouth was against my ear.

'I love you, Lemmer.'

'Cape Town information, Romeo Victor Sierra, good morning,' Lotter said over the radio as the Bokpoort Road slid by below us and my stomach lodged in my throat.

'Romeo Victor Sierra, good morning, go ahead,' crackled a voice over the ether.

'Cape Town, Romeo Victor Sierra has taken off from Loxton at ten zero four Zulu, on flight plan reference zero two five, Romeo Victor Sierra.'

'Romeo Victor Sierra, squawk four zero six six, no reported traffic and call me crossing the FIR boundary.'

It was the language of another world. Lotter repeated the ghost voice's words in confirmation, made a couple of adjustments, and studied his inscrutable instruments. I wondered which one would give the first indication that we were going down in a ball of flame. I looked reluctantly out of the bubble dome. Below us the Karoo had swiftly spread wide and open and the heaven above was deep blue and immeasurably great.

Nausea began to rise in my gut.

I remembered the package on my lap. I unrolled the cloth from the firearm and revealed a peculiar object. It was a MAG-7, the locally manufactured short-barrelled shotgun, like an Uzi on steroids. Twelve-bore, five cartridges in a long box magazine. Serious stopping power. The sort of thing the police task force would use for inside work. There were another twenty cartridges in a plastic bag.

Lotter whistled in my headset. 'I swear, I'm on your side.'

'But who is on Brand's side?'

'What do you mean?'

'These weapons are only for government use. Civilians don't get licences for these.'

Lotter laughed. '*Ja*, that Diederik,' and shook his head. He glanced at me. 'You're a bit pale.' He pulled a brown paper bag from under his seat and passed it to me. 'In case you get air sick.'

Which happened just beyond Hopetown.

'Had a big breakfast?' Lotter asked sympathetically.

I didn't reply, too afraid to open my mouth.

'It's perfectly normal,' he said, with reference to my discomfort. 'You'll feel better now.'

Twenty minutes later another town slid by below us. I took a deep breath and asked hopefully if we needed to land to refuel.

He grinned. 'This thing flies 3,000 kilometres on a tank.'

'That's far for a microlight,' I said sceptically.

'What?' He was insulted. 'This is no *microlight*, this is an RV-7.'

An RV-7 and a MAG-7. Maybe Nicola's game lorry had a seven in its name. I might win the jackpot.

Lotter saw my lack of enthusiasm. 'Best kit plane in the world,' he said. 'She's one of Richard VanGrunsven's designs. Top speed over 190 knots, that's about 340 kilos per hour, she can cruise, she can do aerobatics, hell of a range . . .'

'You mean Wretched VanGrunsven . . . ?' My stomach lurched at the word 'aerobatics'.

Lotter laughed. 'It's the speed and height,' he said. 'Your inner ear says you are moving at a helluva speed, but your eyes don't register it. It's like reading in a car. Just look down often. You will feel better soon.'

Promises, promises.

He busied himself on the radio, talking his unintelligible flight language. 'Cape Town, Romeo Victor Sierra is crossing FIR boundary.'

'Romeo Victor Sierra, call Johannesburg Central on one two zero decimal three, good day,' said the radio voice.

I tuned out, and looked down at the Karoo slowly but surely turning to grassveld. Lotter was right, because after a few minutes my guts began to stabilise. My thoughts began to drift. Slowly. Carefully. To Emma.

I love you, Lemmer.

It was the first time.

Emma and I.

Nine months ago we had been strangers, polar opposites from different worlds. She was tiny, sophisticated, determined, and as lovely as a nymph in a children's fairy tale. She was wealthy, exceptionally wealthy, thanks to an inheritance from her industrialist father. Back then, Emma was on a desperate search for her lost brother – and for someone to shield her from the suspected dangers connected to his disappearance. I was the bodyguard Jeanette had assigned to her. I was dubious, distrustful, sceptical, because Emma was everything my Laws warned me against.

She had conquered me slowly, against my will, against my expectations and, above all, against my better judgement. Firstly she was a client. And secondly I am Lemmer. White trash from the back streets of Sea Point, with serious anger management problems, a powerful affinity for violence, and on parole after four years in jail for manslaughter. I knew my place, I understood the realities of life.

I found her brother. And after all that I went home to Loxton, sure that I would never see her again, and probably for the best. But Emma is never predictable.

She tracked me down. I thought it was just to say thank you, at first, because she was always so painfully polite, faultlessly proper.

I was wrong.

The growth of our relationship had a certain surrealism to it, a dream-like quality, as if I were merely an observer. Perhaps because of my disbelief in the simple possibility that a woman like her would be interested in me. Blinded by the magic of myself with Emma, by my relief and amazement and need. And a morbid curiosity over where and how it would all derail.

Until this morning beside the RV-7. *I love you, Lemmer.*

The trouble is that Emma still doesn't know.

I hid my sins from her. She thinks I live in Loxton because it is a pretty place with good people. She doesn't know I went there to escape the city triggers that set off my firing pins. She doesn't know of my desire to be healed by the peacefulness, patience and integrity of the townspeople. She doesn't know of my stupid quest for their acceptance.

Stupid, because in the eyes of the Bo-Karoo, I was an outsider, a newcomer, an unknown quantity who kept my distance, subtly, politely, and according to my First Law. My strange job also had implications. The freelance bodyguard who worked in other places, stayed away for weeks at a time and sometimes returned with visible injuries. The shadowy figure who rattled off rounds with a handgun every week at the shooting range, and went on long runs at sundown on the gravel roads.

Townspeople like the eccentric Antjie Barnard, jovial Oom Joe van Wyk and my coloured housekeeper, Agatha le Fleur, were the only ones who, despite all that, accepted me without hesitation. But they were the exceptions. Until Emma's arrival.

She was a sign of normality. Through association, she was proof of acceptability, this spontaneous, attractive, well-spoken young woman who appeared out of nowhere and since then visited me once or twice a month. She had swapped her Renault Mégane for a Land Rover Freelander to handle the dirt roads. She had taken my old Isuzu diesel on a Friday afternoon in August to buy groceries in Beaufort West and on the way home had rolled it on the turn near Jakhalsdans, a complete wreck.

The next morning, while looking for a 'green' solution for the ant infestation in my garden, she had made the grizzled farmers laugh hilariously with her tale of how she had taken the corner 'a bit too fast because I was missing Lemmer'.

'And then?'

'Then I rolled the bakkie.'

'And then?'

'I saw I was OK. So I walked the last seven kilometres back to town.'

They shook their heads in amazement: 'And what did Lemmer have to say?'

'Dunno. I don't understand French.'

According to Oom Joe she had them in stitches, and they slapped each other on the shoulder and took great pains to explain to Emma that the Karoo ants weren't really bothered by 'green' poisons.

Emma convinced me to accompany her to the Loxton church on Sundays. She was the reason we were invited to a barbecue at the water ski dam, and a rugby-test dinner in the Blue House. Emma le Roux was my passport to acceptance, my visa to safe asylum. And lost in love, I allowed it all to happen, suppressing the quiet accusing voice that said: What if they all found out who you really are?

Because, like Emma, Loxton had no idea.

I suspected they were vaguely aware of some aspects. Antjie had asked some subtle questions. Emma had glimpses of it while she was a client. In the search for her brother I had occasionally displayed my talents in practice. Maybe the brother had revealed some of those aspects to his sister in relating the events. Maybe they had intrigued her, could that be part of the attraction? When I guarded her, she had slipped easily into the role of the protected – as most women would.

This morning with the Knights, she had seen it. And tried to stop me, without reproach. Maybe she thought she could control me.

But she only knew part of me.

I had to tell her the whole truth.

I wanted to. There were moments when I came so close, the desire for confession so great that I could taste it in my mouth. *I beat a man to death in anger, Emma. And I found satisfaction in it. And enjoyment. Because I am the product of violence. It lives in me. It is me.*

But every time, before it all came out like the evil genie from the lamp, I was stopped by the stifling fear that I would lose her, and with that, all possibility of her love. Even more, losing the potential of her love changing me into someone who would be worthy of it. She was already doing that. She made me laugh, she lured me to make her laugh, to be light-hearted and playful and witty. To forget about the dark alleyways in my head. For the first time in my life I began to like myself. Just a little. I had her approval. And now, her love.

I love you, Lemmer.

I had stood there beside the plane in her urgent embrace, her mouth to my ear, and I had said nothing. I knew, before I could answer her that I would have to tell her everything.

But it was too late now, the potential for hurt and damage was way too great. For me and for her.

I gazed over the endless plains of the Northern Cape and wondered what had made me throw up – this little plane, or my great dishonesty.

23

Trackers will often look for spoor in obvious places . . .

The Principles of Tracking: Recognition of signs

To escape my thoughts, I asked Lotter how he had come to know Diederik.

'Friend of a friend. A few years ago he called me up. He said he had heard that I would fly anywhere. He wanted to inspect a potential investment in Mozambique, but it was too far to drive, time is money, could I pick him up? That was the start of it. Nowadays it works like this, Diederik rings me up and says he urgently needs some tractor parts from Ermelo, or let's pop over to Windhoek quickly, or come and pick up my buddy in Loxton. You know how it is, getting paid for what you love doing . . . Did you know he has a landing strip on the farm?'

I said that in fact I knew very little about Diederik.

'He's a real character. And a shrewd businessman. Finger in every pie . . .'

The tarred runway of Musina lay from east to west, stretched out long and luxurious across the dark brown landscape.

At twenty past two we came in low over the sewerage works and the graveyard, with the town on our right. Lotter touched down as light as a feather, with casual ease, made a U-turn and taxied back to the eastern end, then right on a pipe-stem access road to a collection of low buildings and hangars. He stopped and opened the clips of the cabin dome. Heat flowed in thick and heavy.

'This is it. The lorry will pick you up here.'

But there was no lorry to be seen.

I unclipped the quite considerable seat belt, took my sports bag and the swaddled shotgun from behind the seat and offered my hand to Lotter.

'Thank you.'

'Any time. And good luck.' He pointed at the bundle I cradled like a baby in my arms. 'I hope you don't need to use that thing.' Then, as I stood on the tarmac, and just before he fastened the Perspex bubble again, he called over the idling engine: 'Lemmer, I suppose you already know: with old Diederik, you always take your money up front . . .'

At the gate the tar road stretched out in front of me through the dull brown, dry, hard landscape. Here and there a tree grew. I stopped and unzipped my bag, placed the MAG-7 in it, zipped it shut. Walked on. The heat gradually got the better of me, sweat slid down my back, in thin trickles.

The road was quiet. Deserted. Where was Lourens le Riche?

The whole thing had happened too fast, too uncoordinated. I should have got le Riche's cellphone number. Diederik Brand's too. There were questions I wanted to ask. Such as, why Brand approached me so late, only hours before the rhino were to be loaded? When had he decided to hire me?

I spotted a crossroad ahead. I would wait there.

The only shelter from the excruciating sun was four forlorn, almost leafless trees. I put my bag down and searched for a little bit of shade, leaned against a rough trunk. My shirt was stuck to my back, sweat stung my eyes. I had no hat.

I checked my watch. A quarter to three.

I wiped a sleeve over my forehead. Then I swore fiercely, and at length.

24

> Most animals prefer to remain hidden when feeding, and may take their food to a special feeding place where they can be safe while feeding.
>
> *The Basics of Tracking: Classification of signs*

At a quarter to four I was still sitting on the ground, only the thin tree trunk between me and the pitiless sun. My cellphone rang. I got to my feet and took it out of my trouser pocket, hoping it was Diederik Brand. There was a lot I had to say to him.

It was Oom Joe van Wyk. Of Loxton. 'Lemmer, *ou maat*, I hear Diederik has got you into something.'

'Yes, Oom,' addressing him in the Karoo vernacular.

'Did he pay you up front?'

'I don't know, Oom Joe, he's working through my employer.'

'Oh. No, that's all right then. And what must you do for him?'

'I'm not at liberty to say.'

'Ay, that Diederik,' he laughed his happy laugh. 'Well then, *sterkte*, Lemmer, *ou maat*,' he wished me well as his 'old friend'. 'Tante Anna sends her regards.'

At ten to four my phone rang again. Oom Ben Bruwer, the builder in Loxton, the man who I had consulted about my rotting roof. 'So, you're working for Diederik Brand.' A reproach.

'Only for a day or two, Oom.'

He chewed over the information. 'Nonetheless, if I were you I would ask for a deposit. Fifty per cent up front.'

'He's negotiating with my boss, Oom Ben.'

'Nonetheless, I would ask for fifty per cent up front. Have a good day.' And he was gone.

Loxton was waking from its afternoon nap. News was spreading like a virus.

At half past five the eccentric Antjie Barnard called, seventy years old, a retired international cellist who smoked and drank as if she were twenty. 'Emma is sitting with me here on my veranda, we're drinking gin and tonics and missing you,' she said in her ever-sensual voice.

And here I stood sweating in the Limpopo sun, all my patience exhausted, waiting. I swallowed that thought. 'I miss you both too.'

'She says you are working for Diederik, but she's very secretive.'

'That's my Emma. Always an enigma.'

Antjie giggled. That meant she was on her third gin. 'You know how you deal with Diederik?'

'Take your money up front?'

'Aah, Joe has phoned you already.'

'And Oom Ben.'

'The town is concerned about you.'

'I appreciate that.'

'Do you want to talk to Emma?' So that Antjie could listen and pick up clues to what I was doing for Diederik.

This was not the right time to speak to Emma.

'I'm a little busy, Antjie, tell Emma I'll call her later.'

At ten to five a lorry drove up the tar road. The logo of Nicola's Wildlife Services on the door of the white cab, and a massive bull bar in front. I walked to the edge of the road and waved my arms. If he drove past I was going to take the shotgun and shoot out a tyre.

He stopped.

As I opened the door, swung the bag up and climbed in, Lourens le Riche said: 'I thought Oom would be at the airfield?'

I said nothing. Slammed the door harder than necessary.

'I'm Lourens, Oom,' he put out his hand. 'Have you been waiting long, Oom?'

The le Riche family were a Loxton legend.

My knowledge was limited, from bits of stories told here and there. They farmed out on the Pampoenpoort Road, merino sheep on 6,000 hectares, no labourers on the farm. The family did everything themselves – father, mother, two sons and a daughter. Like their parents, the children were sinewy and tough.

Lourens, the oldest, was a final-year agricultural student at Stellenbosch. He paid for his own studies, taking every possible opportunity to earn a few rand. Like this one. I wondered if he had got his money up front. But I didn't ask because I was sticky with sweat, hot and angry.

'Oom Diederik said you would be here around five o'clock,' he explained his time of arrival as he pulled away. 'So I took a nap, because we're going to pull an all-nighter.' His face was angular: high forehead, a determined chin, easy smile. 'Did you have a good flight, Oom?'

It was the innocence in his voice that stopped me from taking out my frustration on him. I felt the refreshing air conditioning, angled the vent in the instrument panel towards me, turned the knob of the fan up and said, 'No, not really. And you don't have to call me Oom.'

'OK, Oom.'

I shifted the sports bag into the space behind the seats, put on my seat belt and settled into the seat.

'Diederik was a bit vague about our schedule.'

'We are going to get something to eat in town now, Oom, because we are loading tonight after dark. Round about eight. And then we are on our way.'

As the Mercedes diesel growled up the main street of Musina, Lourens le Riche said: 'You must be *lekker* hungry, Oom, shall we go and get a steak?'

To my relief, Lourens was not a chronic talker.

We parked in Grenfell Street. He took two large coffee flasks from behind his seat and locked up the lorry carefully. He was wearing the young Karoo farmer's uniform: blue jeans, khaki shirt with blue shoulder inserts, co-op boots. We walked in silence to the Buffalo Ridge Spur Steak Ranch on the corner. The restaurant was quiet in the late afternoon, the air conditioning mercifully cool.

Lourens ordered a T-bone and Coke, and asked them to fill his flasks with black, bitter coffee. I found my stomach had recovered from the RV-7 experience and asked for a rump steak and a red Grapetizer. When the cool drinks arrived, Lourens asked, 'Which famous people have you looked after?' more from courtesy than curiosity.

'We sign a confidentiality clause . . .' It was my standard answer, but in Loxton it was interpreted as evasive confirmation that I usually went around with American movie and pop stars. The truth was that I tried to avoid the famous as clients. Too much monkey business. So I added: 'I usually work with foreign businessmen.'

'Oh,' he said, vaguely disappointed.

As we waited for our food, he sat and stared through the window at the street outside. Stall traders were packing up, hundreds of pedestrians hurried on their way somewhere. A constant stream of minibus taxis squeezed past with their roof racks piled high, many of them from Zimbabwe. People in transit. A border town.

'This is another world here,' he said pensively.

'It is,' I said.

That was the sum total of our conversation.

The lorry was a Mercedes 1528, a six-cylinder diesel with no seven in sight. No jackpot then.

On the back there was a closed steel structure as high as the cab and painted grey. It had a variety of access panels and wide rear doors. Near the top three slot openings ran the length of the body. There were double wheels behind and single wheels in front.

Inside it was as luxurious as a car. The instrument panel was of black synthetic leather and grey plastic. There was a shelf for two mugs or tins on top, a CD player in the middle. Between the two seats was a half-metre hump at seat height over the engine cowling. Lourens's cellphone and charger lay on it, with a few CDs. I recognised Metallica and Judas Priest, the rest I had never heard of: Ihsahn, Enslaved, Arsis.

The diagram on the gear lever showed a grid of eight gears.

We drove out on the tarred R572 with the setting sun directly in our eyes. Lourens le Riche was a competent driver. His eyes rotated between the road, the mirrors, the instruments. He drove smoothly, evenly, alert.

I took the Glock out of my bag and looked for a place to hide it, within easy reach.

Lourens looked at the weapon, but said nothing, until I began experimenting with the gap between my seat and the engine hump.

'Oom, put it up there.' He pointed at the panels above the windscreen. There were a variety of storage spaces. Right in front of me was an open hollow with enough of a lip to hold the weapon if we braked sharply. Good choice.

'Thanks.'

'What is it, Oom?'

'Glock 37.'

He just nodded.

I took out the MAG-7.

'*Jissie*,' said Lourens.

'It was Diederik's idea,' I said, self-consciously.

Lourens laughed. 'Ay, that Oom Diederik,' and shook his head.

'Why does everyone say "Ay, that Diederik"?'

'Oom, he's a character.'

'A character?'

'An old rascal.'

'What do you mean?'

'Don't you know the stories, Oom?'

'No.'

He smiled in anticipation. I had seen the same expression before on Antjie and Oom Joe's faces, the pleasure that preceded the telling of a good story. Stories were the social currency of the Karoo. Everyone had one. Heartbreak, happiness, triumph and disaster, but it was a story that defined, characterised, gave insight. So different from the stories of city people, now on Facebook and Twitter, dollied up so that everyone looked good, fake and crooked, smokescreens and masks.

'Oom Diederik has many sides. The nature conservation, for instance. He does so much, I don't know of anyone who loves the Karoo more . . . He's very clever too,' said Lourens le Riche. And then reverently: 'As sharp as a needle . . .'

25

> The easiest way to learn how to track is to have an experienced tracker teach you.
>
> *The Basics of Tracking: Learning to track*

He told me the story of the sixteen-ton Toyota Hino double-decker sheep lorry that Diederik Brand had advertised for sale in the *Farmer's Weekly* for R400,000.

'Three blokes phoned him, and Oom Diederik said the first man to pay in cash could come and collect the truck. All three of them deposited the money. Oom Diederik told each of them they could come and collect it. The first bloke arrived and he took the lorry. When the other two arrived on the farm, Oom Diederik said, "I'm terribly sorry, but you are too late". They were angry and Oom Diederik said, "man, it's only business, come, you've driven a long way, sleep here tonight and enjoy Karoo hospitality on the house". He organised a feast, and poured a few brandies and told them stories and jokes the whole evening, and when they were properly drunk he said, "don't worry, tomorrow I'll give you each a cheque for the full amount", and they left the best of buddies. A week later the guys phoned and said the cheques had bounced, where was their money? Oom Diederik said the bank must have made a mistake, he would give the bank manager hell, he would send a new cheque immediately. A week later, same story. So it went on for a month or two, until the men realised they were being taken for a ride, then it was lawyers' letters and threats. But Oom Diederik knows all the tricks, he said his statements showed the payment had gone through, or he asked for proof of the sale contract, of course there was none, because he does everything verbally. Or he wouldn't answer his phone, he strung them along and earned interest on the R800,000 for nearly a year, until it ended up in court. Then on the steps in front of the court, he said, "OK, you can get your money, without the interest, but then you drop all the charges". The men were so thankful, they said all right.'

I began to understand why everyone told me to ask for money up front.

'Clever,' said Lourens le Riche.

Before he could tell me more, his cellphone rang. It was Nicola wanting to know where we were.

'We will be at the loading point in half an hour,' said Lourens.

When he had finished talking I asked him: 'What is this thing's top speed?'

'Depends how heavy the load is, Oom. With game on we drive slowly, between eighty and ninety.'

Racing away from trouble was not going to be an option.

'What does a rhino weigh?'

'I don't know, Oom.'

'How much can we carry?'

'About twenty tons, Oom. But this load won't come near that. In total, I estimate we won't load more than five tons tonight.'

My cellphone beeped. It was an SMS from Jeanette Louw, the standard query this time of the day: 'ALL OK?'

It wouldn't help to saddle her with my frustrations. I replied: 'ALL OK'.

I was expecting a clandestine smuggling rendezvous in the dark, with people sneaking about and urgent whispering somewhere in the thick bush. What we got was the brightly lit, busy yard of an irrigation farm on the banks of the Limpopo River.

A dozen black labourers sat and talked loudly on the concrete edge of a long steel shed, waiting. On the tailgate of a white Land Cruiser sat two white men in khaki shorts, khaki-and-green shirts, long socks, short work boots. As we drove into the yard, they jumped off. One was young, early twenties, the other well into his forties.

Lourens stopped. We climbed out. The white men approached. 'Lourens?' asked the older, and stretched out his hand.

'That's me, Oom.'

'Wickus Swanepoel,' he pronounced the 'W' as a 'V', 'and this is my son, Swannie.'

'And this is Oom Lemmer . . .'

We shook hands. They were two big men with five-o'clock-shadows, farmers' tans, identical snub noses, and bushy eyebrows. Pa Wickus's leather belt was slung low to accommodate a beer belly.

'Their truck is waiting at the border, over there,' he said, and pointed north. 'Are you ready?'

'Yes, we're ready, Oom.'

Wickus looked at his son. 'Tell them they can come. Make sure they have deflated the tyres. And that they know about the poles.'

Swannie took a cellphone out of his shorts pocket and phoned. His father said, 'We thought it better to wait for dark before they came across. Just in case.'

Just in case, I thought. Diederik's words.

The son was talking on the cellphone: 'Cornél, you can come across, they are here. Have you let air out of your tyres?'

'Turn your truck around so long,' Wickus said to Lourens. 'And open the back doors.'

'Right, Oom,' Lourens said. 'How long will it take?'

'They are just here, across the river, in the orchards on the Zim side. If they don't get stuck in the bloody sand they will be here now-now.'

Lourens got into the Mercedes.

'They're coming, Pa,' said Swannie, the son.

'Did you tell them to look out for the marker poles?'

'No, Pa. But they say they can see our lights.'

'No, oh *Koot*, that's just like a woman, the lights won't help fuck all if they don't watch the markers.'

'Don't worry, Pa.'

Lourens turned the Mercedes around so the nose pointed back in the direction we had come. Wickus Swanepoel walked over to where the labourers sat talking. He gave orders in their language. They stood up and came closer. Wickus gave more orders and pointed at some thick metal bars that lay in the doorway of the shed. Half of the labourers went over and got them.

Lourens switched off the Mercedes, jumped down and slid open the bolts of the rearmost grey steel doors.

'I hear they have a Bedford, might be a little lower than your load bed, if so we will get out the pulleys,' said Wickus.

'I hear them, Pa,' said Swannie.

The rumble of a diesel engine could be heard out of the darkness, at high revs.

'Oh hell,' said Wickus, 'I hope the bugger knows how to drive in sand.'

Lourens came closer. We stood four in a row, eyes to the north in the direction of the noise. 'Sand is loose this time of year,' said Wickus. 'Soft. Powder. River is dry. If they haven't let down the tyres they will get stuck. Then we're stuffed.'

'Don't worry, Pa.'

'Someone has to *fokken* worry.'

'Listen, they're through.'

The engine's revs were lower now, more controlled.

'So why doesn't he put his lights on?'

'Don't worry, Pa.'

'Stop saying that to me.'

'But we don't have to worry, Pa. We have all the permits this side.'

'Those people still have to bugger off back to Zim tonight, and they don't have papers.'

Then we saw the lorry, an old Bedford, appear out of the dark at the furthest extent of the lighted circle.

'Thank God,' said Wickus Swanepoel. 'It's an old RL.'

'Pa?'

'Was about the only Bedford with four-wheel drive,' his father said, as the lorry stopped in front of us. It looked like an old military vehicle, the green paint bleached and worn, but there was nothing wrong with the engine. A black driver sat behind the wheel, yellow vest, muscular arms, cigarette in mouth.

The passenger door opened. A woman jumped down lightly. She ignored us, moved straight to the back of the vehicle, which was covered by a dirty grey tarpaulin. She began untying ropes.

'Hell's bells!' said Pa Wickus, fervent, but under his breath. Because at first sight she was spectacular. Shoulders, arms and legs had the muscular definition of an athlete. Pitch black hair pulled back in a careless ponytail, the neck long and elegant, a fine sheen of perspiration on the honey skin, her face dominated by strong, high cheekbones. Lara Croft of the Limpopo, in boots, tight khaki shorts, and a sleeveless white T-shirt that clearly displayed her generous breasts.

'Cornél?' asked Swannie, the son. He sounded overjoyed to connect the voice on the telephone with this apparition.

She looked at him. 'Come and help,' she ordered.

Swannie didn't move at once. 'Flea?' he asked astonished. 'Flea van Jaarsveld?'

She bristled. 'I don't know you.'

'We were in primary school together,' said Swannie, with a tone of deep gratitude that he had a connection to her. '*Jissie*, Flea, you've changed.'

'My name's Cornél. Are you going to help, or just stand there looking?' she said, and turned her attention back to removing the tarpaulin.

'Man, it's so great to see you again.' And Swannie went right over to help her.

26

In order to study spoor, one must inevitably go to places where one will most likely encounter wild and often dangerous animals.

The Basics of Tracking: Dangerous animals

Flea van Jaarsveld, rhino tamer.

She orchestrated the removal of the tarpaulin with an irritated voice and self-important air, as though her responsibility were greater than we could comprehend. She looked disapprovingly at me, where I stood watching with my arms folded, a look that said I too should help. That was when I saw that close-up her beauty was flawed, the impact of the whole more impressive than the parts. The set of the lines of her mouth was somewhat mean, the jaw was a fraction too weak. What saved these features from coldness was the tiny flaw in her left eye, a nick in the lower lid like a tear. It softened everything with a hint of melancholy.

They rolled the big sail off the flatbed of the Bedford, exposing two massive steel cages fitted tightly together. There were only millimetres between the rear flap of the Bedford and the second cage. The rhinos were shrouded in shadows, two chunky, restless shapes behind iron bars.

'I need light here,' Flea commanded, and pointed at the animals.

Young Swannie, suddenly the highly efficient young farmer, sprang into action, barking orders at the workmen.

She clambered back into the cabin of the Bedford, calf muscles flexing, sure movements, full of confidence and focus. When she came down there was a leather case in her hand, the impractical kind that doctors carried as a status symbol. This one had seen some mileage. She swung it onto the back of the Bedford, stepped on the rear wheel and climbed up after it.

'Where's the light?'

'It's coming,' said Swannie.

She checked the chunky watch on her slender arm, pressed buttons on it. Swannie came trotting up with a hunting spotlight, the beam like a searchlight in the night sky. He held it out to her.

'Get up,' she said, her attention on the opened case.

He grinned at his good fortune at being chosen, nodded eagerly, and climbed onto the lorry.

In that moment I saw Lourens le Riche. He stood beside the Bedford. His eyes were fixed on her, an expression of utter fascination on his face.

'Shine here,' she said to Swannie, and pointed at the first cage. She took a syringe and a bottle of liquid out of the case. The needle on the syringe was short and thick.

I came closer to see. The spotlight lit up the foremost rhino. The animal was blindfolded. Bundled material protruded from one ear and hung down over the blindfold. The rhino moved uneasily, stamped a leg on the steel floor, bumped its head against the bars. The skin was lighter than I had imagined, dull grey and deeply textured in the bright lighting, covered with a rash of pinky-red, septic growths on the neck, over the back and the butt of the creature. The growths glistened, wet and sickly.

'Hell's bells!' said Wickus Swanepoel, observing the activity from beside the Bedford. 'What's wrong with them?'

Flea drew liquid from the bottle with the syringe. 'Necrolytic Dermatitis, in the festering stage.'

'You're a vet,' said Swannie, with huge respect.

'Can they die of these sores?' his father asked.

'It usually occurs along with anaemia and gastrointestinal disorders,' she said. 'That is where the danger lies.'

'Hell!' said Wickus.

She pressed the syringe into the rhino's rump, behind and above the powerful thighs. 'They're very weak, very stressed. We can't waste time. Can you shove that sock back in the ear?'

'That's a sock?'

'The only use for a Stormers rugby sock. Dulls sound. Keeps them calm.'

'Well, I never. Sounds like you're a Bulls fan,' said Wickus from below, very happy. 'Just like us.'

She picked up her bag and moved to the second cage. We stood as one man and watched her neat little bottom.

'What are you injecting?' asked Swannie.

'Azaperone. Hundred and fifty milligrams. It keeps them calm, helps with the negative physiological effects of the M99.'

'OK,' Swannie said again, with boundless awe.

And Lourens le Riche stood and stared at her like a buck caught in blinding headlights.

The transfer operation took over an hour, fifteen men sweating, pulling, lifting, putting the cage down and moving it centimetre by centimetre from the Bedford into the load bed of the Mercedes. Wickus organised the labour, in language that was appreciably more socially acceptable now. Flea berated us for the rest of our labours with the minimum words and the maximum scowling. Until Lourens pushed the doors shut and slid the bolts.

Flea walked quickly over to him. 'You're the driver to the Karoo.'

'Lourens,' he said, and put out his hand.

She ignored it, wiped the sweat from her forehead with the back of her left hand, walked over to the passenger door of the Mercedes and said, 'Right, let's go.'

That was the first indication that she was coming along.

We got away at twenty to ten. Flea threw a blood-red travel bag and the doctor's bag in the cab, climbed up after them, and made herself at home in the passenger seat. As I climbed up after her, she looked a me. 'Are you coming too?' Not exactly jubilant about the possibility.

'This is Oom Lemmer,' was all that Lourens said. Then he took out two big soft cushions and put them over the hump between the two seats, stowed her baggage, arranged the cushions properly, one on her seat and one behind her back.

The Swanepoels stood outside, beside my window, with eyes only for her. 'You know where we are now, Cornél. Come and visit,' Wickus Swanepoel called out hopefully. Beside him, his son approved the invitation with a vigorously nodding head, the bushy brows raised high in enthusiasm. Then they waved one last time and we drove away into the darkness.

Her scent drifted through the cab of the Mercedes, an interesting blend of soap, shampoo and sweat. She sat with her legs tucked up, arms wrapped around her knees, her body language showing she was dissatisfied, that she didn't have the luxury of personal space and a proper seat.

Lourens called Nicola, said we were on our way.

Flea consulted the digital watch on her arm. 'Between half past one and two I have to inject them again,' she instructed Lourens.

I sat and waited for his reaction. How would a Karoo boy handle this . . . phenomenon?

He took papers out of his door panel and handed them to her, his movements slow and measured. 'The top one is the route book, the lower one is a map. By two o'clock we should be 300 kilometres from here, maybe a bit more . . .'

She took them in silence, lowered her legs, and studied the uppermost document, a white sheet of paper with columns of places and distances. She unfolded the map and compared the two, her slender finger finding direction on the spider web of roads over Vaalwater, Rustenburg, Ventersdorp . . . until she looked up at him. I couldn't see her face, but I could hear the frown in her voice: 'This is one helluva obscure route. Why don't we just take the N1?'

For the first time I saw the ghostly line of an old scar on her neck. It curled from below her left ear and under her hair, a fine pattern like the outline of a bird's wing, only one shade lighter than her skin.

'Oom Diederik wants us to stay off the main routes. And . . .'

'Why?' Sharp and accusatory.

'Weighbridges,' Lourens said, but calm and controlled.

'Weighbridges?'

'Long distances are all about average speed, and nothing breaks your average speed like a weighbridge. At every weighbridge you lose plus-minus an hour, and there are five between Musina and Kimberley if we take the N1 and the N12. In any case, this route is almost a hundred kilometres shorter.'

I was proud of him: he would not let himself be intimidated, his tone of voice was relaxed, he was not looking for her approval, merely giving information courteously and pleasantly. Impressive for a young man already blindly in love.

She traced the route with her finger again, shook her head. 'No. We will have to drive via Bela-Bela. I need light when I sedate them.'

He looked where her finger pointed. 'All right,' he said. 'We'll stop there.'

She folded up the map, smugly, as if she had won this round. She put it on top of the dashboard, in the hollow behind the cup holders, drew her legs up again and dropped her head onto her knees to discourage further communication.

It was going to be an interesting trip.

The cornerstone of my profession was the art of reading people. To identify threats, to understand the one you protected, to predict situations and prevent them. It had become a habit, a ritual, sometimes a game, to watch and listen and patch the bits of incidental information together into a profile that was continually adapted and expanded, every time one step closer to the truth. The problem, I had learned over two decades, was that we are deceitful animals. We skilfully weave a false front, often extensive and complex, fact and fiction in a delicate blend to accentuate the good and acceptable, and to hide the bad.

The art was to analyse the front as well, since that largely exposed what was hidden behind it.

There was a great deal that betrayed Flea van Jaarsveld: this attitude of irritable superiority. The deliberate distance she maintained between herself and us. The exaggerated use of learned medical terminology. Her nickname. The insistence that she was now Cornél – ten to one her own twisting of Cornelia, as it sounded much more dignified. Add to that the choice of clothing that needlessly accentuated her assets. Because she was pretty, despite the slight deficiencies. Or perhaps because of those negligible imperfections.

The majority of Body Armour's clientele were attractive people who had grown up in wealth. They generally had an effortless assumption of privilege, a natural distance from the common crowd, an ease with, and often a concealing of, beauty.

In shrill contrast with Flea. Therefore I guessed her background was lower middle-class, blue-collar domestic, mine or factory worker, naïve, down-to-earth, a little rough.

Poverty is not necessarily a negative formative element. The problems begin when the desire to escape it becomes all-consuming. In primary school she would already have shown the academic promise that would eventually enable her to be selected for veterinary school. 'You're clever,' her humble, but inherently good parents would have urged her. 'You must get an education. Make something of yourself.' Another way of saying 'you can get out of this'.

But it was the physical flowering that would have been the breakthrough. By inference from Swannie's '*Jissie*, you've changed,' she must have been ordinary at fourteen, dull even, with no great expectation that she would be so genetically lucky. So the metamorphosis, somewhere between fifteen and sixteen, would have taken her by surprise, causing her to change gears swiftly in order to reconsider the potential of it all. Clever and pretty is a strong platform from which to launch yourself.

And she had.

So she would have advanced to this point with fierce determination, and now had the realistic expectation of a Good Catch. She would dream of a fairy tale wedding with the filthy rich owner of an exclusive private game reserve, where she could manage the breeding programme of some exotic threatened species, and occasionally pose photogenically on the cover of conservation magazines, with her attractive, somewhat older husband's arm around her, her own arms protectively cradling a cheetah cub.

But I knew from personal experience: you can't escape your past. It lives in you, woven into every cell. You could say you had lost contact with your parents, you could provide vague answers if Emma le Roux asked, 'What was it like growing up in Sea Point?', you could hide yourself away in Loxton, but sooner or later it catches up with you.

I believe Flea van Jaarsveld knew this, somehow. It was the fear of exposure that drove her, ate at her, it was the mechanism that had turned her into this aggressive, determined young woman.

It was a sentiment I understood. So I would let her be. Accommodate her.

But should I warn Lourens le Riche? Flea *would* break his heart.

No. Lemmer's First Law.

27

> . . . trackers must also be able to interpret the animal's activities so that they can anticipate and predict its movements.
>
> *The Basics of Tracking: Spoor interpretation*

Gravel roads in Limpopo, the occasional stretch of tar, everything deserted in the late night. The headlights of the Mercedes were on bright, lighting up the dull grass at the edge of the road, sometimes trees, cattle, donkeys, villages, poor settlements shrouded in darkness. There was silence in the cab, because The Vet was sleeping.

She had fallen asleep quietly. Her arms slipped off her knees and she concealed her moment's alarm by stretching her legs out under the dashboard, shifting her back irritably against the rear cushion and laying her head on the edge of Lourens's seat.

Only once we turned south on the tarred R561, did Lourens whisper to me: 'Oom, can you get the coffee out, please?'

I worked carefully so as not to disturb her, got hold of one flask.

'The mugs are up there,' he pointed at a shelf panel in the middle, and checked his rear-view mirror. I reached up, unclipped the lid and found the mugs.

'Help yourself too.'

I poured, handed him a mug. He took it, cast a tender look at Flea and said, 'She must be exhausted. I wonder if she's been travelling with them all the way through Zim.'

'Must be,' I whispered.

'It must have been a helluva ride . . .'

He was right. Perhaps I ought to temper my opinion of her. Seven hundred kilometres through Zimbabwe with an illegal cargo would take its toll.

'Where did Oom Diederik find her?' he wondered. Then he checked his mirror again and reduced speed, tested the temperature of the coffee with his mouth, looked at his mirror again and said, 'Why won't this guy come past?'

I poured coffee into the second mug.

'He's been behind us since the other side of Alldays,' still speaking softly, so as not to wake her.

'How far back was that?'

'About fifty kilos.'

That had been gravel road where it was hard to pass, but now we were on the tar and we were driving more slowly, just over seventy. 'What's he doing now?'

'He's dropped back a bit.'

'Do you need this mirror?' I pointed at the one on my side.

'You can change it for now, Oom.'

I wound my window down. The night had cooled considerably since we had loaded the rhino. I adjusted the mirror so that I could see the road behind us. The blast of air woke Flea.

'What?' she said, wiping a hand over her mouth.

I shut the window. 'Just fixing the mirror.'

She sat up, stretched as much as the limited room would allow, and combed her fingers through her hair to neaten up.

'Would you like some coffee?' Lourens asked.

She nodded and rubbed her eyes, checked her watch.

I passed my mug to her and checked the mirror. There were still lights behind us, half a kilometre back.

'Why are we driving so slowly?' she asked grumpily.

Lourens began to speed up. 'It was just to change the mirror,' he said. He caught my eye, conspiratorial.

The vehicle behind us kept its distance. That didn't necessarily mean anything. Some drivers preferred not to pass at night, but use the red tail lights as a guide.

When her mug was half empty, Lourens asked Flea. 'Was it rough coming through Zim?'

'What do you think?'

He didn't allow himself to be put off. 'How do you know Oom Diederik?'

'I don't know him.'

'Oh?'

'I know Ehrlichmann.' A concession.

'Who is Ehrlichmann?'

She sighed faintly and, with exaggerated patience, asked, 'Do you know where the rhino come from?'

'Yes.'

'Ehrlichmann found them in the Chete.'

'He's the one who used to be a game warden?'

'Yes.'

'Aah.' Then in admiration: 'How do you know *him*?'

Again the silent sigh. 'Last year there was a WWF elephant census in the Chizarira . . . that's a national park in Zim. I volunteered. Ehrlichmann was part of the team.'

'OK,' Lourens said.

The lights were still behind us.

She emptied her mug and handed it to me, tucked her legs under her in the lotus position, folded her arms under her breasts. 'Tell me about Diederik Brand.'

'Oom Diederik . . .' he said. 'Where shall I begin? He's kind of a legend in the Bo-Karoo . . .'

'Is he rich?'

Interesting question.

'Oom Diederik? Yes, he's rich.'

'How did he make his money?'

Lourens just chuckled.

'What does that mean?'

'Well, Oom Diederik, how shall I say? He's a . . .' he searched for the right euphemism.

'Black Swan,' I said spontaneously.

They both turned to look at me.

It was because I had been thinking about Emma for the past hour, before Lourens had asked for coffee.

'A black swan is an anomaly, a wild card that changes everything,' I said, and tried to remember what Emma had told me sixteen hours ago in the Red Pomegranate. She had been reading the book all weekend, making frequent comments like 'incredible' and 'so interesting', until by Saturday morning I *had* to ask her what it was all about.

Lourens and Flea waited for me to explain.

'Before they discovered Australia, the Europeans knew absolutely that all swans were white. That's how our brains work: we learn by observation, we draw our conclusions from the weight of probability, we firmly believe that is the only reality. If you only see white swans for hundreds of years, it is therefore obvious that only white swans exist. Then they found black swans in Australia.'

'What has this to do with Diederik Brand?'

Although her attitude was annoying, the question wasn't unreasonable.

'All the Karoo people I know are painfully honest. Honourable. They have a work ethic that says there is only one way to earn your daily bread. I never considered that Diederik could be otherwise.'

'Is he?'

'Apparently,' and I looked to Lourens for help.

'He is.' Then he braked and put on his indicator light. 'We have to turn off here.' He pointed at the road sign that indicated the D579, a right turn to the Lapalala Wilderness Game Reserve.

Flea picked up the map, unfolded it. 'Are you sure?'

'Yip,' he said, continued to reduce speed and turned off the tar onto a broad gravel road. He shot a glance at me, and we both looked at the wing mirrors. He accelerated slowly.

The road behind us remained dark.

Lourens speeded up.

Still dark.

Flea looked up from the map. 'I still don't get this route,' she said.

'We have to go via Vaalwater,' said Lourens. 'Then to Bela-Bela. It's not a big detour . . .'

And then he suddenly stopped speaking, as behind us headlights popped up in the mirror.

28

. . . if you are a keen naturalist who spends a lot of time in the field, the chances of being bitten sooner or later are not insignificant (especially if you try to track down snakes).

The Basics of Tracking: Spoor Interpretation

'What?' asked Flea. She wasn't stupid.

'Don't worry about the route,' said Lourens.

'Why did you look at each other like that?'

'There's a vehicle following us, for the past hour,' I said, because she needed to know.

She looked at me as though seeing me for the first time. Then a short, crude laugh burst from her lips. 'You're joking.'

'See for yourself,' I said, and pointed at the mirror.

She leaned over, saw the lights. 'You say he's been behind us for an hour?' Sceptical.

'He turns when we turn.'

'Big deal,' she said. 'Can I have some more coffee?' And then: 'Do you think I'm going to fall for that one? Do you think I'm stupid?'

'No,' I said.

That seemed to satisfy her.

I considered the terrain. The road climbed up and down, winding between invisible hills. I suspected we were in the Waterberg. In the headlights the thorn trees grew densely up to the road's edge, there was an occasional chunky rock formation. Not ideal.

'I want to make sure about this, Lourens. We'll wait for a long downhill. Don't use your brakes; we don't want to alert them. But slow down, use the gears to stop. Slowly, smoothly. Keep the lights on.'

'OK.'

Flea ignored us, sat there, sulking.

The road made a sweeping turn, first to the left, a kilometre later it curved right, then a long straight stretch with a slight downhill slope. Lourens took his foot off the accelerator, worked down through the gears, put it in neutral. The Mercedes slowed. We watched the mirrors keenly. The lights appeared around the first turn, growing larger initially as they approached. Then they kept their distance.

I looked up at the cab light, moved the switch so it would stay off when the door opened. 'Make sure you know how the road curves, and then switch off your headlights.'

Lourens waited a bit and then turned off the lights. The night was suddenly pitch black. The only lights were the ones behind us, considerably closer now.

'When we stop, turn off the engine and use the handbrake. But stay in your seat and keep your hand on the keys.'

'OK.' Calm, composed. Just what we needed.

I took the Glock out of the storage space, waited until we rolled to a halt, opened the door, leaped out, ran around to the rear of the truck, pistol in hand. Lourens turned the engine off.

The lights behind us, now only 200 metres away, snapped off suddenly.

A very bad sign.

Stars, no moon. My eyes were not accustomed to the darkness, I could only recognise the immediate surroundings, the road, the tall grass, deep shadows of thorn trees across the road.

I listened. The sounds of the truck behind me, metal cooling. Then, footsteps on the gravel.

'Get back in the truck,' I said softly.

She came and stood beside me. 'If the tranquilliser wears off, the rhinos will go into a frenzy.'

I stared into the darkness trying to see them.

'I've seen a rhino smash its sinuses to a pulp against the bars,' she said.

I put my finger to my lips, warning her to be quiet.

'It was dead the next day. I can't inject them in the dark. Can we get moving?'

I knew enough. We had a problem. Someone was behind us, someone with an agenda. And they didn't want to be seen. Content just to follow.

I turned and went back to the passenger door, where I waited for her. She didn't come straight away, wanting to make a point. Then she moved, arms folded and head down, shot me a dirty look as she got in.

I climbed up after her and told Lourens: 'Let's go. Keep the lights off as long as you can.'

She said: 'It's not a joke.'

Lourens concentrated on the road, driving slowly.

I sat and thought things through.

They knew that we knew. They would have seen as little as I did in the dark, but their engine had not been running. They would have heard the Mercedes drive off. They would know we had to switch on our headlights sooner or later, unless we meant to drive this slowly until daybreak. If they were close enough they would be able to follow us without lights, using the truck as a direction finder until daylight.

The question was not what they were after; there was a million rands' of rhino horn within spitting distance from me. The question was rather, what they were waiting for. One vehicle, not a large one, a sedan or bakkie. Or a minibus that could take eight or ten people. Superior numbers if we stopped. Which we had just done. And nothing had happened.

Were they aware we were armed? Or did they just assume? Or was I mistaken entirely.

What would I do if I meant to hijack a twenty-ton truck?

It depended on the purpose. I doubted our pursuers wanted more than the horns. They just needed to force the truck to stop without putting themselves in too much danger, neutralise the people, cut off the booty and get away. There was only one way to do that easily.

I turned around on the seat so I could reach my sports bag and took out the MAG-7.

'Good grief,' said Flea.

I clipped on my safety belt. 'Is there a safety belt for her?' I asked Lourens.

'No, Oom.'

I looked at her. The arrogance was gone, but I saw reproach. For the first time I noticed her left eye from close up. Another faint scar ran from the fold in her lower lid, a centimetre down her cheek, fine as a hair.

'When I say "duck", you get down there,' and I pointed at the foot well in front of my seat. 'I will make room for you.'

'Why?'

I was beginning to question my patience with her, but Lourens preempted me. 'He's a professional bodyguard, Cornél. You should do as he says.'

'A bodyguard?'

'Listen,' I said. 'The chances that they want the rhino alive are extremely slim. Too much trouble, too much time to transfer them, too many tranquillisers and need for expert care. We must assume they only want the horns. That means they must force us to stop. The only sensible way is to block the road ahead. We will have to run a blockade, knock something out of the way . . .'

'No!' she said. 'The animals . . .'

'The animals are protected enough. If we have to stop, we and the animals will be in danger.'

She considered my argument. Then she nodded, to my surprise. She took a deep breath and looked me in the eye. 'What do you want me to do?'

'Give me a chance to think.'

She sat motionless.

I checked the mirror, the road behind us remained dark. I picked up the map again, so I could test my new theory against it.

Lourens said they had been behind us since before Alldays. On the second long tarred road since we had set off, after about fifty kilometres of gravel road. I didn't like to make assumptions, but I had to. Assumption number one: they knew where we had loaded. There were simply too many roads in Northern Limpopo for them to have found us by chance. Which meant at least one vehicle had been behind us from the start. But once they realised we weren't going to keep to the tar, they had to reduce the following distance in order not to lose us on some obscure side road. That was why it had taken Lourens so long to spot them.

Assumption number two was logical: they hadn't known which route we would follow. They would have guessed, and, like Flea, assumed we would take the N1, with the R521 to Polokwane as the second option. If I were in their shoes I would let my other vehicles – three at least, or four – wait near Mokopane. Probably near one of the toll gates, a good place to attack a stationary vehicle, remove the horns quickly and disappear.

Assumption number three: when our route deviated from

expectations, they would have had to reorganise. They would have a map and by now would have plotted the straight line of our planned route – via Vaalwater, Rustenburg and Ventersdorp. Our last turn-off, twenty minutes ago, would have been the final indication.

Assumption number four: the devil works in darkness. They would attack before daybreak. And they would have to work quickly now, before we could reach a police station.

I measured the distances from Polokwane and Mokopane, calculated average speed and probabilities. Every time I reached the same conclusion: Vaalwater. They would have to act before Vaalwater. Within the next fifty kilometres.

I folded the map and put it away. I put the Glock on the seat between myself and Flea, held the MAG-7 in my hands.

'How strong is the bull bar in front?' I asked Lourens.

'That depends . . .'

'If we had to knock a car or a bakkie out of the way?'

'Oom, three weeks ago we hit a kudu beyond Middelburg, and that thing bent back so far it knocked out the windscreen.'

Not what I wanted to hear. 'But the engine is under here?' and I gestured at the bulge under Flea.

'Yes, Oom, but the radiators are in front. If something hits us badly, we're in trouble.'

Flea drew a breath to say something, then shook her head and kept quiet.

I thought. 'If there is no way to get through, we will have to stop. Lourens, they will try to block the road. There might be space to force our way through on the side. Don't let fences intimidate you. If the veld looks good on the other side . . .'

'OK.'

'But you will have very little time to decide.'

He nodded, seated himself more firmly behind the steering wheel, determined.

The mirror attracted my attention. I looked. The lights were there again, much closer.

'They're back,' Lourens confirmed.

'Then it's close,' I said and opened the MAG-7.

Two hundred metres ahead, the road changed from night to day.

29

> ... the tracks of animals fleeing indicates a disturbance, and if no signs of predators are found, further investigation may reveal human intruders.
>
> *The Art of Tracking – Introduction: Poaching*

The headlights of four vehicles blinded us so we couldn't see anything, except the rocky cliff rising up on the left and a black drop on the right. The perfect place.

Lourens hit the brakes, I shouted at Flea to duck, moving my legs to make room for her, wrestling with a plan of action: jump out to distract them, or stay here to protect Lourens and Flea?

She did the one thing I wasn't expecting. Before she wriggled down between the instrument panel and the seat, she picked up the Glock. I grabbed at it, too late. Suddenly outside, to the right, a shadowy figure appeared, out of nowhere, a man with a gun, waving his arm. Lourens jerked at the wheel to avoid hitting him.

The truck skidded on the loose gravel, and for a second I thought he would lose control.

We hit the man, sickening thud.

I decide to get out, create two targets. Fighting the G-force, I unclip the seat belt, shove open the door and jump in the hope that our own headlights will hide me.

A second in the air, my feet hit the ground hard and I use the momentum, roll through the long grass beside the road, stones and grass tufts, the MAG tight against my side, rolling, shock of barbed wire ripping across my back, deep and painful. On my feet, gasping for breath, as the brake lights of the Mercedes halt in a cloud of dust. Ten metres away from me two figures rise from the grass, assault rifles in their arms, charging at the truck. 'Kill the lights,' they yell, 'kill the lights!' One kneels beside the cab, aims the rifle at the door, the other reaches up, pulls it open, jumps down again, crouching next to his partner. 'Kill the lights,' a thunderous order, phantom shapes against the lights and the swirling dust.

Lourens turns off the lights.

'Now get out.'

The dust drifted lazily away. I saw they were black, the weapons AK-47s. In front of the Mercedes another three appeared, rifles to their shoulders, sights aimed at the windscreen.

Flea and the Glock lay there in wait, I hoped she was as smart as I thought.

'Hold up your hands,' someone shouted from the other side of the truck. 'Now, get down.'

Lourens got out.

'On the ground.'

At first I saw only his feet, showing under the truck, then he sank down on his knees.

'Lie down.'

He lay down in the dust, hands on his head.

'You in there,' called one of the men kneeling on this side. 'Get out.'

I raised myself slowly, knelt in the grass, lifted the MAG, thumbed off the safety catch, aimed at the AK closest to me, praying she would obey.

'I said get out!' he shouted.

On the back of the truck the rhinos shifted: stamping, a disturbed snort. The attackers' feet shuffled on the gravel, AKs were cocked. Flea's hands were visible at the window, then her head, fear on her face.

A cold barrel touched the back of my neck. A calm voice behind me, so close: 'Put down the gun.'

I lowered the MAG.

Our pursuers. They must have seen me bail out.

I put the shotgun down carefully, still on my knees. He moved around me, into my field of vision. A big black man, massive silver revolver held with both hands, arms straight, aiming between my eyes.

Then he smiled. 'Mr Stuntman.'

He lunges forward suddenly, kicks me. I fend with my arms, deflecting, so he gets me low, in the belly. I fall over backwards, roll away, but he keeps coming, kicks me again, in the back. I change direction, roll towards him, wait for the next kick, grab his boot and pull with all my strength. Both feet leave the ground, he falls on his back, hard, bellows: 'Hu!' I am on him, my knee sinks into his belly, his mouth wide, croaking for air. My left hand grabs his revolver arm, I bring my right elbow down on his face, smash his nose, feel the blood spatter over me. His revolver hand opens, I grab the gun, shove it to his temple, cock the hammer, throw all my weight on him.

'Amasimba,' *he hisses and touches his nose with both hands. Blood on his mouth. 'You are a fucking fool.'*

A gun against the back of my head, a voice behind: 'You want me to kill him, Inkunzi?'

The big man pushes the revolver away from his temple with an impatient gesture. 'Not yet. If he's stupid, shoot him in the leg.'

'Nazo-ke, *Inkunzi!'*

'Get off me,' Inkunzi says.

I turn my head. There are two of them behind me, AKs at the ready. I stand up. Slowly. Inkunzi's revolver is a Smith & Wesson, the giant Model 500, two kilograms of stainless steel. I drop it in the grass. Inkunzi swears in some African language, bends and picks it up, swings it at my head. It's too heavy for surprise. I duck with ease, grab his arm, pull him off balance. An AK butt hits me in the back. I fall forwards. Instantly, Inkunzi kicks me in the ribs, dull thud, sudden pain. The other two kick me from behind, running shoes, less effective. I kick back, connect with one's knee, try to get up, my only chance. Inkunzi grabs my collar, jerks. I fall back again. Another one joins them, four now. Kicks rain down on me, I roll onto my back, must protect my spine, pull my knees up to my chest, arms over my head. I jerk back and forth, pain everywhere, a dull thud to my head, another, I move my balled fists to protect my skull, I smile faintly, slip away to a safe place in my head, seeing the shoe sole on the way to my face too late.

Buzzing in my head, smell of dust, faraway sounds, shadows leaping in the dancing light, my body a sea of pain.

One swollen eye. Struggle to focus.

Figures.

They slowly took shape.

I was lying on my side in front of the Mercedes, one arm under me, awkward. They must have dragged me here.

To the left of me, Flea knelt with her hands behind her head. Lourens on his knees beside her, Inkunzi's revolver to the back of his head. Between us our belongings were strewn across the road, my sports bag, Flea's medical case, coffee flasks, mugs, cushions, clothing, tools.

Beside me lay the body of the man we had knocked down. As still as death.

Time seemed to stop, no one moved.

Sounds gradually penetrated. At the truck, metal on metal, someone hammering. Men's voices talking.

Flea sobbed.

I had no idea how long I had lain here.

Two men walked past me. A strong smell of diesel. 'Nothing in the tanks,' said one.

'It's not in the lorry,' said the other.

Inkunzi swore. 'Where is it?' he asked Flea.

'I don't know.' Drained.

I lifted my head slowly. A rifle butt hit me in the back. 'This one is awake.'

'Good,' said Inkunzi, and looked at me. 'I will shoot this boy if you don't tell me.'

'Tell you what?' but my voice would not work. I tried again. A hoarse rasp sent flames down my ribcage.

'You know what we want. Where is it?'

'What is he talking about?' Desperate fear in Flea's voice.

'You know,' said Inkunzi.

'I don't,' she implored him.

'Then I will shoot him,' and he cocked the revolver.

'No!'

Someone bent over the motionless figure lying beside me, rolled him over. 'Snake is dead, Inkunzi.'

'Shit. Are you sure?'

'Looks like it.'

'He was a fucking fool . . . Make sure . . . Wait. Where is her pistol?'

The man walked to where our belongings were strewn. 'Over here.'

Inkunzi came closer. 'Give it to me.' He shoved his big Smith & Wesson in his belt, took the other firearm from his assistant. It was my Glock.

'Now why would a lady carry such a gun?'

'It's mine,' I tried to say, my voice hoarse.

'What?'

'It's mine.'

'Good,' said Inkunzi, went to the body of Snake, pressed the barrel to the skull and fired. Blood, fibre, bone spattered. Flea made a high-pitched, frightened mewl. Lourens shouted, bent over, and vomited.

'Now, let's shoot a live one,' said Inkunzi and walked back to Lourens. He stood behind the bowed figure and pressed my Glock against his neck.

'Where is the stuff?' A slight African accent.

'I don't know,' Flea screamed.

'One . . .'

'Please!'

'Two . . .'

'Take the horns,' she screamed, terrified, shrill.

'I don't want the fucking horns.'

'So what do you want?' I groaned.

'You know very well.'

It made no sense. 'No,' I said, trying to shake my head emphatically. Bad choice.

'You stopped, back there.'

'Because you were following us.'

He inspected the defenceless neck of Lourens le Riche thoughtfully. Pulled the trigger. A shot thundered, Lourens jerked, Flea's cry was primitive. Lourens was still sitting, I realised the significance of the dust exploding from the road surface. A deliberate miss.

One heart-rending cry from Lourens. He threw up again.

Flea wept, her shoulders jerked.

The big man looked over us, one by one. Lourens gasped raggedly, he tried to stop his sobs. Then Inkunzi strolled over to me. 'You threw it in the veld.'

'What?' I asked.

He made a noise, a laugh perhaps, but his lip was split, his nose would be hurting. I took satisfaction from that. 'We know all about it,' he said and bent down, a big palm pressed to my chest.

Concussion does not lend itself to clear thinking. I didn't know what to say. 'Take the lorry,' I said. 'Take everything. Take me too. Leave them. Please.'

'No,' he said in a reasonable tone. 'Just tell me if you threw the stuff in the veld. Where must we look? Over the fence?'

'I wanted to see if you were following us. That's all.'

He thought before he answered. 'You're a pro,' he said. 'I wonder why you are here. All that fire power, the route you took. There's a reason.'

'It's because of the rhinos.'

Another grunting laugh, his face not cooperating.

'The horns are worth a lot of money,' I said.

'Chinese witchcraft,' he said and got up. 'Not my business.'

'What is your business?'

He ignored me, getting up slowly. Head bowed, deep in thought, touching his nose carefully, looking across to one of his henchmen: 'You sure there's nothing?'

'Yes, Inkunzi.'

'Shit.' He took a cloth out of his pocket, wiped my Glock with it, then tossed the weapon down with our stuff. 'We marked the place where they stopped. Three rocks on either side of the road . . .'

That's why they had disappeared for a while.

'. . . Take the men, go look. It must be there.'

'Do we kill them now?'

He looked at me. 'This one. I would like to kill him. But first . . .'

He went to Flea, pulled her up by her hair. Stood against her. She twisted, but he held her ponytail in an iron grip, pulled her tight against him. He put his damaged mouth to her ear, his left hand stroked her breasts, whispered inaudibly.

She shivered.

He thrust her away, turned around quickly and came back to me. He took the Smith & Wesson out of his belt, came and stood over me with his legs apart, expressionless. Lifted the revolver.

30

> To minimise the chances of being killed by a dangerous animal you need to overcome an irrational fear of the unknown, while avoiding irrational fearlessness of what you think you 'know'.
>
> *The Basics of Tracking: Dangerous animals*

There is a place I go. I found it as a child, a no-man's-land, a refuge. It has protective walls, but it is not a room. Not an open space, but I can see and hear the comforting sea. I am aware of where my body is, the pain faraway and faint, but I am not there. I know my eyes are hard, they say I don't fear my father's beatings, I endure them, because I have slipped away, one step removed. I am quiet, I don't plead, I don't weep, I don't cry out. My faint smile says hit me some more, come on, lay it on me. One day I'll be back. To offload. To dish it out.

I found my place, looked him in the eye as he cocked his gun. Grinned.

He stood like that for a long time, finger on the trigger.

Then he shook his head. 'You are a mad man.' He lowered his gun. 'I know where to find you.' He walked away. 'Let's go,' he shouted.

I didn't move. Just lay there in no-man's-land.

I heard them drag Snake's corpse off somewhere, then their foot steps moved away from us. Car doors slammed. Engines revved, tyres crunched, gravel clipping against the truck, clouds of dust bloomed. I heard them drive off, saw the lights disappear one after the other, until the darkness descended on us like sweet mercy. Flea van Jaarsveld sobbed quietly. One despairing breath tore through Lourens.

I looked up at the stars, watched how they brightened gradually.

The drone of vehicles died away at last.

Then I came back. In my own time. I sat up in the road. Did not see Flea.

I stood up. Sore, shaky on my feet. I walked over to where Lourens had knelt. I found them both there in the dark. She had her arms around him, her hand stroked the back of his head, comforting. He just sat.

* * *

I gathered our things. Everything was inside out, strewn across the road. My Glock tossed aside. I found a torch among the scattered belongings, went looking for the MAG. It was gone.

I walked around the Mercedes. Tyres were fine. They had left the cap off the diesel tank. I found it behind the wheel and tried to twist it on. Something was in the way – a long wire, bent double, with a hook on the end. I pulled it out and threw it into the veld.

Inspected the cab. Every compartment with a cover was open. More mess. I tidied up, closed everything. Fetched everything that was outside and packed it all away. Lourens and Flea must have nothing to remind them of what had happened.

The rhinos were unhappy, they jostled and stamped and fidgeted. I looked at my watch. Twenty to two. *Between half past one and two I have to inject them again.*

I loaded everything that had been outside back into the cab. Went over to Lourens and Flea. They were still sitting like that.

'I'll drive,' I said, quietly. 'We have to go. The rhinos must be injected.'

Flea got up. She pulled Lourens by the shoulder. He got up. They walked to the passenger door. His head was bowed, in a daze.

I got behind the wheel, slammed the door and waited for them. Then I started the engine, struggled with the gears, switched on the lights and pulled slowly away. Concentrated, trying to get the feel of the vehicle, the full extent of its weight. Tried not to blame myself, but unsuccessfully. I should have protected them. I should never have jumped out. I should have jumped out sooner. We should have stopped, called the police. I should have confronted our pursuers, a few hours before, when there were only two or three.

I should have protected them.

I should have started shooting, created chaos.

We were outnumbered. There was only so much I could do, alone.

Why had Diederik sent me along?

I should have protected them.

Thirty kilometres further, Lourens asked in a whisper, 'Do you have the proper licence, Oom?' his voice was without expression.

'No.'

'I'll be all right soon.'

* * *

At Vaalwater, under the bright lights of a petrol station, she clambered over the cages and injected one rhino, and then the other.

Petrol attendants watched us with wary, shifting eyes. There was blood on my face.

I let them fill up with diesel, checked over the truck again. Everything seemed right. I went to the restroom. Saw myself in the mirror, looked bad. One eye swollen, a deep cut on the eyebrow. Flecks of Snake's brain on my ear. I washed thoroughly and for a long time.

In the café I bought four litres of Coke, they needed sugar.

Lourens said: 'I will drive.'

'Soon,' I said and made him drink some cola. 'You can navigate.'

At two forty-five, we drove out of town. His voice was emotionless as he gave directions.

I wanted to talk to them. I wanted to tell them fear was not a disgrace. I wanted to explain to them how violence and fear stripped you of your dignity, that you mustn't allow that to happen. I wanted to explain trauma to them, the process, the mechanisms to fight it. Like revenge.

I couldn't find the words.

Eventually Lourens fished out his CDs from a compartment. He chose one and pushed it into the player, turned up the volume. I looked at the cover. Arsis. *We are the Nightmare.*

Death metal washed over us, surreal, otherworldly, until there was room for nothing else.

When the CD had played through, the silence was heavy, like lead. Then Lourens said, 'Oom, I'm all right now.'

'I'll drive until just before Rustenburg. Try to sleep a little. There's still a long road ahead.'

He hesitated before saying: 'OK.'

'Do you want a cushion?' Flea asked.

'No, thanks. You should try to sleep too.'

There was a bond between them now.

'I'm sorry,' I said.

'It wasn't your fault.'

I didn't reply.

'There was nothing you could have done, Oom.'

I wanted to believe him. They were too many.

'What were they after?' Flea asked, of no one in particular.

'I don't know.'

She turned to me. 'Are you sure?'

'No,' Lourens stopped her. 'Oom Diederik only asked him to come along yesterday.'

'Why?'

That was the question.

'I will find out,' I said. Diederik Brand had the answer. The old bastard. Black Swan of the Bo-Karoo. 'I will find out.'

They slept, for two hours.

I understood the process Lourens was working through. The closeness of death, the shock of a first confrontation with brutality. The inability to understand or accept that people were capable of such violence. That the world really was a place where the most violent ruled. I was eight years old when my father began to beat me. To punish my mother for her unfaithfulness. A child learns more quickly, adapts more easily if he knows no other life. But Lourens was the product of a stable, loving family that had given him self worth and pride, love and respect for others.

That had all been snatched away.

Seventy kilometres before Rustenburg the sun came up, angled from the left, so that I had to fold down the sun visor. Lourens woke up.

'How do you feel?' I asked.

'Better, thank you, Oom. Ready to drive.' There was a false note to his enthusiasm.

I stopped and got out. Throbbing headache, left eye swollen shut, aching body, but hopefully the worst of the damage was a cracked rib. In front of the truck Lourens put a hand on my arm. 'Oom, there's nothing we could have done.'

I looked at him, saw the earnest expression. I merely nodded.

As we pulled away, Flea woke up with a start, checked her watch and picked up the map. 'Ventersdorp,' she said. 'At six o'clock I must inject them again.'

I made him stop at a garage in Rustenburg so we could use the restrooms. I wanted to see if there was blood in my urine.

There was none. Flea emerged from the café with two brown paper bags. When we drove out again she took out a packet of painkillers for me, sandwiches, coffee and Coke. She plied Lourens with food and drink. There was a determined air about her, an inner strength.

I felt I had been wrong about her.

Lourens turned on the radio. We listened to the news on RSG, all the troubles of the country and the world, self-inflicted, without exception. *Annus horribilis*.

He stopped at twenty to six. They clambered onto the back, she with her medical bag. He helped her to sedate the animals. I stood beside the Mercedes, superfluous, and watched a tractor plough rows in a field.

Just before we got going, Nicola phoned. 'We are behind schedule . . .' said Lourens. 'I guess about seven o'clock tonight. No, no . . . just a bit tired . . . We're OK.'

Which we probably were. No use talking about last night's events.

Beyond Hartebeesfontein, Lourens's silence grew too much for her. She said: 'Tell me about the Bo-Karoo,' her voice was as intimate and soft as a lover's. He took a deep breath before replying, at first just cursorily polite. She kept on questioning him. About his family, about himself. That was her strategy. A good one. Lourens's voice gradually gained momentum, a painfully slow return to who he was. He was still young, I thought. And tough. Maybe he would find his way back home.

The painkillers made me drowsy. I fought sleep, using my frustration, my anger as a counter. Diederik Brand. I looked forward to seeing him again. And Inkunzi. I would go and find him. I would make him kneel with the Glock against the back of his head. Strip him of his self respect, as he had done to Lourens, pull the trigger, watch his body jerk in terror. Give him a taste of death.

My cellphone woke me. Body sore and aching, I felt for it in my pocket, pressed the wrong button, the ringing suddenly stopped.

'Where are we?' The dashboard clock said it was 08.41.

'Coming up to Hertzogville. You had a good sleep, Oom.'

Lemmer, the ever-vigilant bodyguard.

I pressed the keys of my phone to see who had called. Jeanette. I called her back.

'How are things going?' she asked, full of her usual morning fire and spirit.

'We are making progress.' I would tell her everything later, when I was alone.

'Your friend Diederik hasn't paid yet.'

'He is not my friend.'

'I thought you were all friends out there in the boondocks.'

'I will see him tonight. He is going to pay.'

'What gives me the idea that this trip isn't all you dreamed it would be?'

'I'll call you tonight.'

'Lemmer, is everything all right?'

'It will be.'

She caught on quickly. 'You can't talk. Is there something I should be worrying about?'

'No.'

'Call me when you can,' her voice was uneasy.

She didn't let anyone mess with her people.

31

> Virtually all conceivable actions leave distinctive markings, which may make it possible for the tracker to reconstruct the animal's activities.
>
> *The Art of Tracking: Spoor interpretation*

Lourens thawed. He said to Flea: 'You love rhinos.'

A shrug of her shoulders said 'not necessarily'. 'The Hook Lip is endangered.'

'The *who* clip?'

'The Hook Lip. That's the real name of the black rhino. The white rhino is the Square Lip, if you look you can see the difference clearly.'

'How endangered?'

'In 1970 there were 65,000, in 1993 there were only 2,000 left.'

'In the world?'

She nodded. 'Ninety-six per cent murdered.'

'*Jissie*. And now?'

'About 3,700.'

'OK,' said Lourens. 'I get it.' Then: 'It's for the horns? Because the Chinese believe the horns make you . . . fertile . . .'

'*No*, that's a myth. They believe it helps for fever. Most of the horns get ground up for that. About a third are carved. For ornaments. And dagger handles. In Yemen and Oman a dagger with a rhino horn handle is a big status symbol.'

'But numbers are rising again?'

She snorted, indignant. 'Not for long. Last year they shot thirty-six black rhino in our own national parks, another fifty in private game reserves . . .'

'Who did?'

'Thieves. Poachers. Everyone is in on the game, white and black. In the Congo and Zim the slaughter is on a much bigger scale, because nobody cares, nobody stops them. Last year they caught four men in Zim who confessed to killing eighteen rhinos. The police just let them go.'

'That's why you are helping with this trip?'

She nodded. 'You'll see. If these two survive . . . It will make a big difference.'

Diederik Brand was hiding behind that. The Noble Deed. With his charm and acts of conservation. But there was a snake in the grass.

What had Inkunzi and his gang been looking for?

A wire with a hook in the diesel tank? *Just tell me if you threw the stuff in the veld. Where must we look? Over the fence?*

They had searched the truck. Our belongings. Something small enough to be hidden in a sports bag, light enough to throw over a fence?

You're a pro. I wonder why you are here. And that fire power, the route you took. There's a reason.

Diederik had organised the so-called 'pro'. Provided the MAG and, most likely, prescribed the route, with the lame excuse of 'avoiding weighbridges'.

I asked Flea: 'How much does a rhino horn weigh?'

'About three kilos.'

Easy enough to throw a bag of rhino horns into the veld. But he'd said *Chinese witchcraft. Not my business.* He could have been lying deliberately, in case we didn't know what he was talking about.

'Ehrlichmann. What do you know about him?'

'He used to be a game ranger.'

'Who has to survive as a safari guide in a country where tourism doesn't happen any more. Was he there when you loaded?'

'He was in charge of it.' She got my drift. 'Do you think he . . .'

'Who else was there?'

She thought about it. 'Just the workers. And the drivers.'

'You saw the whole loading process?'

'Not everything. I was busy with the rhinos.'

Lourens and I had been there for the transfer to the Mercedes. The only things that had been moved from one lorry to the other had been the two cages.

'When do you have to inject them again?'

She checked her watch. 'In about half an hour.'

'We can stop in Hertzogville. I have to get diesel,' said Lourens.

Something else that bothered me. 'Why hasn't Diederik phoned yet?'

'Nicola is keeping him informed, Oom.'

'You have millions rands' worth of rhinos on a truck, with another million rands' worth of rhino horn, you hire a bodyguard because you are quite concerned. But you get your progress report second hand?'

'Ay,' said Lourens half-heartedly. 'That Oom Diederik . . .' Reluctant to lay any blame on Brand.

While Flea was injecting the animals, I inspected the cages. There were no hiding places. The frame and bars were solid steel, the floor was a single layer of wooden planks with no space underneath.

I rolled under the truck. There were many options, but Inkunzi's henchmen would have searched diligently. I had the advantage of daylight, but found nothing.

What could be so valuable that it warranted the effort of orchestrating a midnight hijacking with five vehicles and twelve men? What would you bring from the north of Zimbabwe, where there was nothing, a land stripped bare?

Before we got back in, Flea quizzed me with raised eyebrows. I shook my head, as I had no answers.

We drove. She got a conversation going again, as though she considered it her responsibility. I stared at the landscape drifting past, trying to make sense of it all. The key was the transfer on the Swanepoel's farm. Was there someone who was not involved, who didn't help to push or pull to move the cages across?

No.

Wickus had been shouting orders from the ground, Flea had been standing on the roof of the Mercedes. Swannie on the Bedford, with half the labourers, while Lourens and myself and the remainder of the men had been pulling on the ropes to shift the rhinos centimetre by centimetre.

Everyone busy, groaning, sweating, focused. The more clearly I recalled the scene, the more certain I became – there had been no chance to transfer anything else, to hide it, attach it.

My cellphone beeped in my pocket. I took it out. An SMS. From Emma. SEE YOU TONIGHT ON D'S FARM. MISSING YOU SO MUCH XXX.

Relief flooded over me, too late I realised Flea was also staring at the little screen.

She looked at me and her crooked smile said she had gained new insight.

At a quarter to eleven we crossed the N8 between Kimberley and Bloemfontein. At eleven Lourens pointed out the signboard to Magersfontein.

'Wasn't that a book?' Flea asked.

'It was a battlefield, in the Boer War,' he said. 'My great-grandfather was there. Paardeberg is also around here. And Modder River.'

'Did we win?'

'At Magersfontein and Modder River we gave a superior British force a good hiding. But Paardeberg . . . that's a sad story.'

'Tell me,' said Flea.

At two minutes past eleven, in the little town of Jacobsdal, something drew my attention away from Lourens's history lesson.

I kept my voice even. 'Could you stop here right now, please?'

'Oom?' he said.

'I just want to say hello to some old friends.' On the main street, in a tidy row in front of a small hotel, stood four Harley Davidsons.

'OK.' He started to brake.

Flea drew a breath to say something.

'I'll be quick,' I countered.

32

Snakes prefer to flee, and only molestation will cause attack.

The Art of Tracking: Dangerous animals

Before I went in I made sure. The number plate on the motorbike closest to the door read NV ME.

I found them in the little bar, all four on high stools, beer in hand, laughing about something. Hu-hu-hu. I went up to Steel Grey and put my hand on his shoulder.

'Are you sober?' I asked.

He looked around irritably, then scowled at my swollen eye, the bruises, trying hard to place me.

'Who mugged you?' he asked. All four were staring at me now.

'Are you sober? I can't *bliksem* you if you're drunk.'

'Loxton,' said Ratface. 'Yesterday . . .'

He could remember. They were sober enough. I pulled Steel Grey by the tassels on his leather jacket, so that he had to get down off his stool. The tassels tore off. 'Hey!' he said and swung at me. An amateur.

I dodged the blow. 'You called Emma le Roux a scrawny bitch,' I said.

'Leave him alone,' said the Big Guy, coming at me.

I hit Steel Grey. There was a lot in that blow. My dilemma at Emma's declaration of love, the stomach-turning flight, hours in the Musina sun, a night of humiliation, pain all over my body, the frustration of unanswered questions.

He dropped. Like a stone.

I turned to the Big Guy. 'Come on,' I said.

* * *

At sixteen minutes past eleven I climbed back into the cab of the Mercedes, experiencing a sense of release, a weight unburdened, a brief taste of paradise.

'Thank you,' I said.

Lourens spotted the blood on my hand and put two and two together. 'Those guys from yesterday?'

'How did you know?'

'Nicola told me over the phone yesterday, before lunchtime already. He heard about it from Oom Diederik.' No secrets in the Bo-Karoo.

I just shook my head.

'I thought they were your friends,' said Flea.

'I think the friendship is over.'

The expression on Lourens's face gradually changed, the laughter crept over him, until he threw back his head, and the hilarity infected Flea, until they were both in gales of laughter. I wanted to smile, even though my sore face protested, because it was then I knew they would get over last night.

Flea insisted that Lourens tell her the whole Harley story, since I refused. It was an interesting experience to hear it from the outlet end of the Loxton pipeline. Four bikers had become six. The story had expanded to include the phrases 'ugly customers' and 'Hell's Angels' – Steel Grey would be flattered by the latter. They had insulted Tannie Wilna and Emma 'dreadfully'. Diederik Brand had stopped my fist in the nick of time, or else, by all accounts, there would have been 'mayhem'.

Lemmer, hero of Loxton.

'They're not Hell's Angels,' I said, when he was done.

'What are they?' Flea asked.

'Rich Afrikaners.'

'What have you got against rich Afrikaners?' Flea asked indignantly.

I shook my head. Unwilling.

'Come on,' she prodded. 'Are you jealous?'

'I'm sure that's part of it.'

'And the other part?'

I sighed, not in the mood for this.

'*Come* on.'

'Ivory tower whingers.'

'What does *that* mean?'

'It means they sit around eating expensive, impress-the-neighbours Woollies' food in their huge, luxurious houses behind high walls and alarm systems, in front of their Hi-Def flat screen TVs, with a Mercedes ML, two quad bikes, a Harley, and a speedboat squeezed into their triple garages, and they bitch about how bad things are in this country . . .'

'But things *are* bad.'

'For them? Rubbish. The point is, they do nothing about it. They don't vote, they don't get involved, they say stuff like "I can't make a difference any more", like vultures, they sit and wait for the government to make a mistake, and then they say, see, I told you so. They are racist, but too cowardly to show it openly. They moan about crime, but not one of them ever thought of starting a neighbourhood watch or becoming a police reservist. They have no culture apart from spending money and drinking. They are scared. Of everything. And these are people . . . Their forefathers at Magersfontein and Paardeberg would spin in their graves . . .'

She was quiet for a long time before she said: 'They're not all like that.'

'That's true,' I said, because Emma was the exception.

Flea nodded, seeming satisfied.

Their conversation took on a natural flow, a rhythm. I became the fifth wheel to the wagon, a spectator to the burgeoning friendship between them. She was a couple of years older than Lourens, wrestling with a few demons, perhaps, but her arrogance had gone. Maybe because she now knew who and what he was. The shared trauma would also play a part, create a foundation.

So I withdrew, let them have room, prepared myself for meeting Diederik Brand again. Emma would be there. I would have to hold back.

We stopped twice more. At Britstown, for pies and cool drinks, at Victoria West, to sedate the rhinos one last time. Flea was worried. 'They are tired and thirsty. The bull should be OK, but the cow . . .'

We drove through Loxton after six, the pear blossoms were a white snowstorm along the streets. Lourens phoned Nicola to give a progress report, then took the shortest route through Slangfontein and the Sak River Poort. At the next junction we turned left one final time to Skuinskop, Diederik Brand's farm in the Nuweveld Mountains, alongside the Karoo National Park.

33

In order to recognise a specific sign, a tracker often has a preconceived image of what a typical sign looks like.

Principles of Tracking: Recognition of signs

They were waiting for us in front of the big shed – Diederik Brand, his wife Marika, Emma, and a horde of labourers. Diederik only had eyes for the rhino, he began opening the rear doors straight away. Emma came to my door full of happiness. That disappeared when she saw my face. 'What happened?'

'We had a bit of trouble,' I said.

'A bit?'

I looked in Diederik's direction and said: 'I will tell you later.'

'Are you . . . ?'

'Nothing serious.'

She hesitated a moment before embracing me. 'Thank God,' she said. 'Thank God.'

'Holy shit,' said Brand from the back. 'Where's Cornél? These animals are sick . . .'

'It's Necrolytic Dermatitis,' said Flea and jumped down. 'We must get them offloaded and relaxed as soon as possible.'

Only then did he come around the truck. 'OK. Then,' said Brand, 'the camp is just around the back here . . .' He saw my damage. 'Lemmer! What happened?'

'Let's offload, then we'll talk,' I said.

At the tone of my voice, Emma stiffened against me.

His 'workroom' was a messy place. Big desk with a PC on top, papers in untidy heaps. Framed photographs on the walls of ancestors, stud rams, hunting parties, and his pretty blonde wife Marika as the Wool

Queen in her young days. One dark wood bookshelf with decorative oil lamps, files, farming and investment guides and a big collection of old *Landbou Weekblad* and *Farmer's Weekly* magazines. In the corner was a golf bag of worn leather, the heads of antique golf clubs protruding. He sat on the edge of the desk, legs straight, arms folded like someone who had something to hide. I sat on the end of the couch. It was covered with Nguni cow hide, brown with white speckles.

'You lied to me, Diederik,' I said.

'No! I can't understand this whole thing,' he said, because he had extracted the story bit by bit from Lourens during the offloading, casting worried eyes in my direction.

'You're lying.'

'Lemmer, I swear.' That was always the first thing they said.

'Diederik, I'm not in the mood for games. I know all your stories. You are a cheat and a liar. You haven't paid my account yet, so you are not a client. Now you have a choice. You can talk, or you can bleed.'

'Lemmer, buddy, looks like this is one big misunderstanding.' Hands raised in innocence, charm turned up to the maximum. 'I haven't got around to the payment yet, I'll do it right now. And that hijacking . . .'

I sighed and stood up.

'. . . if they weren't after the horns . . .' said Diederik. 'What on earth, I mean . . . it . . . I don't understand it . . .'

I walked over to the golf bag and selected a big wood, because my knuckles hurt after the Harley Knights.

'Do you think this is a game, Diederik? Like the time you sold the Toyota truck?'

'What Toyota? There are so many stories, Lemmer, people exaggerate.'

Which was partly true. I pulled the club back and swung at him, aiming for his ribs. For a big man he was remarkably quick on his feet. I missed. 'Lemmer, please,' as he dashed for the door. I grabbed him by the shirt, and dragged him back. I went to the door, locked it and put the key in my pocket.

'Please, buddy . . .' His eyes were wide, charm on the wane.

'Did Lourens tell you how they held a revolver to his head? After they blew the head off the one we ran down with the truck?'

'No . . .'

'Because he's far too *decent*, Diederik. He should have told you what it feels like to hear the shot and believe you are dying. The sound you make, the fear, the humiliation when they deliberately miss. Did he tell you how Cornél begged and cried?'

'Christ, Lemmer, I didn't know . . .'

'Damage has been done. On your account. And now you are going to *pay*.'

'Lemmer, I swear . . .'

I hit him quickly, struck him on the lower ribs.

'Lemmer!' A shriek. 'Jesus, please . . .'

I hit him again. He defended with his hands, the club clipped his forearm.

'Please!' Bellowing, pleading.

'Pappa?' his wife's voice through the locked door.

I raised the club again. 'Tell her everything is all right,' I said softly.

'Everything's OK.'

'Are you sure?'

'Yes, dead sure.' He was breathing fast, his eyes flickering between me and the door.

Silence. Then footsteps on the wooden floor. She believed him.

'Why did you want me to go along?'

He held his hands defensively in front of him. 'You won't believe me . . .'

I lifted the club. 'Try me.'

He retreated up to the edge of the desk. 'Lemmer, I swear to you, it was just about the horns,' he spoke fast, desperately. 'The poachers, things are getting out of hand. And these ones come from Zim, you know how things are there, the police, everyone is involved with the smuggling, I swear, I swear, I only had Lourens and Cornél's safety . . .'

'You're right. I don't believe you. When did you arrange with Lotter to come?'

'Friday night, I phoned him . . .'

'But you wait till Saturday morning at eleven before you ask me?'

'I . . . the thing is, I thought of going along myself at first. But then Marika suggested you, rather get a professional, and so I phoned around, but no one had your number, you're not in the book, and I only got away from here at nine on Saturday, what with all the arrangements, and I went to your house, but there was no one there, and then I found you in the Red Pomegranate . . .'

'And you gave me a MAG-7, just in case?'

'Lemmer, I know how it looks . . .'

'Where did you get the shotgun?'

'It's a long story . . .'

I hit him again, on the shoulder. He made a desperate squeak and fled around the desk, his eyes searching for a place to hide under it. 'What do you want?' he asked in despair.

'The truth, Diederik. Because you are lying.'

'About what?'

I lifted the club again and walked after him.

'OK.' Pleading, retreating all around the desk, as I followed him.

'OK, what?' still on the merry-go-round, a game for children.

'I'll tell you, just put the fucking golf club down.'

I stopped and lowered the stick.

He blew out a long and noisy breath, grinned. 'Look at us . . .'

It was a circus, but I wasn't going to give him any get-out. 'Spit it out, Diederik.'

He sat down in the lovely old chair, worn out. 'I lied about the permit.'

'The permit?'

'It's forged.'

'The import permit?'

'Yes. And the letter from Nature Conservation. I . . . Where's the harm, Lemmer? Nicola . . . He has a rule, he won't transport game unless the permits are correct. There was no way I could get a permit for the rhino.'

'Who forged the documents?'

'I did. Myself.'

'To convince Nicola?'

'Yes. And if you were stopped . . .'

'You never *did* talk to the government people.'

'No.'

'It was smuggling.'

'Yes.'

'Are the animals stolen?'

'No! I swear, Ehrlichmann heard I was looking for rhino, he phoned me, said they were outside the game reserve, belonged to nobody, chance of their survival was nil, just a question of time, Lemmer, it was an emergency, a rescue mission, I swear to you. But I had to be careful, I . . . there were a lot of people involved in capturing the animals, loading them. Any one of them could have decided to take the horns . . . That's why I got you, because you never know, this is Africa . . .'

'What else was on that lorry? What did Ehrlichmann send along, Diederik?'

'I don't know!' he pleaded.

'Pappa?' Marika called, back at the door, deeply worried. She rattled the door handle.

'Everything is fine,' he answered.

'Open the door.'

'Marika, everything is fine.'

'Then open the door!'

I looked at him, the prince of liars who had pushed the 'permit' at me in my house with so much slick dishonesty. He was *still* lying. I took the key out of my pocket and tossed it at him. He missed the catch, bent down to pick it up, and then went over to unlock the door.

'What's going on?' Marika asked, looking at me reproachfully.

'Just a misunderstanding,' said Diederik. 'We're coming now.'

She was reluctant to leave, turning away slowly and disappearing down the passage.

Diederik and I stared at each other. 'Lemmer, on my word of honour, I don't know what they were looking for. I am terribly sorry about what happened, but I am innocent, on my word of honour.'

'The question is whether you have any honour left,' I said. 'You will pay Jeanette Louw now. Before you leave this room.'

'Of course.'

And I walked out to go and fetch Emma.

34

. . . a tracker often has a preconceived image of what a typical sign looks like. Their mind will be prejudiced to see what they want to see, and in order to avoid making such errors they must be careful not to reach decisions too soon.

Principles of Tracking: Recognition of signs

On the way back to Loxton in Emma's Freelander. She drove, I talked.

'Ay,' she said when I had finished, experiencing the same Diederik disillusionment I had, the same sense of something lost, a crack in the honest facade of the Bo-Karoo.

'What are you going to do?'

'Don't know . . . I'll sleep on it. Talk to Jeanette first.'

'Probably best,' she said. 'Lourens said you ran into the Harley guys again . . .'

I should have known.

'I . . .' Groping for an excuse, there was none.

Emma reached out her hand to touch mine gently, with all its ugly cuts and scratches.

Jeanette Louw was a former sergeant major from the Women's Army College in George, and the founder, managing director and sole shareholder of Body Armour. Her age – estimated to be in the late forties – was a carefully guarded secret. She had a taste for Gauloise cigarettes, for bruised, recently divorced, heterosexual women, for men's expensive designer suits, and brightly coloured ties. She was a demanding employer requiring absolute loyalty, integrity and professionalism from her people – because that is what she gave them.

'I hope you gave him a good hiding,' she said over the phone when I told my story.

'With a golf club.'

'Hah!' Her usual laugh, explosive. 'And you won't leave it at that.' She knew me.

'No.'

'Listen to me, Lemmer. I am going to phone the bastard and tell him your account will keep running until you find out what is going on. And if he doesn't pay, I will send two gorillas to collect.'

'Thank you.'

'Are you all right?'

'Just a few marks in interesting spots. Very sexy. I can send you photos.'

'Fuck,' she said. 'How am I going to get that image out of my head?'

Late that night, on my bed's snowy sheets, Emma gasped at the sight of the purple and blue bruises and grazes covering my body. She fetched a little first aid kit and slowly and gently anointed me with oils and ointments. Her hands were soft and cool, her voice melodious as she told me with relish about her afternoon with Antjie Barnard, her morning in the church. Antjie saying through a haze of cigarette smoke: 'Emma, you're the right one for Lemmer. But if I were thirty years younger . . .' And, 'The trouble with Diederik Brand is that he gets bored. He's too intelligent just to be a farmer.'

Before church, Emma said, everyone wanted to hear the story of the Knights and the Red Pomegranate. 'This morning the minister prayed for God's hand of protection over our Lemmer and Lourens on their journey.'

Our Lemmer. That was a first.

And what if I should unmask Diederik Brand?

Once she had finished, she packed away the bottles and tubes, turned off the light and lay down beside me, her hand soft on my chest. 'I have to go back to Cape Town tomorrow,' she whispered. Then sighed in great contentment: 'I love you so much.'

'Emma . . .'

She put her finger to my lips. 'Sleep well,' she said and kissed me on my unscathed cheek.

Tomorrow morning, I thought. Tomorrow I will tell her everything.

At a quarter to seven on Monday morning there was a gentle knock on my door.

Emma was still asleep. I got up and went down the passage to open the door.

Seventy-year-old Antjie Barnard stood there, with hat, walking boots and stick. She looked me up and down. I realised I was wearing only my rugby shorts, displaying the bruises all over me. 'Mmm,' she said suggestively. 'Kinky.'

'Morning, Antjie.'

'Diederik Brand said he doesn't have your number, but would you phone him urgently. He sounded a little alarmed.' She passed me a scrap of paper.

Emma's quiet footsteps behind me. 'Morning Antjie.'

'Morning, Emma. Don't worry, I would have given him a rough time too.'

It took Emma a moment to catch on. She giggled. 'It was only a warning,' she said.

'Oh?'

'In case he pays you too much attention while I'm away.'

'Lemmer, you have to come and see this,' said Diederik over the phone. He sounded more excited than alarmed.

'Why?'

'Lemmer, this is a party line. Please, just come and see. You're never going to believe this.'

I had other plans. I had to talk to Emma. 'I'll see if I can come out this afternoon.'

'I don't think you want to wait that long.'

'Diederik, what's going on?'

He deliberated over his answer. 'The questions you asked. I think I have the answers. The longer you delay . . .'

I was reluctant to believe him, despite the fire and conviction in his voice.

'It's your choice, Lemmer.'

'I'll see what I can do,' I ended the call.

'What is it?' Emma called from the bathroom.

I went to the door. She stood in front of the shower, ready to get in, naked, at ease with her perfect, compact body. It took my breath away. Every time. 'I . . .'

'Concentrate, Lemmer . . .' A mischievous smile.

Unwillingly, I looked away towards the window. 'Diederik Brand wants me to go out there. He's found something, won't say what.'

'I have to leave anyway,' she said.

I had to talk to her first. Not in a rush, I had to say it all in the right way. 'I . . .'

She turned around, giving me a full frontal view as she leaned seductively against the shower door. 'You wanted to say?'

'Emma . . .'

'Yes?'

'I . . .' What had I wanted to say?

'What?'

'Do you want to wash the wounds of a seriously injured man?'

'Actually, I'm keen on the healthy bits. And "washing" isn't necessarily on the agenda.'

'You women,' I said, as I took off my rugby shorts in a hurry. 'No respect for personal hygiene.'

'He's with the rhinos,' Marika said at the front door of the homestead, stiff and unfriendly.

I thanked her and went towards the field where, according to Flea's instructions, the animals had to recover and adapt for two weeks before they were released. This was the first time I had seen the farm in daylight. The farmhouse nestled in a hollow of the Nuweveld Mountains, the bright blue sky and rugged, rusty brown mountain tops were a dramatic backdrop to the simple white building and the lush green garden. A jeep track followed the contour of the mountain past an earth dam where ducks swam under willow trees, then through a valley of thorn bushes. Two black eagles swooped silently along the cliffs, northwards, hunting for dassies.

I found Diederik Brand leaning on the gate of the field, beside the concrete reservoir and windmill.

He heard me approach, but did not turn. I stopped beside him. He pointed, 'Look,' he said.

The rhino grazed between the thorn trees, peacefully.

'What?'

He just smiled, dimples beside the moustache.

Then I saw it.

The animals looked . . . healthy. Here and there their hides were dark and damp. Bits of mud clung to them. But the Necrolytic Dermatitis was gone, the dark pink, septic growths had disappeared overnight.

35

Decisions made at a glance can often be erroneous, so when encountering new signs, time should be taken to study them in detail.

Principles of Tracking: Recognition of signs

Without a word, and with a triumphant gleam in his eye, Diederik handed me something. As large as his thumb, pink, it formed a pocket. It looked like the snipped-off corner of some container. I took it from him. Plastic. Soft, pliable, strong.

I felt it, looked at the rhino again, my brain too sluggish to process it all.

'It was lying here,' he pointed to where the long grass grew lushly in a spot moistened by the leaking windmill beside the gate.

He watched me while I tried to process this.

'Wait . . .' I said, because I couldn't make sense of it. I sniffed the plastic. Nothing.

'She's gone,' said Brand.

I tried to keep up with him. 'When?'

'Some time in the night. She had supper with us yesterday. Then Marika showed her to her room and she said "goodnight" and shut the door. When I got here at six this morning, the cages were open and the animals were out. I went to call her, but her room was empty. She had used the bath, but not the bed.'

'Wait, wait, wait . . .' Gears ground in my head. 'Flea let them out last night?' Last night when the cages were finally on the ground she had explicitly said, 'Leave them like that.' When Diederik asked why, she had answered that the rhinos' sight was poor. 'They will break the fences if they come out at night. Tomorrow morning we can open up. Only after nine. By then they will be accustomed to the smells and sounds.'

'Cornél,' Diederik said.

'That's what I meant.'

'She must have kept them in the cages so she could get these things off,' said Diederik. 'And I think she hoped they would hide away somewhere this morning, so she could buy more time.'

'Shit,' I said as I began to understand.

'I've just called Ehrlichmann on his satellite phone. He says when they loaded the animals in Zim they were as healthy as they could be. Angry and wild, but no skin disease in sight. She must have stuck the plastic on during the trip. Look carefully, they rolled in the mud beside the trough this morning, look at those dark marks on their skin – everywhere they had those sores. I think the glue is irritating them a bit.'

'Only along the top,' I said.

'What?'

'The sores. They were only on the upper sides of the rhino. Over the neck and back and quarters. Where she could reach them through the bars from above.'

He grinned and nodded. 'You have to admit it's clever.'

I looked at the bit of plastic again. 'But what was in them?'

'God knows. But that's what the hijackers were after.'

'Has to be.'

'You owe me an apology, Lemmer.'

'She was working for you, Diederik . . .'

'No! I don't know her at all. Ehrlichmann got her. He pays her.'

'And he says he knows nothing about these things?'

'I told you, he was shocked on the phone.'

'Did you ask Ehrlichmann if she had anything with her when they loaded in Zim?'

'No.'

'How do you know he's not part of this whole thing?'

'Why would he admit the rhinos were healthy?'

Good point. 'I want to talk to him.'

'It's a satellite phone. Calls cost a fortune. What does it matter? The rhinos are here, safe . . . Everyone has been paid. You, Lourens, Nicola . . . Yes, we've been tricked by a girl, but where's the real harm? I mean, by next week your bruises will be gone.'

'It matters to me, Diederik. And to Lourens le Riche. Come . . .' I began to move.

'You still owe me an apology.'

'You forged documents that could have done Nicola a lot of damage. Lourens and I might have spent the night in jail.' And, I could have added, I am on parole.

He looked at the ground, guilty. Possibly afraid I would tell Nicola about his sins.

'Diederik, how did you get hold of the MAG-7?'

'I . . . it's a long story.' With a shake of his head that said he wasn't going to say.

'Have you paid my boss?'

The dimples had disappeared. He nodded sourly. 'Come, let's get this over with.'

We walked in silence. The extent of Flea van Jaarsveld's deception slowly settled over me.

Just before we went in through the farmhouse door, something else occurred to me: how had she left the farm? 'Diederik, it's sixty kilos to town . . .'

'It's ten kilos just to the next major gravel road, Lemmer. And she was tired, I could see.'

'Did you hear anything? A car?'

'You can only hear vehicles once they come through the poort . . .' he said, pointing to where the road emerged from a cleft in the ridge. Then he said: 'Ay, that Cornél,' and he laughed his dimpled laugh, shaking his head.

We couldn't raise Ehrlichmann on the satellite phone. In Diederik's office he pointed the receiver towards me so I could hear the engaged tone.

'But you spoke to him this morning?'

'His phone is not always on.'

I took out my cellphone. 'Give me the number.'

'There's no reception here,' he said.

I checked my phone and saw he was right.

'You don't believe me?' Diederik asked.

'No. Give me the number.'

He looked at me with some amazement. 'You really can't just let this go, can you?'

I didn't expect him to understand my motivation. I was tired of Diederik, tired of his attitude, his evasions, his self-justification.

'I want Ehrlichmann's number. If you give me a wrong number, I will be back. I want Lotter's number and the Swanepoels' number.

And I assume Jeanette Louw called you this morning to tell you your account will keep running until I am absolutely certain you are innocent of this matter.'

'That's blackmail . . . And why would you want Lotter's number too?'

I didn't respond.

He shook his head and sighed, as if he had been done a great injustice. But then he reached for a piece of paper and began to write.

I drove back to Loxton in my new silver Ford Ranger, the four-litre V6 King Cab, knowing that Diederik had paid at least the next instalment.

I thought about Flea van Jaarsveld. About her reaction when young Swannie Swanepoel had recognised her, just before we loaded. *I don't know you*, had been her heated response. It hadn't been bitchiness, it was panic. Her initial, unpleasant aloofness could have been pure tension. She wouldn't want to get involved with Lourens and me, because it is easier to lie to strangers. She didn't want us to stop at the hijacking roadblock. She knew what they were looking for. Inkunzi whispering in her ear . . . Did he know she was the smuggler? How?

Her thoughtfulness towards Lourens after the hijacking. Not compassion, but guilt, because his humiliation, his terror, was all due to her. That meant she had a conscience. Not a hardened smuggler. But a very clever one. And nasty. She tried to put the blame on me when she asked, 'What were they looking for?' And she was quite happy for me to suspect Diederik.

What had she been smuggling? I looked at the little piece of plastic in my hand. How many of these . . . sachets were stuck on each rhino? Fifteen, perhaps, about thirty in total. Someone must have designed them, filled them with something so valuable that a gang of thirteen men raced a hundred kilometres through the night to intercept us.

Why go to all that trouble to smuggle something out of a country with a border as secure as a sieve?

Agatha, my coloured housekeeper, was tidying up the house. She gave my face a long, disapproving look. 'I heard about the scooter people. Ay, ay. I don't like this fighting.'

Before I could explain, she said: 'Now, we have to unpack that bag, so I can get the washing done.'

I nodded like a scolded child and went to the bedroom, I picked up my bag from where I had left it against the wall, put it on the bed, unzipped it. I started to unpack, my brain occupied with rhinos, bits of pink plastic.

Only when I had finished, did I realise my Glock was not there.

I searched through the clothes, with sudden urgency. I *had* put the pistol in the bag, while I was tidying up after the attack. Or had I? Racking my brain, anxiety slowly descending on me. After the attack in the night: it was lying there among the clothes, in the headlights of the truck. I had picked it up, dazed. Put it on top of my T-shirt, which was lying beside it. Shoved both items in my bag, last, so that the firearm was on top. Definitely.

I couldn't find it.

I took a deep breath, put everything to one side and looked through it all again, slowly, carefully.

The Glock was gone.

36

> Creating employment opportunities for trackers provides economic benefits to local communities. In addition, non-literate trackers who have in the past been employed as unskilled labourers can gain recognition for their specialised expertise.
>
> *The Art of Tracking*

'Fuck, Lemmer,' said Jeanette Louw over the phone, worry in her voice. 'There's a story in the Beeld this morning, an unidentified black man found beside the road near the Lapala Game Reserve. Bullet wound in the head.'

'My fingerprints are on the Glock. And the man's blood, his DNA.'

'Fuck.'

'Flea is the only one who could have taken the Glock. If she . . .'

'Then you'll have to find her.'

* * *

Ehrlichmann's satellite phone stayed engaged.

I phoned the Swanepoels. It rang for a long time before Pa Wickus answered. 'Swanepoel?'

I explained who I was, asked if they would be on the farm over the next few days. 'We are always here. Is there a problem?'

'Not at all. I want to drop in for a quick visit.'

'Oh?' He waited for me to explain why.

'Do you have a landing strip on the farm?'

'Sort of. But there are no lights or anything.'

'I will ask the pilot to phone.'

'When are you coming?'

'Tomorrow, I hope.'

He was quiet for a long time before he said: 'Well, then,' but he sounded worried.

I left it at that.

I phoned Lotter.

'So how was the trip?' he asked.

'Interesting,' I said. 'Diederik Brand wants you to take me to Musina again. And then to Zimbabwe.'

'And you are prepared to fly in my Vomit Comet again?' Enjoying himself at my expense.

'Prepared' was not the right word, but his RV-7 was the quickest way to get into Zim and I had a few questions for Lotter. 'I'm pinning my hopes on a smaller breakfast,' I said, which was more or less the truth.

'Where exactly in Zim?'

'Near the Chizarira National Park, provisionally. I will let you know if it changes. But we have to land on a farm near Musina first.' I gave him Wickus's number.

Once he had written that down he asked: 'And when?'

'Tomorrow morning.'

'I will have to check the weather again. And Zim . . . Getting flight clearance can take time. I'll call you back.'

I tried Ehrlichmann's satellite phone again. Still engaged. Had Diederik written down the correct number?

Why?

* * *

At ten to three Emma called to say she had arrived safely back at her house. 'How are you feeling?' she asked.

'My whole body misses your healing hands.'

'Your *whole* body?'

'Head to toes.'

'Unfortunately, Dr Emma's healing hands are only available in Cape Town this week, at a special price for Karoo boys.'

'This Karoo boy has to go to Zimbabwe first.'

'Lemmer.' Suddenly serious. 'You will be careful.'

'I will.'

Which was close enough to the truth.

'His name is Julius Nhlakanipho Shabangu,' Jeanette Louw said over the phone. 'His nickname is "Inkunzi". That means "bull" in Zulu. He comes from Esikhawini, a township near Empangeni in KwaZulu-Natal, but he lives in Sandton now. Filthy rich, divorced, a playboy with the Jo'burg girls, a criminal record as long as Jolene's legs . . .'

'An interesting comparison,' I said. Jolene Freylinck was Body Armour's efficient, sexy receptionist.

'You know what I mean, Lemmer. Listen: Julius is not the sort of guy you want to fuck around with. He's organised crime, specialising in cash-in-transit robbery, in cahoots with a Mozambican car theft syndicate, they think he and his gang does forty per cent of car hijackings in Gauteng. And he has political connections.'

'So why is he messing around with a game truck in Limpopo?'

'That is the question.'

'Which I am going to ask him.'

'You're out of your fucking mind.'

'That's why you find me irresistible.'

'Hah!' she said. Then: 'Go and find Flea van Jaarsveld and your firearm. That's all Diederik Brand and I are going to finance.'

'Just in case, Jeanette,' I used my new favourite phrase, 'if I wanted to talk to Julius-the-Bull, how would I go about it?' I knew she would know all about him. Her network was impressive.

'Get Flea first.'

'Come on, Jeanette . . .'

'Christ, Lemmer . . .'

I waited.

'The Bull Run. It's a restaurant, beside the Balalaika Hotel in Sandton. Specialises in steaks. He hangs out there, announcing to all and sundry that the place is named after him.'

I would have to call Lotter again. Johannesburg was now part of our flight plan.

When I came back from my late afternoon jog, there was a message from Lotter on my cellphone. 'Weather is looking good, still waiting for flight clearance for Zim. I'll pick you up at half past nine.'

I tried Ehrlichmann again. The satellite phone rang.

'Base camp,' a man's voice answered.

'Ehrlichmann?'

The satellite delayed his reply. 'Yes?'

'My name is Lemmer. I worked with Diederik Brand to get the rhinos here.'

The moment of silence again, the signal bouncing through space. 'This is not a secure line.' Rhodesian accent, modulated, slow and patient.

'I need to come and see you.'

'Why?'

Because I wanted to look him in the eye, to see if he was lying. 'Diederik didn't tell you?'

'Tell me what?' he asked, very careful.

'The . . . our cargo. How miraculously they healed.'

'I don't know what you're talking about.'

'Did you speak to Diederik this morning?'

'Yes.'

'What did he tell you?'

He was quiet so long that I thought the connection was lost. 'I'm sorry. I don't know you.'

'Call Diederik. He will tell you I rode shotgun on the lorry. He says you spoke about the health of the cargo early this morning.'

He considered that first. 'He asked me if they had a skin disease when I last saw them. I said no.'

'Nothing more?'

'No.'

'I'm flying up there tomorrow morning. I need to talk to you.'

'You're flying to Harare?'

'I'm flying to wherever you are. Do you have a landing strip?'

Another long pause. 'I hope you have a very good pilot.'

37

While basic tracking skills can be trained in a short period, the more sophisticated aspects of tracking could take many years to develop. Furthermore, the intuitive and creative aspects require an inherent aptitude, so only some people have the potential to become expert trackers.

The Art of Tracking

I watched *7de Laan* on TV first. Then the aromas lured me to the kitchen. Agatha's note on the kitchen table:

Dear Mister Lemmer,

I made your favourite, Mister Lemmer, to build up your strength. I don't like the fighting, but thank you for restoring Miss Emma's honour.

Yours sincerely,
Agatha le Fleur

She was short and round, sixty-five years old, had brought five children into the world, and treated me as the sixth. She made liberal use of the royal 'we' in her scolding and care. 'We must put the washing in the laundry basket, we spend so much on these clothes, look how they are just thrown down here.' On a Monday morning: 'We can't leave the whole weekend's cups and glasses all over the house.' Whenever I came back from a contract, she always inspected me from top to toe: 'Ay, ay, we are getting too thin, tomorrow we will have meat, Miss Emma likes a strong man, we can see that.'

And if there was something serious to communicate, then there'd be the letter on the table, formal, then it was 'Mister'.

I opened the oven door. Lamb rib, slow roasted, crackly on the outside, butter soft on the inside, the taste . . . indescribable. That meant there was salad in the fridge, since, 'We must have a balanced diet,' even though no scrap of salad ever passed her lips. Tonight it was baby beetroot, round as billiard balls, and feta. I dished up, opened a bottle of Birdfield red grape juice and poured a glass. Emma had brought me two bottles in July. Since then I had been addicted. I ordered it by the case from Klawer.

I took my plate, glass and the bottle and went to sit at the table on the back veranda.

Thank you for restoring Miss Emma's honour.

She understood because she knew about life without honour. She knew about poverty and humiliation, she knew first hand the terrible struggle to maintain her humanity, her dignity. She knew what it was worth.

Diederik Brand had asked: 'You really can't just let this go, can you?' without understanding. *He* had never lost everything.

The answer to his question lay in Agatha le Fleur's letter. And in my childhood. And on a dark road in the Waterberg.

I finished the food, poured the last of the grape juice into the glass, looked up at the stars, the unutterably beautiful firmament of the Karoo. Despite the lack of sleep and the pain in my body I found pleasure in this moment, this place. My house, which I had rebuilt bit by bit, like my life. Still so much to do, but it was my safe haven, my castle, my refuge. *My* key that fitted in the lock. I knew the sounds of my house, the creak of old roof beams, the ticking of the zinc roof as it cooled at night, the moan of antique water pipes. I knew the smell of each room, the cool corners in summer, the warm glow of the Aga stove in winter. And under my bare feet the feel of the floorboards in the passage, the carpet in the bedroom, the stone on the veranda. My sweat and blood and labour was in the renovated parts, the demolished walls, the calluses on my hands from carrying bricks and pushing the wheelbarrow and swinging the hammer, until the house had become part of me.

And all around me, the village, so perfectly silent now. Here and there a light would still burn, a television flicker: vulnerable, good people whiling away the hours before bedtime. Soon the speckled eagle owl would hoot, two lonely syllables from his nest in the pine tree opposite the old-age home. Two porcupines would push their way under my fence and raid my garden. The wind would rustle through the pear trees, a truck would drone past on the tar road on the way to Victoria West. Predictable, routine, ordered, a rhythm that had not changed in a hundred years. I was crazy about it, I couldn't live without it any more.

I would be careful, because Diederik Brand was part of this whole. He might be a cheat and a rascal, but he was Loxton's. His pedigree went back four generations in this district, he was part of the local DNA. Here he was tolerated and forgiven, here with a wry laugh they said: 'Ay, that Diederik,' because there was loyalty forged over decades, forebears who died together in the Boer War, the shared hardship of drought, pests and plagues, the isolation that made everyone dependent on each other, tomorrow they still had to get along, at the co-op, the church bazaar, the livestock auction.

I would need more than a forged permit to punish Diederik.

Sleepless. Emma's scent was still on my bed, the house incomplete without her, as if the structure and the spaces sensed her absence. I missed her.

I would drive down to Cape Town, stand in front of her and lay my life out before her, so that she could say that she just couldn't deal with it. Then I would live with the consequences. No other choice.

But first I would go looking for Flea and Inkunzi. Get my Glock. And answers.

I thought of all the unanswered questions, relived the past seventy-two hours, searching for sense, a tangle of interwoven events, knotted threads and wires. I picked at it, tugging at ends here and there, and only pulled the knot tighter. Until I wondered where Flea van Jaarsveld had disappeared to in the night – sixty kilometres from Diederik's farm to the nearest town, ten kilometres to the nearest larger gravel road, not even cellphone reception. She didn't know the area, she didn't know anyone . . .

Then I realised that she did know someone, someone who had made calf's eyes at her, someone who had tried to explain her attitude with a compassionate, 'She must be tired.' Someone who had forged a bond with her over 500 kilometres.

I got up and looked at the clock. A quarter to ten. He might still be awake. I called the regional exchange, asked if they had the number for the le Riches of Pampoenpoort.

'I'm ringing . . .'

It rang, far-off and monotonous, the static on the line chirped and crackled. 'Hello, this is Lourens.' Excited, wide awake, hopeful.

'Lourens, it's Lemmer.'

'Hello, Oom, how are you?' Just a touch of disappointment, as if he had hoped it would be someone else.

'Very well, thanks.' There was no sense in beating about the bush. 'Lourens, did you pick up Cornél at Diederik's last night?'

A long silence, before he said: 'Oom . . . Can I call you back? From my cellphone?'

He didn't want to answer over the party line. That alone spoke volumes.

'Of course.' I gave him my number.

It was twelve minutes before he called, in a muted tone. 'How did you know, Oom?'

'I suspected it, Lourens.'

'Oom, I . . .'

'This is just between us, Lourens. I give you my word. Did she ask you to fetch her?'

Hesitation before he answered. 'Yes, Oom.'

'All I really want to know is where you took her.'

'Ay, Oom, I . . . She . . . To town, Oom. I didn't want to just . . . But she said someone was coming to pick her up. Why are you asking?'

'We're just worried about her. She didn't tell Diederik she was leaving.'

'She said she left them a note.'

Flea van Jaarsveld, queen of the white lie. 'It must have got lost. What time did you drop her in town?'

'It was about three in the morning, Oom.'

'You don't know who picked her up?'

'She just said a girlfriend, Oom. She waited outside the police station.'

'And she told you to go?'

'Yes, Oom . . .' Something in his voice told me there was more.

'This is just between us, Lourens.'

'The thing is, Oom, she says she is in a relationship, she didn't want . . .'

'The friend to see you?'

'Yes, Oom,' relieved I understood.

'Last question. What did she have with her?'

'Shoo, um . . . Bags, Oom, two bags, a red one and a yellow one.'

'What happened to her doctor's case?'

'Shoo, Oom, that's a good question.'

'And the yellow bag? How big was it?'

'Oom?'

'The yellow bag. Bigger than the red one?'

It took a while for the penny to drop, but despite his state of infatuation and the minimum of sleep, he did work it out: 'Fu-uck,' he said softly. 'The yellow one. She didn't have . . . At Oom Wickus's place she just had the red one and the doctor's case.' Then in sudden concern, 'Oom, is she in trouble?'

'How big was the yellow bag?'

'About . . . How shall I say, about as big as a fleece, Oom.'

'A fleece?'

'Yes, Oom, the fleece of one sheep.'

I tried to imagine it. 'How heavy was the bag?'

'Oom, what has she done?'

'Lourens, it's a long story. When I find out I will let you know. How heavy was the bag?'

'I don't know, Oom, she loaded and offloaded it herself, when I tried to help she said she was a strong girl.'

'Have you got her number?' Just in case.

Another hesitation. 'Oom . . .'

'I won't tell her where I got it.' I searched for pen and paper in the kitchen drawer.

He gave me the number. I let him repeat it. Then he asked: 'Oom, please, what's going on?'

'Lourens, I really don't know. But I am going to try to find out. Thank you very much. I promise you I won't breathe a word.'

'Thanks, Oom.' Genuine relief. Then: 'I nearly forgot. She said I must tell you . . .'

'Oh?'

'She said, if Lemmer is looking for something, tell him I've got it.'

I keyed Flea's number into my phone and called.

'The number you have dialled does not exist . . .'

No big surprises there.

If Lemmer is looking for something, tell him I've got it. It was a message. It read: 'Leave me alone, or else . . .'

That was a chance I would have to take.

When I got into bed again, I wondered if she had a real conscience. She had played Lourens, all the way. The attack had been a bonus for her.

Did she know that a man who has looked death in the face is more receptive to the temptations of the flesh?

I would get her.

38

> Tracking requires intermittent attention, a constant refocusing between minute details of the track and the whole pattern of the environment.
>
> *The Art of Tracking: Principles of tracking*

Lotter landed at twenty-seven minutes past nine, taxied the plane alongside my Ranger, unclipped the bubble and shouted, 'Howzit, Lemmer, not bad timing, is it? Jeez, what happened to your face?'

'I walked into a door.'

'You do know they come with handles . . .'

I decided to trust my instincts about Lotter. I told him about our journey with the rhinos, leaving nothing out, not even my suspicions about his involvement, and my doubts about Diederik's truthfulness. He mulled it over for quite a few minutes, and then he laughed, first in disbelief, then in comprehension.

'That explains it,' he said.

'What?'

'Diederik, last night. When I phoned him to check if he was going to pay for this flight. He said "I suppose I'll have to".'

'When did he ask you to come and pick me up, the previous time?'

'Last Friday afternoon. But that's par for the course, he's always in a hurry and late.'

'What did he say?'

'He wanted to send someone along with a game truck. Maybe himself, maybe someone else.'

So Diederik hadn't lied about *that*. But then, what *did* he lie about? Because he had, about something.

'You said you've flown him to Mozambique before?'

'Sure.'

'What was he doing there?'

'Listen, by now you should know that Diederik is a bit of a bullshitter. He's all about insinuation and overstatement. That Mozambique affair, all he said was, "Big bucks, Lotter, wish I could tell you". You just have to take him as he is. He's entertaining, he's charismatic, he's a character, first time I flew him, he didn't pay, all charming over the phone, "Still not got the money?", went on like that for three months. Till the next time he wanted to fly, I told him, "No offence, but for you it is pay as you go, and only after you settle your prior account", and he laughed and said "Sure, Lotter", and I never had trouble with him again. And what he does once he gets off my plane is his business. But he knows: I fly by the rules.'

'You must have wondered about his business.'

'Of course. We have this thing, Diederik and I. When he phones and says he wants to go somewhere, I ask him, "Who are you conning this time?" and he says, "You know how it is, Lotter, there's a sucker born every minute". But exactly what he does, I don't care.'

'I do,' I said.

'I can see that.'

The Swanepoels' landing strip was a broad, straight length of farm road a kilometre from the farmyard.

Lotter flew low over the house before setting down the RV-7 with ease. When Swannie fetched us a minute later with the Land Cruiser, Lotter was busy anchoring the plane with pegs and ropes.

Swannie admired the plane. '*Jissie*, that's a sexy little thing.'

'American,' I said, 'wretched VanGrunsven design.'

'Really,' said Swannie. 'What happened to your face, Oom?'

'He walked into a door,' said Lotter, tapping the side of his nose conspiratorially.

'Genuine?'

'Genuine,' Lotter was enjoying himself. 'I make a point of avoiding doors in the Karoo. They can be lethal.'

Swannie looked to me for a sign that Lotter was pulling his leg. I looked away. He gave up. 'Ma says you must *sommer* come and have lunch, Oom, how are the rhinos, what does Flea, I mean Cornél, say, when is she coming to visit, did you all have a good trip to the Karoo?'

'The rhinos are alive and kicking,' I said. 'And when I see Flea, I'll ask her.'

'Ma's name was Lollie, and she didn't match the rough simplicity of the Swanepoel men – she was a slim, dignified woman, not pretty in the conventional sense, but skilfully groomed. There was humour in her eyes, as though she would laugh easily, and an ease, a contentment with herself and her life. The interior of the farmhouse was a surprise. I had expected hunting trophies and crocheted doilies, but found tasteful old wooden furniture, oriental carpets on polished wood floors, original paintings on the walls, and a long bookshelf filled with hardcover books.

Her influence on Pa Wickus was good as well – he was the epitome of the courteous host, offering drinks and making polite conversation. At the table he said grace, short and serious. In the middle of the table was a chicken pie, golden crusted. Lollie removed the lids from the other serving dishes to display sweet pumpkin, steamed green beans, baked potatoes and rice.

'*Jissie*,' said Swannie with gusto and reached for a serving spoon.

'As if I don't cook every day,' Lollie said.

'Let the guests serve themselves first,' said Wickus.

Also to his credit he waited patiently until everyone had finished eating before he brought up the burning question: 'And what brings you here?'

Since yesterday I had been undecided, still unsure how to approach him. The problem was that Wickus and Swannie were involved, but I had no idea at what level. There was something about them, a naivety, that made me feel their role was incidental and merely superficial.

'It's Flea,' I said.

Both Swanepoel men's eyebrows lifted in tandem.

'She left Diederik's farm in the middle of the night. Without saying goodbye . . .'

'Ay,' said Lollie.

'So was there trouble?' asked Wickus.

'No. But she was supposed to look after the rhinos yesterday morning. Now Diederik is worried . . .'

I hoped it was enough. But Wickus was not stupid. 'That's not the whole story,' he said, though without reproach. 'Your face, the fact that you flew here . . . I won't ask you what happened, perhaps it's better that we don't know. But just tell me: How serious is it?'

'Serious enough.'

'Flipit,' breathed Swannie. His parents exchanged a significant glance, as though they knew something. Wickus nodded slowly. 'How can we help?'

'I got the impression she came from this part of the world. Weren't you at primary school together?' I said, looking at young Swannie.

'That was twelve years ago. They left here in . . .'

'Nineteen-ninety-eight,' said Lollie.

'Where to?' I asked.

Wickus and Lollie exchanged another look. 'There was a lot of gossip,' she said softly.

'It's a sad story,' said Wickus.

'Flip . . .' said Swannie.

'You were too young to know these things,' his mother said.

Wickus pushed his plate away and put his elbows on the table. 'Tell him, Lollie. I don't know if it will help, but tell him.'

39

Most animals continually move their sleeping quarters, and may only have a fixed home during the breeding season to protect the young.

The Art of Tracking: Classification of signs

They played it like a duet.

She began with: 'Her father was Louis, a free spirit . . .' and Wickus added: 'He was a tracker, but the thing you have to understand is that he was a master. These days you get different levels, with the training they do now, level one and two and three, then Senior Tracker and finally Master. Now Louis would have been a Master, Hell's Bells, but he was good.'

'He came from the Kalahari,' she picked up the story. 'They say he grew up very poor, his father was a drifter, a loser, doing piece work here and there on farms. Louis's childhood was half wild, with the Bushmen. He learned to track from them. Not much schooling, only passed Standard Eight, then he went to help his father, who died when Louis was seventeen. Somehow or other he ended up in our area.'

'He wanted to get a job with Nature Conservation, but he didn't have the qualifications, you don't get in there without official papers,' said Wickus.

'So the hunting people used him. Here, Botswana, Zimbabwe . . .'

'The professional hunters, the guys who find the biggest elephants and lions for the American and German trophy hunters . . .'

'Not always legally,' said Lollie.

'What could he do? He wanted to live in the bush, he had to make a living.'

'A handsome young man, he was, rosy cheeks, a bush of thick blond hair, but he lived in another world. Apparently he found a python near Phalaborwa once, and went all strange, said it was his ancestor. Got that from the Bushmen, they believe men are descended from the python . . .'

'But the best tracker you could get, highly regarded, sought after.'

'Then he got mixed up with Drika. No, let me put that differently. He fell in love with Drika. And she . . . the trouble was, she was barely nineteen, and she was the daughter of Big Frik Redelinghuys and she got pregnant . . .'

'Hell's bells,' said young Swannie, sounding just like his father.

Wickus looked sternly at his son: 'Yes, as I've always said, some women may be hot, but they can also be hell. Be careful you don't burn your . . .'

'Wickus . . .' Lollie cautioned.

'Anyway, Big Frik farmed in the Lowveld, six, seven farms, oranges, nuts, bananas, game, he used Louis when the overseas people came hunting, very rich, three daughters. Drika was the youngest. Pretty girl, Flea got her dark hair and figure from her, but spoilt . . .'

'Very. Knew she was beautiful, not afraid to show it. And she had a bit of a wilful streak, wanted what she couldn't have. She was barely out of school, didn't know what she wanted to do yet, stayed at home that year, horses and parties. And then Louis came along . . .'

'Ma, how do you know all this stuff?' Swannie asked.

'People talk, my child. It was such a big scandal, daughter of a prominent man. They said Frik found out about their love affair before she fell pregnant. He sat her down and said over his dead body. And *then* she slept with Louis, to show her father she would do as she pleased.'

'So she fell pregnant with Flea,' said Wickus.

'Flipit,' said Swannie.

'Frik was furious, such shame on the family. He resigned as a church elder, didn't set foot in church for over a year, we heard. He disowned his daughter entirely. Later, when one of his daughters married a Delfosse, and he had another grandchild, Helena, he sort of recovered. Helena became the apple of his eye. Anyway, Louis and Drika were married in the Magistrate's office and they came to live here, on Elandslaagte, a big farm about twenty kilometres outside Musina, on the charity of others. In those days they still spoke of *bywoners*, sharecroppers. Louis had to work where and when he could, so it was Drika and Flea alone in a little house in the middle of nowhere . . .'

'A recipe for trouble,' said Wickus.

'Drika was still a child herself, accustomed to wealth and glamour, not very keen on raising a crying baby on her own, the romance of running away with her lover did not last. If you have had attention and admiration all your life, and suddenly it dries up, you go looking for it. She was in town more than she was on the farm, she started phoning Big Frik and saying she was sorry, wouldn't he help her, and Frik said "you made your bed, lie in it" . . .'

'Which is right, children have to learn: everything has consequences.'

'But, Wickus, she was his child . . .'

'I'm just saying.'

'If he had helped, who knows . . . Drika began leaving Flea on the farm with her *Venda* nanny more often, and she flirted with every man, gate-crashing parties, drinking, having a good time, and Louis knew nothing about it, because when he came home from the veld, she stayed at home and whined about how awful it was to raise a child alone. It went on like that for more than two years; everyone knew how she was carrying on, except Louis. Nobody had the heart to tell him.'

'Until the guitar player.' Wickus spat out the words, as if it were a sinful occupation.

'He was a chap from Port Elizabeth, long hair, tight jeans and big loose white shirts open to the belly button . . .' said Lollie.

'Big gold chain on his hairy chest. What would a man want to wear jewellery for?'

'He had sung in clubs and bars all over, but he wasn't very good . . .'

'You know the kind, the audience has to be a bit drunk . . .'

'. . . so he came to play in the Intaba, it was a sort of bush pub outside town . . .'

'Wicked place.'

'. . . and one of Drika's haunts, and he and Drika linked up, a red-hot affair, she was with him more than with her own child. Late nights, she would end up in a drunken singalong with him. That was when people decided enough is enough. First a couple of the men threatened the guitar man and told him to pack his stuff, and two of them went to fetch Louis. He was up in the northern Tuli with a Scandinavian hunting party, and they told him he had better come home, his wife was creating a scandal.'

'Flea's father chased them away,' said Wickus.

'Louis didn't want to believe them, poor man. But two days later, he came. Must have been brooding over it. By the time he got home, Drika and her guitar man were gone. Louis was crushed, he loved that woman with all he had. But the great tragedy was, he went looking for her, but by the time he found her, she was dead, she and her guitar man, this side of Sun City, drove off a bridge in the night, probably drunk, and they were both killed instantly.'

'Hell,' said young Swannie.

'Bad, bad,' said Wickus.

'Louis brought his daughter up alone, and let me tell you, it must have been very hard, because he mourned Drika for years. He withdrew entirely, he only went to work when the money ran out and then he took Flea with him . . .'

'That's how she learned to track . . .'

'She just about grew up in the bush . . .'

'Some people say she is better than her father.'

'I know there was an issue when she had to go to school, Louis wouldn't hear of it, Welfare had to go and talk to him. Eventually he put her in boarding school, although he didn't want to. She was with Swannie until standard . . . ?'

'Grade Six,' said Swannie, eager to contribute. 'You hardly noticed her, she was a loner, a skinny girl who talked to no one, just kept to herself. *Jissie*, she's changed,' he shook his head in disbelief, the impact the adult Flea had made on him clearly visible.

'Louis found a permanent job. That's why they moved away,' said Wickus. 'That was the time when private game reserves were shooting up everywhere, and the concessions. Guys like Louis were suddenly very sought-after, there were lots of new jobs, good money. They came to find him and offered him a job up there in Moremi . . .'

'In Botswana,' said Lollie.

'Okavango.'

'Private tuition for the children.'

'That was the biggest thing for Louis, he could see Flea every day.'

'Must be where she got her opportunity to study veterinary, through the private schooling.'

'They left the area. Overnight almost. That's about all we know really,' Lollie said.

'There were other stories . . .'

'I don't know if you can always believe them . . .'

'The one about the crocodile is true, Lollie. Div de Goede heard it personally. And he knows Big Frik well.'

'Maybe . . .'

Swannie couldn't suppress his curiosity any longer. 'What crocodile story?'

'Div pitched up here with the story, must be six or seven years ago. He's the rep for AgriChem, their head offices are in Nelspruit, Frik is one of his big clients. He said the people from the Moremi concession turned up at Frik's door one day and told him the whole story. How Louis grew odder and odder with every year that passed. Sometimes he would just disappear, then he would reappear a month later smelling like a native hut, all sweat and woodsmoke, and then they would hear that Louis had been with the Bushmen again. Sometimes Louis would make a big fire in the bush and then dance around it until he went into a trance . . .'

'I don't know if I believe that,' said Lollie.

'I'm just repeating what Div said. The thing is, apparently, Louis began to unravel after the baboons attacked Flea . . .'

'Hell!' said Swannie.

'That's just nonsense,' said Lollie.

'I don't know,' Wickus shrugged. 'They said it had been a bad drought up there, late winter, the baboons were very aggressive, because there was nothing to eat. Flea went walking with this little dog, a Jack Russell terrier or something, she was terribly attached to it. Then the baboons came across them and they went for the dog, blood lust, they get that way. And Flea tried to stop them and a big male attacked her, terrible scratches and cuts across her torso and face. You saw the eye, while she was here. Anyway, some of the natives came across them and they threw stones at the baboons and saved Flea, but the little dog didn't make it. But that's when Louis started to talk about how he was to blame, the gods were angry with him because of something he had done as a child. When they asked him what it was, he said he had eaten tortoise, that is a great taboo with the Bushmen, only old people may eat it, or something like that. The more they told him it was nonsense, the more he said the gods were punishing him, that's why Drika died, why she messed around with other men, why his father had died, why the baboons had attacked Flea. He said he must sacrifice himself, it was the only way . . .'

In a barely audible whisper, Swannie sighed, 'Hell.'

'That's nonsense,' said Lollie.

'It wasn't nonsense to Louis. Anyway, they told Div, there in that bar, that Louis had gone out into the bush, and had sat on the river bank, and waited until a huge crocodile had dragged him into the waters of the Okavango, because Louis was dead, and they didn't know what to do with Flea. She must have been, I don't know, seventeen, eighteen. Frik was the grandfather, could they bring the child to him? Frik just stood and looked at them, and without a word, he shut the door in their faces. The Moremi people went to Nelspruit in the hopes of finding someone there who could help, maybe one of Frik's other daughters, they were Flea's aunts after all. Div bumped into the men somewhere, probably a bar, he does like a good time, and they told him the whole story.'

'But why?' asked Swannie. 'Why did Louis let the croc get him?'

'To free his daughter from the curse.'

40

> . . . trackers should place themselves in the position of their quarry in order to anticipate the route it may have taken. They will thereby be able to decide in advance where they can expect to find signs and thus not waste time looking for them.
>
> *The Art of Tracking: Principles of tracking*

Lollie took Lotter to 'the office' to finalise the fax for our flight clearance. I drank coffee with the Swanepoel men in the sitting room. 'And where will you go from here?' Wickus asked.

'To Ehrlichmann,' I said deliberately.

'Aah . . .' he said. Which meant he knew who that was.

'How do you know Ehrlichmann?'

'Through helping the Zimbabweans,' he said. 'Ehrlichmann was involved in that from the early days.'

'Helping the Zimbabweans?'

'When that dirty rotten Mugabe started taking people's farms, lots of the Zim farmers knew they had to get their stuff out of the country quickly. We smuggled it out. Furniture, livestock, machinery, cars, tractors, trailers, implements. Dollars, a few times, cardboard boxes full, you wouldn't believe. Hell, once we brought a whole bloody cigarette factory through here, I have no idea where they went with that. Anyway, Ehrlichmann was one of the men on that side who helped organise the whole operation.'

I mulled that over before asking: 'And Diederik Brand?'

'Diederik was a buyer.'

'A buyer?'

'I thought you worked for him?'

'Since Saturday.'

'Oh. Look, the stuff that came from Zim . . . The farmers over there were looking for cash, what could they do with their machinery and livestock in South Africa? Diederik bought them up, he was one of a few who helped out that way. Then he would resell, on auctions and suchlike. I never met him, just talked over the phone. A good man . . . Once he even sent food and medical equipment back to Zim, when Mugabe and his gang plundered the Red Cross aid for their own benefit.' Wickus laughed softly and shook his head. 'I still wonder where Diederik got the stuff . . .'

'He's an operator,' said Swannie, equally delighted.

'Heck, that's true. How does a Karoo farmer get his hands on medical supplies from Norway?'

A mental alarm sounded in the back of my head. 'Norway, you say?'

'On the crates, large as life. Karma or Karmer or something . . . And "Oslo, Norge".'

'Kvaerner?'

'Something like that.'

Kvaerner was the Norwegian company that actually owned Techno Arms, the manufacturer of the MAG-7. 'Did Ehrlichmann help with those medical supplies?'

'Yes, he did,' said Wickus Swanepoel. 'Zimbabwe needs more people like that.'

* * *

All three of them came to see us off in the plane. Lollie kissed us goodbye, Wickus and Swannie gave us warm, friendly handshakes, as if we had become part of their social circle.

As Lotter circled back above them and waggled his wings in a final salute, we looked down on the three small figures waving with outstretched arms, and Lotter said, 'Good people.' He, the Swanepoels, Emma, spontaneously saw the good in others, they believed that people were inherently good, or at least interesting, fascinating. I refrained from speaking, because I'm not like that. I had sat and listened to the story of Flea van Jaarsveld and wondered why no one had stepped in. Why had no one gone to Big Frik Redelinghuys and said, 'It's your daughter and your grandchild, you idiot, wake up'? Why hadn't the keepers of Musina's morals talked to Drika or warned Louis earlier? When the people from Moremi came looking for Flea's next of kin after Louis died, why had no one stepped forward and said, 'bring the girl to me'? Why hadn't Wickus and Lollie done something themselves? It was no good telling the story with quasi-altruistic remarks like, 'It's a sad story', more than ten years after the damage was done. That was the trouble with our society; we had become spectators, sideline critics. We couldn't wait to read about other people's hardships, hear about them and pass on the stories. Always from the moral high ground, of course. 'They got what was coming to them'. But no one had the guts to step in.

Granted, My First Law was: Don't get involved, but the critical difference was that I did not seek the moral high ground, I didn't pretend to be 'good' . . .

I became aware I was angry. I knew where it was coming from. Wickus and Lollie had deprived me of something: my motivation to . . . well, what *did* I plan to do when I caught up with Flea? Punish her? Expose her? And now? Now that the parallels had been drawn so clearly between us – a slut for a mother, a madman for a father, a youth effectively ruined by parents who should never have reproduced, and a family and society that chose to look the other way, because it wasn't their problem. Now I wished I would never find her, I hoped that whatever she had stuck on those two rhinos would bring her escape and release.

I felt like turning around and going home.

But I couldn't. I had to get my Glock back. My whole life depended on it.

Lotter looked down on the strip of cleared bush in a shallow valley between high hills and he said: 'This is going to be tricky.'

'How tricky?'

'Very tricky.'

'We don't have to land,' I said, beginning to think of alternatives, mainly involving road travel.

'Shut your eyes if you like,' with a grin that said he always wanted to test the RV-7's limits.

He flew over the landing strip again, dipping a wing to see better.

'What are you looking at?'

'There's no windsock . . .'

'Is that a problem?'

'Naah . . . not really.'

Then he made a wide turn before diving, aiming for a cleft between two hills. 'Hold tight.'

I seriously considered shutting my eyes.

Rocks, bush and trees only metres from the wing tips, then he turned sharply left, dropping even lower. The valley widened, the tree tops too high, too near. The engine tone dropped, he worked the pedals and joystick, the landing strip straight ahead, too short. We hit the ground with a jarring bump. Lotter braked hard, my body strained against the safety webbing. The wall of trees was coming up too fast.

I closed my eyes.

'Jeez,' said Lotter.

We stopped. I opened my eyes. The plane's propeller was not much more than two metres from the massive trunk of a baobab tree.

He turned off the engine, breathed a long sigh.

'That wasn't so bad,' he said.

'And what about taking off tomorrow?'

'Naah . . . Piece of cake.' But even he didn't sound convinced.

41

In difficult terrain, where signs are sparse, trackers may have to rely extensively on anticipating the animal's movements.

The Art of Tracking: Principles of tracking

Ten minutes after we landed, a battered Land Rover came rattling through the grass and thorn trees. Two black men got out and welcomed us shyly in English. Visitors weren't an everyday occurrence, it seemed.

'We will take you to camp.'

Lotter looked at the vehicle with deep interest. 'Amazing,' he said, 'Series II station wagon, the two-point-two-five diesel. This thing must be at least fifty years old.'

He was in raptures. You'd never have guessed we'd just defied death.

We each took a bag, climbed in and were shaken about on the barely discernible jeep track through the bush, disturbing a small herd of blue wildebeest and their swarm of accompanying birds. Three giraffe, aloof, ignored us. The heat was bearable here, less oppressive than in Musina.

The camp was situated on the side of a hill, a circle of light green canvas tents on wooden platforms in the shade of massive msasa trees. Beside the road was a rough sign, the words *Chinhavira Camp* carved out of a block of teak. There was a *lapa* in the middle, a few tables and chairs, a huge hearth. A man was raking the red earth between the tents. At a table beside the *lapa*, two other men were peeling vegetables.

Our driver said: 'Shumba will come later. I will show you your tents.'

'Shumba' had to be Ehrlichmann.

We followed him.

He appeared at sundown, a big man walking through the long shadows, crooked walking stick in hand, khaki shorts and short-sleeved shirt, sandals, a broad-brimmed hat and long silver hair down to his shoulders. A clean-shaven Moses in safari gear.

Lotter and I sat in the *lapa*, he had a beer, I had a Coke, since there was no Birdfield or Grapetizer. The man propped his staff against the encircling ring of wooden poles, took off his hat, smiled broadly and held out his hand as he approached us.

'I'm John Ehrlichmann,' he said in the same pleasant, modulated voice I had heard over the satellite phone.

We rose to meet him, introduced ourselves.

'Lotter.'

'Lemmer.' I expected him to ask about the state of my face, wondered what witticism Lotter had ready.

'Alliteration,' said Ehrlichmann. 'We have a lot of that up here,' and then he laughed gently. 'Welcome to Chinhavira. I see Chipinduka and Chenjerai have taken care of you.' He was close to two metres tall, his face deeply lined. He had to be on the shady side of sixty, but he made an impressive figure, vigorous and fit. The long grey hair formed a halo. An array of armbands circled his left wrist.

'Please. Sit. Enjoy your drinks. I'll be with you soon.'

'Thank you,' said Lotter.

'My pleasure.' He turned and walked slowly and solemnly towards the tents. Once he was out of hearing, Lotter said quietly: 'You know who he reminds me of?'

He liked people. So I was expecting some noble comparison. I gave him my best attempt: 'A sober Nick Nolte?'

'No,' he laughed. 'That mandrill-baboon in *The Lion King*, the one with the walking stick, what was his name . . . ? This guy has the same loping gait . . . Rafiki! He's bigger and he's older, but he reminds me of Rafiki.'

Rafiki Ehrlichmann was the perfect host.

When he came out again, he was showered and in his wilderness evening wear: long-sleeved khaki shirt, blue jeans and *velskoen* leather boots. The cascade of hair was tied back in a ponytail, the shirt sleeves turned up just enough to show the armbands. They glittered and shone in the light of twenty paraffin lamps and the big campfire. First he made sure our glasses were full, then ordered a whisky and soda for himself before joining us. He stretched out luxuriously on the camp chair and enquired delicately about our journey, seeming to want me to reveal our purpose. I wanted him to have a couple of whiskies before raising the subject. So I left Lotter to describe the flight, and our visit to Wickus and family.

Every now and then Ehrlichmann would comment briefly, with a sage nod of his grey head. Diederik Brand is a 'fine man'. On the subject of the Swanepoels he said, 'wonderful people' – clearly a popular view. When Lotter, equally intrigued by the lives of others, began asking about Ehrlichmann's, he told his story as though it were commonplace and insignificant. Born on a farm outside Gweru, boarding school in Bulawayo, BSc at the University of Cape Town, Game Warden in the Matobo National Park in the old Rhodesia days. After that he was Senior Warden at the newly established Mana Pools Park in the early eighties, later Deputy Head of the Chizarira National Park, until the Mugabe witch-hunts began. Since then he had been a concession hunter and walking tour guide. The black men who worked with him were all field guides or support personnel from his Chizarira days.

By his second whisky he skilfully steered the conversation to stories of his experiences. He had two mannerisms – stroking his right hand over his hair, and a set of his mouth, a sardonic half-smile when he came to the finale of every anecdote, an expression that said, 'There you have it'. His stories were about elephants and lions, crocodiles and hippopotami, fish eagles and dung beetles. I wondered how many times he had related them, how many foreign tourists he had regaled with them around the campfire. But he was masterful, had perfect dramatic timing, a fascination for nature, and a studied modesty, as if it were mere chance that he was so privileged.

We drank *Nhedzi* soup of wild mushrooms. We ate *sadza*, made with maize porridge and pork, served with green beans and pumpkin fritters by his quiet, efficient team. Then a bottle of French cognac appeared on the table.

'Wow,' said Lotter.

Ehrlichmann looked at me. 'I do believe you don't take alcohol.'

'No, thanks.'

Then, as he poured a quarter glass each for himself and Lotter, 'But you did have some questions regarding the rhino.'

No, I said, my questions were about Cornél van Jaarsveld.

'Mmm . . .' he said, and got up slowly, walked thoughtfully over to the glowing coals and threw on more wood. He poked a stick in the fire, waited until the flames began to lick the logs, came back to the table. 'May I ask exactly what happened?'

Sometimes you have to trust your instincts. I told him, without unnecessary detail. About the rhinos' 'dermatitis', the journey, and the attack, the amazing recovery of the animals, Flea's disappearance. I took the scrap of pink plastic out of my pocket and showed it to him. Throughout, I observed him closely, his eyes, his hands, his body language. His only reaction was raising his eyes when I described the hijacking, and a fleeting glance at my face, as if the damage made sense to him now. He took the plastic and rolled it between his fingers. He asked a few questions, about the numbers of sores, the exact size of them.

I played open cards about my suspicions about Diederik, and the Swanepoels. I told him I already suspected that he himself was involved in some way. That produced a serious nod of the head.

When I had finished, he looked away and stared into the night. 'She has such potential,' he said, to himself.

He picked up the cognac glass, rolled it between his palms, sipped at it. Rolled it again, deep in thought.

He made his 'there-you-have-it' grimace.

'I think . . .'

Stroked a hand over his hair, looked at me.

'I think I know what she was smuggling.'

42

> The average person should by practice and experience be able to become a fair tracker, but really outstanding trackers are probably born with the latent ability.
>
> *The Art of Tracking: Learning to track*

He paused for dramatic effect before he began.

'It will be conjecture, but I'm pretty sure . . . Let me tell you the whole damn story . . .'

He said it was, like everything in Zimbabwe nowadays, a bit of a circus. Two game rangers from the Chizarira National Park had been caught two years ago with twenty-two elephant tusks. There was intense international reaction from the Green faction, but only once tourism boycotts began to threaten the only remaining source of foreign currency, did the Mugabe government respond. Their conciliatory strategy was to agree to the elephant census that the WWF insisted on. This organisation approached Ehrlichmann because of his background. Flea van Jaarsveld was part of the team of more than thirty who set up camp in the national park in April.

He only really noticed her after she had outshone the other three trackers. 'She was phenomenal, I've never seen anything like it. That sixth sense . . . her knowledge, detailed knowledge about the veld and the animals, insects, birds, you name it. I started keeping an eye on her. As you know, that was no hardship . . .' He smiled with old man's nostalgia.

She was driven, working from sunrise to sundown. At night she mixed with different groups by turns – the WWF people, the game wardens, the volunteers, labourers and helpers. One evening she was at the table with Ehrlichmann and two spirited young veterinarians, a Hollander and an Austrian. There was a discussion about the sedation of elephants, the Europeans were full of book learning and big theories. Flea silenced them with one word: 'Bullshit'. And went on to tell them with some annoyance and in fine detail how it was done in Africa.

'So, obviously, I thought she was a vet. I asked her if she had studied at Onderstepoort. No, she said, she worked with Douw Grobler for three years. Now, Douw used to be the head of Game Capture in Kruger, probably the best of the best. But even so, for her to assimilate so much in-depth knowledge . . . She's a very smart girl. But I digress . . .'

'Are you saying she isn't a veterinarian?'

'No, she isn't. But she could hold her own with those two guys. On everything. When it came to wild animals in transit, she knew much more. That's why I called her when the two rhinos became an option for Diederik.'

I almost missed it, still pondering Flea's false career. 'You're a vet,'

Swannie had said respectfully when we loaded the rhinos. Her answer had been a string of big medical words, anaemia and gastrointestinal diseases. A delicate way of avoiding the truth. Then I registered what Ehrlichmann had said.

'You called her? How did you contact her?'

'She left her card with just about everybody after the census. I called her cellphone.'

'Do you still have the card?'

'Of course. I'll find it for you. But first, let me tell you what I think happened. And then you can draw your own conclusions. In the first week or so, I was impressed by how she mingled with everybody, quite deliberately, and with such consummate skill and charm. After a while I realised that there was method in this socialising, because she started to ignore certain people, even snub them, and shift her considerable focus onto others.'

It wasn't difficult for him to grasp her purpose: the people she spent more and more time with were those who were useful to her. Someone who might use her services in future, or at least provide access to other, more important people. But her most peculiar choice was the final evening, the closing function at Kaswiswi camp number one.

'We had this huge barbecue, lots of booze, your typical VIP bush bash, because a number of government people had flown in by helicopter: the Minister of Environment and Tourism, his three directors, the Head of Parks, the regional chief of the Wildlife Fund . . .'

Ehrlichmann cast a quick glance over his shoulder, leaned across the table, and dropped his voice as if sharing a secret. 'But the one guy Cornél spent the most time with that night, was Johnson Chitepo.'

He saw the name made no impression on us.

'You've never heard of Johnson Chitepo?'

'Nope,' said Lotter.

'He is Mugabe's crony-in-chief,' with a reluctant admiration. 'He is the key man in the Zimbabwean Central Intelligence Organisation, the head of the Joint Operations Command, and the man with whose blessing almost any crime in Zimbabwe can be committed with impunity. If you believe the rumours, he is also the guy who rigged the last elections, and the leading candidate to become the next president.'

Like his wildlife tales, he was building up to a climax.

'But it's not so much what Chitepo is doing now. The key to all of this lies in his history, and the history of the region. You see, back in 1998, President Laurent Kabila of the Congo needed an army. Urgently. His former allies, Rwanda and Uganda, had just turned against him, they had reached the outskirts of Kabila's stronghold in Kinshasa, and he was desperate for help. So, Kabila called his old pal Mugabe. And Mugabe sent Johnson Chitepo with a very clear directive: go and find out what's in it for us. As it turned out, Kabila was more than ready with an answer. He offered a mining concession at Mbuji-Mayi, in exchange for the loan of Mugabe's army. And you know what they mine at Mbuji-Mayi?'

We shook our heads.

'Diamonds,' Ehrlichmann whispered.

'Aha,' said Lotter.

A slow nod. 'Diamonds,' he repeated. He downed the last of his cognac. 'And that, I believe, is what our Cornél was smuggling out of here.'

He let it sink in before stretching out his hand for the bottle, picking it up and holding it out towards Lotter's glass.

'No thanks, I'm flying tomorrow.'

Ehrlichmann nodded and poured another for himself.

I wasn't entirely convinced by his story. 'The war in the Congo was ten years ago . . .'

'Forget about the war. That's just where it started. Think now. Think noose around the neck of Zimbabwe. Think millions of American dollars' worth of diamonds extracted from Mbuji-Mayi over the years, and fewer and fewer buyers. Because of the increasing isolation of Zimbabwe. There have been sanctions, the EU has frozen all the assets of Zimbabwe's ministers abroad, and the Kimberley Process is making it very difficult for them to find a market for their dirty stones. And then, there's the weighty matter of international terrorism. You see, there is a connection between the Mbuji-Mayi concession and al-Qaeda.'

'You're kidding,' said Lotter.

Ehrlichmann shook his head. 'I'm not. Back in 1998, Mugabe and Chitepo had one big problem: they didn't have the technical know-how to extract the diamonds. But in Africa, carrion is always guaranteed to attract the scavengers. Enter Mr Sayyid Khalid bin Alawi Macki, a businessman and mining magnate from Oman, with all the technical expertise needed for the job. Within a week, they had created a joint venture between Osleg, the business wing of the Zimbabwean armed forces, the Zim government, and Macki. And our Mr Macki, apparently, is the one with ties to al-Qaeda. Through his many companies, he not only launders money for the terrorists, but also directly supplies, funds, arms, and equips them. So now you will understand how difficult it has become for Chitepo to get rid of the diamonds. Everybody has been watching, including the CIA. All the usual channels are blocked, all the border posts are being monitored. According to the bush telegraph, Chitepo is getting more and more desperate to sell the diamonds, and time is running out. For him, for Mugabe, for Zimbabwe. I mean, who knows where this new coalition government will lead? It's every man for himself now, and even they are watching each other like hawks . . . Anyway, that night, during the Big Barbecue, Johnson Chitepo was spending a lot of time with Cornél. As a matter of fact, when I left just before midnight, they were sitting, just the two of them, heads together, very deep in discussion. And I think I know what they were talking about. I mean, she would have been perfect – a South African, white, no obvious ties to smuggling. And using the rhinos . . . Well, that's very, very clever.'

I asked him about the rhinos.

He said it was more than a year ago that word had reached him that Diederik Brand, a benefactor to Zim farmers, was most eager to acquire a breeding pair. When he came across the two animals in June, barely twenty kilometres from where we now sat, he realised their chances of survival were slim. Poaching of Black Rhino was intense, organised, and executed with the full knowledge of the Zimbabwean police. That was why he sent word to Diederik via the channels: if Brand financed the operation, Ehrlichmann would do the rest to get the animals to the border. When a positive answer was returned, Cornél van Jaarsveld was the obvious choice, because of her knowledge of sedation of game in transit. He had dug up her visiting card and called her . . .

'When was this?' I asked.

'Early July. Two days after I called her, she was here. Quite the little negotiator. If I supplied a team to help load the rhinos, she would organise everything else – the lorry, the drugs for the animals. But she didn't come cheap. Two hundred and fifty grand . . .'

Flea had nearly three months and a quarter of a million rand to organise it all. And most likely the cooperation of Johnson Chitepo and the Zim authorities, to have the plastic holders manufactured, to manipulate roadblocks, to get them safely to the border. If Ehrlichmann was right.

'I kept track of the rhinos, we arranged a final date for the capture, and last week, we did it. Cornél darted them, we loaded, and off she went. Pretty uneventful, really. And those two hook-lips were in fine health when she drove down that road,' he said, pointing in the direction of the jeep track that led away from camp.

'When *she* drove down that road?' I asked.

'That's right.'

'No driver?'

'She said she had a relief driver waiting in Kwekwe. That's about 150 clicks from here.'

43

Every person has an individual mannerism in the way he or she walks, leaving a 'signature' in his or her spoor.

The Art of Tracking: Introduction

I couldn't sleep. I lay in the tent listening to the sounds of Africa, recognising only the howl of a jackal. The other sounds were indecipherable: birds, insects, night creatures living their secret lives in darkness. Like so many of us.

Before we finally left the dying campfire, I asked Ehrlichmann two more questions. The first was whether Flea ever talked about her home, her background.

'Funny you should ask,' he said. 'The night before we captured the rhinos, I asked her where she came from. And she pointed to this red carry bag of hers and she said, "That's my home". So I said, no, I meant where did she grow up? And she gave a rather strange laugh and said, "purgatory". Never quite figured out what she meant.'

Then I asked him about Diederik Brand and the 'Kvaerner' crates.

'Well . . .' he said, looking at his glass as though there was something very significant to be found in it. 'This is Africa.'

Did he know they contained weapons?

'Yes, I knew.'

Where were the crates bound?

He stood up, not entirely steady on his feet now and said to me: 'Come.'

He took a paraffin lamp from one of the tables and walked away through the dust. I followed, Lotter remained seated.

He headed away from the tents, up the slope of the hill. Behind dark thorn trees and a rocky outcrop, hidden in the dark shadows of trees, were two low-roofed corrugated-iron buildings, the sort that construction companies frequently used as temporary workshops. Painted a dirty green, the strokes of hasty paintwork were visible. The double doors of one stood open. In the faint light of the lamp I could see two Land Rovers, one raised on wooden blocks. Parts, old tyres, tools. Ehrlichmann went to the other building, passed the lamp over to me to hold, took a bunch of keys from his pocket, fiddled with them and unlocked the door. He pulled the door open, took the lamp back and went inside. He lifted a tarpaulin and the dust drifted up into the lamp beams.

'Here they are.'

The crates were there.

I looked. Two of the crates had been broached. The others were still untouched. He opened one. Guns, packed in bubble wrap, a few gaps where some had been removed.

'Are they for sale?'

'Do you want one?'

'Depends on the price.'

'Help yourself. It's free.'

I stared at him. He grimaced at my disbelief, bent, took out a MAG-7, opened another crate and picked up a box of ammunition, propping it all in my arms. He draped the tarpaulin over again and walked out. Outside he put the lamp on the ground while he took his time locking up. We walked back. Halfway he stopped, held up the lamp and had a good look at me. 'You are quite a piece of work, you know. So righteous.' No reproach, just an observation. He began to turn away, but reconsidered and confronted me again. 'I do believe you have your own demons.' He lifted his other hand, and for a tiny surreal moment I thought he would strike me. But he just loosened his ponytail, and shook his head lightly, so the hair tumbled over his shoulders. He said: 'I distribute the guns. Amongst my farmer friends. The few I have left. That's what Diederik wanted. That is why he made this gift.'

Then he turned slowly and walked back to the campfire. To Lotter he said, 'I bid you goodnight,' collected his staff and did his dignified Rafiki shuffle over to the tents.

I lay listening and thinking of night animals and secret lives. Of impressions. And the stories we weave, so frequently embellished in the telling. Of the layer upon layer of camouflage we paint on, creating our facades with such practised skill that the brush strokes go mostly unseen.

Diederik Brand. The rascal. The farmer con man. A 'character' Lourens le Riche and Lotter had called him. Not the Black Swan I had taken him to be. His paint was grey, the shades just light enough to evoke the good-natured Bo-Karoo smile that said, 'Ay, that Diederik'. I suspected he had created this image deliberately, his wicked deeds bordering on crimes, in the barely safe no-man's-land of social acceptability. It was, as Emma would say of her clients and their products, his unique selling point, the quality that made him stand out from the crowd. His story.

Was he hiding his role of benefactor from Loxton deliberately, the emergency aid to Zim farmers, the gift of a consignment of MAG-7 shotguns, because it would alter his image, make him less interesting?

How strange. Will the real Diederik Brand please stand up. Or is that who he *really* is, the sum of his contradictions, the man who felt such contentment standing at the gate and watching the two rhinos grazing peacefully, knowing *his* money saved them, *his* work, *his* intervention, *his* white lies and forgeries.

And Ehrlichmann, with his hair and bangles and long staff. A trademark, unsubtle, unapologetic, the image strengthened and refined by his sagacity, the mannerisms, emphases, voice, spellbinding tales. By nature I was wary of his kind, always suspecting them of hiding something. Or at least living in a fantasy world, either option a danger in my profession.

I do believe you have your own demons. That had many implications: that he had his. That he had the insight – and interest – to notice mine. That he wasn't judgemental. Characteristics that made him both more interesting, more acceptable than the carefully cultivated, exaggerated image. Which made me wonder: *Why* then?

The answer was, just as it was in Diederik's case, in his desire to be noticed.

Emma had a theory that this need was at the heart of every brand name – people's need to stand out, to escape from the homogeneity of the masses. We wanted to create an image through all that we purchased, hold up a placard of ourselves to the world that said 'this is me'. It was an interesting, exciting concept to Emma. For me it was plain depressing, because no longer were we defined by what we did, but by what we owned. It was the engine of consumerism, superficiality and greed, the origin of all the lies and subterfuge.

That, I realised, was what motivated Flea van Jaarsveld. It was her remedy for the tragic past, the trauma, the humiliation. I remembered when we talked about rich Afrikaners in the lorry. They are not all like that, Flea had said. Because she so badly wanted to be one. She believed it would ease her pain.

She was incredibly focused, relentless in her deception. In my mind's eye I could see her throughout the elephant census, in her tight-fitting clothes, busy, busy, busy, searching out opportunities, making contacts. The disdainful cold shoulder for the useless, the warm courtship of the useful.

She had manipulated me, and particularly Lourens, with skill, handled us flawlessly through her suggestions, her careful approaches. She must have been terrified, there on the ground in front of the truck, as Inkunzi and his henchmen searched it, all her plans hanging in the balance, lives on the line. But how quickly she had recovered and adapted.

The theft of my Glock. Was it the delay at the Knights of Harley that gave her the idea I would come looking for her? So that she made provision for that as well?

'She has such potential,' Ehrlichmann had said. But it was much more than potential. She had set up the entire operation, planned it and carried it through.

I wondered what she would do when she realised that money would not heal her wounds.

44

The shooting of dangerous animals should be left to experienced rangers who know what they are doing.

The Art of Tracking: Dangerous animals

We ate breakfast alone. Chipinduka, the Land Rover driver said: 'Shumba has gone walking. He sends his greetings, he says goodbye, and you will always be welcome.'

'He walks a lot?' Lotter asked.

'Every morning and every afternoon.' He took something out of his breast pocket. 'Shumba said I must give you this.'

I took it and had a look. A business card, the colour of sand. The image of a paw print. *Cornél van Jaarsveld.* A Googlemail email address, and a cellphone number. *Not* the same one I got from Lourens.

I heard Lotter ask Chipinduka 'What does "Shumba" mean?'

'It is Shona for "lion". For the hair. He has the hair of a lion.'

'Do you know animal tracks?' I asked him.

'I do.'

I showed him Flea's card. 'This track? Which animal is that?'

He studied the paw print. 'I think that is the brown hyena.'

'The *brown* hyena?'

'Yes. It is not like the other hyena.'

'Why?'

'It walks alone.'

While Lotter loosened the plane's guyropes, he asked: 'What's the plan, Stan?'

I examined the short landing strip, the hills around us. 'Step one is to survive takeoff.'

'And if, by some miracle, we make it?'

'Can you drop me off in Jo'burg, please.'

'You think she's there?'

'Probably not. But my last lead is.' Inkunzi, who had pressed against Flea and whispered in her ear.

'And you have a score to settle.'

'That may have to wait.'

He raised his eyebrows at me.

'I will probably have to choose between information and satisfaction. Tough choice.'

'I've noticed that about you,' he said, and began going through his pre-flight checks.

Both Shonas watched him with great interest. 'You want to go for a spin?' Lotter asked Chipinduka.

Wide, white smile, heads shaking. 'We are not crazy.'

'Exactly,' I said.

They laughed.

Once Lotter had finished, we said goodbye and got into the plane.

He was still irritatingly cheerful. 'Ever experienced a miracle?'

'Not really.'

'Then this should be a big moment for you . . .'

The miracle occurred, but I don't know how, my eyes were tightly shut.

When we reached cruising altitude and Lotter finished talking pilot dialect over the radio, I asked him if he had ever thought of himself as an animal.

'What sort of a girly-man question is that anyway?' he asked in a perfect Arnold Schwarzenegger-accent.

'I think it's the new fashion. Shumba the maned lion, Flea the brown hyena. Snake was the one who was killed in the hijacking, and I am on my way to visit Inkunzi the bull. What is it with these people?'

'It's part of our culture, I suppose,' said Lotter, philosophically. Then, a few minutes later: 'You ever read Laurens van der Post, the naturalist?'

'No.'

'He wrote about an encounter between a little meerkat and this six-foot cobra . . .'

'And?'

'That's you, right there. And I don't mean the cobra.'

'Did the meerkat win?'

'Thing is, I can't remember.'

We landed at Lanseria just after twelve. 'I will have to drop you on the apron, I have to refuel. By the way, is that shotgun in your bag?'

He had said nothing last night when I came back from my walk in the dark with Ehrlichmann carrying the MAG-7 and the box of ammunition.

'Yes.'

'Then just tell them we've come from Musina. We don't want you to go through customs.'

'Thanks, Lotter.'

He shook my hand. 'It's been a pleasure and an education.'

'I can almost say the same, if we leave the Zim airstrip out of the equation.'

He laughed. 'Good luck, mate. And when it's all over, gimme a call. I want to know what happens.'

At the car rental I asked if they had a Ford.

'A Ford?' It seemed to be an indecent suggestion.

'Yes, please.'

'Why?' Very dubious.

'I like Fords.'

She peered sidelong at my battered face while her computer completed its search. 'I can give you an Ikon.'

'Thank you very much.'

She held my ID book up to the light to make sure it was genuine. The price of loyalty to Ford. Along with visible wounds.

I drove to Sandton on a freeway that was overcrowded and slow. Wondered when the Gautrain would start running, because that was the only thing I had against Johannesburg: this frustrating traffic.

At the Sandton Holiday Inn they didn't discriminate against my choice of car or my appearance, they gave me a room on the second floor with a street view. When I had put my bag on the bed, I took out Flea's card and used the hotel phone to call her cellphone.

It went straight to voicemail. 'This is Cornél. Please leave a message.' Businesslike, a little hasty. Flea in her efficient vet mode. I ended the call. Then I called Jeanette to bring her up to date.

My employer was a woman of many talents, but the one that impressed me most was her unbounded ability to adapt the word 'fuck'. She used it four times in the course of my narrative, every time with a different emphasis and meaning. The last one, when I came to the part about the diamonds, was long and drawn-out, which meant she was deeply impressed by Flea's entrepreneurial initiative.

'That is why I have to talk to Inkunzi. He is the last remaining link.'

'Talk, you say?'

'I will also explain politely to him that Body Armour's personnel should be left in peace.'

'And you expect me to believe you?'

'Jeanette, Nicola's game truck . . . Inkunzi could have had the registration written down. If they want to find us, they will. As much as I would love to rearrange his face, it's not a sensible option. Lourens and I would spend the rest of our lives looking over our shoulders.'

'Shee-it,' she said. 'Expect a big storm: Lemmer used the word "sensible".'

'If something happened to Lourens or Nicola . . . Loxton would never forgive me. In any case, the greater priority is to get the Glock back.'

'Mmm . . . ' she said. 'And what gives you the idea Inkunzi will want to talk?'

'I've got a plan.'

'Tell me.'

I did. Once I had finished she said: 'You call that a plan?'

'It could work. Have you got a better idea?'

'My plan is for you to go back to the boondocks and drop the whole thing. But I know you won't do that. I'll get his home address for you. Is there anything else you need?'

'Yes. I need a make-up artist, please. My face is a bit too conspicuous at the moment.'

'Let me see what I can do.'

45

Because they rely on their camouflage to remain undetected, Puff Adders account for the greatest number of serious snakebite cases.

The Art of Tracking: Dangerous animals

I drove to the address that Jeanette had sent via SMS. The Bull's kraal, Gallo Manor, a rich man's neighbourhood within spitting distance of the Johannesburg Country Club, quite a long way down a dead-end street. Big trees on the pavement, a two-metre plastered wall without electrified wire, the house barely visible behind it. Shrubs, trees, climbing vines on the other side of the wall. It would be a dense, tidy garden, filled with shadows.

Electronic gates with CCTV camera, and two signs: *Python Patrols – Alarms & Armed Response*. And *Python CCTV – Your 24/7 security eye*.

I was expecting the alarms. I had planned for them. The camera was an additional risk, but not insurmountable.

The patrol vehicle of a private security company drove past. *Eagle Eye*. More animal associations. Perhaps Lotter was right, it was ingrained in our culture.

I turned at the end of the street, pretending to be looking for an address, came back again, had another good look. Then I drove off; stopping and staring was not an option in this neighbourhood. And that presented my biggest problem.

At Sandton City I bought a Panasonic fx37 digital camera, an Energizer head lamp with a red filter option, a baseball cap, a cheap plastic spectacle frame, a pair of thin leather gloves and a book to read – *Of Tricksters, Tyrants and Turncoats* by Max du Preez.

Late that afternoon the make-up artist knocked on my door. Her name was Wanda and she had a sense of humour. She saw my face. 'I hope the other guy looks worse.'

She sat me down on the high folding chair she had brought along. Her aluminium case with brushes, powders, paints and lipsticks was on my hotel bed. She stood close to me, an attractive woman in her thirties, round angel face, dark hair, soft eyes, and patted a little round sponge on my face. She smelled nice.

'How do you know Jeanette?' I asked her.

'In the Biblical sense.' Not a hint of embarrassment.

'Divorced?'

'No. Born that way. And you?'

'Beaten up this way.'

She laughed, a lovely, deep sound.

When she had finished and stood back to admire her work, she said: 'Don't rub your face. Don't sweat, don't brush against people, don't scratch if it itches. When you go to bed, wash it off with soap and water.' Then she held up a hand mirror so I could see her handiwork.

'Brad Pitt,' I said.

'*Bad* Pitt.' She laughed and began to pack away her stuff.

'Jeanette did tell you it could be a contract for a few days?'

'She did. I am available in the late afternoon, so that's OK.'

'What do you do usually?'

'I freelance. Mostly in the TV industry.'

'Did you ever work on *7de Laan*, the soapie?' I asked hopefully.

'No. Do you watch *7de Laan*?'

'Absolutely.'

She shook her head in amazement. 'What a wonderful world,' she said, and I wondered what Jeanette had told her about me.

I carried her folding chair to her car, said goodbye, went back to my room, closed the curtains and tested the Panasonic camera in the gloom. Ten megapixels and five times optical zoom, intelligent autofocus, which controlled almost everything when an idiot had only one chance to take a picture.

Exactly what I needed.

Then I took the Yellow Pages out of the drawer and looked up a taxi service that operated in Sandton.

The Bull Run was a pleasant surprise. It was opposite the Stock Exchange, right next to the Balalaika Hotel, the decor was tasteful and simple, the walls bare brick and there was a fire burning in the hearth, a butcher's counter where you could buy fresh meat to take home.

By half past six it was half full. The bar had the best view over the restaurant, but would make me too conspicuous. I asked for a table in the corner. The young waitress in white shirt and black apron, looking curiously at the black sports bag that I had brought along, showed me to a table. I sat down with my back half turned to the room, and opened the menu. I studied it for a long time before raising my head to look around.

Julius 'Inkunzi' Shabangu wasn't there.

I asked if they had Birdfield grape juice. No, the waitress said. I ordered salad with deep-fried haloumi and a red Grapetizer and asked the waitress what time they closed. That depends, she said. Usually late, around one a.m.

I started the book, wondered whether I should contact the writer and tell him about the new generation of tricksters.

The Grapetizer arrived, later the salad. I ordered a pepper-crusted steak, medium, said there was no hurry.

No sign of the Bull.

By half past eight the place was full. Two big groups of businessmen, quite a few tables for six with laughing, chatty twenty-year-olds, black and white, so easy in each other's company, as if our country had no history. It was like that in the shopping centres and the streets, as though this city was a vision of what we could be if the dark shadow of poverty could be wiped away.

The steak was perfect, the chips hot and fresh, the side dishes of baby corn and roasted sweet peppers not really to my taste.

I began to doubt he would ever show up.

At ten to nine Inkunzi and his entourage walked into the restaurant – four young women, three henchmen. I recognised one of them. He was one of the kickers that night in the Waterberg.

They sat down at a table to the left of me. I turned my back to them, pulled my sports bag closer and unzipped it.

The MAG-7 lay there. Just in case.

They were loud. Laughing, talking, expansive gestures. Very much at home.

I finished my main course, declined the dessert, asked for the bill. When it came, I paid at the table.

I picked up the bag, swung it over my shoulder so the gun was close to hand, turned around and strolled out, keeping my face turned away from them.

It wasn't hard to find his car. A black BMW X5 with extravagant wheel rims. The number plate said INKUNZI. A modest man.

No other bodyguards or sentries. I sat down at the Village Walk fountain, phoned the taxi company on my cellphone and asked them to send a car. I took the baseball cap out of my bag and pulled it over my head, put on the glasses. Ten minutes later the taxi arrived. I got in, asked the driver to park so that I could see the interior of the restaurant.

'The meter is running,' he said.

'Let it run.'

I gave him Inkunzi's home address. 'Do you know where this is?'

He pointed at the GPS against the windscreen. 'I know where everything is,' and he typed in the address. The device showed it was 6.9 km from where we were now, with an expected drive time of fourteen minutes.

'When I give you the signal, we need to get there fast.'

'Yebo.' Seen everything, heard everything. This was Johannesburg.

Ten minutes later he asked whether he could put some music on.

Of course, I said. He tuned to a station playing *kwaito*, sat listening, unconcerned.

At half past ten he asked: 'Woman trouble?'

'Yes.'

'Welcome to the club.' With a sigh.

At a quarter to eleven I saw Inkunzi and company approach the door.

'Let's go,' I said.

He switched on the engine, pulled away smoothly, following the GPS directions, quickly and surely, without exceeding speed limits.

The streets of Gallo Manor were quiet, the residents safe behind walls and security systems. On the way we saw two private response vehicles on patrol. Neither paid us much attention.

'Right there,' I pointed at the deep shadow beneath one of the trees in the street, and pulled my bag close.

The fee was R265. I gave him R350. 'Buy her some roses. It works for me,' I said, before getting out.

'Doesn't look like it, but thanks.' He cast a sidelong glance at the black bag I was holding, shook his head and drove off.

46

In order to come close to an animal, trackers must remain undetected not only by the animal, but also by other animals that may alert it.

The Art of Tracking: Principles of tracking

Timing is everything. And a little bit of luck.

I assumed Inkunzi would have the best available alarm system – wide-angle motion sensors outside, the smaller infrared eyes inside. I was counting on him turning them off via remote control when he came home. That was my window of opportunity.

There were two major risks: that a patrol vehicle would challenge me before he arrived, or that he or one of his cronies would spot me scaling the wall. That's where luck came in.

The trouble was that he took longer than I expected. I stood in the shadow of a jacaranda tree, twenty metres from Inkunzi's wall, took out my gloves and put them on. Hitched the black bag over my shoulder. I waited. I could hear the hiss of traffic from the N1, a car alarm complaining monotonously, an accelerating motorbike screaming through the gear changes.

Ten minutes. No movement, no patrols.

Fifteen minutes.

Did they go somewhere else? Drop someone off? Pick someone up?

Twenty minutes. My luck was running out.

At twenty-two minutes, lights appeared at the end of the street.

I moved behind the trunk of the tree, hoping it was wide enough.

The lights washed over me, and disappeared. I peered out. Three of them in the BMW, waiting for the gate to slide open. I had to move fast.

The gate was open. He drove in. I ran.

I spotted another vehicle approaching. Slowly. Security patrol?

I threw my bag over, leaped, grabbed the top of the wall, running shoes slipping against the plastered smoothness, pulling myself up, desperate.

On top. I slid across, rolled off the other side. Too exposed, looked for the bag. It lay on a patch of lawn. The sound of a garage door closing automatically. I grabbed the bag, darting between the shrubs towards the house.

How much time did I have before they activated the alarm?

A massive house, modern design, three levels following the contours of the land. The lowest point was the furthest from me, east, a long way around the back. I ran along the southern side of the building, where the smaller windows would be, the bathrooms and store rooms.

Lights went on inside, to the left of me, on the level closest to the front gate. I would have to move further along, away from the activity.

Sprinted full speed on the paved pathway right next to the house. Windows, too high to reach.

A set of steps, I nearly fell. Level two. Windows still too high. The sand was running through the hourglass.

More steps, third level, windows within reach, I was out of time. The first window, chest high, was just big enough for me to get through. I took a T-shirt out of my bag, twisted it around my hand, and hit the glass hard. It fell inwards, a single crash, loud in my ears. I reached through, opened the catch, pulled the window wide, threw the T-shirt in, then the bag, wriggled through. I pushed the window shut.

There was a contact sensor. Was the interior alarm off?

It was a toilet, interior door shut. I knelt and shoved the T-shirt back into the bag, took the MAG out, pumped a round into the chamber.

Seconds ticked away. Nothing happened.

Phase One successful.

I hoped.

Phase Two would be easy bar one complicating factor: I needed personal one-to-one time with Inkunzi. I had to conduct my business without his henchmen knowing I was here, because if I dented his ego in front of his companions, if I made the gang leader lose face, he would come looking for me.

But I could use his status to my advantage, put it on the line. I had to prove he was vulnerable. That would give me leverage. Another reason to isolate him, confront him alone. Which made it all much more difficult.

I was counting on two basic assumptions: that people felt safe behind security systems, and that this house had a typical layout – reception and entertainment areas up front near the garage, personal areas, such as bedrooms, at the back. And Julius would have the biggest one, the throne room.

This part of the house was dead silent.

I took out my camera and put it in my shirt pocket. Then the Energizer torch, twisting the looped cord around my left hand.

I reached my left hand up and opened the toilet door quietly, still crouching.

A dark passage.

I snapped on the light on the red filter to maintain my night vision.

The bedrooms should be to the right of me. I shuffled forward, peering first left in the direction I suspected Inkunzi and his buddies were still partying.

Nothing.

I looked right. A long dark passage. I illuminated it quickly with the torch. Doors led off to the right and left.

I moved, vaguely remembering response team training from twenty years back, the MAG leading every move. The passage was wide, at the far end was the door I guessed would be the master bedroom.

It was shut.

A noise behind me. I pressed the torch to my shirt to douse it, spun around and dropped to my haunches, MAG to my shoulder.

A voice, someone appeared at the end of the passage, opened a door, switched a light on and disappeared into a room. I rolled to the open door nearest to me. A bedroom, big. Massive bed, lots of pillows. I sat down against the wall beside the door and listened.

I heard the door at the end of the passage close. Quiet again.

I peered cautiously around the door jamb. There was no one to be seen. Did he come to fetch something?

I waited for fifteen seconds, then jogged down the passage, to the closed door at the end. I put my hand on the lever and pressed down. The door swung open.

It was dark inside.

I slipped inside, shut the door behind me.

An enormous room. The northern side was glass, a sliding door behind a light lace curtain. Outside, lights twinkled in a swimming pool. In front of the window stood a couch and two chairs, a coffee table. Against the eastern wall was a giant bed with wooden headboard. I shone the torch on it. A charging bull was carved in it, ominous in the red light. The southern wall consisted of white louvre doors from end to end: the two in the centre stood open, leading to a bathroom where marble and stainless steel were dimly visible. To the left of me, on the western wall, was a large flat-screen TV with surround sound speakers.

I jogged over to the louvre doors to the left of the bathroom entrance and opened them. A walk-in wardrobe. Clothes hung in neat rows, impressive in their excess. Below were shoes, above were jackets, trousers, shirts, ties, belts.

Against the rear wall was a gun safe. I would have to keep him away from that.

I stepped out, back into the room. Opened the doors on the right side. Another walk-in wardrobe. Here and there hung the odd woman's garment. This one was clearly not used much. Just what I was looking for.

I closed the door behind me, sat down in the middle of the space, took the camera out of my pocket, put it down in front of me on the thick white carpet, cradled the MAG in my arms. Switched off the torch.

I would have to wait till he came.

47

> Mock charges, especially by old and lone bulls, are characterised by the ears spread out and a loud trumpeting display, and may end a few metres from the intruder, after which the Elephant retreats. To run away may be fatal. If it demonstrates, stand still until it stops, then slowly move away downwind.
>
> *The Art of Tracking: Dangerous animals*

I had a long wait.

Just after twenty past twelve I heard the bedroom door open. He switched on the light and closed the door. I stayed seated, pointing the shotgun at the entrance to the wardrobe.

Strips of light shone through the slats. Suddenly the sound of the TV, a soccer channel, the sound just loud enough that I could not hear his movements.

Three minutes later, water began to run next door. Sounded like the shower. This was the perfect Kodak moment. I gave him enough time to get the water temperature right and get in. I stood up, picked up the camera, switched it on, choosing the auto mode. Held it in my left hand, the MAG in my right, stepped out, walked across to the door leading to the passage, turned the key to lock it. Then I went into the bathroom.

Inkunzi was in the shower, his back to me, busy soaping himself. Broad shoulders, strong arms, good muscle definition. The scars of old knife fights.

He was singing softly in Zulu.

I raised the camera, let it auto-focus. Aimed the MAG.

'Julius!' I called out quietly.

His head jerked around. I clicked, the flash catching his indignation.

He swore, annoyance turning to rage. I clicked again, pushed the camera in my pocket and held the gun firmly in both hands, lifting it to my shoulder and aiming for his face.

'Blast from the past,' I said.

'What?' The water was still streaming over him, his face still dumbfounded.

'Close the taps.'

He took a while to gather his wits, and turn the water off.

'Another MAG-7,' I said. 'Not very accurate. But at this distance it will blow your knee away. So we are going to have a quiet little chat, but if I hear anyone outside I will start shooting. Do you understand?'

He was uncomfortable in his nakedness, exposed, his red eyes showed he had been drinking. There was still dark bruising on his slightly swollen mouth and nose from our previous encounter.

'Sit,' I said.

He sank slowly to his knees, keeping his hands high. Sensible. He sat down, instinctively angled so that his private parts were shielded.

He looked at me with calm hatred. 'You are a dead man.'

'That's one of the things we must talk about Julius. No one needs to know about this . . . uncomfortable moment between us. Oh, before I forget . . .' I took out the camera, aimed so that the barrel of the gun and Inkunzi were in the picture and took another photograph.

He cursed, colourfully and at length.

'If I ever get the idea you are looking for me, or for anyone that I know, I will put these up at the Bull Run, the Sandton police station, I will put them on your X5's windscreen, I will send them to the tabloids and to every rival and accomplice you have, and I will put them on the Internet. And I will tell everyone who wants to know how easy it was to tame the Bull in his own *kraal*. On the other hand, if you want to keep our chat confidential, you have my complete cooperation.'

I let him chew over that, but didn't get a positive response. His face showed only hatred.

'Come on, Julius, you have a reputation to uphold. Especially after Flea van Jaarsveld, also known as Cornél, fooled the both of us.'

I saw his recognition at the name.

'The diamonds were on the lorry,' I said.

Surprise. 'You lie.'

'Remember the sores on the rhinos, those sickly pink growths? Plastic, all along, Inkunzi. The diamonds were inside them. I had to go all the way to Zimbabwe yesterday before I could work it out. But you knew about the cargo. The important thing is, I want you to ask yourself why I went to all this trouble to come here tonight if I already knew about the diamonds. Why would I lie? The truth is, Flea has taken something from me, and I want it back. You want the stones. We can help each other.'

He digested this, straightened up a little. 'Give me my bathrobe,' he said, his voice reasonable, pointing at a white garment hanging from a hook against the wall. Negotiation is give and take. I tossed it at him. He draped himself in it. 'How can we help each other?' The change of gear was too rapid. I didn't trust him.

'Help me track her down.'

He laughed without humour.

'Funny?'

'Impossible.'

'Nothing is impossible. How did you know about the diamonds?'

'Let me get dressed first.'

'That is not going to happen.'

'Then it will be a long night.'

'Only if you have lost interest in the diamonds.'

'I don't negotiate in a shower.'

I liked the shower. It reduced his options. But I would have to let him restore some dignity. As long as I kept him away from the gun safe in the walk-in wardrobe. 'Come,' I said, 'but slowly.'

He rose, and put the bathrobe on. I walked backwards into the big bedroom. He followed me.

'I want a smoke.' He gestured at his bedside cabinet where a pack of Camels and a Zippo lighter lay beside a bunch of keys.

I nodded, keeping the MAG trained on him, and moved across to the couch against the window. Inkunzi had closed the curtains behind it. I sat down. He tapped out a cigarette, lit it, sat on the bed.

'The ashtray . . .' He pointed at the coffee table in front of me, where there was a heavy glass one.

'Use the carpet.' I didn't want to give him anything he could throw at me.

He blew smoke through his nose. Angry.

'How did you know about the diamonds?'

He drew deeply on the cigarette, stared at it, seeming deep in thought. 'I hear a lot of stories.'

'It's a story you must have heard in great detail, because you knew exactly where to find us.'

'There are Zimbabweans on my team.'

My team. The sport of organised crime.

'And they heard about Flea and Johnson Chitepo?'

He gave me a look, impressed. 'You know a lot.'

'Not enough.'

He rested his elbows on his knees, bent over away from me, as if he were thinking. Drew on his cigarette, blew the smoke out in a long slow stream. 'We heard about a deal. Chitepo and some others. The first story was it was coming through the Kruger Park. Then, a day before the time, we heard it was one Cornél van Jaarsveld behind the plan, and they were coming across the border near Musina. In a Bedford truck. Later that night, they said no, it's a Mercedes.'

'How did they know?'

'The man who Cornél hired to drive the Bedford. But first he had to get away from you before . . .'

The driver of the Bedford, the man in the yellow vest, muscular arms, cigarette in his mouth. I put two and two together. 'She made him wait in Kwekwe so she could stick the diamonds on the rhinos first. That's why you didn't know.'

Inkunzi just nodded.

'And you heard nothing else? Who were the people Chitepo made his deal with?'

'I don't know.' But he was lying. I let it go for now.

'And then you just let us go, without encouraging Flea to tell you where the diamonds were? It doesn't make sense to me.'

He shrugged.

'Come on, Julius. Why didn't you shoot me? Why didn't you torture Flea just a little? You're not the kind of guy who has a problem with violence.'

He had finished the cigarette. He looked around for a place to dispose of the stub. He wasn't keen to answer my question, which confirmed my suspicions.

'You knew who the final buyer was, Julius. You knew where she was going. And the only reason you were prepared to let us go was so you could put Plan B into action. But Plan B was not as profitable or as easy as Plan A . . .'

'I want to put this down,' he waved the stub at the bedside cabinet.

'Slowly.'

He stretched out an arm, put the stub down carefully beside the bunch of keys so that it stood upright, the glowing end upwards. Then he pressed a finger on something in the bunch of keys and the alarm began to wail in the roof above us and he looked at me and said, 'You're fuckin' dead.'

He threw the keys at me and jumped up, moving towards the wardrobe.

I ignored his projectile, pulled the trigger.

Nothing happened.

48

Unless one is an excellent marksman and knows exactly when and where to shoot an animal, it may be better not to shoot at all, since there is nothing more dangerous than a wounded animal.

The Art of Tracking: Dangerous animals

The MAG's safety catch is on the left of the trigger, but it also has a locking catch on the grip below the barrel. That is the one I had forgotten, accustomed to my missing Glock, which has no safety mechanism bar the stiffness of the trigger.

In feverish haste I press the chunky shotgun's locking catch as I jump up, aim, see Inkunzi jerk open the louvre door to the wardrobe. He dives, I shoot, too soon. Splinters, dust, big hole in the wood. Run, have to get him before he opens his gun safe, precious seconds.

Must count my shots, just six rounds in the magazine. Five to go.

He's at the door, big Smith & Wesson Model 500 in his hand, I drop flat, he shoots. Ear-splitting thunder, a miss. He must have had it hidden under a shirt. I dive, roll, aim for the light in the centre of the ceiling, pull the trigger, keep rolling.

Four left.

Still too light in the room. The TV. I turn, shoot it out, roll.

Sudden darkness. Three left.

The telephone starts ringing. Security company.

His revolver thunders, bullet cracking beside me. I roll towards the bed, knowing I'm in trouble, both his companions will be coming, the passage door is not an option, the security company will be on the way if no one answers the phone. Only one choice: take Inkunzi out, use the sliding door to the swimming pool.

They hammer on the door to the passage, shouting. I turn, shoot through it, a henchman screams on the other side, falls.

I only have two shots left.

Roll behind the bed, jump upright fast, beam of light through the hole in the door, see Inkunzi as he sees me, no choice, shoot him in the chest. He falls, pulling off a shot, it hits the ceiling.

I swing the MAG at the passage door, there is one more out there.

One shot left.

I hear Julius choking, gurgling. This is not what I wanted.

Voice from down the passage. 'Inkunzi?'

I crawl over the bed.

The Bull lies there, big hole next to his heart, blood pumping onto the carpet. That terrible rattling in his throat.

Then he is quiet.

'Inkunzi?' Urgently.

I point the gun at the door, nothing to be seen.

He would crouch or kneel, stay out of sight.

I have to get away from here. I clamber over the bed, take the Smith & Wesson out of Inkunzi's hand, can't remember how many times he fired. I jump up, towards the curtains, pluck them aside, unlock the sliding door.

The passage door splinters behind me, I spin around, shadow rolling in, I shoot. He bellows. Got him.

I throw the empty MAG to the right, against the wall. He shoots at it. Swap the revolver to my right hand, lift its weight, see him struggle upright. I pull the trigger, two shots. He drops.

I run to the sliding door, push it aside. The alarm and the telephone clamouring inside. How much time do I have?

Stop and think. Black bag still in the toilet. Inkunzi's keys on the floor. I snap the Smith & Wesson's cylinder open. All five rounds fired. Throw it down, go back in the room. Silent inside. I climb over the bodies, slipping in the blood. Find the keys, pick up the henchman's handgun. Smaller revolver, looks like a Colt. Out through the passage door. The one lying there is not dead. His right arm is shot away, he holds the stump with his left hand, trying to stem the blood.

'Help me.'

It's the one who helped kick me during the hijacking. He stares at me, his eyes narrow. He recognises me. Reaches quickly for his pistol on the carpet.

'No,' I say.

He knows this is about survival, his fingers wrap around the grip.

I shoot him in the heart.

Then I throw the Colt away in revulsion and rage, because I didn't plan it like this, this is not what I intended.

I run down the passage, into the toilet, grab my bag, head out. Look for the garage, find a door leading out of the spacious, modern, spotless kitchen.

Telephone stops ringing. Bad sign.

Look for the remote control on the keys. Four buttons. Press the red one. Alarm stops.

Press the other buttons one by one. Hear the gate slide open. Then open the garage door. I jump into the BMW, push the key in, switch on. Automatic gearbox, put it in reverse. Drive.

Unarmed. If the response team arrives . . .

Out of the gate, jam the X5 into gear, pull away, accelerate.

A security van approaches from the front, siren wailing.

I put my foot down. Pull my cap down.

Past them.

Watch him in the rear-view mirror.

He turns in at the Bull's house.

'Fuck,' said Jeanette Louw. Disgust in her voice.

In my hotel room I held the cellphone to my ear, but said nothing.

'Where is the fucking BMW now?'

'In front of the Bull Run.'

Her voice softened. 'You know you're trouble.'

'I know.' But I don't go looking for it, it comes looking for me.

BOOK 3: MILLA
(A Theory of Chaos)

19 September to 11 October 2009

We must live so that we leave tracks on every day

Photostatic record: Diary of Milla Strachan,
27 September 2009

49

Photostatic record: *Diary of Milla Strachan*
Date of entry: *19 September 2009*
My book is not progressing. The story is insignificant, too careful, fearful, just like my life.

From: *t.masilo@pia.gov.org.za*
To: *quinn@pia.gov.org*
Cc: *director@pia.gov.org.za; raj@pia.gov.org.za*
Sent: *Sat 2009-09-21 11.31*
Marked: *Urgent*

Operation Shawwal

Quinn
Please note that the surveillance of the Supreme Committee, the Restless Ravens, Julius Shabangu and our fishing expedition in Walvis Bay will henceforth fall under the auspices of 'Operation Shawwal'. It shall enjoy the utmost focus, and the highest priority. Brief daily reports are essential.
Furthermore:
1. Please ensure that Reinhard Rohn understands the urgency. He has six operatives at his disposal, but is there a detailed plan? Let him draw one up, and supply him with everything he needs. We absolutely have to intercept that arms shipment.
2. I am not satisfied with our intelligence on the Restless Ravens, and need a plan of action before the end of Monday 21 September to dramatically improve this.
3. We cannot afford to lose three days of calls on the Shabangu wiretap every week, especially in the next two to four weeks. How do we rectify this?
4. Please report in full, before Wednesday 23 September, on the security measures for the Cape Town Stadium, re the Fifa visit on 12 October.

21 September 2009. Monday.

'The American soccer team? Pure speculation, Tau. Where is your proof?' Janina Mentz asked.

'We can't just do nothing, the risk is too great.'

'So what do you want to do? Talk to the newspapers?'

'We will have to inform the Commissioner of Police, take him into our confidence.'

'That is as good as going to the tabloids.'

'Ma'am, we can't simply do nothing.'

'What do you want to do, Tau?'

'Arrest the Supreme Committee. Take them out of circulation, tie them up in court appearances, put them under a spotlight so bright that this whole affair burns clean.'

'No,' she said.

'Why not?' Masilo asked.

She was annoyed. 'We'll end up looking like fools, Tau. You're the lawyer, you should know. What do we do when the judge dismisses the case, because he *will*, you know that very well. Where does that leave us? With disaffected friends in the Middle East, a President who will have lost all faith in us, and Muslim extremists going deeper underground. Is that what you want?'

'I want to prevent the attack, the far greater damage of an act of terror.'

'In an idiotic way?'

'That's unfair . . .'

'If your people had done their work, we wouldn't be in this position.'

'My people do their best . . .'

'Their best? Sorry for the bloodbath, Mr President, sorry for the humiliation and the shame, but we did our best. You might as well merge us, we are just as useless as National Intelligence.'

'Is that what this is about?'

'May I say something?' said Raj. He had never seen the phlegmatic Masilo like this. It made him uneasy.

'What are you insinuating, Tau?' Mentz asked.

'I'm not insinuating, I'm asking . . .'

'I have an idea . . .' said Rajkumar.

'And what are you asking?'

'I am asking what is most important to us.'

'We can track the ships,' said Rajkumar.

'You're implying that . . .' Suddenly she looked at Rajkumar. 'What did you say?'

'We can track the fishing vessels of Consolidated. In Walvis Bay.'

'How?'

'We've done some probing into their systems, their digital security is pretty ordinary, which is not really surprising, I mean, they catch fish, after all . . .'

'Raj . . .'

'They use Lloyd's MIU, specifically the Automatic Identification System Fleet Tracker, or AIS. It's a real-time system, they log onto the Lloyds website with a password to see where their ships are, at any given moment. It's satellite based, sort of like GPS tracking for grown-ups, very sophisticated, very accurate. If we can get in, we can see where their vessels have been, where they are at any given moment, and, hopefully, plot where they are going. Of course, we need to get the password. And then we simply mask our IP, or we use theirs.'

'How do we get the password?'

'We'll have to plant a key logger. But I'm thinking, let's do more. I mean, with all due respect, we now have six operatives there, but no guarantees. Let's go the whole hog. Let's get a pipe into their system. Let's see the whole damn picture.'

Mentz thought for a long time. Eventually she nodded. 'OK.'

Rajkumar glowed.

Just before they walked out, she said to the Advocate, 'I'll talk to the Minister. About October twelfth.'

50

25 September 2009. Friday.

Operation Shawwal
Transcription: *Audio surveillance, J. Shabangu, cellphone conversation*
Date and Time: *25 September 2009. 12.42*

(Unknown): Mhoroi, Inkunzi, how are you?

JS: You tell me.

(Unknown): I have big news, Inkunzi.

JS: Yes?

(Unknown): It is not Kruger Park, Inkunzi, it is Musina, and it happens tomorrow, Inkunzi, maybe tomorrow night . . .

JS: No maybe, I don't want any maybe, I want definite.

(Unknown): Inkunzi, they will be coming down from Kwekwe tomorrow morning, definitely, in an old Bedford truck. Colonel van Jaarsveld, a South African, is the smuggler. My man is the relief driver, he says they have to take the back roads, they have to keep away from the roadblocks, so it will take all day to get to the border. They can't be there before five o'clock at the earliest.

JS: And they are coming through the Musina border? Beit Bridge?

(Unknown): No, Inkunzi, they are smuggling, they won't go through the border post. My man says, some illegal crossing, somewhere between Beit Bridge and the Botswana border, we think Mapungubwe National Park, it is the obvious place.

JS: You think? You fucking think?

(Unknown): Please, Inkunzi, this Colonel did not tell my man where. But there are not many roads for a big truck on your side. Look at the maps.

JS: You sure it's a Bedford?

(Unknown): Dead sure, Inkunzi.

26 September 2009. Saturday.

Once everyone had taken their place in the Ops Room, Masilo said: 'Listen to me very carefully. We have only one goal – to intercept the diamonds. And we have only one chance. The operators in the field are totally dependent on us. They cannot intercept Julius Shabangu and his troops unless we tell them exactly where to go. So I want absolute professionalism, absolute focus. If you get tired, if you lose concentration, come and tell me and we will bring in a relief. There is a great deal riding on this. A great deal.'

Then they set to work. The audio feed was relayed so they could listen to Julius Inkunzi's cellphone when he used it, so they could keep in contact with the seven teams of PIA operators – a team for each possible route in the Musina area, and an extra team as backup.

They listened to Shabangu directing his people and their vehicles like a general.

'He has ten vehicles,' said an audio surveillance operator.

'He wants the diamonds real bad,' said Rajkumar.

At twelve-thirty p.m., after a one-sided telephone conversation, Quinn reported: 'There is no South African who goes by the rank and surname of a Colonel van Jaarsveld who has entered Zim in the past six months. We have twelve van Jaarsvelds crossing the border, nine men, three women.'

Advocate Tau Masilo murmured something inaudible, took a deep breath and said: 'Bring me the original sound file.'

Wearing earphones, Masilo sat in front of the laptop, writing pad beside him. At a quarter to one he took the headset off and asked: 'I want the details of all the van Jaarsvelds with names starting with a "C" or a "K".'

'I'll print it,' said Quinn.

Everyone in the room looked at Masilo expectantly.

'Might not be a rank, might be a name, badly pronounced,' he said.

'Aah,' said Rajkumar.

At one o'clock Masilo looked up from the list of names and asked Rajkumar: 'The Afrikaner guy on the Report Squad, what's his name?'

'Theunie.'

'What's his extension?'

'You want to talk to him now?'

'Yes.'

'Hang on,' said Rajkumar, then dialled Mother Killian and asked to talk to Theunie. He held the receiver out to Masilo.

'Theunie . . . ? We have a woman with the name of Cornelia Johanna. Is it possible that she would be called Cornel? Or something?' Masilo listened a while, said, 'Thank you,' and put down the phone. 'Cornelia Johanna van Jaarsveld. Her ID number is on the list. Get a home address, get people there. I want to know everything there is to know.'

The day was a slow poison, gradually paralysing everyone. Tension, boredom, frustration. At ten past three, a little excitement.

Over the loudspeaker, Shabangu's voice as he answered his cellphone: 'Stop fucking calling me.'

'*Ouboet*, I am just as tired as you are. Let's get this thing behind us . . .'

'Fuck you,' said Shabangu, and ended the call.

The operator who had sent Quinn the original sound files, looked up and grinned. 'Becker,' he whispered.

Quinn nodded.

'Who?' Rajkumar and Masilo asked in unison.

Before they could answer, there was another call. Becker again. '*Ouboet*, I'm not going to stop calling until this thing . . .'

Shabangu: 'Where did you get this fucking number?'

'One of your men gave it to me.'

'Which one?'

'He says his name is Kenosi.'

Shabangu cursed over the ether in Zulu, a stream of words that cracked like a whip. Then: 'I'm going to come and get you.'

'*Ouboet*, bring the money when you come.'

'Fuck you, Boer.'

'*Ouboet*, should I rather come to your house? Kenosi told me where you . . .'

The call was abruptly cut off by Shabangu.

The surveillance operator laughed. 'Guy's got nerve.'

'What the hell was that all about?' asked Masilo.

'Who *is* this guy?' Raj asked again.

Shabangu's voice interrupted them again: Becker was calling a third time. 'Fuck off, just fuck off, I will not answer again.'

End of call.

'You *know* about this man?' asked Masilo.

They filled him in, briefly, about the white man who wanted his money back, apparently after a car hijacking.

'Why must I only hear about this now?'

Before anyone could explain, an operator said: 'Guys, we have a problem.'

Everyone looked at him.

'Shabangu has just sent an SMS. It reads: "Cellphone now off. Call Thato."'

'Shit,' said Rajkumar. 'Shit, shit, shit.'

'That's it. He's off-line.'

'What are the implications?' asked Masilo.

'Big,' said Rajkumar. 'Bad. He's been our primary, the number we've been tracking.'

'Can we intercept the other numbers, the recipients of the SMS?'

Rajkumar jumped up, waddled over to the door. 'We need more equipment in that area. It's going to take hours. I'll get on it.'

Tau Masilo slowly lowered his head into his hands. 'Beckett? Is that his name? Will no one rid me of this turbulent priest?'

'No,' said Quinn. 'Becker. His name is Lukas Becker.'

The big electronic clock on the Ops Room wall read 23.35.

They were tired and fed up, because they knew it would fail. Not one of the PIA's seven teams on the Zimbabwe and Botswana borders had seen a Bedford truck.

Masilo did not hide his disappointment. In them, in everything.

Suddenly in a clear, optimistic tone an operator said: 'Shabangu is back on-line.'

'Thank God,' said Rajkumar and took another bite of his hamburger.

'Amen,' said Quinn, quietly.

'SMSs coming in.'

'Read them to us.'

'The first says, "Mercedes 1528".'

Quinn Googled the message.

'Second SMS is just numbers.'

'Read them!'

'S23 54.793 E28 27.243.'

'Jesus,' said Masilo, and looked at Quinn: 'GPS coordinates.'

'Mercedes 1528 is a truck . . .' Quinn added.

'Shit,' said Rajkumar, putting his hamburger aside hurriedly, his fingers dancing across the keyboard to pinpoint the coordinates. 'The coordinates are way south of the border . . . way south, shit, T-junction where the R518 and the D579 join.'

'Then let's get people down there. Now.' Masilo leaped up and began pacing up and down.

Quinn barked orders over the radio.

51

27 September 2009. Sunday.

Masilo got to bed at four in the morning. At 08.07 Rahjev Rajkumar's phone call woke him. 'The boss says she wants to see us and our department heads in the Ops Room at 10.00.'

Masilo rubbed his eyes, cleared his throat. 'I'm not going to accept unfair criticism.'

'We will have to accept whatever we get,' said Rajkumar soothingly.

'No,' said Masilo.

The informant and the agent had their heads together as if they were gossiping. They stood in an alley near the pavilion of the De Grendel sports complex in Parow, only 300 metres from the station where the informant had got off the train.

'Tweetybird's wife and children are gone, my *bru'*, got on a plane yesterday, to Paraguay or Uruguay. And everyone's saying The Bird will fly tomorrow, false passport, permanent exile. And now they say, it's Terror versus the Money Man, it's gonna be a war, I'm telling you.'

'Hang on. Terror Baadjies. He's the Restless Ravens' strongman, the Enforcer.'

'Yes.'

'And the Money Man is Moegamat Perkins. Tweetybird's accountant.'

'Yes.'

'Where is Tweetybird now?'

'He's lying low.'

'But where?'

'Not a clue, he's afraid the Prosecutor will lock him up for tax evasion before he can leave the country.'

'And Terror Baadjies? We can't find Terror.'

'They say he's the one who has to see that Tweetybird gets safely on the plane. They are hiding somewhere, but nobody knows where.'

The agent took five 100-rand notes out of his pocket and slipped them into the waiting hand of the informant. 'If you can tell us where they are I will give you 5,000.'

'*Jissis*, my *bru'* . . . I'll try . . .'

Late that morning Mrs Killian phoned Milla. 'I know it's Sunday, but we need you. Can you come to the office, please?'

'Of course.'

Half an hour later she walked into the Report Squad. With the exception of Jessica, all the others were there.

'What's going on?' Milla asked.

Donald MacFarland sighed deeply, looking worried. 'If they call us in on a weekend, the shit has hit the fan.'

The Goddess only arrived an hour later. 'I was on a yacht, for God's sake. Don't these people have a life?'

'Welcome to my world,' said Mac the Wife.

It was a day of whispering about The Great Confrontation. It was a day of writing short reports, slowly, with odd fragments of information that trickled in hour after hour.

Oom Theunie was working on the profile of a young woman.

'Where do they *find* these people?' he asked. Later, shaking his head, he tested aloud the phrase 'disappeared without trace'.

'What?' asked Mac, irritated.

'Cornelia Johanna van Jaarsveld seems to be a professional tracker, Mac. But the irony is that she has disappeared without trace herself.'

Milla smiled. She was busy with a report on one Ephraim Silongo, also known as 'Snake'. She added to it systematically as the agents' reports were sent in. Snake Silongo's body had been found on a deserted gravel road in the Waterberg of Limpopo Province, bones broken, bullet wound to the head. Police information was that he was an armed robber, part of Julius Shabangu's syndicate.

'Didn't we do something recently on a Julius Shabangu?' she asked.

'We did,' said Oom Theunie. 'It will be in the database.'

While she searched, she thought again about the bubble she had lived in, her ignorance of the undercurrents in this country.

It was Donald MacFarland who told them, after a whispered phone call, about The Great Confrontation. 'I hear the Iron Lady exploded this morning,' he said.

'What?' asked The Goddess, always inquisitive when she heard Mac's gossipy tone.

'Apparently, my dear, the much venerated Director threw a tantrum, amongst other objects . . .'

They all huddled around, and in muted tones and with frequent glances at Ma Killian's door, Mac repeated the rumour with as much verbal embellishment as possible. Something that happened last night, an operation had gone horribly wrong. And this morning Janina Mentz had called all senior personnel into the Ops Room, Mother Killian included. She stood in front of her audience, glared at the latecomers, waited till everyone was seated. Then she began to berate them. '"Never in my life have I seen such mediocrity, such inept imbecility," that's how she started, and it went downhill from there,' said Mac with great relish. 'She really *did* throw things. And then Mr Nobody dared to take her on, and she asked the rest to leave, and then the two of them had a showdown behind closed doors, they say you could hear them shouting at each other down the hall.'

Masilo walked into Janina Mentz's office with a single sheet of paper in his hand. He stood in front of her desk and said: 'Here is my letter of resignation. It is dated the fourteenth of October. If I can't prevent the terrorist attack, I will leave. If I am successful, it will be up to you to decide whether you accept this or not.'

Mentz stared at him, her expression impenetrable.

'We can't trace Willem de la Cruz or Terrence Richard Baadjies.' Masilo's monotone betrayed his weariness, his resignation. 'We suspect they have gone somewhere to receive the consignment of diamonds. We also suspect that de la Cruz is only waiting to complete the trade with the Supreme Committee before he flees to South America. Consequently, we are monitoring all international flights from Cape Town and Oliver Tambo Airport. We have liaised with traffic authorities in the Western Cape; they will hold every Mercedes 1528 truck that stops at a weighbridge on the way to Cape Town, until one of our agents has searched it. We have intensified the surveillance and tracking of Suleiman Dolly, Shaheed Latif Osman, Ebrahim Laattoe and Baboo Rayan. The reaction unit is ready if there is any contact between the Supreme Committee and the Restless Ravens. The operation to gain access to the computer system of Consolidated Fisheries will take place on Monday just after midnight.'

Still Mentz sat there, sphinx-like.

'Currently, we are investigating the feasibility of a plan to insert an electro-acoustic microphone in the cellar of 15 Chamberlain Street. The only way is to keep Baboo Rayan away from the house for at least an hour, possibly by a sham robbery of the café he visits every morning. It will have to be done with great circumspection as we don't know what security measures are in place inside the Committee's house. Finally: we will maintain the surveillance of Julius Shabangu until the thirteenth of October.'

Then he turned and walked out.

52

Photostatic record: *Diary of Milla Strachan*
Date of entry: *27 September 2009*

Leaving tracks, creating some impression on the surface of this earth, is a way of saying 'I was here'. Something to give meaning to this fleeting existence.

How do you leave a track, a trail, a spoor?

And what sort of spoor do I want to leave? What sort of traces *can* I leave? Why would I want to leave my mark? Is it just fear, fear of being forgotten, since being forgotten makes a whole life pointless. Is that my actual fear? Is that why I want to write a book, my only (last!) chance to leave something tangible, a small scrap of evidence that I was here?

And what is the point of that?

I should also ask, then, what is the point of this diary? Is this not evidence? I was here, this is what happened to me. And how many of my journals are merely the writing down of nothing. Thoughts, sighs, murmurs, but nothing happened, nothing was done.

Because some days leave no tracks.

They pass as though they never existed, immediately forgotten in the haze of my routine. Other days' tracks are visible for a week or so, until the winds of memory cover them in the pale sand of new experiences.

How many of the average 22,000 days of our lives do we remember, date and day? Maybe ten or twelve, birthdays, weddings (desertions and divorces!) and deaths, a few of the First Times. The traces of the others wear away, so that a life really only consists of a month of specially commemorated days and a host of dateless recollections.

We must live so that we leave tracks on every day.

But how?

The Pilatus PC-12 landed at Walvis Bay at 13.52. It was the 'Combi' model, fitted out for four passengers and considerable cargo – in this instance, 200 kilograms of computer hardware.

The four men, respectively, two break-in specialists and two of Rajhev Rajkumar's best technicians, climbed out, offloaded the crates of equipment and waited for Reinhard Rohn, who came towards them over the tarred surface, with an import permit in hand and two customs officers at his side.

It took ten minutes to deal with the formalities. Rohn fetched his bakkie to transport the crates. Once they were loaded, the break-in specialists and technicians, each with an overnight bag slung over the shoulder, walked off to the car hire section. Rohn watched them go, noting the lean bodies, the brash self-confidence.

I was like that too, he thought. Long ago.

Operation Shawwal
Transcription: *Audio surveillance, J. Shabangu and L. Becker, cellphone conversation*
Date and Time: *27 September 2009. 17.21*

JS: I don't have your fucking money and I'm telling you now, if I get my hands on you, you are going to bleed . . .
LB: Ay, *Ouboet*, that won't get us anywhere. Who has my money then?
JS: Fuck off.
(Call terminated.)

Operation Shawwal
Transcription: *Audio surveillance, J. Shabangu and L. Becker, cellphone conversation*
Date and Time: *27 September 2009. 17.29*

LB: *Ouboet*, what a surprise . . .
JS: I'm going to tell you who has your money. Then you leave me alone.
LB: On my word of honour.
JS: Shaheed Latif Osman. Go and ask him.
LB: Who is Shaheed Latif Osman?
JS: He's a fuckin' *isela*, he lives in the Cape. He's got your money. Every fucking cent. I'm going to SMS you his number. You tell him, he and Tweety the Bird must give you your money. Tell him I said they should do it.
LB: *Ouboet*, I thank you . . .
JS: Don't phone me again, fucking never again!

At 23.00 Quinn went to the office to monitor the break-in and installation taking place in Walvis Bay.

The operator had him listen to the conversation between Gauteng crime boss Julius Shabangu and the mysterious Lukas Becker. When it had finished Quinn shook his head in concern and disbelief. He wrote a quick email to Masilo and Rajkumar. He said that Becker was no longer just comic relief, since it was his call to Shabangu that had upset the Musina interception so dramatically. He was an unknown factor, with the potential to derail the whole operation. Consequently, they urgently needed to find out more, do an in-depth profile on him. And seriously consider intercepting him.

He sent the email and went to the Ops Room. Fifteen minutes before the Walvis Bay break-in. He sent up an emergency prayer. Dear Lord, please don't let there be any mistakes tonight. Amen.

28 September 2009. Monday.

Twenty past twelve at night, Milla's cellphone dragged her from sleep and she stumbled to the sitting room with a feeling of foreboding. She saw it was Barend calling and her stomach contracted.

'Are you OK?' was the first thing she asked.

'It's Pa,' he said.

Milla had to sit down suddenly. 'What happened?'

'He's been assaulted. He's in hospital.'

'Assaulted? Where?' She couldn't understand the reproach in her son's voice, it was not her fault.

'In Jacobsdal, but the ambulance took them to Kimberley . . .'

'Barend, how serious is it?'

'Serious. They broke his cheekbone and nose and his ribs . . .'

'How do you know this? How did you hear about it?'

'He phoned me, just now . . .'

'Your father phoned you?'

'Yes . . .'

Relief, and she nearly said, 'It can't be too bad then'. She sank back slowly on the couch. 'Who assaulted him? Why?'

'A bunch of guys just walked in and started beating them up . . .'

'Them?'

'Oom Tjaart and Oom Langes and Oom Raynier, they were on the Harleys, they stopped in Jacobsdal to have a drink, then these freaks came into the bar and started beating them . . .'

That was why Barend had to go to his grandparents for the holiday. So Christo and friends could go on a Harley road trip. He was still not taking his fatherly duties seriously, he still put himself first. But she would have to restrain herself, her son needed her.

'Does Granny know?'

'No.'

'I'll phone the hospital and find out how serious it is, then I'll call you back.'

'Ma, why don't you phone Pa?'

'A doctor would . . . we need an expert opinion.'

Only once she had rung off, did she realise Barend's question meant that he still had hope, that he saw the assault as an opportunity to bring her and Christo back together.

Half an hour later she phoned Barend. 'I spoke to the ward nurse. She says none of their injuries are serious, they will all be discharged later today.'

'How will Pa get home, Ma? He can't ride his bike with broken ribs. Can't we go and fetch him?'

'There are regular flights between Kimberley and Cape Town, Barend . . .'

'Ma, how can you be so unfeeling?'

Rajkumar was not good with conflict management. So this meeting was painful to him, the oppressive atmosphere, the obvious antagonism between the Director and Masilo. A contributing factor was that there would be no praise, despite the good work of the previous night.

Masilo was stubborn. He stood throughout the meeting. It was a form of protest, Raj thought, a way of saying: if I sit down at a table with her, it indicates consent, solidarity.

And Mentz would not look at Masilo. She sat beside Raj, her eyes on the wall, while Rajkumar gave his report. 'The operation at Consolidated Fisheries was a resounding success, beautiful teamwork between Tau's operatives and my technicians,' he said and looked at her, saw it made no impression.

'Go on.'

'We are now cloning all their drives. Some of the software is proprietary, some is custom written, but we will be up and running in record time,' said with all the optimistic enthusiasm he could muster. 'The really great news is that we are already logged into their Fleet Tracker website. We will have a full report on all vessels' patterns for the last month by lunchtime.'

She merely nodded. 'Anything else?' she asked without looking at Masilo.

'Only bad news,' the Advocate said. 'We can't trace de la Cruz or Baadjies. Our attempt to intercept the truck has produced nothing. That is all.'

Milla was the first one in the office. Mrs Killian hurried in carrying a thin file. She greeted her, and placed the folder in front of Milla.

'Theunie will explain to you how a new profile works, look at this until he gets here. We only expect the first reports from the operators tomorrow, the idea is that you add to the document as you receive new information . . .'

Milla opened the file. Just one sheet of paper, the original instruction under the title: *In-depth Profile: Lukas Becker.*

'This is an important one, Milla. You need to focus . . .'

Operation Shawwal

Transcription: *Audio surveillance, A. Hendricks and L. Becker, cellphone conversation*

Date and Time: *27 September 2009. 17.41*

LB: *Kan ek met Shaheed Latif Osman praat, asseblief?*

AH: I'm sorry . . . ?

LB: *Verstaan jy Afrikaans, Ouboet?*

AH: Who is this, please?

LB: My name is Lukas Becker, I'm looking for Shaheed Latif Osman.

AH: I think you have the wrong number, sir.

LB: Tweety the Bird? Is he available?

AH: You definitely have the wrong number.

LB: Are you sure?
AH: There's nobody here by those names.
LB: OK. Sorry.

In the office of the Minister, over a cup of tea, Janina Mentz chose her words carefully, as she had prepared thoroughly. 'Sir, we have a potential target for the act of terror, and it seems to be a highly sensitive one. Of course, our first priority is to secure the target, But we have two dilemmas. Firstly we have no incontrovertible evidence that it *is* the target. We are speculating on the grounds of a date that we intercepted from the extremists. Secondly, to secure the possible target, we would need the assistance of our colleagues at law enforcement, with the possible inclusion of certain *local* authorities. As you know, the DA provincial government in the Western Cape will try to gain political advantage out of anything. We simply can't trust them.'

The Minister nodded his agreement.

'I am here for advice, sir. How can we prevent the terrorism, without jeopardising the whole operation?'

29 September 2009. Tuesday.

'If there was contact between the Ravens and the Committee, we've missed it. Or maybe there was no contact,' Quinn said.

'So where are the diamonds?' asked Rajkumar.

'On their way to Oman.'

The two deputy directors looked sharply at Quinn.

'Think about it,' he said. 'They are Muslim extremists. The stones are tainted. Sinful. They don't want to touch them. And they want as little contact with the Ravens as possible, for all the obvious reasons. So what are the options? You tell Terror Baadjies to pack it all into a strongbox, and DHL the thing to Macki in Oman. The minute it arrives, the money is paid over. Or something like that.'

Masilo just sat there.

Rajkumar said, 'Shit.'

Quinn said, 'We have to assume that the deal is done and dusted. We need to focus on the weapons now. Or explosives. Or whatever the hell it is they're going to smuggle in. And the 12th of October.'

53

30 September 2009. Wednesday.

Milla showed Oom Theunie the four new documents for the Lukas Becker dossier – a single sheet from the National Population Register, a concise bank report, a SAPS query, and a printout of an email from a R. Harris. 'It reveals nothing,' she said. 'And . . . it's not very good.'

He took a look at them, then explained. 'R. Harris is the PIA operator, he sits in a little office somewhere, receives an instruction that says go and find out more about so-and-so, and make it snappy. It's not his job to interpret or organise, he's just the collector of information. So he sends every bit as he goes along. It's our job to put the pieces of the puzzle together. Some of these profiles can look like mangy strays for weeks, then suddenly a whole bunch of meaningful data comes through. It's normal. Don't worry about it, you do what you can, with what you have.'

'I understand,' Milla said. 'Thanks.'

Report: *Profile – Lukas Becker*
Date: *30 September 2009*
Compiled by: *Milla Strachan. Field report: R. Harris.*

Background

Lukas Becker (42) currently of no fixed address, was born on 23 July 1967 in Bloemfontein, the son of J.A. and E.D. Becker, apparently from Smithfield. Credit card expenses indicate a presence in Johannesburg, especially the Sandton area, since 13 September 2009. Purchases include clothing (R2,118.64) and meals.

Criminal record

None. (According to ID number Becker was the victim of a car hijacking in Johannesburg.)

Education and Training

BA degree in History. (Unconfirmed.)

Finances

Becker has four accounts at Standard Bank:

A cheque account. Balance: R2,294.60.

A Mastercard credit card account. Balance: R4,646.27.

An investment account (32-day notice). Balance: R138,701.89.

An investment account (Fixed deposit). Balance: R1 425,007.22

Transfers to and from a current account with Wells Fargo in the USA (balance unknown).

Late that afternoon Mrs Killian gave Milla new documentation on Lukas Becker. She saw there were two field operators working on the profile. She wondered what that meant. What could a man with a degree in history have done that was so bad?

She read, in a hurry and inquisitive.

She saw the study majors first, and that fascinated her. When she came to the information on Lukas Becker's parents, she lowered her head and read more attentively.

Report: *Profile – Lukas Becker*

Date: *30 September 2009*

Compiled by: *Milla Strachan. Field report R. Harris and P. Lepono.*

Background

Lukas Becker (42) currently of no fixed address, was born on 23 July 1967 in Bloemfontein.

He is the only child of Johannes Andreas Becker (1934–2001) former owner and farmer of the farm Rietfontein in the district of Smithfield, and Esther Debora Becker (née Faber, 1941–1999), former teacher, later housewife. (Mostly unconfirmed.)

After his school education (Smithfield Primary School, and Grey College, Bloemfontein) he matriculated with a distinction in History in 1984. After two years' compulsory military service in the SA Navy, he completed a full-time degree in B Agric at the University of the Free State in 1989. A BA degree in History and Anthropology (part time, UNISA, 1994), and post-graduate study in the USA followed. (The latter unconfirmed.)

Parents

Around 1995 Esther Debora Becker was committed to an institution for the mentally disturbed, allegedly Witrand in the former Transvaal, and later to a private clinic in Johannesburg, where she died of natural causes in 1999. (Unconfirmed.)

Johannes Andreas Becker was allegedly declared bankrupt in 2000, and the farm Rietfontein was sold to W.E. Stegmann, who continues to farm the property. Becker Senior committed suicide in 2001 in Margate, KwaZulu-Natal – See list of references.

Working career

After his full-time studies for B Agric degree at the UFS, Becker joined the Navy again (Permanent Force), and worked at Simonstown from 1990 to 1994, achieving the rank of Lieutenant. (Unconfirmed.)
After that he worked overseas.

54

1 October 2009. Thursday.

Past midnight, when he was deeply, soundly asleep, Quinn's cellphone rang.

The noise – and his wife's elbow in his ribs – woke him. He got up hurriedly, confused, fumbled for the phone twice, and scrambled groggily down the passage peering blearily at the screen. It was his bureau chief in Johannesburg.

'Yes,' he said.

'I'm really sorry, but it's Inkunzi Shabangu. He's been killed. Massive bloodbath at his house. I thought you'd want to know right away.'

'When?'

'About an hour ago.'

'How?'

'Looks like Shabangu was killed with a shotgun, some of his people with a handgun.'

'How did you find out so quickly?'

'We were the first on the scene. One of our cellular surveillance vehicles saw a white male coming past him at high speed in Shabangu's BMW, and went to the house. Everything was open, the gate, the garage door . . . Then the security company arrived, and went in. My guy called me, and I told him to follow the security man inside. They found three bodies, Shabangu and two cronies.'

'Are the police there?'

'They arrived ten minutes later. Place is now swarming.'

Quinn was wide awake now. 'Tell me about the white male.'

'Not much to tell. He went past at high speed. Surveillance guy can't give a description. There's a bulletin out on the BMW . . .'

'OK,' said Quinn. 'How are your police connections?'

'Pretty good. I'll keep you posted.'

'Thanks.'

Quinn went to the kitchen, sat on the high stool in the breakfast corner, his brain racing.

Ouboet, *should I rather come to your house. I know where you live.* Becker had said something like that to Shabangu last week over the phone.

Becker. He had phoned the number he got from Shabangu, day before yesterday, the number for Supreme Committee member Shaheed Latif Osman. And he had been told it was the wrong number.

Did he go to Shabangu's house last night? His patience exhausted?

What had Shabangu said to him before The Bull was shot? About Osman and the Committee.

Quinn picked up his cellphone and called the PIA office, got the Ops operator on night shift. 'I want a general and comprehensive red flag warning for a Lukas Becker, his ID and credit card details are on the system. If he moves an inch I want to know about it. And phone the Bureau in Bloemfontein. Tell him I want all his people on the Becker investigation. Now.'

Quinn propped his elbows on the kitchen counter and rubbed his eyes. This had suddenly become quite complicated. They had intelligence on a serious crime. Someone would have to decide what they shared with the police. And when.

Not his problem. Time to disturb the Advocate's sleep as well.

* * *

The red flag was digitally hoisted at seven o'clock that morning, at the Oliver Tambo Airport when Lukas Becker used his credit card at the 1time airline counter to buy a ticket for flight 1T 103 to Kaapstad.

'It departs at 09.25 and arrives at 11.35,' Quinn told Masilo over the phone. '1time has agreed to an IFI, I'm sending my best teams to begin observation once he lands.'

'Good,' said Masilo.

'And the police?'

'The risk to the operation is too great. We say nothing. But you must not let Becker out of your sight. Not for a second.'

The air hostess on the 1time flight did the IFI, the in-flight identification, forty minutes after the jet had taken off. She consulted the passenger list and saw there was only one Becker on the flight – a Mr L. Becker in seat 11A. She made certain that he was sitting in that seat by asking a few passengers in Becker's area for their boarding passes, including Becker himself. She memorised his appearance and clothing.

Just before Flight 1T 103 landed in Cape Town, she looked at the man, who was calmly reading, one last time.

When the plane stopped and she and a colleague opened the door, she saw there were two extra, unfamiliar ground staff in 1time uniforms at the top of the stairs. One of them made eye contact and nodded at her.

She nodded back.

She waited until Mr Becker came past. She put out her hand in a friendly gesture. 'Did you enjoy your flight?' and she touched the man's elbow.

He smiled at her. It was a genuine smile. 'I did, thank you very much.'

Then he was out.

She looked at the unfamiliar ground staff member who waited until Becker had passed. Then he looked at her, and nodded again.

He walked after Becker.

Mrs Killian put the new information on the desk and said: 'Milla, the status of this report was raised this morning. In the next twenty-four hours a lot of material will come in. I'm going to ask Theunie to help you.'

'What did the guy do?'

'I don't know.'

Milla looked at the new information. She saw there were four operators working on the report now. There was an analysis of a bank statement and official documents from the Navy and a hospital. There were also short snippets, taken from websites, transcribed interviews, long and short, with acquaintances and former friends and neighbours. One was an interview with an academic from Bloemfontein, a woman who had been a student with Lukas Becker.

I was his dance partner. He loved dancing.

And:

No, we were just friends. We all knew, back then, Lukas was on the move. Always. It was safer . . . to just be friends. I always wondered, was he running towards something, something that drove him, or was he running away from his parents . . .

She worked through the documents systematically, quickly and efficiently, wholly captivated. She added the new snippets of information to the report, making changes where speculation became confirmation.

Finances

Becker has four accounts with Standard Bank, with current cash assets of R1,570 649.98. Transfers to and from a current account with Wells Fargo in the USA, as well as income from at least two American investments indicate a net worth of more than R2 million.

She also added the information about his parents:

Becker's mother, Esther Debora Becker, was admitted to the Witrand Care and Rehabilitation Centre on 17 April 1995 for observation and treatment of a psychiatric disorder. She was transferred to the Janet Steinmetz Private Clinic in Johannesburg on 1 December 1995, and was in treatment until her death from natural causes on 27 September 1999.

Under 'Background':

During his compulsory military service (1985–1986) Lukas Becker was trained as a diver in the SA Navy at Simonstown. (The South African Diving Unit trains teams of combat divers in mine-countermeasures, search and recovery and underwater explosives as a wartime role – See references.)

And:

Becker earned a Masters Degree in Anthropological Archaeology at the University of South Florida (At St Petersburg in the USA) in 1996.

Below 'Working career':

After his full-time studies for B Agric at the UFS, Becker joined the Navy again where he served from 1990 to 1994 as an instructor and later training officer (Lieutenant) at the Diving Unit.

From 1994 to 1996 Becker worked part-time in the marina in St Petersburg (USA) as deck hand, skipper and diving instructor to pay for his studies at the University of South Florida. (Unconfirmed.)

From 1997 to 2004 he took part in various American inter-university archaeological expeditions, including trips to Israel, Egypt, Jordan, Iran and Turkey, while he worked extramurally on a thesis about Human Prehistory, with specific reference to the Paleolithic period. (Unconfirmed.)

In 2005, he accepted a position with the American military servicing company Blackwater (now known as Xe Services LLC), and has since worked for them under contract in Iraq.

Two teams followed Becker from the airport. One took photos as Becker collected a car from Tempest Car Hire, a white Toyota Yaris 1.4, and noted the registration number.

They remained on his tail unseen on the M29 in the direction of Parow, then along the M16 past Tygerberg Hospital, the M16 past Karl Bremer and finally the M31 and M13 to Durbanville.

In the quiet suburban streets they had to drop back, nearly missing him turning in at the Vierlanden Garden Cottage.

They stopped and consulted before phoning Quinn. He gave one team orders to enquire about accommodation at the guest house – and book in if there was room. He also gave immediate orders for a new surveillance team to go to the address without delay.

'The piece about the parents is superfluous,' said Oom Theunie.

'Don't you think a disturbed mother has an influence on someone's psyche?' Milla asked.

'You only need one sentence to say his mother was mad and his parents are dead.'

'OK.' With a touch of reluctance.

Then the photo came through.

55

The report was a live document in the PIA database. Milla Strachan sat and wondered if anyone was reading her updates. And why.

What had Lukas Becker, historical anthropologist, done to make an intelligence agency interested in him? Was it his contract work with Blackwater, now known as Xe Services? She had read up about this company on the Internet. There was nothing under the new name, only a website under construction. Under 'Blackwater' there was a lot, mostly controversial. They trained mercenaries.

At 14.27, while she was rewriting the report, the software indicated that someone had made an external update. Milla clicked the Refresh icon. The new material was a photograph. She could not curb her curiosity, and clicked on it.

The photo opened.

Caught in the bright sunlight, beside a white Toyota, stood a man with dark hair in a brush cut. His body was lean, his head turned half towards the camera, as he looked at a black man in a car hire uniform.

There was something about the smile, the good-natured eyes, his way of looking, that captivated her. In that second something was said between two strangers, a moment of understanding and recognition. She stared at it for a long time, looking for traces of *that* life on *this* face, the unstable, deceased parents, the man who was someone's dance partner at university, the fascinating, exotic studies, the archaeological expeditions, the job as soldier and later mercenary, but there was nothing. Just the smile and the compassion. When Jessica the Goddess suddenly touched her shoulder and asked, 'Who's the dish?' Milla was brought back to reality with a bump.

Just before five Quinn walked into Masilo's office and said: 'We have trouble. Lukas Becker has just driven slowly past Shaheed Latif Osman's house.'

'And then?'

'Then he drove off, towards the city.'

'Do we have a tracker on his car yet?'

'Before the end of today.'

'And his cellphone?'

'We are listening. But that's not all, the Johannesburg bureau has let us know that Julius Shabangu was shot with a MAG-7, an automatic, short-barrelled shotgun . . .'

'And . . . ?'

'It's a weapon with baggage. Smuggling and military baggage. Becker was with Blackwater and in Iraq . . .'

'What are you saying, Quinn?'

'This guy is armed and dangerous . . .'

'We are not sure it was him who shot Shabangu. The evidence is circumstantial.'

'And if Osman is next on his list?'

Masilo did the one thing Quinn did not expect. He shrugged.

Quinn realised the Advocate was hoping for exactly that. And Masilo still did not trust Janina's motives.

Photostatic record: *Diary of Milla Strachan*
Date of entry: *1 October 2009*

Life is a four-letter word, without dimensions. You live. Or not. Like a switch, on or off. The dimension comes from what we do with it. That makes the difference between living, and a life.

I told Jessica I wanted to do things, to experience. I wanted to live.

I thought my new beginning, my new job, my dance classes and plans for a book constituted life. And then I compared it with the life of one Lukas Becker and I knew then that my switch was not yet on.

2 October 2009. Friday.

When Baboo Rayan's Elantra disappeared around the corner of Chamberlain Street, the Telkom bakkie stopped at number 15 – right opposite the front door.

Two technicians got out, one with a small toolbox in his hand, the other with a larger bag and a roll of telephone cord. They went in through the gate and walked purposefully up to the front door.

One technician began unrolling the telephone cord while he examined the wall of the house speculatively as though he intended to install something there. The other crouched down at the front door, his back to the street so that passers-by could not see what he was doing. He opened the toolbox and took out the fibre optic scope. It was a long, thin tube, called a snake cam at the PIA. He slowly pushed the end of the fibre optic scope under the front door, his eyes on the colour screen in the box.

Then he moved the point of the scope back and forth to see as much of the interior as possible.

'Shit,' said Rajhev Rajkumar.

He and Quinn sat watching the monitor in the Ops Room. It showed an enlarged image of what the snake cam recorded in Upper Woodstock.

'These guys are paranoid,' said Quinn. The living room of 15 Chamberlain was a model of security – contact alarms at the doors and windows, motion sensors in two corners – and a CCTV camera in another corner.

'You can't blame them,' said Rajkumar.

'That's enough,' said Quinn over the radio to the technicians. 'Let's get out of there.'

Rajkumar got up with difficulty. 'Well, there goes the mike op . . . You know, I've never seen this . . .'

'The security?'

'That too. But this streak of bad luck. Never seen it this long, so much of it. Fluke. The good news is, it will have to change, sooner or later.'

* * *

At the Arthur Murray Friday social, Milla Strachan saw Lukas Becker walking across the dance floor towards her.

She was seated at a table with other students, old and young, waiting for the music to begin, making the usual chitchat 'Where are you from?', 'How long have you been dancing?' The lights dimmed, only the dance floor left brightly lit, and the movement caught her eye, so that she looked up and saw him.

Her first, instinctive, impulse was to wave at him, since she knew him. Then she placed him, the circumstances dawned on her and her heart shuddered.

The music began. A foxtrot.

'Shall we dance, Miss Strachan?' Mr Soderstrom, her instructor's voice beside her. She sat dumbstruck for a second. Then she stood up.

The 'bus stop' was designed to allow the Arthur Murray students to dance with multiple partners. The women lined up, the men came past and took the first woman for a circuit, then came back for the next one.

Milla was intensely aware of Becker. Aware of his presence, his dancing ability, his gallantry. And of everything she knew about him. She tried not to look at him.

The timing of the first bus stop ensured that she didn't dance with him. Twenty minutes later, halfway through the second, she was at the front of the row. He approached her, that photo smile on his face, fine perspiration below the hairline of his brush cut, a small bow and then they were dancing and he said, 'I'm Lukas.'

'Milla,' but it came out too quietly. She was weak with nerves, and struggled with the dance.

'Millie?' He was a head taller than her, looking down at her.

'Milla.'

'Milla,' he repeated it, as if he wanted to remember it.

She smelled him. She realised she wasn't dancing well. 'I'm still learning,' she said, apologetic and shy.

'Me too.'

That was the sum total of their first conversation.

* * *

'And now, an American line dance,' said the announcer.

Milla hadn't learned it yet. She remained sitting. The music began to play. 'Cotton Eye Joe', country music. She saw Lukas Becker standing in one of the rows with his back to her.

She watched him, saw he was a bit rusty, made a couple of errors. And then it was as if he began to remember, and he danced with more abandon, with pleasure, carefree, near exuberance.

She could recall his scent.

At the end of the line dance he caught her eye and smiled at her. She looked away quickly.

56

Photostatic record: *Diary of Milla Strachan*
Date of entry: *2 October 2009*

Should I report it? What would I say to Mrs Killian? You'll never believe who came waltzing into the Friday night social?

And then? Then they would send people around to talk to the Arthur Murray studio, like they talked to Christo before? No thank you.

Ten to one I will never see him again in my life.

3 October 2009. Saturday.

Crazy Mamma's Pizzeria and Restaurant in Walvis Bay is a cheerful place on a Saturday night, packed and noisy.

Reinhard Rohn walked in and saw the woman sitting at the long counter at the back of the restaurant. There wasn't a chair vacant near her, so at first he found a place at a table.

He ordered a beer and a pizza, keeping a careful eye on her. She didn't look any better than her photo, late forties, slightly overweight, the hairstyle not flattering.

But she was alone.

Later a chair beside her became available.

He stood up, took his second beer and the half-eaten pizza along.

'May I sit here?' he asked her.

'Be my guest.' Eyes summed him up, a reflex, without much interest. She had finished eating, was drinking something with Coke.

He sat down and ate.

She looked the other way.

'Good pizza,' he said.

At first she didn't realise he was talking to her. 'Oh . . . *Ja*.'

'I usually eat pizza at La Dolce Vita, in Windhoek, in the Kaiser Krone Centre . . .'

She shook her head to say she wasn't familiar with it, and evaluated him with more focus.

He pointed at the pizza in front of him. 'This is just as good.'

'You're from Windhoek?' she asked.

'*Ja*. Here on business. And you?'

'Been here nine years already.'

'Oh? What do you do?'

'I work for a fishing company. Head of Admin.'

4 October 2009. Sunday.

In the morning Milla Strachan sat at the small writing table in her bedroom, in front of her laptop. She had Microsoft Word open. She typed, a new title page:

At Forty
By Milla Strachan

She inserted a page break, then wrote: *Chapter 1*

And underneath, the first two sentences of her latest attempt, which she had pondered over for a long time – and still wasn't sure if it would work.

Hannelie, older and wiser, had often warned me: everything changes at forty.

I didn't believe her.

The head of Admin for Consolidated Fisheries phoned Reinhard Rohn after eleven in the morning. He took the call in his room in the Protea Hotel.

'It's Ansie.'

'Good morning.'

'What are you doing?'

'I'm sitting here working. And you?'

'I'm lying here remembering.'

'And what do you remember?'

'Everything.'

'You're a naughty girl.'

'And when will this naughty girl see you again?'

'What's the naughty girl doing tonight?'

5 October 2009. Monday.

Janina Mentz's agenda for the day was peace. She walked into Advocate Tau Masilo's office, sat down opposite him with a sense of purpose and asked: 'What would you have done if you were in my position?'

He betrayed no surprise. 'I would have done everything in my power to scuttle this terrorist act, even if it meant the amalgamation of the PIA. I would have had understanding of and appreciation for the work my people did.'

'Would you have considered searching for a solution that would prevent the terrorism and ensure our future?'

'Of course . . .'

In a soft voice she played her trump card. 'The Minister announced this afternoon that the FIFA visit of October 12 would coincide with a massive security exercise, to test the readiness of the SAPS, the Metro police and certain elements of the Defence Force. He would request the public to be patient in this regard as there would be extensive roadblocks and the closing of certain routes could cause delays.'

Masilo tried to hide his relief. 'Thank you,' he said.

'For the record, Tau, I have great appreciation for the enthusiasm and dedication of our personnel. But if it does not produce the desired result, it is my duty and responsibility to say so. That is the most unpleasant part of my job, but I do it with the same vigour and dedication.'

Masilo sank slowly back in his chair.

'Tau, I need you. I rely heavily on you. We may differ in our opinions, but we must trust each other, in order to carry out our respective duties.'

He nodded. 'You're right.'

'Would you consider sitting at my table again?'

57

During her dance class at seven o'clock, something inside Milla broke loose.

Maybe it was because she was late and distracted, didn't have time to think, and just started dancing. Maybe it was that two months of dance classes, theory, practice, determination and desire, eventually came together, so that she moved without thinking, the music took control of her. And Mr Soderstrom, her instructor, had the insight not to say anything before the end, didn't make her do school steps, didn't give her pause to breath, or think.

Only once the hour was over, did he say: 'Miss Strachan, that was magnificent.'

Milla, with the bloom of exertion and pleasure on her cheeks, suddenly realised what she had achieved. 'It was,' she said. Emotion welled up in her, euphoria. 'Thank you,' she added, 'do I say that enough?'

She took off her dance shoes, said goodbye, picked up her handbag and walked out with an energetic bounce, the bag swinging gaily, down the steps, through the banking corridor, out, the evening quiet and lovely. She walked across the access road to her Renault.

Someone called her name.

She turned her head, her heart still light and full.

Lukas Becker walked across the tarmac towards her.

A laugh seemed to bubble up inside Milla, the knowledge that this meeting was meant to be and that it was good and right, and she said, 'Hello,' and waited.

'I was just on my way to Woollies, and I saw you go in . . .'

She just stood there smiling.

'So I decided to ambush you, in the hope that you would come out thirsty, tired and vulnerable,' with enough caution *and* courage in his tone.

'You waited a whole hour for me?'

'Actually only the last ten minutes. There against the pillar.' Boyishly embarrassed. Then he laughed.

She laughed with him. 'I am very thirsty. And a little bit vulnerable.'

Photostatic record: *Diary of Milla Strachan*
Date of entry: *5 October 2009*

Dear Jessica

You once asked me if I have ever lived dangerously.

Tonight I did. A little. And it was good.

In the Thai restaurant in Main Street, just a block away from Arthur Murray, they sat on the balcony.

'What do you do?' he asked her.

'I allow stalkers to buy me mineral water and sushi.'

'Touché. What line of work are you in?'

'I'm a professional journalist. I work for the Government Department of Communication, for a newspaper called *News This Week*. If I resign tomorrow, the government will collapse. And you?'

'I've been overseas. For about thirteen years.'

'What were you doing over there?'

'The first seven years, archaeological digs. From 2005 I was in Iraq. Small boat training on the Euphrates. For the Iraqi government.'

'When did you come back?'

'About three weeks ago.'

'Why?'

'It's a long story.'

'Then we had better order sushi.'

Photostatic record: *Diary of Milla Strachan*
Date of entry: *5 October 2009*

He was genuine. Honest. And so very at ease with himself, with me, with the waitress (he called her 'ousus', and the wine waiter 'ouboet'), he didn't try to impress anyone, he didn't try to be overly clever or serious, he talked easily about himself and he showed an easy interest in me.

I like his voice.

I gave him my cellphone number.

'I came back to buy a farm.'

'In the Cape?'

'No. In the Free State. Between Philippolis and Springfontein.'

'Why there?'

'That's more or less where I come from – and it's a pretty farm. It's the landscape I love. The South West Free State, grass veld and hills, thorny thickets, a stream with willows . . .'

'But what are you doing in the Cape?'

'You *are* an inquisitive woman.'

'That's what my father taught me: if a man is stalking you, find out as much about him as you can.'

'Your father is a smart man. I'm in the Cape to retrieve some money that someone . . . borrowed from me. I need it to pay for the farm.'

'Is that why you went to work overseas? So you could buy a farm?'

'That was one of the reasons.'

58

6 October 2009. Tuesday.

Milla slid her identity card through the slot of the security door, listened to the click of the lock, and went in. She looked up at the CCTV camera in the corner, and felt a prickle of guilt.

If these people only knew . . .

For just a second she considered the possibility that someone might have seen them last night. Her heart began to race, it made her suddenly aware of the few people in the corridors, on their way to the office. She searched for signs of interest, or disapproval, from her colleagues as well.

They greeted her with the usual rituals.

'Good morning,' said Mac, his nose pressed to his computer screen.

Oom Theunie looked up from cleaning his pipe and smiled at her. 'Carmen. You look particularly lovely this morning.'

And Jessica was late. Like every morning.

Milla gradually relaxed.

Maybe the profile was all they wanted. Maybe Lukas Becker had been forgotten already.

* * *

Quinn didn't recognise her in the photo because the light was poor: Becker and the woman on the restaurant balcony at night.

It was only once he had read the report of the surveillance team, the registration details of the white Renault Mégane, that he saw the name. Milla Strachan. It sounded familiar.

He had to think hard to place the name: at the top of a few recent PIA reports, if he remembered correctly.

He looked it up on the computer, saw it was indeed the same name as the new woman on the Report Squad. Coincidence, he thought? It wasn't a common name, he had better make sure. Wouldn't that be something, wouldn't that let the fox into the hen house?

He called up the PIA personnel record of Milla Strachan, and the car and colour and registration number were identical. He looked at the head-and-shoulders picture, compared it to the woman on the balcony of the restaurant.

It was her.

He asked the database to display the reports that she had worked on.

Lukas Becker's was the most recent.

Quinn didn't say anything, just blew through his teeth, a hiss of astonishment, and a kind of amazement at fate, which just would not leave Operation Shawwal alone.

'Quinn called in the surveillance team and interrogated them thoroughly,' Tau Masilo said to Mentz. 'They say Becker waited for her, outside the shopping centre. There was a gymnasium and a dance studio, she could have been at either of the two. When she came out at 20.00, he began talking to her. Then they walked to the restaurant where they ate and talked until 22.40. After that he went back to the guest house. There weren't enough men to follow her.'

Janina Mentz sat and stared at the opposite wall for such a long time that Masilo said: 'Ma'am . . . ?'

She got up swiftly, angrily, walked around her desk and sat down at her computer, did something with the mouse. She looked intently at the screen. Masilo saw a blush slowly spread across her face.

She looked at him. 'CIA,' she said, as though the word were a curse.

Masilo, trying to keep up, admitted defeat. 'I don't understand.'

'Did you read his profile? He works for the damn CIA.'

Masilo recalled Becker's conversations with Inkunzi Shabangu, how he had been looking for his money after a hijacking. 'I'm not sure I agree.'

'Put it all together, Tau. What do Becker and America have in common?'

He tried to remember what was in the reports, but she answered the question herself. 'Israel, Egypt, Jordan, Iran, Turkey. And now Iraq. Doesn't that tell you something?'

'CIA hotspots . . .'

She shook her head, picked up the photograph, the one of Becker and Milla on the balcony. 'Look at her, Tau. Look at the way she looks at him.' The Deputy Director sank slowly back into his chair. 'I am very, very disappointed in her.'

Masilo and Quinn were behind the closed door of the Advocate's office.

'Did you discuss the Strachan event with anyone?' the Advocate asked.

'Only the surveillance team.'

'Is there a dossier? Anything on the system?'

'Not yet.'

Masilo nodded in relief. 'Keep it that way. Quinn, this is a very sensitive issue. There is a strong possibility that he targeted her. That he isn't who we think he is.'

Quinn considered that. 'I would be surprised . . .'

'We can't afford to make a mistake. The damage to the Operation, the damage to the Agency's reputation . . .'

He looked at Quinn, made sure it all sank in.

'The Director's orders are most specific. Nothing on the system. Keep everything in your drawer. Strachan's name is not to be mentioned anywhere. From now on she will be known to us as "Miss Jenny". That is how all those involved will refer to her, that is the name that will be on all instructions to other departments. From now on we drastically limit the number of people who know – the Director, me, you, and a small task team that you will put together immediately. A few operators you trust, Quinn, three or four people with good judgement. Hand-picked. They must do the monitoring, write the reports. Manually.'

'I understand.'

'We want her flat searched, we need microphones in every room. Today. And only your task team listening in. And we want to know exactly what she looks at on her computer, what material she requests here, digitally, or hard copy. And we want to listen to her cellphone conversations.'

'Visual monitoring and tracking?'

'No. Keep the focus on Becker. And speaking of him: we want you to trace the two Shabangu henchmen that Becker worked with . . .' Masilo consulted his notes. 'According to the transcripts Becker told Shabangu, *I have one of them here. He says his name is Enoch Mangope, the one with the white eye. He says he works for you.* And the other one's name is Kenosi, that's all we have. Find them, Quinn, we want to know exactly what Becker said to them. Any questions?'

'No.'

'The next order is for Rohn in Walvis Bay. He will have to exploit his resource . . .'

'It might be too soon.'

'We don't have a choice. Seven days to go, Quinn. We don't have more time.'

'I'll tell him.'

'That is all, thanks.'

Quinn stood up and walked to the door, where he stopped. 'Why "Miss Jenny"?'

'It was the Director's idea. Apparently someone who spied on the Americans. A long time ago.'

Quinn frowned.

'You'll figure it out,' said Masilo.

Mountain Street in Newlands was rich in trees, big houses, high walls.

The operators who were watching Shaheed Latif Osman, did it from a vacant bedroom on the top floor of number twelve, with the permission of the mostly absentee owner. It wasn't the ideal vantage point, because Osman's house was diagonally opposite, down the street, so that they could see the entrance, part of the driveway, the garage, a piece of lawn and the front door, just. But it was all they could get.

Just after nine they saw the white Toyota Yaris stop in front of the entrance. The operator swivelled the powerful binoculars on the tripod and focused on it.

He saw Becker get out and walk to the gate, where the intercom was mounted on a shiny steel stand. Becker pressed a button. Waited.

Bent down to talk into the intercom. Straightened up again, looked through the gate.

The operator swung the binoculars at the front door. Seconds ticked by. Then it opened. Shaheed Latif Osman came out wearing his Muslim robe, walked to the gate. With an attitude.

He said something to Becker, stopped in front of the gate, but did not open it.

Becker talked back.

Osman shook his head.

Becker spoke again.

Osman said something, his body language aggressive.

Becker spoke.

Osman made a gesture with his arm that said Becker should go.

Becker said something again.

Osman turned and walked back to the front door. On the threshold he turned, called out something, went in and shut the door.

Swivelled the binoculars back to Becker. The man stood still a moment more, then walked to his car.

The operator swore he could see a smile.

The search team unlocked the door to Milla's flat at 14.03. They were skilled and experienced. First they took digital photos of every room, of every cupboard and drawer. Then they began to search.

The one who found the diaries phoned Quinn. 'There are twenty-four of them. They date back to 1986, it's going to take a long time.'

'Photograph the last . . . six months' pages. We can copy the rest bit by bit. From tomorrow on.'

Only once the search team had finished, at 15.32, every room arranged as the original photos depicted them, did the technicians arrive to plant the microphones.

* * *

At 15 Chamberlain Street in Upper Woodstock, the members of the Supreme Committee began to arrive.

The operator opposite immediately notified Quinn, and made certain all the equipment was working.

She sat listening, without much hope, to the concrete microphone in the base of the satellite dish.

To her surprise, at 15.59, she heard the voice of Shaheed Latif Osman, indignant: 'He said Shabangu told him I've got his money. Tweetybird or me.'

'Take it easy, Shaheed, your heart . . . Did you get the car's number?' the Sheikh, Suleiman Dolly, asked.

'I did.'

'Let's go and talk down below.'

He phoned her after six.

She was sitting in front of the laptop in her bedroom, thinking of working on the book.

She didn't recognise the number. 'Milla,' she said, careful.

'The chips at Fisherman's Choice are always golden brown, crisp and very hot and fresh, the hake just melt-in-your-mouth. And it's a lovely evening.'

'What would a Free Stater know about hake that melts-in-your-mouth?'

'Absolutely nothing, I had hoped my winged words, my poetic touch would be irresistible.'

'It's very evocative . . .'

'We Free Staters don't know such big words. Is that a "yes"?'

'Where is Fisherman's Choice?'

On Quinn's computer screen the photos of the pages of Milla Strachan's diary were displayed.

He read the entries for the past week first.

He saw she had already met Becker, for the first time, on Friday evening at a dance.

Becker had orchestrated it.

He saw traces of Milla's conscience, saw how events pulled her along. He went back to the beginning, read the entries for the past six months. She was still a housewife then. Lonely. Lost.

He followed the tracks of her words, to freedom, to the PIA, he read about her struggle over her child, her intimate thoughts, her slow emancipation.

Against his will he liked her. And he became all the more convinced of her innocence. She was a chance piece of flotsam washed along by the flood of Operation Shawwal.

Then his phone rang. 'Becker has just phoned Miss Jenny. They are going to eat out again.'

Reinhard Rohn lay on the bed. Ansie, Head of Administration at Consolidated Fisheries, rested her head on his stomach. She was smoking a cigarette, the ashtray on the rounding of her body.

He said: 'I hear one of my old friends was here with you not long ago.'

'Who?'

'Shaheed Osman. From Cape Town.'

'You know Osman?'

'More of a business acquaintance, to be honest. I happened to mention to him over the phone yesterday that I was in Walvis Bay, and he said he came and did business here a month or so ago. With you guys.'

'Small world,' she said.

'I didn't even know he imported fish.'

'He doesn't.'

'Oh?'

'What work does the Osman you know do?'

'Imports.' Deliberately vague.

'That's not what he said to us. He said he's a broker. A speculator.'

'In fish?'

'No. In boats. He bought one of our vessels.'

59

At the Cape Town Waterfront, where a thousand lights swam in reflection in the still waters beside quay number four, Milla listened to Lukas Becker. She listened to his voice, the tone and inflection – relaxed, peaceful, soft. There was a hint of self-denial, as if he and his life only had worth via her interest. And something else, a sense of being in tune that resonated in her, a warmth, for her, for *them*.

Tell me about the archaeological digs, she asked him, as though she knew nothing about them.

He said they were among the most exciting experiences of his life.

Why?

I would bore you.

You won't.

He ate a little more first. Then he said, have you ever walked across the Free State plains and wondered what it looked like, 100,000 years ago? Have you ever walked in the veld and seen something shiny, picked it up and rolled it around in your fingers? A piece of ostrich eggshell, rubbed smooth, with a tiny hole through it, and wondered, who wore this around their neck? What was it like, to live like that? When the springbuck in their thousands trekked across the savannah, when people made fires at night to keep the lions away, where now there are only sheep and cattle and civilisation. Have you ever wondered why this world, this Africa, speaks to our hearts, we, who are from Europe? I used to wonder, ever since I was young, about seventeen or eighteen. Where does the love for this landscape originate? Why do we want to *own* it? Why do Africans, and especially the Afrikaner, have such a strong connection, such a deep longing for land. For a farm, specifically. Where does that come from? My father had it and so do I. And I went looking for answers and I realised, increasingly, that it is a new thing. Ten, maybe 12,000 years old. Before that people were drifters, nomadic hunter-gatherers who populated the whole planet while following their food sources. Everything belonged to us, the whole earth. For 200,000 years, if you just look at *Homo sapiens*. For two and a half million years, if you include *Homo habilis*. The world was our home, the crossing of horizons, the freedom, the movement, was in our genes, it drove us. And then, between eighteen and fourteen thousand years ago, the Kebaran of the Levant made way for the Natufians' first sowing of grasses . . .

The Kebaran? (She asked in a whisper, a little apologetic, because she didn't want him to stop talking.)

* * *

He walked her as far as the security gate.

She wanted to invite him in.

He said: 'Milla, I want to see you again tomorrow night.'

She said: 'That would be lovely.'

They stood together a moment in silence. Then he said, 'Goodnight, Milla.'

7 October 2009. Wednesday.

Rajkumar knew it wasn't his technology that made the breakthrough. It was the old-fashioned methods of Masilo and Quinn's man, the middle-aged and practically forgotten operator, Reinhard Rohn. He tried to make up for that, with information quickly collected that morning: 'We got all of this from their systems. It's called a stern trawler fishing vessel, and it's not a boat, it's a ship. Length of forty-four meters, breadth of ten meters, draft of five meters. Quarters for some fifteen crew, it can carry almost one thousand tonnes of cargo. But the real problem is, it's equipped to stay at sea for up to forty-five days. And Osman's people took commission of the ship on 21 September, so they've been out there for about three weeks. They could be anywhere in the world,' Rajkumar said. Then, quickly, because Mentz was glaring at him, 'I know that's not what you want to hear . . .'

'You are missing the point.'

'Ma'am, there was no reason to look at ships they have sold . . .'

'No, Raj, that's not the point either. You are asking, "where?", when what you should be asking, is "why?".'

'Oh . . .'

'Why do they need a ship this big? What do they want to transport? Let us assume Tau is right, the target is the American soccer team, or the Cape Town Stadium, or both. They don't need a thousand tonnes of weapons and explosives . . .'

'People,' the Advocate said. 'They're bringing in people.'

'Exactly,' said Mentz.

Raj brushed his hair back over his shoulder, angry at himself.

'They're bringing in a hit squad,' said Mentz. 'Probably al-Qaeda trained. The ship explains everything. It explains why they needed that much money. Why Macki was so deeply involved . . . They might have used the diamonds as direct payment, Walvis Bay is a smuggling haven. It explains why they had such limited contact with the Ravens . . . But the main issue is, we've been watching the Committee, but the Committee's role is basically over. They can just sit back now and wait for the hit squad to arrive . . .'

'With respect,' Rajkumar said, 'that makes the question of "where" even more vital.'

'Absolutely right,' said Masilo.

'So how do we find it?'

Rajkumar was ready for the question. 'It's going to depend on how much they want to be found.'

'Why?'

'SOLAS. The International Convention for the Safety of Life at Sea. Since 2006, it requires all vessels bigger than 300 tonnes to operate Long Range Identification and Tracking equipment, amongst other things. If they have their LRIT and AIS transmitters switched on, we can submit a Chapter Five request through the Minister – or any cabinet member – to the International LRIT Data Exchange, to get their current position.'

'And if they are not running the transmitters?'

'Then we'll have to find reports of ships that have disregarded the SOLAS regulations, which will take time. The only real solution is to talk to the Americans, ask them to look with their satellites.'

'I'm not going to talk to the Americans.'

'I know how you feel, ma'am,' said Tau Masilo, 'but we have no choice. We are running out of time. And they don't need a harbour to unload a terror squad. They can be transferred at sea, to a smaller vessel, somewhere – anywhere – off the coast. And we have a very long coast line.'

'Why is asking the Americans for help an issue?' Rajkumar asked, in all innocence.

'Because they are snakes,' said Mentz.

'Oh . . .'

'We have no choice,' Masilo repeated.

Mentz looked at the Advocate in disapproval, but eventually she capitulated, 'Raj, prepare the Chapter Five request. I'll go talk to the Minister.'

* * *

'No,' the Minister said, greatly displeased.

'Sir . . .' Mentz said.

'No, no, no. What do we say to the Americans? Someone is bringing a boat full of mad Muslims to blow up your soccer team, please give us a hand? Because we are too useless to stop a bunch of old bearded men? Have you any idea of the pressure at the moment, from the news vultures circling up there in the sky, over this World Cup, all those Afro-pessimists? They *want* us to fail. So they can say, look, Africa is still Africa, rotten with crime and corruption and stupid black people. Now you want us, nine months before the tournament, to tell the Americans your team is in danger and we are too stupid to handle it ourselves? The next thing would be Obama announcing they aren't coming any more. The risk is too high, no, Janina, no, no, no . . .'

'Sir, no one has a greater distaste . . .'

'Why didn't you just arrest the Muslims, Janina? When there was time?'

'Sir, you know . . .'

'I know what you are telling me, I trusted you.'

'We don't have to tell the Americans anything, sir.'

'Nothing? We ask them to turn all their satellites to look at our waters and we tell them nothing?'

'Sir, we have a trump card.'

'What?'

'The CIA have just begun a process of infiltration. Of the PIA.'

'You're not serious.'

'I am.'

'Do you have proof?'

She put the photos on the desk. Lukas Becker, at Cape Town International Airport. 'He is a former South African with a military background. In 1994 he left for the USA . . .'

'In 1994?' Indignant. 'One of those who didn't like our new, democratic South Africa?'

'Most likely. We are still busy investigating his ideology, but we are reasonably certain he was recruited by the CIA in the period 1994 to 1996, because from 1997 to 2004 he was deployed in all the CIA focal points: Israel, Egypt, Jordan, Iran and Turkey, under the cover of archaeological digs. From 2004 till earlier this year he was working full-time in Iraq, as an "employee" of Blackwater. He has at least one American bank account and two investment accounts, and his cash assets are over two million, conservatively estimated. And a month ago he was suddenly back in the country, and assassinated a major figure in the organised crime arena, coincidentally, one that we were investigating for his connection with the Supreme Committee.'

The Minister dropped back into his chair, shaking his head. 'CIA,' he said, with new understanding.

'He is currently making himself agreeable to one of our administrative workers.'

'And then they sit in the liaison meetings and pretend they are our friends.'

'Exactly, sir.'

'How do you want to use this, Janina?'

'Leverage, sir. I don't want to play the trump card before it is necessary.'

60

'Shall I make us some coffee?' Milla asked when they reached the security gate to her flat.

'Please,' he said.

She typed in the code and opened the gate. Her heart thumped.

'Milla,' he said.

She turned to look at him.

'Will you tell me about yourself?'

The operator was a woman, thirty-four years old. She was one of Quinn's trusted, dependable people.

At 22.48, in her cubicle at the PIA, the surveillance team let her know Becker and Miss Jenny had just stopped in front of her flat. Audio surveillance could begin.

She hurried to the Ops Room, strongly aware of Quinn's orders: no recordings on the system. Just a digital audio file on a memory stick, for his attention, on his desk. And a handwritten note to indicate its importance.

She tuned to the correct channel, fired up the computer, put on the headphones.

She knew nothing of the man and woman whose voices she was hearing. She only knew their code names.

She was aware of the impressive sensitivity of the high-tech microphones, picking up every sound with great clarity – the soft footstep on the floor, the creak of a chair, the clink of mugs, the tinkle of teaspoons. And the voices. The woman telling the story of her life, the man asking gently probing questions. They talked about the pros and cons of a small-town upbringing. About parents. They moved to another room. She said: 'They were two *Afrikaner*-hippies, my mom and dad. Very eccentric, very different from other children's parents. I still don't know if it . . . what effect it had on me. There was a time when I was so ashamed of them . . .' The sound of a car passing in the street.

The operator listened with an open mind: her only focus was registering information that could be relevant to Operation Shawwal. But what she heard was a man and woman talking about life, about childhood and growing up, about all the things that had shaped them.

And later, to her discomfort, she heard a man and woman's intimacy. She heard them go quiet after midnight. And then the subtle sounds began to tell a story of physical contact and caresses, until the woman, the mystical Miss Jenny, gave utterance to her intense pleasure, in breath and voice, the sounds from her throat.

The operator found little eroticism in that. Because tomorrow, when Quinn listened to it, he would know that she had heard it too.

8 October 2009. Thursday.

When the American team walked in, there were four of them.

Mentz was surprised, as she knew only two of them. 'My, my, how you've grown,' she said.

'Janina, how are you? Tau, good to see you again. I'd like to introduce two of my colleagues,' said Bruno Burzynski, the Bureau Chief of the CIA in Southern Africa, big, athletic and bald. 'This is Janet Eden, and this is Jim Grant. And you already know Mark.'

When the greetings were over and they were seated around the table, she said to Burzynski, 'And what is it that your colleagues do, Bruno?'

'Agricultural secretaries, of course.'

She smiled. 'On behalf of the Minister, thank you for coming at such short notice. He sends his regards.'

'It's always a pleasure. Tell him we said "hi".'

'Anybody for coffee? Tea? Water?'

'We're good, thank you.'

'Please help yourself to the refreshments behind you if you change your mind . . . Now, if I may, let's get right down to business. As you probably know, our government submitted a SOLAS Chapter Five request internationally yesterday, for a fishing vessel. The matter at hand concerns this ship, a stern trawler,' and she clicked the remote to activate Powerpoint on the big screen. 'The Vessel Identifier is ERA112, and it's registered under the Namibian flag, the name on the bow is *The Madeleine*. It was sold by a Walvis Bay company about three weeks ago. Unfortunately, a preliminary SOLAS report indicates that it is not running LRIT and AIS, which makes it very difficult to find. And we need to find it as a matter of great urgency. That is why the Minister suggested that we ask our good friends, the United States Government, for assistance in this matter. He and the President would appreciate it very much.'

'It would be an honour to help, if we can, of course. May I ask who the new ship owners are?'

She had expected the question. 'A rather unsavoury group of people who are intent on undermining our national security.'

'I see,' he said, once he realised she was not going to add anything more. 'And what sort of assistance did the Minister have in mind?'

'The Minister has great respect and admiration for the vast array of technological wizardry at the disposal of the United States Government, particularly the ability of BASIC, the Broad Area Surveillance Intelligence Capacity.'

'The Minister is well-informed.'

'He prides himself on it. And he was wondering whether the United States would be willing to help protect our budding young democracy, by making these facilities available to us. To find the ship, of course.'

Burzynski nodded slowly, as though he were first thinking it over. 'Janina, as you know, The US Government, and particularly the CIA, is dedicated to maintaining and strengthening the friendship with our much valued allies in South Africa. And if we can help in any way, we will most definitely do our very best, as always. But you do understand the costs involved, in terms of both manpower and resources, should we agree to a satellite search? Especially if they are not running LRIT. The ship has been missing for weeks, and there is time pressure.'

'Please educate me.'

'It becomes a world-wide search, Janina. They could be anywhere. The logistics are huge.'

'I understand . . .'

'I'm not saying we can't help. But in order to . . . shall we say, motivate my superiors, I'm going to need ammunition.'

'Of course you are. That's why the Minister has prepared this letter . . .' She pushed it across the table to Burzynski. 'You will see that he refers to the case as a matter of both national and international security, and of the utmost urgency.'

'And?'

'And he expresses his most heartfelt gratitude.'

'So noted. But with all due respect, Janina, we are going to need more than that.'

'Such as?'

'The nature and scale of the threat. Especially concerning the international implications.'

'Unfortunately, we are not in a position to give you much more at this time. But if you can help us find the vessel, and we unearth any intelligence the CIA might be interested in, I give you my word that we will pass it along.'

'Janina, that's not going to cut it.'

'That is a real pity. I would have thought it the ideal opportunity for the CIA to . . . regain our trust.'

'I'm not following you.'

'I'm sure you do, but it's not all that important right now. May I ask you to take the request, as it stands, to Langley?'

'Are there trust issues I'm not aware of, Janina?'

'I honestly don't know what you are aware of, Bruno. Will you forward our request?'

'Of course, I'll do my very best.'

'Thank you very much.'

61

There was a gap between Milla and reality, a soft cushion, a light mist.

Her body could still feel him, she could still smell and taste him. His words, his stories still swirled in her head.

Oom Theunie stood beside her and put his arm around her shoulder. 'Is everything OK?'

She reacted slowly, looked up, smiled. 'Oh, yes.'

'You seem a bit absent this morning.'

'I'm fine.'

And she thought, so this is what it feels like to be in love. At forty.

'We lost Becker,' the operator said.

'How?' asked Quinn. He kept the disappointment out of his voice.

'At the airport. He took the Toyota back to Tempest Car Hire. Then he went to the departures hall. We didn't expect that, by the time we got there he was gone . . .'

'How long ago?'

'Five . . . six minutes. The check-in queues are long, he wasn't in one of them. I don't believe he took a flight. I think he left the building somewhere.'

'That means he saw you.'

'Sir, that's impossible . . .'

'Keep looking. I'll get back to you.'

Quinn cursed, stood up and jogged over to Rajkumar's team. He wanted to know if Becker had bought a plane ticket, and why they didn't know about it.

'*Jissis*, Quinn,' said Masilo.

Quinn knew under how much pressure his boss was operating. He kept his voice calm. 'We'll find him.'

'You will, indeed. I am *not* going to walk into that woman's office and tell her we don't know where he is.'

'We will get him, because we have a point of reference,' he said quietly.

'What?'

'Miss Jenny. He spent the night with her. We will wait for him there.'

'I'm not so sure.'

Burzynski phoned her just after lunch. 'Janina, I'm assuming the line on your side is secure as well?'

'It is.'

'Good. I've just had a lengthy video conference with Langley, and I have some really great news. We are going to help you find the ship.'

'Bruno, that is great news. I am deeply in your debt.'

'No, Janina, please. In matters of friendship, debt is irrelevant.'

In Masilo's office, Janina Mentz was surprised that the Advocate didn't respond happily to the CIA news.

'That confirms it all,' she said.

'I had my doubts about Becker and the CIA,' he said. 'But you were right. They warned him. That we know. He shook off our team, this afternoon. He's disappeared.'

'Christ, Tau . . .' She sat down.

He lifted his hands in justification. 'In retrospect it was to be expected. But Quinn says it is temporary. He will make contact with Miss Jenny again.'

'I doubt it.'

'So do I. But there are questions, ma'am, things I don't understand. Why was the CIA interested in Shabangu? Why would they want to eliminate him?'

'I don't think it was an elimination,' said Mentz. 'Look how it happened. In his bedroom. Why go to all that trouble if you could shoot him on the street? Or put a bomb in his BMW?'

'Valid point.'

'I think it was a negotiation that went wrong. Or an interrogation.'

Masilo pondered that. 'We will find out.'

'If he contacts Miss Jenny . . . don't let Becker out of your sight.'

Becker phoned Milla as she drove her Renault back to the flat.

'When last did you climb Lion's Head?'

She had been looking forward to this moment all day, the joy inside her was instant. 'Never.'

'It's full moon, and I have a bottle of champagne.'

'I'll buy some food at Melissa's.'

'Perfect. Not too much, we will have to carry it. See you in an hour.'

Milla stopped in front of the apartment building, cellphone in her hand, and only then did she think how there had been something in his tone, in the voice she had listened so carefully to for the last three evenings and now knew so well. A discordant note, subtly different. As though he were straining for enthusiasm, but just not quite making it.

Was she imagining it? Was it just that the signal was weak?

She looked at the phone in her hand, noticed for the first time that it was not the usual number, the one that she had saved with such a sense of significance in her contacts under 'Lukas'.

'He's using another cellphone and SIM card,' the surveillance operator said to Quinn. But we've got it now.'

'Do you have his position?'

'We do. Milnerton. Marine Drive, he's mobile, but the cellphone is off now. We will keep scanning.'

Quinn looked up at the TV screens in the Ops Room. The video feed showed the outside of Milla's apartment block – the camera was mounted on the roof of the apartment building across the road. He had three teams in cars nearby. 'Did you hear that?' he asked them. 'He's on his way.'

'We heard. We're standing by.'

At 18.17 the taxi stopped in front of Daven Court. A man got out.

'It's him,' said Quinn.

'He's taking a taxi now?' the female operator beside him asked.

'Get the number of the taxi. I want to know where he was picked up.'

Quinn stared fixedly at the image. 'And take note that he has only a rucksack with him.'

'Sir?'

'He checked out of the guest house this morning. Where's his luggage?'

It was a moment before she registered. 'He's not moving in with Miss Jenny. He's found somewhere else to stay.'

'Precisely,' said Quinn.

* * *

When he came in, he embraced and kissed her, the Lukas of last night, all the warmth there.

It was just the phone, she thought.

They busied themselves in the kitchen, packing the rucksack. 'I'm temporarily without transport, would you mind if we took your car?'

'Not at all.'

On the way to Lion's Head she realised he was quieter than usual, though he held her hand. She asked him: 'How was your day?'

'It was busy,' he said.

He was tired, she realised. Of course he was tired, they hadn't had much sleep, he must have had a difficult day, she didn't even know what it was that kept him busy.

Relief. She squeezed his hand and said, 'If you would prefer to relax, we don't have to climb the mountain.'

He laughed, full of tenderness and gratitude. 'It wasn't *that* busy, thanks.'

'They have parked. They are going to walk up the mountain. What shall we do?' the operator asked.

Quinn considered the risks. 'Stay with the car, let's not take chances.'

'OK,' said the operator, thankful.

It was the third night that Becker had taken her somewhere public, out in the open, thought Quinn. Was he avoiding the flat? Did he suspect anything, that it might be tapped?

They leaned against each other on a rock, each holding a glass of champagne, the food laid out in front of them. The moon was a silver coin above, Sea Point and Green Point spread out in front of them, the city to the right, the N1 a worm of light creeping to the dark Hottentots Holland mountains. There were other people with them on the crest, small groups that, like them, spoke in muted tones.

He told her about the article in *Die Burger*, that morning, about the British scientist who believed that mankind had reached the end of the evolutionary road, because there was no more real natural selection. He said it was an interesting point of view, but not one he fully agreed with.

Then he stopped talking and she wanted to ask him about his day, what he had done, but he shifted away from her and said, 'Milla, there is something I need to tell you.'

She saw how solemn he was. 'What?' and reached for her cigarettes.

'I have to be careful how I say this, Milla, because I need to get it right. I owe you that.'

'Just say it,' she said, suddenly worried about implications of the word 'owe'.

He saw her discomfort and put out his hand to her, then let it drop as though he had changed his mind.

'I went to draw money in Durbanville. I saw the sign for the dance school. It's been five years since I last danced. I went to enquire and they said there was a social, and I was welcome to come as a guest. And then I saw you. And I danced with you. When I sat down, I thought . . . I wanted to dance with you some more. So, on Monday, when I saw you, purely by chance . . .'

'Why didn't you?' She suddenly understood, he wanted to back off. Now. After he had slept with her. She couldn't keep the distaste out of her voice.

'What do you mean?'

'Why didn't you dance with me again on Friday?'

'That's what I wanted to explain to you. My circumstances were not good . . .'

'Circumstances? What circumstances?' She felt anger now at his betrayal, his lame excuse.

He weighed his words. 'I see you misunderstand me. I don't want to stop seeing you. I can't stop seeing you. It's the timing, Milla . . . It's because of these people that owe me money. It would be better if I didn't see you for the next few days, and I want you to understand why. I don't want to expose you to any danger.'

'It would be better . . . ? What danger?'

'Can I tell you the story, from the beginning?'

She looked at him, then at the pack of cigarettes she was still holding in her hand. She took one out, lit it, drew deeply and exhaled slowly. 'Tell me,' she said.

'Will you bear with me until I'm finished?'

She nodded.

He put down his glass of champagne. 'Over the past few years, I tried to spread my investments, not to have all the eggs in one basket. One of my investments was with Northern Rock, the British bank that landed in trouble with the credit crunch last year. When that happened . . . I took a flight to London, and I withdrew the full amount, because I wanted to wait and see. So I had all this cash, and in Iraq . . . all I could do was lock it away. Until I landed here three weeks ago. With the money in my rucksack. That was my first mistake. Then I made another one. In Johannesburg. I hired an expensive car at Oliver Tambo Airport. I didn't plan to, it was a spur of the moment thing, they offered me an upgrade and the roads of the Free State lay ahead. So I took a Mercedes SL and drove to Sandton to find a hotel, to get some sleep. I was hijacked. Four guys with guns, there was nothing I could do. The money was in my rucksack, in the back. I asked them if I could take my baggage out . . .'

'So they stole the money?' The question burst out involuntarily, she saw him smile at the interruption. 'Sorry,' she said.

'Yes. They stole the money. Forty thousand pounds sterling. Half a million rand.'

Milla caught her breath, she suppressed her words with difficulty.

'It was an interesting experience,' he said, 'to see them drive away. I ran after them, for a few hundred metres . . .'

Milla looked at him, in wonderment now. Her heart had slowed down a bit.

'In any case, I reported the hijacking, waited a day or two . . . No, let me backtrack a bit first, please be patient, this part is important . . . for us. I want to explain to you why I have to do certain things. It comes partly from my childhood, from my mother's illness, my father's helplessness, neither one of them had control, Milla, circumstances overwhelmed them. I remember how I experienced a sort of revelation at fifteen, that I didn't want to live like that. That I could only truly rely on myself, with the . . . absence of both of them. At university I read Voltaire, where he said you can't choose the cards life deals you. But it is *your* choice how you play them. If you want to win. I made up my mind then, Milla. To decide my own fate . . .'

She nodded, because she understood.

'When they stole the money . . . I realised the police in Sandton were dealing with two or three hijackings a day, they don't have enough manpower, too much other crime . . . and even if they caught the men, there was little chance of getting the money back. I had to have the money to pay for the farm, otherwise the sale would fall through. So I decided I would have to get the money back myself. The first problem was to track down the hijacker. One of them had a serious eye defect, a white discolouration of the cornea. I knew if I described him to the right people . . . It took a few days, I asked around, I paid people for information, until I found him. And then, another day before he told me who he worked for. And then I began negotiating with the boss, Julius Shabangu . . .'

It was the name that shocked Milla, because she knew it.

'. . . and the trail of my money led me to Cape Town, that is why I am here. The trouble is these are difficult people, syndicates and organised crime in Johannesburg, and PAGAD here in the Cape, I suspect. Yesterday . . . I think someone is following me. That's why I want to get this thing sorted first. But I promise you, when I'm finished, I will come back . . .'

'Wait,' she said. 'Tell the police. Now that you know who has your money.'

'Shabangu is dead, Milla. He was shot last week in his house. If I go and tell the police that it was he that . . . You *do* understand?'

62

The realisation of her own dishonesty dawned slowly on Milla, a dark stream flowing through her, pressure building up; she must tell him that she knew about Shabangu, PAGAD, organised crime, and more – of the PIA profile on him that she now began to vaguely understand.

But she couldn't, she would lose him.

The evil that lay just beneath the surface of her world reached out now and touched her. She tried to force it back. She offered to lend him the money. She tried to argue, tried to convince him that there would be other farms, it was only money, it wasn't worth it. But he just shook his head and reassured her and touched her gently saying, don't worry. He knew what he was doing.

Finally, just before they had to go back, he put both hands on her shoulders and said: 'Milla, I'm going to play this hand. I can't walk away from this. That is not who I am.'

They walked down Lion's Head in silence, her heart heavy.

When they stopped in front of her flat she said: 'Stay with me tonight.'

Half an hour after they went in through the gate, Quinn saw Milla Strachan's bedroom light go on.

He stood up. 'Looks like he's going to stay. I'm on my way.'

'Sleep well,' said the female operator.

'If he moves, call me.'

'I will.'

They lay in her bed just before midnight, his arms around her. She thought through everything. She compared Lukas Becker to her ex-husband, thought about her struggle to direct her life, to gain control of her destiny.

'Are you still awake?' she whispered at last.

'I am.'

'I understand who you are. And I don't want you any other way.'

9 October 2009. Friday.

She slept fitfully, so terribly aware of him lying next to her.

Some time after four she woke when he moved, she heard him get up quietly and go to the bathroom. Then to the kitchen.

He spent some time there.

She heard him come back, get dressed. She felt the light kiss on her cheek. Silence, a rustle beside the bed, before she heard his soft footsteps leave the room.

The front door opened, and shut.

She lay there for another second, then leaped up and ran to the window. She wanted to see him. She pulled the curtain aside, her eyes on the security gate below.

He emerged from it, rucksack over his shoulders, and walked purposefully down the quiet street without looking back. His pace accelerated, he disappeared around the corner. She stood there until emotion overwhelmed her. She had to lie down again.

She saw the letter on her bedside cupboard.

Her name was written on the white envelope. She opened it.

Dear Milla

My head tells me it's too early to say I love you, but my heart speaks another language. There is a cellphone number below, in case of an emergency.

Lukas

She read it three times. Then, knowing she would not be able to sleep, she sat down at her writing table and reached for her diary.

She began to write.

The female operator saw Becker emerge from the security gate. Her drowsiness vanished. She grabbed the radio, spoke urgently to the three teams: 'Becker is on the move, he's out of the gate, walking in a westerly direction towards Highlands Avenue.'

Silence.

'Are you there?'

It took a while before someone answered, a voice still croaky with sleep, with a rushed 'We see him.'

'He's beyond my field of vision, tell me where he's going.'

'He's coming down Highlands, towards the city.'

'Don't lose him.'

'He'll see us. It's as quiet as the grave, nobody's moving, just him.'

'No, he mustn't see you.'

'Now he's running. He's fucking running.'

At 05.19 the female operator phoned Quinn.

She could hear by the sounds that he was fumbling with the phone.

'Just hold on,' he said in a muted tone. She heard his breathing, then: 'Any news?'

'We lost him.' Businesslike. She knew there was no way to soften it.

A long silence, then the barely audible sigh. 'Where?'

'In the Company Gardens. There were too many exits. They're still looking, but I don't think they'll find him.'

'Did he see us?'

'We think so, sir. That was part of the problem.'

Quinn took it all in. 'I'm coming.'

Masilo presented the mitigating circumstances; the hour of the night, the silent streets, the fact that he was on foot and must have realised he was being followed.

Mentz was remarkably calm through it all. 'Does it really matter? Now the CIA knows we know about him?'

'Probably not. What bothers me, is why he was still so eager to shake off our tails.'

'The Americans have their own agenda.'

'Which I cannot fathom. I went through all the transcripts and reports again and, in my mind, there is only one scenario that fits.'

'And that is?'

The Advocate referred to his notes. 'Their records show that Becker flew from Baghdad to London on 12 September, and the same evening to Johannesburg, where he landed on the morning of 13 September. The SAPS file says his hired car was hijacked just before nine o'clock that same morning in Sandton. He phoned Bull Shabangu for the first time on 18 September, and asked for his money. That was the only subject of all their conversations. And we have a recording from 6 October, when Osman told Suleiman Dolly in Chamberlain Street that "Shabangu told him I've got his money. Tweetybird or me." Now, let's assume the hijacking was genuine. And let us examine the manner of his contact with Shabangu and Osman. There is only one conclusion we can draw. There was something in that hijacked car. Something that Becker and the CIA want back very badly. And it's not money.'

Mentz nodded, slowly.

A knock on Masilo's door.

'Come in . . .'

Quinn opened it and put his head through. He saw Mentz. 'Morning, ma'am.'

'Morning, Quinn.'

'Shall I come back later?'

'No,' Masilo said. 'Any news?'

'It's Miss Jenny. She is opening a bunch of reports and documents on the system.'

'Which ones?'

'Shabangu, the Supreme Committee, PAGAD, Tweetybird, organised crime. She seems to be following a trail.'

Mentz was the first to respond. 'That's good news,' she said. 'She's doing it for him. For Becker. That means he will contact her again.'

The PIA team following Shaheed Latif Osman, sitting a block away from the Coronation Street mosque, beside the school grounds of the Zonnebloem School for Girls, lulled by Osman's strict routine and the knowledge that there was a GPS sensor on his car.

'Fuck,' the one with the binoculars said suddenly.

'What?' asked the driver.

'Start the car . . .'

'What do you see?'

'There's a guy . . . shit, call Quinn, someone just hijacked Osman. Go!'

'Keep your distance,' said Quinn. 'We'll track him with the GPS.'

He watched the flickering arrow icon on the Cape Town map, saw that Osman's car was driving in the direction of Woodstock.

'Did you see what the guy looked like?'

'He's white. Dark hair, that's all I could see.'

'I'm going to send a photo to your cellphone. See if you recognise him.' Quinn nodded at the operator beside him to get going.

'Roger.'

'It will take a little time, we have to reduce it first . . .'

'Roger.'

Quinn watched the progress of the car on the screen. They seemed to be on the way to Chamberlain Street. Why?

But the icon moved north along Melbourne Street, past the possible routes, into Victoria.

Where were they going?

Quinn spoke into the microphone. 'The photo has been sent, let us know when you receive it.'

On the screen Osman was travelling along Plein Street, then turned left into Albert.

To the N1?

'It might be this guy, I'm not sure,' the passenger in the tracking vehicle said.

To get onto the N1, the logical route was from Albert to Church Street in Woodstock, but the GPS showed Osman turning in the opposite direction.

Then left in Treaty. Inexplicable.

'Hang back,' said Quinn to the tails. 'It's circular, they will have to come out the other side.'

The icon stopped.

Quinn stared at the screen, frowning.

'Is it an industrial area?' he asked.

'Arse end of the world . . .'

Osman's car was still stationary.

Then Quinn realised what Becker was up to, because he was certain it *was* Becker. He didn't curse, it wasn't his way. He just said, into the cellphone, 'Go! Now, go to Osman's car. Hurry.'

63

Quinn's verbal report to Masilo was businesslike, he hid his disappointment.

He said Osman and Becker had stopped in Treaty Street, right beside the railway line. The surveillance team was just in time to see Becker forcibly dragging Osman across four rows of railway track, the two men on foot passing through previously prepared gaps in the high fences. Becker seemed to have a rucksack, another carry bag over his shoulder, and a weapon in his right hand.

They ran after them, but he had too much of a lead. At a distance of a hundred metres, past factories and warehouses, they saw Becker shove Osman into a car on the other side, at the Eastern end of Strand Street. It was a blue Volkswagen Citi Golf of indeterminate model. It was too far off to see the registration.

The Golf pulled away with screeching tyres and drove west, since

Strand ran into a dead end to the east. Becker could easily reach the N1 via Lower Church Street.

This, Quinn said in his calm way, is a well-trained man, a man who planned intelligently, who knew that he and/or Osman were being followed, who suspected Osman's car was being monitored. A man who wanted to shake off the trackers, and knew how.

Milla Strachan was proofreading for Oom Theunie, a review of South Africa's weapons transactions with Iran, Libya and Venezuela. She looked up when both men came in with Mrs Killian, recognising one of them. It was Nobody's Perfect, Advocate Masilo, the one wearing braces. She realised they were focused on her.

'Milla,' Mrs Killian said.

She felt the sudden claustrophobia, the tightening in her gut. 'Yes?' she said, alarm in her voice.

'They want to talk to you.'

'Would you come with me, please,' said the other man, the one wearing the black polo-neck sweater.

'Why?'

'Nothing to worry about,' said Mrs Killian.

'We just want to talk,' said Polo Neck.

At Janina Mentz's insistence, as Deputy Director at the time, the Presidential Intelligence Agency's interrogation room was pleasant. There were three stuffed beige chairs, bolted to the floor. They formed an intimate communication ring, a hospitable triangle. The floor was covered with wall-to-wall carpet, unpatterned, unobtrusive. The microphone was hidden behind the soft fluorescent light in the ceiling, and the CCTV camera placed in the room alongside – the observation room, as it was called – its lens directed through the one-way window at the three chairs.

Milla sat in one of them.

Masilo, Mentz and Quinn were in the observation room.

'Let her simmer,' Mentz said. 'For an hour or two, before you talk to her. Quinn, send some people to her flat in the meantime. Bring back everything that could be of value, let them go through it with a fine-tooth comb. And it must be obvious they were there.

Let them mess it up a bit. Tau, you break the bad news to her. And then let her go.'

Milla sat in the chair, her thoughts racing, panic inside, a chorus that kept echoing in her head, *they know, they know, they know* . . . until the questions took over: how long had they known? How did they know? What did they know? What did they want from her? What were they going to do with her? What was going on? This morning she had feverishly read the reports, about Shabangu, PAGAD, searching for reasons why the PIA was interested in Lukas. She had only seen spectres, ghostly possibilities that evaporated when you looked too sharply at them. What had Lukas done to them?

She still had no answers. She thought about what they would ask her, thought about possible answers, and gradually realised she had only done one thing wrong. She had not reported her contact with Lukas. Why not? Because no one had said she must. Was it such a great sin? Truly? Because it was not a crime, what could they do to her, what was the worst? Fire her?

Eventually she calmed down, and resistance grew in her: let them confront her, let them question her, let them discharge her, she didn't give a damn, she had committed no crime. Eventually Milla stood up and, resolute, went to the door, tried to pull it open, only to find it was locked. The sparks of anger leaped higher, who did they think they were? They couldn't do this, she had rights, she was no imbecile, no fool who would reveal state secrets. She was neither a criminal nor a child.

She sat down again, and heard the door open behind her. She looked around and saw it was Mr Perfect, Mr Nobody, Masilo in his braces. 'You don't have the right to lock me in here,' she said and stood up from the chair.

He smiled at her, locked the door behind him. 'Calm down,' he said, smoothly, as though they knew each other.

'Unlock the door,' she said.

He went to a chair opposite her. She smelled the aftershave, just a hint. 'That I cannot do.' He sat down. 'Please, Milla, let us talk, I am sure you realise there is much to talk about.'

She stood beside the chair. 'No, I don't think so.'

'Oh?'

'I have done nothing wrong.'

'Even more reason to sit and have a chat with me.'

She knew he was trying to manipulate her, but her choices were limited. She sat down reluctantly, and crossed her arms.

He said nothing, just smiled benevolently.

Until she could stand the silence no longer: 'What's going on?'

'You know very well.'

'I have no idea.'

'Lukas Becker.'

'I've done nothing wrong.'

'Then why your reaction. Earlier on?'

'How would you feel if someone did that to you? Out of the blue?'

'But I don't have secrets, Milla.'

'Everyone has secrets.'

He laughed softly. Then his expression turned serious. 'Milla, you're a pawn. A tool. He's using you, and I am sure you are completely unaware of it.'

'Lukas?'

'That's right.'

'Oh, please!'

'There is a lot about him that you don't know.'

'I wrote his profile. He . . . He doesn't even know where I work.'

Masilo laughed, long and heartily. 'You are very naive.'

'Why?'

'Milla, your Lukas Becker works for the CIA.'

It was her turn to laugh, uneasily. 'You're paranoid.'

'I must be honest with you, I was also sceptical at first. Until we let the Americans know we knew about him. The same day, only hours later, he suddenly disappeared. New accommodation, new car, new cellphone number . . .'

'And now you think . . .'

He didn't give her a chance. 'Did you know he's a murderer?'

'Rubbish!'

'The Julius Shabangu you so loyally read up on for him this morning. Who do you think eliminated him?'

'It wasn't him.'

'How do you know, Milla? Because he said so? Is that the evidence you have? Because we have a whole lot more.'

'No . . .'

'Milla, Milla, you trust so easily. You know he was in Israel, Egypt, Jordan, Iran and Turkey. But do you know why? Think a little about the places in conflict with America. What about his bank accounts? Doesn't that make you just a little suspicious? How does a man accumulate millions of rands in just six, seven years? Doing archaeological digs for universities? Look at the strange coincidence that he turned up at your dance school. Twice. Look at how he took you somewhere else every time, somewhere in the open, away from the microphones . . .'

'Microphones . . . ?' She didn't immediately grasp the full portent.

'Milla, we're not asleep . . .'

'You have no right.'

'We have. This is national security at stake, it is international . . .'

'You have no right.' There was a new note in her voice, anger and shame combined, and she half rose from her chair.

'We have your diaries too.'

It sank down slowly inside her, like a depth charge. Then it exploded. Milla Strachan sprang from the armchair, and leaped right at him.

64

'Thanks for returning my call, Janina,' said Burzynski, the Bureau Chief of the CIA.

'Of course, Bruno. As a matter of fact, we were just talking about you.'

'All good, I hope. Janina, I have a report from Langley, and I'm happy to say we are making progress. Let me briefly attempt to explain what they've tried to do. Step one was to make absolutely sure *The Madeleine* is not running LRIT and AIS, and I can confirm that it definitely isn't. The last record of a signal from this ship was received on 22 September at 23.30, from waypoint S13 34.973 W5 48.366, which is about one thousand five hundred miles west-northwest of Walvis Bay, in the Atlantic Ocean. Then it just stopped transmitting.

Went off the radar completely. We've checked with the SOLAS authorities, and they say they duly notified the owners of the vessel, but got no response . . .'

'It's a dummy corporation. All the registration details are bogus.'

'So we gathered. Step two was to plot all LRIT-silent vessels of the right size against possible matches for satellite imagery, and we identified sixteen potential candidates, of which fourteen have already been vetted through hi-res visual material – we've found some pretty interesting specimens, some smugglers in the Andaman and South China Sea, one ship being held by Somali pirates, but the majority are experiencing equipment problems, and are all accounted for. The last two are a bit of a problem. Adverse weather conditions, bad visibility from space . . .'

'Where are they?'

'North Atlantic, I'll have to check. Grand Banks, something like that. The weather should clear within the next twelve hours, and we'll be ready.'

'Bruno, I can't thank you enough.'

Milla Strachan struck Advocate Tau Masilo on his left cheekbone. She hit out again, but he stopped her, grabbing her wrists.

'*Thiba*!' he shouted in his mother tongue, shocked. He pushed her away, straightened up and forced her back into her chair. She struggled furiously, kicking at him.

'*Se ke* . . .' He let go of her suddenly, raised his hand to slap her, but stopped himself, and went over to the door.

'*Nkwenyane*,' he said, out of breath. 'What a fishwife!'

'I quit,' Milla screamed, her blood still boiling. 'You can keep your job.'

Masilo, gingerly probing his cheekbone, looked at her and smiled slowly.

'Very well,' he said and took the key out of his pocket. 'Let me get someone to escort you, and you can pack up your things.'

The Director phoned Rajkumar in his office. 'I need to know what the weather is like in the North Atlantic right now. The Grand Banks area.'

'Call you back?'

'I'll hold.'

'OK.'

She heard the click of Raj's mouse, his laboured breathing. 'Getting there . . . getting there . . . OK. I have a satellite image of . . . twenty minutes ago . . . looks pretty good . . .'

'No bad weather? No clouds?'

'Just a second . . . Weatheronline in the UK says . . . nope, no bad weather, let me just check the NASA Earth Science Office . . .'

She waited.

'Clear as a bell, a few clouds off Canada, but that's it.'

'Could you double-check and get back to me?'

'Absolutely.'

She put down the phone.

Why would Burzynski lie?

With anger and shame burning inside her, and two muscular officials walking behind her, Milla collected her handbag and the few items in her drawer.

Dead silence hung over the Report Squad, only Donald MacFarland challenging the two escorts with a look, and then giving her a slight nod, in sympathy. The others avoided her eyes and only later, when she sat beside the sea at Milnerton, did she realise someone must have talked to them. She wondered what they had been told.

But now she put only the personal items in her handbag, gave Mac one last look, and walked out.

At the security door one said, 'Your card, please.'

She took it out and threw it down in front of him.

The other one opened the door for her.

In the flat Milla found chaos. Cupboard doors stood wide, the floor was strewn with articles.

In her bedroom she saw they had taken her diaries. And her laptop. Helplessness and rage and injustice overwhelmed her, but she knew there were microphones somewhere in this place, and she wept silently, her fists clenched.

She suddenly had to get out, this space was polluted now. She picked up her handbag, took out the things she had packed up at the office, threw them hastily down on her writing table and left. Just before she got to her car, she stopped with a sudden anxiety. She opened her handbag, searched furiously for her purse, found it. She opened it carefully, to see whether there was evidence of some other fingers going through it.

Lukas's letter was there, beside the banknotes, still folded up as she had placed it there that morning.

She took it out and thought back, her handbag had been in the office, hanging over the back of her chair.

Would they have searched it?

She was going to memorise the number, get rid of the letter.

Quinn and Masilo watched the screen, saw over the video feed how Miss Jenny suddenly stopped to look in her handbag.

It was Quinn who read her body language, put her urgency and the object of her interest together.

'We didn't search her handbag,' he said, in self-reproach. 'It was here, in the office.'

'Ay, ay,' said Masilo, and touched the slight swelling on his cheek with his fingertips.

'Looks like it's a piece of paper.'

They saw her fold it up again, put it back in her purse, and continue to the car. He picked up the radio and said: 'Stand by, Miss Jenny is on the move.'

'How many teams?' Masilo asked.

'All three who were following Becker.'

'And lost him.' No reproach, just a statement of fact.

'And they know how unacceptable that is. Becker was on foot, in the early hours, he knew we were tailing him, and he is a pro. She isn't. We have GPS on her car, we are plotting her cellphone for position, we hear every call, we have microphones in her flat . . .'

'OK,' said Masilo. He watched the screen where Milla's car was now a moving arrow on the map. 'Where is she going?'

At first she just drove, instinctively, in the direction of Durbanville. Until she realised what she was doing, and why. A sense of panic came over her, she turned off at the Koeberg exit, not knowing where she could go, no place was safe, she must phone Lukas now, right now. She reached out her hand for the phone in her bag, found it, the number in her head, typed in the first three digits.

A car beside her hooted, shrill and sudden. She looked up, shocked, saw she was veering across the lane, jerked the Renault back, looked across at the other car: a man grimacing, arm waving, finger raised, angry words forming soundlessly.

Then he was past and her hands were trembling. She knew she must stop, first stop and then phone. She saw the Caltex service station beyond the traffic lights, she would turn in there. And only then, from somewhere, a voice in her head said don't phone, they're listening.

The realisation reverberated right through her.

Lagoon Beach was the first place she could park, she turned off without thinking, she just wanted to get off the road, get out of the car. She got out, locked the Renault, and walked blindly, her handbag over her shoulder, her hand clutching it desperately, as though it were her sole possession.

Masilo's allegations were flickering, blinding lights that obscured everything, so that she could not think at first, could neither recall her conversations with Lukas nor the content of the reports she had read, only see the fireworks that had just exploded into her life.

She walked for six kilometres, past the golf course, the houses, past other people, unaware of the four men trailing her on foot. Then she sat down without warning, in the sand some distance from the sea, handbag on her lap, chin in her hands, eyes gazing over the ocean, and she thought, long and hard.

The agent lowered his binoculars and told Quinn over the cellphone: 'No, she's just sitting there.'

'Listen carefully: we suspect she is waiting for Becker. You all know what he looks like. Let me know immediately you see him, but lie low. He's a professional, and most likely armed.'

'Roger.'

'The reaction unit is on the way. If Becker comes, they will bring him in. Stand by.'

* * *

It was the knowledge that she had come so close to phoning Lukas that forced Milla to try to calm down.

She sat with her eyes closed, trying despairingly and at first in vain to suppress everything: the fears, emotion, the doubt, the humiliation and self-pity.

It was the pain in the knuckle of her right hand that gradually penetrated, shifting her focus: why was it so sore? Then she remembered how she had hit Masilo, and recalled the sudden, deep sense of injustice that she had experienced at that moment. She saw herself again, striking out at him. 'What a fishwife.' And she couldn't help smiling; Lord, Milla, was that *you*, the little housewife from Durbanville?

It lifted the awful tension – not entirely, just enough for her to breathe out slowly and deliberately, find a foothold against the storm in her head. She thought, I have made progress after all, I have grown: in that blow-striking moment I fought back, instinctively. And it was good.

She clung to the positive thoughts, she tried to recall others, like the entry in her diary, *This morning I found a piece of myself. I have a habit. To suppress fears, to hide them from myself. And then to do strange things.* And, *Milla, the anxious cat, takes anxious leaps, and mostly I don't know that I am anxious.*

She decided she wasn't going to suppress these fears. She wasn't going to deny these anxieties, she was going to tackle them head-on, she was going to plan her leaps. She was going to find the truth, she was going to make a plan. In the words of Lukas Becker and Voltaire, she was going to play the cards that life dealt her in a reasoned way.

She sat there for over an hour, a lonely figure on a wide beach.

65

'She's standing up, she's walking back to her car,' the agent said.

'Nobody came near her?' Quinn asked.

'No one. Hold on . . . Looks like she's phoning . . .'

Quinn turned to one of the team members in the Ops Room. 'I want to hear the call.'

The technician nodded and made the adjustments.

'Yes, she has the cellphone to her ear . . .' the agent on Milnerton Beach confirmed.

Milla's voice came over the sound system. 'This is Milla Strachan, may I speak to Gus, please?'

'Hold on,' said an unfamiliar voice.

Music on the line.

'I want to know whose number this is,' Quinn said to his team.

'Milla, how are you?' A male voice.

'Fine, thanks. Gus, I need your help . . .'

'Don't tell me Christo is giving you trouble?'

'No, this is work related. The place I began working at on the first of September is the PIA, the Presidential Intelligence Agency. Their offices . . .'

'The PIA, the spy guys?'

'Yes. Their address is . . .'

'You became a spy?'

'No, I just wrote reports. Their offices are in the Wale Street Chambers, on the corner of Wale and Long Street . . .'

'Hold on, I want to write this down.'

Someone whispered to Quinn: 'The number belongs to a firm of attorneys in Durbanville. Smuts, Kemp and Smal.'

'Get one of the surveillance teams to drive in that direction.'

'OK,' the man's voice said over the phone.

Milla's voice: 'I will SMS you the telephone number of their switchboard, and the name of the Deputy Director involved. They broke into my flat this morning and stole my laptop and all my diaries. I want them back, Gus . . .'

'*Jissis*,' someone in the Ops Room whispered.

Quinn raised his hand to request silence. It was the calm in Milla Strachan's voice that worried him the most.

'. . . and then I want someone to come and remove the bugs that they have planted.'

'Fuck, Milla,' said the one she called 'Gus'. And then, a short, hard laugh.

'And I want you to know,' said Milla, 'the chances are good that they are listening to this call, but it doesn't really matter. I want my things back, and the more public and open the process is to get them, the better. Gus, they mustn't be able to hide.'

'An urgent interdict is completely public. If you want I can phone

one of my buddies at Media24 . . . but you must know, tomorrow it will be all over the papers.'

'Let me just call Barend first and tell him that his mother is going to be in the news.'

Masilo told Mentz about Miss Jenny's call to Kemp, the attorney, and ended with: 'She SMSed my name to him. I think it's personal because I told her about Becker's misdeeds.'

Then he waited for the explosion, but it didn't erupt.

Mentz stared at him. For a long time. Then she said coldly: 'The Americans are lying to us.'

He had to make the mental leap first. 'What about?'

'About the weather in the North Atlantic Ocean. It's a delaying tactic, Tau. It has something to do with the fact that Becker has given them Osman, or that they still haven't retrieved what was stolen from Becker. We will have to get Becker. And fast.'

'Miss Jenny is the way to him.'

'And the little bitch is phoning her lawyer,' said Janina Mentz, but without venom.

'I should have read the signs better when she assaulted me,' said Masilo, and he stroked his cheekbone again. 'I miscalculated.'

'We should have read the signs better when we employed her. She had the courage to walk out of her marriage . . .'

Masilo thought back to the rumour that Mentz, too, a decade ago, had left behind an unhappy marriage with a straying husband, and wondered how much the Director identified with Milla Strachan.

Operation Shawwal

Transcription: *Audio surveillance, M. Strachan. No 14 Daven Court, Davenport Street, Vredehoek*
Date and Time: *7 October 2009. 23.19*

LB: Why did you wait so long?

MS: I wonder about that every day. But then . . . I think it was . . . there are so many reasons. I didn't know how a functional marriage worked, I only knew my parents' one and I knew, at least, that that was not normal. But what is normal? I mean . . . When I looked around, everyone had a marriage like that, the man and his career, the wife at home complaining she didn't get enough attention. Two worlds, it was the norm, everyone experienced it, everyone just got on with it. But it was more than that. If you are depressed, if you lose your self-confidence, if you live in this daze, if you don't have meaning and purpose, then every day just slips through your fingers. It's the routine as well, so soul-destroying . . . You don't think, you don't really feel, even, I don't know . . . if you've never experienced it, it's probably hard to . . . I . . . It's such a slow, silent process, like the lobster in the pot of boiling water, you get used to it, you don't realise it. And even if you . . . I think Christo had his first big affair ten years ago, but I was too naive then. Or maybe I didn't want to . . . I only realised last year, when . . . Lord, it is all so suburban . . .

LB: If you would rather not . . .

MS: No, no, I want to, I've written about it in my diary, but when I read it again lately, it's just so . . . pathetic. I . . . all the signs were there, I was just . . . blind is not the right word. Blunted? Absent? I don't know, I was so awfully introverted . . . He was in the shower, one evening, he had to go out again for a business dinner, his cellphone was lying on the table, downstairs. I heard the SMS. I still don't know what made me look, I had never . . . It was just so banal. About what she wanted to do with Christo, that night. I remember how I thought it must have been sent to the wrong number, it wasn't Christo. I mean, our sex . . . when it still happened was so . . . proper.

LB: Milla . . .

MS: I drove after him. To the Tyger Waterfront. Not even far away. Just around the corner. Out in the open, at a restaurant. She looked so . . . I don't know, ordinary, younger than him, but not . . . not someone who would send an SMS like that. I still wonder if she knew she wasn't the only one, that he had three or four others, Barend saw him with another one, a blonde, even younger, that's how he knew . . .

'Are we going to negotiate with her?' Tau Masilo asked.

'Absolutely not,' said Mentz. 'Let Mrs Killian call her. And say something like "You've been cleared, but we had to be sure. We will deliver everything to your flat this evening".'

'And the microphones?'

'Leave them. Let's see how many they find.'

* * *

Milla drove through Table View in the five o'clock traffic. She kept an eye on her rear-view mirror with the strong suspicion that they were behind her, somewhere. But she saw nothing.

She crossed the N7. At Bothasig she turned left onto the N13. She still couldn't spot any tails. It meant either that they weren't there, or a bit further behind, and that was all she needed. She accelerated, driving as fast as the traffic allowed, flashing her lights at slow cars, shooting past.

At the Altydgedacht junction, as she was about to turn right to Tyger Valley, her cellphone rang.

'Hello?'

'Hello, Milla, this is Betsy Killian.'

Milla remained silent.

'I just want to say that the team and I are very sorry about what happened.'

'Thank you.'

'And I can also tell you, your diaries and your laptop will be delivered to your flat this evening.'

'So they *are* listening to my phone calls.'

'Excuse me?'

'It doesn't matter. Mrs Killian, thank you for phoning. Just ask them to tidy up everything, please.'

'I will pass the message on. They want you to sign for delivery. What time will you be home?'

'No, Mrs Killian,' Milla said. 'I don't know when I will be home. Tell them to put everything back where it belongs. They know how to get in. Oh, and tell Advocate Masilo, if they return everything, I will drop the interdict.'

'I will tell him.'

When she rang off, Milla wondered whether there was any other reason for the call. She knew, from the operator's reports, that it was possible to determine someone's position from a cellphone signal.

It didn't matter either. She would leave the phone in the car when she went to call Lukas.

Transcription: *Interrogation of Enoch Mangope by S. Kgomo. Safe House, Parkview, Johannesburg*

Date and Time: *9 October 2009, 14.14*

SK: You were one of those who hijacked Becker's car on 13 September.
EM: (No response.)
SK: I am not from the police, it doesn't matter.
EM: (No response.)
SK: So, afterwards, where did Becker find you?
EM: Joel Road. Berea.
SK: Was he armed?
EM: *Yebo.*
SK: With a shotgun?
EM: *Hhayi*! *iSistela*.
SK: A pistol.
EM: *Yebo.*
SK: And then?
EM: Then he said, come with me.
SK: Where did he take you?
EM: Indlu. In Randburg. A town house.
SK: Would you find the place again?
EM: *Kungaba* . . .
SK: Then, what did he do?
EM: He tied me up. To the chair. Then he talked a lot.
SK: What did he say?
EM: He wanted his money.
SK: What money?
EM: The money that was in his bag.
SK: Did you see the money?
EM: (No response.)
SK: Come on, Enoch, I told you, we are after Becker, not you. Did you see the money?
EM: *Yebo.*
SK: How much was it?
EM: Lots. English money. Pounds.
SK: So, what did you tell him?
EM: I didn't have his money.
SK: And then?
EM: He asked me, who did?
SK: Yes?
EM: Then I said nothing.

SK: And then?

EM: Then he didn't talk again, the whole night. No food, no water. He kept me awake, *kaningi*, I couldn't sleep, because I was sitting like this.

SK: When did you tell him Enoch? About Shabangu. Inkunzi.

EM: The third day. He took me to the *amaphoyisa*.

SK: The police? I don't understand . . .

EM: He took me in the car, to the police. Then he said, I must talk, or I would go to *ijele*, the jail.

SK: In the police station?

EM: *Hhayi*. Outside.

EM: And then you told him?

EM: What could I do?

SK: And then?

EM: Then he phoned Inkunzi. And he let me go.

SK: Did he torture you?

EM: *Kungani*?

SK: Did he hit you or something?

EM: *Hhayi*.

SK: Not at all?

EM: (No response.)

SK: Did he ask you about anything else? What was in the bag?

EM: Like what?

SK: Anything.

EM: He just talked about the money.

SK: Nothing else? Nothing?

EM: *Mahhala*.

66

'She's stopped,' said Quinn over the car radios to her trackers. 'In the Tyger Valley parking lot, the eastern side. Team One, how far are you from the shopping centre?'

'About a kilometre . . .'

'Hurry up. Park, and go and find her. Team Two, do the same. Team Three, let us know when you get there, you have to cover her car.'

'Roger,' they responded, one after the other.

'We're plotting her cellphone now, we'll let you know more or less where she is.'

She knew the Tyger Valley shopping centre, every nook and cranny of it.

She hurried into Entrance 8, stopped abruptly and looked around. People everywhere, walking in, walking out, but nothing that looked suspicious.

She walked into the centre, slipped left into the Pick 'n' Pay side entrance, then out again at the Durbell Pharmacy end, down the escalator, turned left, ducked under the barrier at the cinema.

'Madam!' shouted one of the movie ticket collectors. Milla began to jog, just waving her hand at him.

Out the other side, she turned right, up the steps, then left again in the Arena. The telephones were there, near the escalators, as she had recalled. She opened her handbag, took out her purse and went to the coin-operated phone furthest away. She took out the coins. Had one good look around, tapped in the numbers one by one.

It rang.

She put the coin in the slot. It dropped.

'Hello?' Lukas's voice was brusque.

'I don't have much time, I'm calling from a payphone. I'm going to ask you two questions. Just answer them. Nothing else.'

'Milla, what's . . .'

'Nothing else.'

'I'm listening.'

'Do you work for the CIA?'

She listened with every fibre of her being, heard the sound he uttered, astonishment and amusement combined, as though she was making a joke. 'Do I work . . .' Another noise, a little concern now. 'No. The answer is no.'

He's telling the truth, Milla thought. She knew it. 'Did you shoot Julius Shabangu?'

'No!' Fervent. 'Milla, you have to tell me . . .'

'Lukas, just listen. The flat was bugged, they're listening to my cellphone calls, I think they're following me. They're looking for you. I want to warn you, and I want to help you.'

He was quiet a moment. When he spoke again, his voice was suddenly calm. 'Do you know who they are?'

'Yes. The Presidential Intelligence Unit.'

Another silence. Then, 'How do you know . . . Wait, that's not important now. Where are you?'

'In the Tyger Valley Centre. No one followed me when I came in.'

'Where is your cellphone?'

'In the car. Outside.'

'Good. Listen very carefully, I'm going to tell you what to do.'

Rajkumar waddled into the Ops Room out of breath, holding a memory stick in his hand. 'You had better listen,' he said to Quinn and Masilo, and pushed it into a computer.

'Patch it through to the system,' said Raj. 'News bulletin on Kfm, five minutes ago.'

He got the audio file playing. The newsreader's voice, clear and solemn: *Local police are calling on the public to help in the search for Cape Town businessman and Muslim religious leader Mr Shaheed Osman. Osman was reported missing after an apparent car-jacking outside the Azzavia Masjid mosque earlier today. Several witnesses saw a man forcing Osman into his late model Toyota Prado. Family members have told Kfm news they are deeply concerned about Mr Osman's health, as he suffers from a serious heart condition.*

She walked briskly out through the Game exit, through the underground parking, to the slope down to Hume Street. She looked for a pedestrian path, spotted one to the right and jogged over to it. She skidded down the incline to the bottom.

The street was busy, just as she had hoped. She waited for the first gap in the traffic and sprinted. A motorist hooted sharply at her, she stood on the island for a second, then ran across the other lane, to the ugly steel fence of Willow Bridge. Only then did she stop and look around, out of breath, searching, as Lukas had coached her. *Were there any other people walking too fast? Or running. Identify them. Colour, gender, clothing, height, appearance.*

There were none.

She ran to the corner and turned left.

* * *

'Nothing?' Quinn asked over the cellphone.

'It's a big centre,' the operator said. 'There are only four of us.'

'Keep looking.'

'What about her cellphone?'

'We suspect she left it in the car.'

First she bought a bright red headscarf, and a white jacket. She asked for the largest shopping bag they had. Then, the sunglasses with outsize white frames. *If you don't have cash, use your credit card. It doesn't matter now.*

Then she bought a cellphone.

Where is your cellphone?

In the car.

Good. Leave it there. Buy a new one. They will ask for your ID, tell them you will bring it tomorrow, it's an emergency, your . . . your phone has been stolen, you have to let your family know urgently. Buy a charger that works in a car. Then find a place, somewhere in a shop, where you can watch the doors, somewhere quiet . . .

She walked down to the basement parking, ran to the back, against the wall. On the back of a blue Mazda she put down the box with the cellphone, opened it and assembled.

There is usually enough power in the battery to last an hour or two . . .

When she was finished she sent the SMS. HAVE PHONE. NOW FOR STEP 2.

She wound the scarf around her head, put on the dark glasses and slipped into the jacket.

At Pick 'n' Pay she quickly bought the bare essentials – a toothbrush, colourless lip gloss, mascara and deodorant. A writing pad and pen. She asked one of the bag packers where she could find a minibus taxi.

'Where to, madam?' Amused.

'To Bellville.'

'Up in Durban Road, at the Engen garage. But it's a long walk.'

'It doesn't matter. Thank you.'

Walking out of Willow Bridge was a problem, there was only one route in and out.

Get something to change your appearance, a jersey or a jacket, something bright. And a big shopping bag, anything to change your silhouette. From then on try to walk differently, slower, head down, like you are tired, on your way home. Don't look back, don't look round, just walk . . .

It took her just over fifteen minutes to reach the filling station. There were three taxis there. She approached the rear one. 'Where are you going?' she asked the fare collector.

'Is that a philosophical question, or does madam want to ride with us, genuine?'

67

She took the Metro train from Bellville to the city.

There were few people travelling in that direction this late in the afternoon. She sought out the busiest compartment, as Lukas had instructed her. She kept her eyes on the floor, her handbag on her lap, holding it with both arms. Most of her fellow travellers were young men. Milla thought about the report on organised crime.

She SMSed Lukas: ON THE TRAIN.

Minutes later came the response: WAIT IN FRONT OF STATION IN ADDERLEY. BLUE VW GOLF.

She replied: OK.

Then she put the cellphone in her handbag, sat hunched over in her seat and wondered what he would say when she told him everything.

'We can't find her,' the operator told Quinn.

'They have CCTV. I'm going to phone the shopping centre office and ask them to let you look at the tapes. She must be there somewhere, her car and cellphone are. But two of you must keep looking. What about fitting rooms . . . ?'

'It's difficult.'

'No it isn't. Look.'

She didn't have to wait long before the blue Golf stopped next to her. The car's paint was faded, it had rust spots, a few dents. She bent down, saw it was Lukas wearing a baseball cap, opened the door and got in.

He pulled away immediately, but put out his hand and grasped hers, looked at the headscarf and the dark glasses. He grinned and said: 'Mata Hari Strachan.' She saw the tension in his face, thought she was to blame. She squeezed his hand and said, 'I'm sorry.'

'No, Milla, I am.' His eyes on the busy traffic.

'Lukas, there are things you don't know.'

He glanced fleetingly at her, worried.

Then she told him, from the beginning.

They drove towards Blouberg, in the last crush of rush hour. Past Milnerton Beach where she had come to her senses a few hours before, though she was barely aware of her surroundings. She let the words tumble out of her, too fast, the pressure to confess her deceit was too great, she stumbled over the sentences. The sun was setting over the sea, Lukas's face was grim in the soft light. He listened in silence, not looking at her.

When she was finished, he just said, 'Milla . . .' with a weary admiration.

She felt the relief of a burden set down, the suspense of waiting for his reaction. It didn't come quickly.

He sighed. 'I don't work for the CIA and I had nothing to do with Shabangu's death.'

'I believe you.' Then: 'Was it coincidence, Lukas? When you went dancing?'

'Yes.'

'And the Monday night?'

He lifted his hand from the steering wheel in a gesture of helplessness.

She waited, increasingly aware of his tiredness.

'One night in New York,' he said quietly, 'I was thinking about a university girlfriend. Just incidentally wondering what had become of her. And the next day I bumped into her on Lexington Avenue . . . What are the chances . . . ? I can't explain it . . .'

She understood what he was trying to say. 'I know.'

'It just happened . . .'

'Do you still think of her?' Her attempt to provide relief.

It worked. He turned his head and smiled. 'Not so much any more.'

'You're tired,' she said.

'No,' he said. 'I'm in trouble. And I'll have to tell you about it, because you are part of it now.'

At half past six the operator told Quinn they had studied the video material. They had seen Milla Strachan walk into Entrance 8 of the Tyger Valley centre just after 14.00. They could determine her route more or less, she had been responsible for a small flurry of excitement at the cinema, she had walked past a camera in the Arena. It was fourteen minutes before they saw her leave via Exit 6 on the western side. One last camera had followed her trail in the underground parking lot, apparently to the outside.

They suspected someone had picked her up there.

Lukas Becker told Milla about the kidnapping of Shaheed Latif Osman.

It was supposed to be over within a couple of hours, he said. He wanted to intercept Osman and his car outside the mosque, get him into the Golf in a way that ensured no one could follow them, drive to Blouberg, tie Osman to a chair in the rented apartment and say as soon as they paid the money back he would release Osman.

It had initially run according to plan. Outside the mosque Osman had been very frightened, then he recognised Lukas from their previous confrontation outside Osman's house, and calmed down a bit. He had got into his Prado, followed instructions and driven off, saying over and over, 'Shabangu is lying, I don't have your money.' To which Becker had patiently replied: 'Then you will have to get it.'

The first problem arose when he had forced Osman out of his car next to a railway line in Woodstock. While he was getting out, Osman had put his hand in his pocket. 'Don't,' Becker shouted and pointed the pistol at him, but the man ignored it. Lukas tackled him to the ground, pinned his hands and pressed the pistol barrel to his cheek.

'Lie still.'

There was dreadful tension in Osman's body, a desperate look in his eye. Becker, acutely aware that his time was running out, ripped off the jacket and searched it. He found only a cellphone, tossed it over the fence.

Osman jumped up then, but strangely did not run away. He struggled back to his car.

'What are you doing?' he shouted, stopping him.

'The bag,' Osman said urgently.

The bag. The shoulder bag Osman had carried out of the mosque.

Lukas turned back swiftly, pulling Osman with him, and collected the bag from the Toyota Prado. He had to be quick, because his pursuers were coming.

Once they were over the railway tracks, in the alley between factory buildings, Osman tried to take the bag from Lukas. 'Give it to me!'

Lukas jerked it away and said: 'Come.'

Osman, despair etching his face, walked more slowly and grabbed his chest. 'My heart,' he said.

'Stop lying. Come on!'

In the Golf, Osman had sat hunched up, waxen, wet with perspiration, breathing rapidly. A trembling hand reached out for the black bag in slow motion.

'Leave the bag.' Then he looked into Osman's eyes, saw his wild panic. The hand jerking back to Osman's left shoulder, face distorted in pain. Still, Lukas Becker did not believe him.

'I have to have my medicine,' Osman groaned.

Lukas ignored him, concentrating on the road ahead, and the rear-view mirror.

Then Osman collapsed. Becker cursed and stopped. Picked up Osman's head, saw the eyes rolled back. He grabbed the man's wrist, felt the dreadful pulse and knew it was a heart attack, he had training in basic first aid, he knew the next fifteen minutes meant life or death to Osman.

That changed everything, he raced into the city, to the nearest medical help, the Chris Barnard Memorial Hospital, with an unconscious Osman. He stopped at Casualty, carried Osman in with a fireman's lift and called for help. The medical personnel rushed up to them, ordering him to put Osman down on a hospital trolley. He explained that the man had had a heart attack, he lied and said he had found him just down the street.

They ripped open Osman's Muslim robe, pressed stethoscopes to his chest, put an oxygen mask over his face and pushed him through the swing doors.

'I phoned the hospital just before I picked you up. They still haven't identified him, but they say his condition is critical. If he dies . . . I thought the people following him were his people. His bodyguards. I thought the people following me were his people. But when you spoke about the PIA over the phone . . . That changes everything. They can connect me. They think I murdered Shabangu. Now they will think I killed Osman as well.'

Janina Mentz threw the stapler first. The paperweight followed, leaving another mark in the door of her office.

Then she said, 'Jesus Christ,' before striding up and down her office, her face crimson with fury.

Tau Masilo just sat there. He had no defence.

A housewife, a report writer, an amateur, had evaded the professional surveillance teams of the Presidential Intelligence Agency.

What was there to say?

He unlocked the door of the holiday unit at the Big Bay Beach Club and let her walk in. The interior was gaily decorated, cottage furniture, sea-blue and white walls, an open-plan sitting room and kitchen. She put her shopping bag on the kitchen counter beside a black carry bag.

She turned to him, held him tightly. His arms wrapped around her, but with tension in his body. 'Milla, you can't stay here . . .'

She looked up at him in query.

'This is *my* trouble,' he said. '*My* problem. *My* risk. They can't do anything to you, you are not guilty of anything. You have to walk away from it all, until it's over . . . You . . . Your circumstances . . .'

She just shook her head, knowing that she couldn't answer him now, the words would come out wrong, like when she had confessed in the Golf.

'When did you last eat?' she asked.

68

Lukas, my love,

Alliteration, unintended, but I am immediately delighted by it. And therein lies the root of the problem.

Because my life is a flood of words, a stream, a river that never stops flowing. I am not a drowning person being washed along, but a water-word creature. I frolick here, in the words of my thoughts, the words I hear, the words I read and write. The words are in me and around me and through me and they never stop. I bob and swim and dive in them, splish and splash, this is the world I live in, my natural habitat, I can see the words and feel, hear and taste them.

The word-water is brown; a thousand drops of colourless conjunctions, and in-between words, and only-there-to-serve-other words. But some words are silver, like fish that dart and leap, glittering bows in the sun. Action words, wholly dynamic. Verbs. Living words. And others are heavy, dark, riverbed words, round rolling boulder words that scrape and chip and erode, and here I go again, compulsively, I am an addict, this letter is my intravenous feed, my dose for the day.

Speech is different. There the current frequently drags me away, there are whirlpools and rapids and submerged rocks; then the words slip away. But when I write, when it is just me and the river and I can open my eyes under the surface, I see every word, and search and select.

So I write. Much, and often, and have done for a long time. It gives me control. And that is the dilemma.

Thoughts and written words don't make a life. They can tell the stories, but they can't make the stories. They can fantasise (and I am good at that), but fantasies are phantom stories, word shadows, mirages that fade away when you get too close. They are rivers that dry up.

I don't have a story, Lukas. I began to write a book, the other day, and my best resource was to tap everything from my single major act – my running away, my making-life-new-at-forty. That is the sum total of my doing, my single source of character conflict, the climax of my existence and the depth of my story river. Perhaps you will understand better if I say, before I knew you, I was in love with your story, the one I was required to write as a profile and a report. You are everything I wanted to be, everything I fantasised for my own life: a discoverer, a doer, a traveller, a risk-taker, you followed your heart and passions and interests, you experienced, lived. I sat in front of that computer and thought, how eagerly would I love to write your story. How wonderful your book would be.

This morning (it feels a lifetime away) I sat on Milnerton Beach and the pain in my hand rescued me – because it reminded me of something I did. And in that act, never mind that it was through shame and anger, I did not walk away, I fought back.

And this afternoon I fought back again; through a phone call to retrieve my diaries, since then I have sneaked, evaded, camouflaged and outmanoeuvred. Action words. My heart beat, my hands shook, I rode in a minibus taxi, sat in a suburban train – both firsts for me, what would the Durbanville wives say? I discovered another world, I crossed borders, I lived (just a little bit dangerously) and I can write about it, Lukas, one day I can use these small scraps of experience.

By now you must be able to guess what I am trying to say: that I dare not, in your words, 'walk away from it all'. That I want to have more, to live more, to experience more.

I know what you meant to say with 'your circumstances . . .' and I can't blame you. You wanted to say that I am a mother, I have a child, I have responsibilities, I don't have to (or can't, or ought not, or must not) stay in this great adventure. It is a question I have been wrestling with for months, and I still don't know where the truth lies. For seventeen years I lived for my son and my husband. Now, for Barend's sake as well, I must live for myself.

You said, 'you can't stay here'. But I must.

Please . . .

10 October 2009. Saturday.

She came out of the bedroom wearing one of his shirts. She saw him at the breakfast counter, his bare back to her, bent over, all attention on the disassembled parts of a laptop, tools spread over the counter top.

And her letter nearby.

She leaned against the door jamb, looking at him, at the long muscles of his back, at his neck, his dark hair so neat in its military cut. She wanted to touch him, went closer.

His head jerked around, and he looked at her for a second. 'Milla,' he said, stern and urgent, scaring her. 'Stop right there.'

'What?'

He turned back to the innards of the computer. 'Explosives. It's Osman's laptop . . . Just let me . . .' She saw him carefully pull out a thin, silver tube, with two thin wires attached. He put it to one side, with great respect. Then he slowly lifted out a thin worm of greyish white stuff, it looked like children's modelling clay.

'C4,' he said, keeping it still, touching it respectfully. 'There might be another detonator here . . .'

Until he was satisfied, had taken the clay out of the interior of the computer and put it aside. He wiped perspiration off his forehead and turned to her.

'Good morning,' he said.

She came close, leaned against him, her hand on his bare back, kissed him on the cheek. 'So that's what you do before breakfast . . .'

He held her tightly, said nothing.

'Did you read my letter?'

'I did.'

'And?'

He let go slowly. 'Look,' he said, and pointed at the explosive.

'I understand. But . . .'

He shook his head, put his hands on her shoulders, his face solemn. 'Milla . . .'

'I can help you,' though she knew what he was going to say.

'Milla, I want you, I want to be with you and I'm coming back to you when this thing is over, I swear to you. But look at it objectively, please; if things get rough . . . I can't afford to worry about your safety, I can't allow that to affect my choices . . .'

She couldn't keep the disappointment from her face.

'I'm sorry,' he said.

Later, while she drank coffee and he put the computer together again, he told her about the laptop, how he understood now why Osman reached for his cellphone first during the kidnapping.

'This receiver was on top of the computer lid. Osman wanted to phone a number that would activate the explosive. The charge is small, just enough to destroy the computer. And when I took the phone away from him, he tried to get to the computer, because there is a switch as well . . .'

'But why?' she asked.

'That is what I want to find out.'

When he had finally put the computer back together, there was another obstacle.

'It needs a password,' Becker said.

Milla came to look. A box on the screen. *Enter your Windows password.*

'You don't know what it is.'

'No idea.'

'Perhaps I can help.'

'You know about computers?'

'No, but I know someone.'

Janina Mentz and Tau Masilo on one side of the table, the Americans on the other, in a meeting room at the Department of Home Affairs in Plein Street, the nearest to neutral ground that Mentz could find at short notice.

From the outset she was cool towards the four CIA people. Burzynski's reaction was a small, secret smile, as though he knew something. It irritated Mentz, she decided to fire the first salvo: 'Bruno, I haven't informed the Minister about the CIA's shenanigans yet, but if we can't find a resolution by lunchtime, I will have no choice.'

'Shenanigans?' with the surprise of the innocent.

'Please. I really don't have time to play games.'

'Janina, I honestly don't know what you are talking about.'

'Adverse weather conditions in the North Atlantic? Do you honestly think we are so backward that we don't know how to check the weather?'

'I said I wasn't sure exactly where . . .'

'Oh, nonsense, Bruno. You knew exactly. You always do. You were playing for time, and I deeply resent that, because it is putting South African citizens in harm's way. Do you really want that on your conscience?'

'There's risk to your public? You never said that. Perhaps, Janina, you could start by levelling with us, especially in view of the fact that you expect us to throw all our resources at your problem.'

'Here's a bit of levelling, Bruno: We don't have an operative snooping around the CIA at the moment. We don't do that with our allies.'

'Are you suggesting what I think you are suggesting?'

She clapped her hand on the file that lay before her, decided to play her trump card. 'Be careful now, Bruno. I have some very interesting information in here.' She saw a momentary hesitation, and she thought, *I've got you.*

'Then, by all means, share it with us,' said Burzynski.

She opened the file, took out the photograph of Lukas Becker and skimmed it across the table to him, keeping her eyes on him like an eagle.

Burzynski gave nothing away, squared up the photo slowly, and studied it. Then looked up at her, the little smile back again. 'So who's this guy?'

'He's the one who's been working for you since at least 1997. Israel, Egypt, Jordan, Iran, Turkey, and, more recently, Iraq.'

'Not for me, he hasn't.' Burzynski slid the photo across to one of the new people, Grant, a middle-aged man with a big half-grey beard and an intense gaze.

'Oh, please, Bruno. We know about his attempts to befriend one of our staff members, we know about the very important item he lost in Johannesburg, we know he eliminated Julius Shabangu. And you've paid him a small fortune. So stop insulting my intelligence, and let's move on . . .' She watched Grant, saw the negative shake of the head. Then she asked: 'Where are you keeping Osman?'

It was with this last name that she finally spotted a reaction, slight, a narrowing of Bruno's eyes, just as quickly it was gone. He looked at his three colleagues. The two new ones, Eden and Grant, nodded at him, one after the other.

They were Burzynski's seniors, she realised. Interesting.

Finally he looked back at Janina, and cleared his throat. When he spoke, the annoyance was gone from his voice, it was suddenly calm and serious. 'I'm going to tell you three things, Janina, and you should seriously consider believing me, for the sake of your government and your country. Number One: I don't know who this man is,' he tapped a finger on Becker's photo, 'but if you want us to investigate the matter, we will. Number Two: we believe *you* have Osman, and we're very keen to get access to him. And Number Three: your ship, *The Madeleine*, has completely disappeared. It's like it never existed.'

'You can't find it?' In disbelief.

'That's right. And to say we did our best is putting it mildly. We want to find it, even more than you do. So, here's the deal: you show me yours, and I'll show you mine.'

Tau Masilo had been following the full interaction with great interest. At that moment his cellphone rang in his jacket pocket.

'I am sorry,' he said, took it out and checked the screen. It was Quinn calling. 'This might be important,' he said, 'excuse me.'

Masilo got up and walked out quickly, closing the door behind him, and then asked: 'Any news?'

'Osman,' said Quinn. 'He's in hospital. Intensive Care Unit at the Chris Barnard Memorial. Heart attack. A man corresponding to Becker's description dropped him off yesterday afternoon. Osman only regained consciousness this morning . . .'

Masilo laughed, abruptly. 'Unbelievable.'

'That is not the big news. Osman asked the nurse at Intensive Care to phone Suleiman Dolly, via land line to his house. Probably he couldn't remember the Sheikh's latest cellphone number. We intercepted the call. First she told Dolly that Osman was in hospital. Then, and I quote "Mr Osman asked me to say the dog has the laptop" . . .'

Masilo quickly made the connection. 'Becker.'

'That's right. We suspect it was in the shoulder bag that Osman was so attached to. The hospital staff said that was the first thing Osman asked for when he woke up. But there is something else. The third thing that the sister told Dolly was that "the dog is driving a blue Citi Golf, CA 143 and another four numbers".'

'They're going to look for him.'

'I think so.'

'Do you have people there?'

'I have eight people at the hospital now, Osman is isolated. In the meantime, Dolly has also arrived, threatening interdicts . . .'

'Let him threaten, just keep them all away from him.'

69

iThemba Computers was on the first floor of Oxford House in Durbanville's main road. The young man behind the counter recognised Milla, despite the headscarf. 'Hello, Tannie,' he said, using the respectful Afrikaans form of address.

'Hello,' said Milla. 'My neighbour,' she gestured at Becker, 'has a problem with his laptop . . .'

'What can I do for you, Oom?'

'I forgot my Windows password,' said Lukas Becker.

'XP, Vista or Seven?' the young man asked.

Burzynski was talking when Masilo came back. '. . . have an interest in Osman, so we both know this is about local Muslim extremism, Janina. I really don't see the point of being coy about it.'

Masilo sat down, pulled his notepad closer and wrote the words, *Osman found. In hospital. We have him under guard.*

Mentz read as he wrote, nodded slightly.

Masilo turned the notepad over

'You can't find the ship,' Mentz stated sceptically.

'We have located every single vessel of that approximate tonnage not running LRIT and AIS. And believe me, it wasn't easy. The fact of the matter is, there are three possible explanations. The first is that they are hiding somewhere. Not terribly likely, I know, but if they've switched off the transmitters, if they are completely stationary, and well camouflaged, they might get away with it. The second option is that they've scuttled her. Which begs the question of "why", of course, and we're not seriously considering it. The third is that they're running a false LRIT, and if that is the case, we're basically up the creek. It could take weeks to cross-check every ship out there.'

'You said you want to find it even more than we do.'

'Yes.'

'Why?'

'We knew you would raise that question, Janina. I've been on the line with Langley all night about this, and the bottom line is that I'm not cleared to say more than this: we believe the cargo on *The Madeleine* is of vital importance to both American and South African national security.'

'So you know what we know.'

'I don't know what you know. But let me formally and fully introduce you to my two colleagues,' and he gestured at the two new people who Mentz knew absolutely nothing about. 'Janet Eden is a senior analyst at MENA, our Office of Middle East and North Africa Analysis. Jim Grant is at the Office of Terrorism Analysis. And they both came to South Africa because of your SOLAS request. Janet, would you do us the honour?'

She was a slim, attractive woman, well-groomed, in her forties. 'Thank you, Bruno.' She addressed Mentz and Masilo. 'I'm not going to apologise for the fact that we won't be able to share all our intelligence. We're all big girls and boys in the same line of work. We know the rules.' She was businesslike and self-assured. 'So let me tell you what I can. About ten weeks ago, both Jim and I independently became aware of higher levels of communication between suspected al-Qaeda cells in Oman, Pakistan and Afghanistan, and, to our surprise, in South Africa, particularly Cape Town. We've seen communication between Somalia's al-Shabab and Cape cells before, low level, easily decoded, but the al-Qaeda stuff was very different. When we took this information to our superiors, a task force was created to focus on the matter exclusively, which also included Bruno and his colleagues down here. Much to our frustration, the communication is using a cypher discovered by Dr Michael Rabin at Harvard back in 2001, and it is probably unbreakable. I won't bore you with the details – which you can Google quite easily – but it entails two parties setting up a source of genuinely random numbers, then broadcasting those numbers to each other . . .'

'We know about the encryption,' said Mentz.

'Good, then I don't need to explain. Last week, we followed the trail of the communication to, amongst others, Shaheed Osman, hence our recent interest in him. But electronic communication is not our only source of intelligence. Assets in Pakistan and Afghanistan have been picking up snippets, and we accumulated enough to know that something very big is brewing, that a fishing vessel is involved, and that it will happen within the next seventy-two hours, in or near Cape Town. Bruno . . .'

'Thank you, Janet. Janina, let me be frank: we want Osman, and we want him badly. We have little doubt that he has the cypher keys, and this is a real emergency situation, our time is running out. Yesterday, Langley asked me to submit to you a formal request for the apprehension of Osman, with your approval and cooperation. You can imagine our surprise when we received news of his abduction late yesterday. We honestly believed it was you. That's why we asked for this meeting . . .'

Burzynski stopped talking when he saw Tau Masilo writing frenetically on his writing pad.

Mentz read the four words: *Becker has Osman's laptop.*

She looked up at the Americans. 'I'm going to need a few minutes to think this over.'

It took the young man at iThemba Computers only eleven minutes to retrieve the password for Shaheed Latif Osman's laptop. He wrote it down for them: *Amiralbahr.*

'There you are,' said Milla, with a happy, effervescent feeling, as though she herself had provided the solution.

'What does it mean, Oom?'

'Nothing. That's why I forgot it. Thanks a lot.'

'Oom, should I leave the script like this?'

'What script?'

'The formatting script.'

Becker scratched his head. 'Remind me.'

'Oom, the script you have here that says, *control*, *alt* and *home* will format the hard drive, delete everything.'

'Oh, yes . . .'

'And two wrong passwords too . . .'

'You can take all that off.'

'Bruno,' said Janina Mentz, 'you are playing a dangerous game. Your man Becker has Osman's laptop, you now have the decryption key, and yet you are sitting here, deceiving us, and wasting precious time. Why?'

Indignation infused Burzynski's face, he wanted to reply, but Jim Grant got in first and spoke for the first time. 'Madam,' he said in a deep, authoritative voice, 'I am the Deputy Director of the CIA's Office of Terrorism Analysis. I am fully informed about every intelligence and counter-intelligence operation the Agency is currently running in Southern Africa, as well as every single agent and asset involved. And I wish to most categorically state that this man is *not* one of them. If he were, I would have told you right now, because the greater and common cause necessitates it. If you're going to insist on doubting us, I'll have to ask you to take this matter directly to your President. We might respectfully ask that he calls our Secretary of State for clarification . . . But I beg you, if we go that route, let's do it immediately. As everybody seems to be pointing out, we are running dangerously low on time.'

It was the combination of his gravity, authority and solemnity, and their repeated denials, even though Becker had the laptop, which made Janina Mentz wonder, for the first time, whether she might be wrong. She hesitated a moment before she said: 'If he's not working for you, the next question is, who *is* he working for?'

'We don't know. But we would love to find out, if you'll supply us with more intel.'

'In that case,' she said, and leaned back in her chair, 'we all share the same problem. We have to find Becker. Because he has the key.'

At the Bayside Centre in Table View she bought clothing and groceries with cash she had drawn from an ATM in Durbanville. Then they drove back to the Big Bay Beach Club, so she could cook, and he could explore the laptop.

Lukas was quiet. She knew it was the circumstances, the odds that he would be able to get his money back growing ever slimmer. She wanted to encourage him, but she didn't know what to say.

Mentz and Masilo walked back to the PIA offices.

'You realise this is your fault,' she said.

'What?'

'Becker. And Osman's laptop. You wanted to keep Becker in play, Tau. When I wanted him taken out. Neutralised. You hoped he would force me to act.'

'Yes,' he said.

'I appointed you because you're not a "yes-man". Because you're strong enough to disagree with me. But please do it openly and honestly.'

'It was a mistake. It won't happen again.'

70

At the deserted pavilion of the De Grendel Sports Complex in Parow the informant smoked a cigarette in short, nervous puffs, blowing the smoke out audibly between sentences. 'They say it's the Sheikh, calling in a favour.'

'Suleiman Dolly.'

'They say he phoned Terror personally.'

'And?'

'The Committee is looking for a laptop, stolen by a whitey in a blue Citi Golf, tall and dark, a Boer. Registration number is CA 143 and something.'

'And Terror and the Ravens have to help look?'

'*Ja*, that's the favour. And the word is, they don't want the whitey alive, it's the laptop that counts. There's a hundred K bonus for the one who brings it in, fifty more if you *blaas* the whitey. This news is travelling fast, every wannabe on the peninsula has got his eyes open now.'

'Do you think they'll get the guy?'

'Sooner or later.'

Janina Mentz sent for Quinn as well, to save time. Now they sat around the Director's round table with Rajkumar and Masilo.

'Our first priority,' said Janina, 'is to track down Becker and Strachan. Quinn, I want their photos in the Sunday papers, supply all the information: he's armed and dangerous, wanted for kidnapping and murder, she's the accomplice. Publicise the Golf's details as well, but talk to the Western Cape Commissioner of the SAPS, so that we work through their public relations department.'

Quinn made notes.

'The first thing she'll do when she sees her photo in the paper is phone her son. Are we prepared?'

'We are,' said Quinn.

'Keep the Reaction Unit ready, and tell the Police Commissioner to keep their hands off. We will take Becker out.'

Quinn nodded.

'Tau will set up and manage the coordination office with the CIA, and I will keep him updated from the Ops Room. One channel of information only, through me. I hope everyone understands that.'

She looked at Rajkumar. 'That's the brawn of the operation, Raj is going to head up the brain. I need you to select the best minds in the agency, Raj, get a think tank going. You will be concentrating on three issues. If anyone can figure out how the Supreme Committee can make a fishing trawler disappear off the face of the earth, it's you. It must be a question of technology, and I need you to show that we are smarter than the CIA. I want you to find *The Madeleine*.'

'OK,' said Rajkumar, delighted.

'Secondly, Becker. There's a lot about him that still doesn't make sense. If he's not working for the CIA – and I have to accept that for now – then who the hell is he working for? The third matter is related. The CIA's reaction on Thursday and again this morning, leads me to believe they have an asset in our midst, or they're fishing for one. Let's assume it wasn't Becker trying to recruit Strachan. So, who is it? Could you look into it?'

Milla stood at the stove, spoon in hand. She was making spaghetti bolognese with Ina Paarman's sauce, aware of Lukas sitting nearby at the counter, glued to the computer, a frown of concentration on his forehead. Aware of the irony, here she was again, reduced to cook and housekeeper, excluded from men's work.

And later that afternoon she had to go home, that was the agreement they had reached. She didn't like it.

She reached for the box of spaghetti and opened it. The water in the pot was boiling.

'Seven minutes till we eat,' she said.

He nodded absently, absorbed in the screen in front of him.

She let the spaghetti slide into the boiling water, added a little olive oil, then the salt.

'*Jissis*,' said Lukas, softly.

'What?' she asked.

'They . . . There's something here . . .'

She stirred the meat sauce, looked at him and saw a new focus.

'*Jissis*,' he said again, fingers moving quickly over the laptop's touch pad, to click, and click again.

The sauce simmered. She turned the heat off, took out two plates, then the parmesan and the grater.

Lukas looked up at her. 'They . . . They talk about a shipment, they are bringing something in under the radar, smuggling something in. A woman by the name of Madeleine is going to . . . No . . . It's a ship, they are bringing something in by ship. Haidar . . . that's what they're bringing in . . .'

'Haidar?'

'I think it's an abbreviation . . . But the date makes no sense. It says here Monday 23 Shawwal 1430 A. H. . . .'

'Shawwal,' said Milla, suddenly excited. 'That was the name of the operation, the whole PIA operation . . .'

'What does it mean?'

'I don't know.'

The Ops Room was full, sixteen people manning computers and systems, Quinn in the middle, Mentz right at the back, on her own.

'There is no Volkswagen Golf on the system with a registration number beginning with CA 143,' one of Rajkumar's team members told Quinn.

'Maybe Osman didn't remember correctly . . .'

'Maybe not. According to the SAPS database, the theft of a set of number plates was reported on Thursday evening, in Table View. CA 143 688.'

'Table View,' Quinn said.

'That's right.'

'Can you compile me a list of all places offering accommodation in Table View? Short term. Hotels, guest houses, holiday apartments.'

'It will take a while.'

'Then we had better start. You coordinate it, everyone who doesn't have a specific task: start phoning. You have Becker and Miss Jenny's descriptions . . .'

Becker used his cellphone to Google. 'It's the Muslim calendar,' he said urgently, 'Twenty three Shawwal 1430 is the twelfth of October 2009. That's the day after tomorrow. Monday.'

He turned back to the computer, read more emails. 'Monday. Two in the morning . . .'

'What about the abbreviation? Anything on that?' Milla asked, and walked back to the stove, ready to dish up.

He typed in the letters, clicked on the search button. 'Haidar,' he read, 'means "lion" in Arabic. This was the name of Ali, the husband of Fatima, the daughter of the Prophet Mohammed.'

'Lion . . .' said Milla. In the PIA reports there was no mention of the word.

Becker was back at the laptop. 'It's a code word. For the cargo . . . It . . . Here are some coordinates, Milla . . .' He grabbed his cellphone again, pressed the keys in a hurry, until he looked up and said to her: 'I've got the bastards, I've got them.'

She smiled at him. 'Welcome back,' she said.

The operator phoned Quinn from the hospital, his voice urgent. 'There is a call for Osman, it sounds like a white guy.'

'Tell the team with Osman that I want him to take the call. Then put him through, we are listening this side,' and he gestured to the technician to get it on the Ops Room loudspeakers.

It took valuable seconds, they were just in time to hear Becker's voice. 'Shaheed, this is your friend from yesterday. I know about the ship, Shaheed, the date and time and place. Is it worth 500,000 to you?'

Then the click of a phone call being cut off. And silence.

Quinn wanted to swear, stopped himself, since Mentz was right behind him. He grabbed the phone and called the operator. 'What are you doing?'

'It wasn't us, it was Osman. He put the phone down.'

71

Milla ate alone. She was rinsing her plate when she heard the unfamiliar ring tone of the cellphone, not realising at first that it was her new one. She had to run to the bedroom where she had left it on the bedside cupboard the night before. She answered with just a 'Hello?'

'It's Lukas. I think they were with him, Milla. The PIA, or someone. He put the telephone down. I'll have to make another plan.'

'What kind of plan?'

'I'll have to get some weapons.'

'Weapons? What about your pistol?'

'I'm going to need more than that.'

Fear took hold of her. 'Why?'

'To get my money . . . I'll have to intercept that ship's cargo.'

'Becker made the call from a public phone box at Eden on the Bay in Blouberg,' the operator told Quinn.

'A hotel?'

'I think it's a new shopping centre . . .'

'Another one?'

'I'm trying to find out.'

'Get me a map on the big screen,' Quinn said. 'Mark the place where the number plate was stolen. Then the shopping centre. How are we doing with the guest houses?'

'We've phoned more than twenty. Nothing so far.'

'Make sure you include Blouberg as well.'

Then silence, until Janina Mentz's voice came from the back. 'Good work, Quinn.'

Masilo had hurriedly set up the coordination office on the ground floor of the Wale Street Chambers. Network cables snaked across the floor along with temporary phone connections, a long table stood in the centre, a few chairs gathered around.

Burzynski came in carrying files and a laptop, talking before the door even closed behind him. 'Your man Becker works for himself,' he said and put the stack on the table, the laptop on one side, and picked up the uppermost file.

'My man?'

'Figure of speech.' He handed the file to Masilo. 'We received this from the FBI an hour ago. Turns out, Lukas Becker is a smuggler. Of ancient and historic artefacts.'

Burzynski sat down and pulled his laptop closer. 'I'll be using wireless and my mobile, if you don't mind. Not that I don't trust you, of course, standard operating procedure . . .' He pointed at the file: 'As you'll see, the FBI opened a file on Becker in 2004, after he was sacked by an archaeology professor from the University of Pennsylvania during a dig in Turkey. They caught him with a two-thousand-year-old pendant, worth a small fortune. The prof fired him on the spot, and, as he didn't want to report it to the Turkish authorities for fear of losing his excavation license, he made a call to the FBI. Told them other artefacts went missing too, but they couldn't pin it on Becker. When the Bureau started looking at Becker's past, they found that he was under suspicion at earlier digs, too, but nobody had any proof.'

'And then he went to Iraq.'

'Exactly. He must have known he had no hope of working in archaeology again. So, he joined Xe Services to train Iraqi boat crews patrolling the Tigris. Which runs all the way down to the Persian Gulf, a highway to smugglers' heaven. A month ago, Interpol started uncovering a massive syndicate trafficking in ancient artefacts, starting at the museums in Baghdad, pipelines to New York and Amsterdam, ancient Persian stuff, art, jewellery, you name it. Somehow, the info leaked, and the network started disbanding very rapidly. And your man Becker resigned from Xe overnight, and caught the first flight home, via London . . .'

'Ahah . . .' said Tau Masilo.

'But there's one more thing. When Interpol and the US Military Police started questioning some of the smugglers they arrested, they were told Becker got away with a tidy sum belonging to the syndicate bosses. Sterling. And, apparently, the syndicate caught up with your man in Johannesburg, where he told them a sad tale of car-jacking, and a fortune lost. Word is, he has six weeks to repay them, or they take him out.'

'*Jeso*.'

'*Jeso*, indeed,' said Bruno Burzynksi. 'Now that we've cleared the air, let's catch us some extremists.'

'Sir,' said another operator, 'here's a call from Jarryd January, he says it's urgent.'

'Put him through.' He waited for the little light to flash, and answered. 'You've got news?'

'My informant with the Ravens just phoned. He said someone told Terror Baadjies and them that the Golf has been spotted . . .'

'In Blouberg?'

'Yes.' Surprised.

'Where exactly?'

'The guy drove out of the shopping centre, Eden on the Bay. They were too late to tail him. But now everyone is on the way there, every gangsta on the Flats.'

Quinn swore, barely audibly. He turned to Mentz. 'Ma'am, I want to move the Reaction Unit to Blouberg now.'

'Do it.'

Right at the back of the FBI report Masilo found a paragraph that made him suddenly pick up the phone and call Mentz's Ops Room extension.

'Mentz.'

'Becker worked for himself. Smuggler in antique artefacts, I've got a dossier here from the FBI, a report from Interpol. But tell Quinn, he has three aliases, all with forged passports . . .'

'Let me write them down.'

'John Andreas, Dennis Faber . . .'

'His parents . . .'

'Excuse me?'

'Those are variations on his parents' names.'

'Oh . . . Yes . . . The last one is Marcus Smithfield.'

'I'll tell Quinn. Any other news?'

'Nothing.'

She had asked Lukas over the phone, where would he get weapons?

For the first time there was irritation in his voice, impatience with her, as though she was a bothersome child. '*Jissis*, Milla, five years in Iraq, you get to know people,' and then, 'I have to go, see you as soon as I can.' Brusque and hasty.

She dropped down in an armchair, hurt, she had just been asking, she just wanted to know, there was no need to talk to her like that. Self-pity clashed with a desire to be understanding of his tone with her, indignation and the impulse to pack up and go against the knowledge that she didn't want to return to her flat. She knew they were waiting there for her, the ones who had bugged her, the ones who had studied her whole life in her diaries, she never wanted to see them again.

She had to go back. She had to collect her car, and her cellphone, there would be a message from Kemp, the attorney, about someone who could find the microphones in her flat. She would have to clean up and tidy up, she would keep the cellphone close at hand to call Kemp if they tried to interrogate her again. This time she would fight back, let them go ahead and charge her with something, she had broken no laws.

She would have to sit and wait until Lukas was finished, until he came back from this other world, the one where you got weapons because you knew people, the one where ships carried smuggled cargo, where people hijacked and stole money. A man's world of organised crime in Gauteng and the Cape Flats, and Muslim extremists. And poverty and unemployment and drugs, a reality she was only vaguely aware of, because she had been locked away in the prison, the fort of Durbanville, behind walls and alarms, a pseudo world built on ignorance, denial and enclosure, by huddling together with others who helped preserve the phantom of prosperity and security.

The irony was that she hadn't felt at home there. Durbanville was just as strange a landscape as this other one that Lukas wanted to expose himself to. And here she stood, a foot in each of these worlds, and she belonged in neither. Milla Strachan, permanent outsider. Her instinct was to get up and pick up pen and paper and write about it until it made sense, but she suddenly realised she was doing it again, trying to create a safe haven with words, a home, a place she belonged, a universe that made sense, even if just to her. Was that all she was destined to have?

She rose from the chair with the urge to do something, to take part in some sort of action that would save her from this limbo, a lifebelt in the river of words.

Her eye fell on the laptop on the counter, the one from which Lukas had extracted the explosive and the equally dangerous information, and she thought, let me take a look, I can at least know what he knows, it will make the wait for him more bearable.

'I've got him,' an operator called, hand cupped over the telephone receiver. 'Under the name of Dennis Faber, in the Big Bay Beach Club.'

'Hotel?' Quinn asked.

'No, it's self-catering units . . .'

'Where is it?'

'Last place on the right when you drive out of Blouberg towards Melkbos.'

'Which number?'

'Sir?'

'Which number is Becker in?' Quinn lifted his phone receiver, called Major Tiger Mazibuko, commanding officer of the Reaction Unit.

'Oh . . . hold on . . .' the operator said. 'Ma'am, Dennis Faber, what is the number of his unit . . . Twenty-seven . . .'

'Mazibuko.'

'The Big Bay Beach Club, it's a holiday resort just outside Blouberg. He's in number twenty-seven . . .'

'We're on our way.'

'How long?'

'Fifteen minutes.'

72

Milla read the emails between Osman and one Sayyid Macki.

Shipment arrives Monday 23 Shawwal 1430 A.H. at 02.00 (GMT +2).

Day after tomorrow, at two in the morning.

She looked in the *Sent* mail folder, found Osman's answer:

Alhumdulillah. We will be ready. The Madeleine to anchor at S33 49.517 E17 52.424, we will have transfer vessel waiting, to transport Haidar to fully equipped reception team at S33 54.064 E18 24.921, OPBC.

OPBC? What did that stand for? Was it also Arabic, like Haidar, which meant 'lion'?

She recalled the password on this computer. *Amiralbahr*. Another word with a Middle Eastern feel.

Words were what she knew, she would try to unravel this one. She would have to Google it, like Lukas. But how? She wasn't familiar with her new cellphone.

Milla got up and fetched her new cellphone and the box it came in, found the manual and started to read. 'Use your mobile phone as an Internet modem,' was all she could find. She followed the directions, plugged in the USB cable and activated the modem.

Network connection successful.

Pleased with her success, she opened Internet Explorer on the laptop and went to the Google website.

She typed in 'Amiralbahr'.

Did you mean amir al-bahr?

Perhaps. She clicked on it.

Facts about amir al-bahr: etymology, as discussed in admiral (naval officer): the title of admiral has an ancient lineage. It apparently originated before the 12th century with Muslim Arabs, who combined emir, or amīr ('commander'), the article al, and bahr ('sea') . . .

It meant 'admiral'. In Arabic. The origin of the word.

She typed in the Google window: 'Significance of lion in muslim extremism'.

She scanned the first results. Only one was of interest:

Babur Cruise Missile Pakistan The Babur missile (Babur means lion in the Turkic language Chaghatay; it is also suggested that the missile was named after the first Mughal Emperor Babur) is the first cruise missile to be fielded by Pakistan. The Babur is capable of carrying either conventional or nuclear warheads and has a reported range . . .

Suddenly a new window popped up on the computer screen and hid the web browser: *Command Prompt. Running email decryption script.*

She saw white letters on the black background, lines of code appeared rapidly, one after the other, then the window closed automatically.

A small notification appeared at the right bottom corner. *New Mail Message.*

Email. The computer must have downloaded mail automatically, since it was connected to the Internet now.

She opened Microsoft Outlook.

Right at the top, a new message, from Macki.

She opened it.

Allahu Akbar, amir al-bahr
We agree with your assessment. Arrival of The Madeleine and Haidar now 24 hours earlier, at 02.00 (GMT +2) on Sunday 22 Shawwal 1430 A.H.

They had moved the arrival time of the ship a day earlier. Then it hit her. That was tonight. Tomorrow morning. Her stomach contracted as she looked at her watch. Seven minutes past seven in the evening . . .

She heard a car door slam outside. Lukas. She would have to tell him right away. She jumped up, walked to the front door and opened it. She saw the Golf parked there, the boot open. Lukas was busy behind it. She walked out to meet him.

A movement caught her eye, on the right, down the road. Men were running towards them from the gate 200 metres away.

Then she saw they were carrying guns.

'Lukas!'

He appeared suddenly from behind the Golf, saw her pointing down the road. His head jerked around towards the men.

'Inside, Milla!'

She hesitated, frozen, her eyes on the young coloured men who sprinted faster, five, six, seven of them, Lukas pulled something out of the back of the Golf.

He had a firearm in his arms, short and chunky. 'Go inside!'

She saw the men lift their weapons, saw Lukas cock his. Shots, something smacked into the Golf, glass shattered behind her. She stood still, unable to move, a cry in her throat. Lukas fired. Two of the men fell, the rest swerved sharp right, looking for the cover of parked cars.

'Christ, Milla!'

This time she responded, turned and ran back to the front door, her legs like jelly.

Shots thundered from the cars, a bullet smacked against the lintel ahead of her.

Then she was inside.

Janina Mentz sat at the back of the Ops Room and listened to the radio connection between Quinn and Major Tiger Mazibuko.

'ETA five minutes.'

'Roger.'

She would wait. Until Mazibuko personally confirmed that they had Becker and the computer. Only then would she tell Masilo that he could inform the Americans.

She got up and walked to Quinn, stopped beside him and said, quietly and firmly, 'Tiger has permission to use all necessary force. All we want is the laptop, undamaged.'

Quinn nodded and switched on the radio microphone.

She stood in the sitting room with a racing heart, her breath was shallow, hands instinctively shielding her head, knowing it must be Osman's men. Lukas rushed in, short rifle in one hand, a dirty canvas bag in the other.

He turned around and pointed the weapon out of the door, fired off a burst.

'Come, Milla.' He was next to her, grabbing her arm, pulling her towards the bedroom.

'Get the rucksack.' He pointed the rifle barrel at the bag lying beside the bed and shoved the sliding door of the bedroom open.

She grabbed the rucksack and her handbag next. He was outside already, looking back at her. 'Come!'

She ran.

Ahead of them was a wire fence, high. Behind that a big sand dune, densely overgrown.

He hurled the grubby canvas bag over, straining with the effort, took the rucksack out of her hand and threw that after it. 'Climb,' he said, his expression fierce.

She threw her handbag. Not hard enough, it hit the top of the fence and dropped back.

'Fuck,' he said, picking it up and throwing it over the fence. 'Now climb.'

Shots from behind in the flat.

She scrambled up the fence, propelled by adrenaline, a part of her amazed that the wire didn't hurt her hands, that she could be so quick. Then she was at the top. She swung her leg over, and slid, so that she dropped into a thick green bush on the other side, the smell of wood and leaves suddenly filling her nostrils, sharp points jabbing into her. For a moment she felt disorientated, tried to stand up, her blouse ripped.

Lukas was with her. He pulled her up, shoved her handbag into her arms, grabbed his rucksack, swung it onto his shoulders, took the canvas bag and wormed his way into the shrubbery. 'Just stick with me.'

She pressed the handbag tightly against her body.

Shots cracked, she heard the whine of bullets, looked back, could see nothing, just the greenery; looked forwards, Lukas crawling along like a snake under the branches.

She dived in after him.

73

'Shots being fired, repeat, shots being fired, it's a hot zone,' Mazibuko's voice was high-pitched and excited over the radio.

'They're shooting at you?' asked Quinn.

'Negative, we're at the gate, no visual, we're going in . . .'

The drone of the military vehicle's engine filled the Ops Room.

'Two down, middle of the road, two coloured men . . .'

'Shit,' said Quinn.

'Terror's men,' said Janina, standing beside him now.

Shots sounding across the ether, unimpressive, like crackers.

'Taking fire now,' said Mazibuko. 'Combat deployment . . .'

Janina Mentz took the microphone from Quinn. 'I want that laptop, Tiger. I want it intact.'

'Roger. Out.'

They heard the shooting escalate when they were halfway up the slope of the dune, invisible in the depths of the bushes and trees. Lukas was right in front of her, she could see the soles of his boots, he lay still suddenly, listening to the clatter, back and forth.

'Christ,' he said, looking back at her. 'Are you OK?'

'Yes.' Her voice sounded peculiar and shaky. 'Yes,' she tried again, more firmly, and that gave her something to cling to, a consciousness that penetrated the fear and shock, *so, this is what it feels like, mortal danger.*

He looked ahead again, moved with increased urgency, and Milla slithered after him, with thin bloody scratches on her hands and arms.

Deadly silence in the Ops Room, minutes ticking away.

Then static filled the room, a wave of sound. Mazibuko's voice, excited: 'Number twenty-seven is secure, we have one man wounded, seven bogeys accounted for, five are dead, two wounded, one seriously, they're fucking teenagers, Quinn, coloured kids with semis . . . We have one laptop, all shot up, no sign of Becker and the woman, but they must have been here very recently, there's leftover food, some clothing, a cellphone, I think they went out the back, we are securing the whole complex now, over . . .'

'The laptop,' said Mentz. 'I want to know how badly damaged it is. But get Raj here first.'

She saw Becker stand up at the crest of the dune, and survey the surroundings. He spotted something to the right.

'There,' he said, muted.

She stood up, looked in the same direction. Between the branches she saw the shopping centre 500 metres to the south, the big red and white logo of Shoprite high up on the wall. And down below them, a sandy footpath like a snow-white snake, winding down the flank of the dune.

He took her arm and looked at her with great intensity.

She tried to smile. 'I'm fine,' she said.

He waited another moment, and nodded. 'We'll have to run.' He turned away and moved down the dune, weaving through the bushes.

'It's got three nine-millimetre rounds through it,' said Major Mazibuko.

'Can you see if the hard drive was hit?' asked Rajhev Rajkumar.

'I don't know . . .'

'It's about six or seven centimetres, by four or five, it should be the biggest thing you see in there . . .'

'Shiny metal casing?'

'That's right.'

'*Yebo*, it took a hit.'

'Shit. Right through?'

'No, sort of on the front end, where the little wires connect, only, they're not connected any more.'

'Is that it, just the wires gone?'

'No, it's sort of bent as well. The casing.'

'Just in the front?'

'*Yebo* . . .'

Rajkumar looked up at Mentz. 'Maybe,' he said. 'If we're lucky.'

'Tell him to get it here.'

They ran down alongside the wall of the shopping centre to the edge of a big wide street that bordered it. Becker stopped, put down the canvas bag and then the weapon he was carrying. He unzipped the bag. Milla saw more guns inside, two large automatic rifles, and Lukas's pistol.

He took the pistol out, tucked it under his belt behind his back, zipped the bag closed again.

Then he peered around the corner of the wall.

'We're going to walk calmly now. We don't have much time . . .' He held his left hand out to her.

'Where are we going?' She took his hand.

'We need a car. We have to get away from here.' He began walking up the pavement in the direction of the shopping centre.

'Where will you get a car?'

'We're going to steal one, Milla.'

'Oh.'

Quinn pointed the laser at the big screen, on which a map of the area was projected. 'This area is dune veld, up to the R27, about a kilometre away. Here is a shopping centre, here is a town house development. His other option is north, there's a small residential area next to the Big Bay Beach Club. Tiger will try to cover the residential area, we have asked the police to close off the town house complex, the R27, Otto du Plessis north and south, and Cormorant Avenue east. They say it will take a while to close all the gaps, however.'

'A while? How long is a while?' Mentz asked.

Quinn shrugged. 'Ten, fifteen minutes . . .'

'He knows what's on that computer, Quinn. He told Osman over the phone . . .'

'We'll have to get helicopters in too. This whole section, up to Melkbos, is dune veld. And not much daylight left.'

Becker decided on an old white Nissan Sentra from the early nineties, dented in the front mudguard.

Sirens were wailing in the distance.

He stopped beside the car's rear door and looked around.

Milla saw the nearest people were a hundred metres away.

He took the pistol out of the back of his belt, banged it hard against the window.

It broke with a dull crack. He reached inside, unlocked the door. Milla ran to the front passenger door, watched Lukas take the rucksack off and toss it on the back seat, then the canvas bag, before he unlocked the driver's door and got in. He leaned over, unlocked her door. She got in.

He put the pistol down in the foot well in front of his seat, gripped the plastic under the steering wheel with both hands and jerked. It came free. His fingers searched frantically through the tangle of wires that hung there, followed it to the ignition. He picked a wire, ripped it loose, bent, bit the insulation off. Then another wire.

Milla looked up towards the shopping centre.

There were people approaching, a man and a woman with a full shopping trolley.

The Nissan's engine turned, and fired.

Lukas took the steering wheel in both hands, and jerked it hard and suddenly to the right.

Something snapped and broke.

He put the car in gear, and pulled away. The tyres screeched. They shot past the couple with the trolley, watching them wide-eyed. The sirens were louder now, closer.

Lukas raced to the exit, hesitated for a second then turned left away from the sea, in the direction of the R27.

74

The roar and whistle of the wind through the broken window, the high, determined revs of the engine, the sun-cracked plastic of the instrument panel, the musty smell inside, the fine network of bloody scratches on her forearms, handbag clamped on her lap. A swinging, silver cross hung by a string of beads from the rear-view mirror, the radio was missing the knob on the volume dial. Lukas crouched forward, concentrating hard, the fabric of his shirt was torn, there was a small, dark red mark where a bullet had grazed him.

It was surreal.

In this instant she remembered The Bride at the dance classes. A lovely young blonde woman, about twenty-three, slim, athletic and graceful, who had come to Arthur Murray with her fiancé to learn the steps so the bridal pair could open the dance floor at their reception. The aspirant bridegroom was somewhat shorter than the young woman, with a chunky farmer's build. His face, Milla had thought at the time, was that of a cartoon character, one of the smaller creatures that provide comic relief. And he had absolutely no coordination, his movements across the floor were rigid, clumsy, stiff, despite the enthusiasm, the frowning dedication. While the instructor patiently coached him to one side, The Bride went through the steps flawlessly in front of the large mirror – but lost in her own world, a flight of fantasy about The Great Day, wishful thinking of how it could be, her arms bent as though a dream prince were leading her.

Now, in the valley of an adrenaline low, Milla saw a vison of her own life, unexpected but clear as crystal, her self-deceit, her acting out of how-it-ought-to-be, her blindness to reality. The disillusionment was massive, it flooded and overwhelmed her so fast, it made her feel useless and lost, so many years wasted. She longed, inexplicably, for Barend, with a painful intensity, she wanted to go to him now and say she was so terribly sorry, without knowing why she felt she should apologise to her child.

Lukas spoke. She came back to herself in the Nissan, realised her eyes were wet, tears running down her cheeks. She wiped them away angrily with the back of her hand and said: 'What?'

'They saw you.'

She didn't understand, looked at him in question.

'Osman's people saw you, Milla. We'll have to drop this. Until . . . Until it's safe.'

Her understanding came slowly. 'Until it's safe?'

He took his gaze off the road for the first time and looked at her. 'Are you OK?'

'Until it's safe? Until it's safe?' indignation exploded. 'Safe? What kind of word is that, Lukas, what kind of word? What does it mean, in this country? Where do you find it? Safety?' Tears of rage, she couldn't stop them. 'How could you *say* that? It doesn't exist. You know that, you *know* that, but you talk of "safe", it's empty, it's a naked word . . .'

He put out his left hand, but she slapped it away, her voice jumping half an octave higher. 'Don't, Lukas, don't try to console me, don't . . . Why do you do it? Why do you try to exclude us, why do you deceive us, we have a right to know . . .'

He tried to protest, but she drowned him out with her dark flood of words. 'You hide it from us, you men, who have created this world. You, who made this country, this mess of hatred and envy, crime and violence and poverty and misery. And now you're trying so hard to cover it up, to disguise it behind stuff. You think you can give us shiny trinkets, glitter, shops, magazines, hiding our heads in the sand, just don't see the truth. It's lies, it's all lies and now *you* are lying along with them. Safe! "Until *I'm* safe," is what you mean to say. Do you want to go and pack me away somewhere, Lukas? Do you want to take me somewhere and brainwash me and calm me down behind high walls and alarms and then you go creeping back to their world? You want to drop this thing, because you have a *woman* in your stolen car? It's not *your* choice. You are *not* going to drop it and you are *not* going to dump me somewhere, I want to see it, I want to see *everything* . . .'

She became aware of the pistol that lay beside his feet, she reached down and picked it up. 'Look,' she said, 'I'm not helpless, I can . . .'

'Milla!' He grabbed her forearm with his left hand, pushed it so the barrel swung away from him, she tugged, but he was too strong. She pulled the trigger, nothing happened. 'Let me go,' she screamed, wild, furious. She saw the safety catch, pressed it with her thumb, pulled the trigger again. The shot boomed deafeningly, a star in the window, and she squeezed it again. 'You see, I can shoot too,' but he braked hard, she fell forward, he held onto her arm, the Nissan's tyres squealing off the tar onto the verge of sand and grass. He let go of the steering wheel, took the pistol in his other hand, twisted it out of her fingers and she hit out at him with her fists balled, a lifetime of rage behind her actions as he raised his arm to shield himself.

She wept and hit and screamed, deep, unearthly cries that boiled up and out of her, filling the interior of the car. And he just sat there and endured it.

'I think I know how they did it,' said Rajhev Rajkumar. 'They're using another ship's LRIT and AIS transmitters.'

'How can they do that?' asked Mentz.

'The SOLAS treaty has a few loopholes. The major factor to keep in mind is that the ship owners do the actual tracking of their vessels, the SOLAS authorities just verify signal authenticity against global position. So, let's say you're a ship owner in . . . Durban, for argument's sake, running a few boats in the greater Indian Ocean. So I approach you, and I say, my Muslim brother, I want to borrow the AIS identity of one of your ships for a month or so, and I'll pay for the pleasure. So, I install the equipment on *The Madeleine*, and you turn a blind eye to the movements of your tracking signal. SOLAS won't know a thing, because the signal is for the route you filed with them, everything looks kosher . . .'

'What about my original ship? It will show on the system, because it's not transmitting. The CIA would have picked it up.'

'Only if your ship is actually in the water.'

'But . . .'

'Ships must get serviced. Refurbished, repaired, in dry docks. That is only filed with the local harbour authorities.'

Mentz considered his argument. 'You do realise you are a brilliant man,' she said, eventually.

Rajkumar nodded, self-conscious. 'There are a number of ways to narrow it down. The Committee would have had to work with someone they know, and trust. The AIS will have to be attached to a ship with South African harbour clearance, which normally operates in the Indian Ocean, as far as the Arabian sea, and it would have to be a vessel of the same tonnage, more or less, preferably a fishing trawler.'

'So let's start looking.'

They drove in silence, only the noise through the windscreen and the open window behind. First along the R27 north, and then right at the Melkbos traffic lights, to the N7.

Milla stared out over the wheat fields in the twilight. She was empty, the emotion expended. On the other side of the eruption she had found calm, a small hard nucleus of indignation and determination. With her head turned away from Lukas, calmly and precisely and loud enough to be heard over the wind noise, she said, 'The ship is arriving early.'

He was slow to respond. 'No, Milla . . .'

'Another email came for Osman. I connected my cellphone to his laptop. I also know what they are bringing in.'

'What?'

She played her trump card. 'I'm coming along.'

'No.'

She just stared at him.

His anger rose. 'Didn't you notice? They shot at us.'

'You don't have the right to decide about my life. No man has.'

'Christ, Milla . . .'

'You are not going to shut me out.'

'When is the ship arriving?'

She ignored him.

He drove in silence for a long time. Then he said, 'OK.'

'Say it.'

'You're coming along.'

'I can't hear you.'

'You're coming along. We're going to get the money.'

'On your word of honour?'

'Yes.'

She waited until he looked at her, she gauged his sincerity. 'Tonight. Two a.m. *Arrival of The Madeleine and Haidar now 24 hours earlier, at 02.00.* At the same place, same coordinates. I don't know what OPBC means.'

'Nor do I. What are they bringing in?'

'I think it's weapons. Missiles. From Pakistan.'

Rajkumar turned the hard drive over in his fingers, a sceptical expression on his face. 'Maybe,' he said. 'But it's going to take time.'

'How much time?' asked Mentz.

'Five, six hours . . .'

'That's more than enough. We have about forty-eight hours before *The Madeleine* arrives. And we might just find it before you're finished.'

75

For the first time he asked her advice, at the N7 junction – he wanted a back road to Parow or Goodwood. He drew her in with his explanation: they had to dump the car at an unobtrusive place, then get into the city.

She described the route via Philadelphia to him.

'What weapons did you get?'

'Assualt rifles.'

'What are their names?'

Her attention to detail evoked a half-smile that came and went. 'The small one is a Heckler & Koch UMP, that's short for "Universale Maschinenpistole", because it's a German machine pistol. This one is adapted to shoot .45 ACP rounds, not the usual nine-millimetre. ACP stands for Automatic Colt Pistol, it has more stopping power than the nines. The other two are AKs, a 4B and 2A, I only wanted one, but they sold them as a parcel.'

'They . . . ?'

'Nigerians. In Parklands.'

'How much did they cost?'

'The H&K was expensive. Four thousand. The AKs were seven-fifty for the two. The ammunition was included.'

'Seven hundred and fifty rand for two AK-47s!'

'I could have got them for 500 if I wasn't in such a hurry.'

'What happens after we ditch the car?'

At 19.37 came the news of the Nissan Sentra stolen at the Eden on the Bay shopping centre.

In the Ops Room, in front of the big team, Janina Mentz responded with stoic self-control – a small nod, a request for a wider search for the vehicle.

At 20.14 the agent phoned Quinn. 'I'm standing on the bridge of *The Trident*, it's a stern trawler from United Fisheries, it's been lying in the Robinson Dry Dock at the Waterfront since the thirteenth of September, total refurbishment. On the sixteenth of September someone broke in and stole all the electronics, radios, computers, navigation, the lot.'

'Excellent. Do you have the AIS identity?'

'No, we will have to get it from the United people, there are only guys here from the refurbishment company. He gave me the numbers, but it's Saturday night, there's no one in the office.'

'Give me the numbers,' tossed over his shoulder as he hurried across to Janina Mentz.

They left the Nissan Sentra in Dingle Street in Vasco, in front of a church, and walked to the minibus taxis at the station two blocks away. He carried the rucksack and gun bag, she had only her handbag. He held her hand.

They travelled along with nine coloured passengers down Voortrekker, Albert and Strand Street. The atmosphere was dampened by their presence at first, inquisitive, fleeting workmen's eyes were cast at Milla's soiled blouse and grazed arms, and Becker's shoulder. Until one of the men asked: 'Wicked weekend, *bru*?' and Lukas grinned and nodded, Milla laughed. Then came the wisecracks and speculations and stories, and by the time they stopped at the station, one woman said seriously: 'Go well, you two.'

They took a taxi to the Waterfront, just before the shops closed. They only bought the bare essentials – a small rucksack for Milla, shirt and blouse, dark anoraks, toiletries. They put on the new clothes in the public restrooms, then they walked through the Red Shed to the outside, up the stairs, to Portswood Street and the Commodore Hotel.

Rajkumar put down the phone and said to Mentz and Quinn, 'He says they've cancelled the Lloyds account for *The Trident*, because it's a waste of money while they're waiting for the new AIS equipment. So we won't be able to track the ship through them.'

'And the electronic ID?'

'He's on his way to their offices, we should have it in an hour.'

'And then?'

'Then we will have to talk to the Yanks.'

'Is that our only choice?'

'Yes.'

In the big hotel room Becker put the bags down, wrapped his arms around Milla and held her tightly, not speaking. They stood that way for a long time, until he said: 'You'll have to eat something.'

With his hands on her shoulders he looked at her, his eyes searching her face, for something.

She stroked his cheek with her fingers. Then she said: 'I want to have a quick bath. I won't be long.'

He let her go reluctantly.

Then he ordered sandwiches from room service.

'Jesus, Janina,' said Bruno Burzynski, indignant, astounded.

'Let's try and stay calm . . .'

He rose from his chair in the coordinating office, cracking his knuckles on the table, his face reddening. 'I just don't get you,' he said in a monotone, straining for self-control. 'Honest to God, I just don't get you.

You've just wasted two hours, we have little more than one day left, and you're still playing games. Have you got any idea what's at stake here?'

'Despite my third-world simplicity and my gender, I think I can grasp the stakes, Bruno.'

'Can you? Because I'm starting to think that chip on your shoulder is seriously impairing your ability to grasp anything . . .'

'The chip on *my* shoulder? How about the monkey of superiority on your back . . . ?'

'Enough,' barked Tau Masilo and stood up. 'That is more than enough.' He walked between them. 'Now, sit down, both of you.'

He gave Milla a short course in the use of the AK-47. He pressed the rounds out of the magazine with his thumb while explaining to her that it was a simple weapon, robust, reliable, but not very accurate. He showed her how to click home the magazine, how to cock the rifle, and push the safety catch down.

He explained the settings for semi-automatic and automatic fire, he showed her how to hold it, how to lean her body forward, how to press the trigger rather than pull it.

He made her do it over and over, until he was satisfied.

Burzynski was the first to react. He took a deep breath, sat down slowly, his face still red.

Mentz remained standing.

'Janina, please,' said Masilo.

'I grasp things better when I stand,' she said, with thin sarcasm.

Masilo visibly gritted his teeth, addressed himself to Burzynski. 'We would be very grateful if you could pass on the new information, and help us find the ship.'

Burzynski nodded, put out his hand to his cellphone.

'And then, I think it's time to put our cards on the table,' said Masilo, without looking at the Director.

'It doesn't make any sense,' said Becker. 'There are too many people here.'

At 21.38 they were standing in front of the Radisson Hotel, looking out over Granger Bay harbour, brightly lit. There were people everywhere: on the balconies of restaurants, on the walkways of the long, narrow quays, on the decks of the yachts that lay in long rows, masts and tackle in line.

'Is this the right place?' Milla asked.

He looked at the cellphone again. 'According to the GPS coordinates. It's here. Definitely.'

'They'll only be here at two. That's another four hours . . .'

Becker pointed at a party on the deck of a yacht. 'Those people will still be here at two o'clock . . . I should have written the coordinates down.'

'OPBC,' said Milla. 'Is that a navigational term?'

He shook his head. 'I don't know. Let me Google it.'

She watched him connect via his cellphone, and search.

The very first result was 'Oceana Power Boat Club'. He activated the link. A website opened, a small photo of the sea in the foreground, cranes and the buildings of Sea Point in the background. The accompanying text was barely readable it was so small on the screen. 'The Oceana Power Boat Club (OPBC),' he read, 'located at Granger Bay within the V&A Waterfront environs, is the only slipway for small craft in the Cape Town precinct. It has provided a valuable service to boaters for more than twenty-five years.' He studied the photo, then looked up, towards the sea. 'This is Granger Bay. It must be here.'

'Wait,' said Milla and walked down the steps to the wooden deck, where two men with beers in their hands stood at the gangway of a yacht. She heard them speaking English. 'Could you tell me where we can find the Oceana Power Boat Club?'

'You've got it wrong,' said Bruno Burzynski. 'They are not after our soccer team. It's a coincidence of dates. Our intelligence indicates something entirely different.'

'And what would that be?'

For the first time Burzynski looked uncomfortable. 'I'm sorry, but I'm not at liberty to share that with you.'

Mentz made a sound of scornful disgust.

'So we can call off Tuesday's security measures?' asked Masilo. 'You don't want your soccer team protected?'

'Go ahead.'

Masilo shook his head in bewilderment.

Mentz broke the silence. 'Let me try and figure this out. You were very keen to talk to us when you thought we had Osman,' she said.

Burzynski did not react.

'And the only thing you really want now, is the new electronic identity of *The Madeleine*. Which means you don't need us once you've found the ship.'

Burzynski stared at the table. Mentz walked towards them slowly, with growing certainty in her voice. 'You've got a boarding team standing by, haven't you? What are they, Bruno? Navy Seals? Did you bring in your own little fast boats, or did you buy them here? Chartered a few choppers? Because you're planning on taking the ship. And telling us about it afterwards.'

'That's absurd.'

'No, it's not,' said Janina Mentz, and sat down at the table. 'And that begs the question: what is on that ship that is so valuable that you would risk a huge diplomatic row, that you would sacrifice your relationship with us and with our government?'

'You've got it wrong,' he said, but she heard the faint traces of discomfort in his voice.

'I've got it right. At last.' Janina reached for the telephone, drew it closer and called a number. Burzynski followed her movements with his eyes. 'Raj,' she said into the instrument, 'we've just given the new AIS identity to the CIA. How long would it take them to find *The Madeleine*?'

She listened, then said, 'I see. You have four hours to decode the hard drive. Can you do it? . . . Good.'

Mentz slammed the phone down and smiled at Burzynski.

'Hard drive?' asked Burzynski. '*What* hard drive?'

'What's the cargo on *The Madeleine*?' Janina Mentz shot back.

76

The Oceana Power Boat Club was an ugly dark lump of coal between the diamond clusters of the Victoria and Alfred Waterfront and the Granger Bay yacht marina.

There were three identical OPBC signboards in white on the high, neglected wire fence, as though one was not enough to convince visitors.

It did look temporary, primitive, shabby, like a hidden building site – bare gravel, ships' containers scattered randomly, a long, nondescript flat-roofed building with a single light burning at one corner. Right at the back, a high breakwater of concrete dolosse, huge jumbled Xs like a giant child's carelessly thrown jacks, outlined against the phosphor glow of the sea. The double gates were locked, all was quiet and deserted.

They stood in the deep shadow just to the left of the gate. Milla watched Lukas's body change subtly, his shoulders and neck and head, as though he were making himself smaller, hiding, alert. His eyes took in everything, in front of them, around them, assessing and measuring.

'I need to know what it looks like inside,' he murmured. He started walking along the fence to the right.

'Tell Tiger to split his team in two,' Janina Mentz told Quinn. 'I want half of them at Ysterplaat, the helicopters will be ready in an hour. The other half must go to Simonstown, the captain of the Corvette SAS *Amatola* is expecting them. Raj says he should have the information . . .' she checked her watch, 'by two o'clock.'

Quinn wanted to ask her how sure she was that the ship was coming to Cape Town, but he assumed it was a calculated, optimistic guess. The Americans had the same dilemma, if they traced the ship first, they had to cover the same distance.

'Anything on the stolen Nissan?' Mentz asked.

'Nothing,' said Quinn. 'Absolutely nothing.'

They followed the fence for a hundred metres down to the sea. The wire ended there, before the steep slope down to the water and the chaos of the heaped up triangular dolosse. To the left was a way through to the Oceana Power Boat Club – a narrow sill, overgrown with weeds, along the short side of a ship's container. He began to shuffle along it, chest against the container, using the metal ridges for hand grips. He looked back at her. 'Come. It's easy.'

She followed him.

On the other side of the container there was a small, sheltered bay. The slipway into the sea was barely ten metres across, the bay itself just big enough to accommodate six or eight motorboats at a time. In the middle there was a narrow quay of cheap wood, floating on steel drums. Beyond that, a concrete surface with a gradual upward slope away from the water.

From here the club's shabby simplicity formed an even greater contrast. To the right the highest levels of luxury apartments were visible at the yacht marina, to the left the glow of the Waterfront. To the south, 500 metres beyond a grass bank on the other side of Strand Road, the new soccer stadium towered, spectacular, surreal, a glowing spaceship floating against the darkness of Signal Hill.

He stood considering it with a calculating eye. 'They know what they're doing,' he said.

'Why?'

'This is an almost perfect smugglers' cove; looks like something about to be demolished, no one would look twice if they drove past it. If your boat comes in here – you are practically invisible. But you have a good view over everything, you can see anyone coming 200 metres away. And you're five minutes from the N1, ten minutes from the N2, you're right in Sea Point and the city, get in quick, get out quick . . .'

'How are we going to . . . ?' She didn't know how to complete the sentence, because she didn't know how you would steal a missile and exchange it for money.

'It's nearly perfect. Look there . . .' He pointed at the two half-moon arms of the dolosse-breakwater. 'Easy to hide there. From that point you control the whole area. The big problem is there are only two exits, and both are narrow: the gate, to the street, and the slipway, to the sea.' He checked his watch, suddenly hasty. 'We have nearly two hours. Let's go and get coffee.'

'Another four hours,' she said.

'No.' He walked back to the narrow ledge.

On the table between the computers, tools, and equipment, the hard drive lay, incredibly small, connected to two thin wires.

'The drive is slightly buckled, so we had to get it out of the casing first,' said Rajkumar, and he picked up the dented black metal box, showed it to Mentz. 'And then we built a new, modified casing, to accommodate the warp, because the drive still needs to spin. It's the only way to get to the data quickly. Problem is, the disk is definitely damaged . . .'

'How much?'

'We just don't know. Depends on how full the disk was, how often he defragged . . . We're going to need a bit of luck.'

Mentz looked at him without expression.

'Wheel of fortune's got to turn, ma'am. Sooner or later, wheel's got to turn.'

They sat in the Mugg & Bean and drank coffee. She asked: 'Why do we only have two hours?'

'The rendezvous is at two o'clock. If they arrive too early, the wait is long, the people get bored and impatient. Careless. The risk is greater – security patrols, the police, a club member who has forgotten something. You send a couple of men around about one o'clock to secure the place, to have eyes on the look-out. And the rest of the team, along with the trucks or bakkies or whatever they use, only turn up at a quarter to two. But these are Muslim extremists, extra cautious, since their laptop has been stolen. They might send their eyes from twelve o'clock. Maybe earlier. We shall see.'

'What are we going to do?'

'We are going to take the money.'

'What money?'

'There is always money, at this kind of transaction. Cash. This is a world where no one trusts anyone, you don't pay in advance, you don't pay by cheque, you don't believe it when a guy says he will make an electronic transfer. You want to see the money in your hand and you want to count it. One guy will bring something in, the other inspects the goods and hands over the money. Always. And if it is weapons, they will pay in dollars.'

'There are only two of us.'

'We're going to wait until the deal is done. We aren't interested in the weapons, we're after the guys who are going out with the boat again. Through that narrow slipway. They will have the money . . .'

He took a pen out of a side pocket of his rucksack. He pulled the serviette closer, drew on it, quick lines for streets, the sea, the breakwater.

'I'll be here in front, on the point of the breakwater. You'll be here on the other side of Strand Road, behind the grass bank. That way we will cover both exits. The way this sort of thing usually works, the bringers in and the takers out all help to transfer the goods, it's in everybody's interest that it happens quickly, that the goods are delivered safely . . .'

'Why?'

He smiled again at her compulsion to understand everything. 'Because they want to do more business in future, there are reputations to protect, a code of honour. So, with a bit of luck, the boat will go back to the ship with the money at the same time as the load goes out the gates. I will stop them at the breakwater. All you have to do is fire off a few rounds. Here, in the direction of the gate, low, into the ground . . . It's dark, it's a hell of a surprise, we want to create the impression that we are many. I'll fire a burst with the AK, then with the H&K. You take the other AK and the pistol. Wait till I fire, then shoot first one then the other, single shots, five or six, completely different sounds, create the impression of superior numbers. That's all we need.'

He picked up his cup and took a big gulp.

'Lord, Lukas,' she said.

Extract: *A Theory of Chaos, Coronet, 2010, pp. 312–313*

He made the logical assumption. He thought my concern and uncertainty was about what lay ahead, he put his hand on mine and he said, 'If everything goes haywire, leave the weapons there and walk away. Go to the lights. To the hotel. Wash your hands and your clothes to remove the residue. Wait there for me.'

'No,' I said, because I couldn't contain it any longer. 'I wrote your report. I know what you learned in the Navy. How . . . ? Why do you know about things like everyone helping to offload, and about shaking off tails and buying cellphones without ID and getting guns in the Cape and about stealing cars,ripping parts off and connecting the right wires? And washing residue off your hands?'

Later, on the grass bank, I felt ashamed of my fervour and how badly I had expressed it. I found the words that I had wanted: 'It doesn't matter where all your knowledge comes from, it doesn't matter where you were and how you learned it. But why won't you trust me with the truth? Why don't you trust my love?' But it was too late by then.

I watched how he first looked past me at an invisible horizon. His face slowly changed. It became softer, like someone who was bringing sad tidings. In a voice the colour of a rainy day, he said the strangest thing: 'I went to study to find out when we lost our innocence. And I did.'

Only then did he look at me. 'For fourteen thousand years we have been heading for chaos, Milla. From the first settlement, the first town, the first city. So slowly that no one noticed it. But that's changed. It's pushing up like a tide, everywhere. In America, in Europe, here, ever faster, ever closer. In ten years, twenty, maybe fifty, it's going to swallow us up. You saw it, you know now. You will regret that, yet, you will still wonder whether it is better to be blissfully ignorant. You just have to get to the point where you realise the chaos is inevitable. Then you have to ask yourself, what are your choices? Can you afford to ignore it? Or should you utilise the chaos to escape it?

He picked up his coffee cup, drank the last of his coffee. He said, 'That's what I did. I learned from the chaos, so I could use it. And soon you will do that with me.'

77

He lay beside her on the grassy bank, the soccer stadium behind them, the street in front of them, the boat club to the other side. He held to his eyes a small pair of binoculars that he had dug out of his rucksack. He scanned the Oceana Power Boat Club, slowly, from end to end. Then he said, 'They're not here yet,' and he explained to her exactly what he wanted her to do. He told her how time stood still, how it disappeared when adrenaline flowed, a minute could feel like eternity, she must not be misled by that. She must look at her watch when she heard the first volley. They had easily ten, maybe twenty minutes before the police would arrive. Stay aware of the time, keep your cool. When she saw he had the money, when he was out of the gate, she must not go to him. Walk along behind the grass bank. To the light. To the hotel.

She nodded, a frown of great seriousness on her face.

He said the most difficult time would be the two hours of waiting. It was hard to lic still, so make sure you're comfortable, scratch open a place to lie in. Your greatest enemy is your mind. You're going to feel sleepy, you're going to doubt, you will see phantoms, you will think of everything that could go wrong. Just stick to the plan, forget about everything else: just stay awake, and stick to the plan.

He let her go through the rifle drill of the AK-47 one more time. Just before he got up and jogged expertly down the slope, he put his arm around her shoulders and kissed her in the neck and then on the temple. 'See you soon.'

She followed him with her eyes, across Strand Road, to the OPBC gate, until he disappeared in the shadows along the fence.

In the coordinating office, at a quarter to one in the morning, Masilo watched Bruno Burzynski. The CIA man walked up and down the opposite wall, restlessly, holding his cellphone to his ear. He kept repeating, 'Uh-huh', with varying pauses, his face betraying nothing.

He rang off, turned back to the table and sat down. His elbows on the table, his hands open in a gesture of conciliation. 'You have to talk to her, Tau.'

'She won't budge, Bruno. Not unless you tell her what the cargo is.'

For the first time the tension showed on Burzynski's face. He made a gesture of frustration and helplessness: 'I can't, it's not my decision, and this thing is so fucking politicised, so fucking *invested* . . .'

'That's not going to cut it.'

Burzynski regained control, his body still. He leaned back in his chair, visibly tired. 'I know.'

Extract: *A Theory of Chaos, Coronet, 2010, p. 317*

The last half-hour before they came was the most difficult.

The ache in my body from lying too long on the invisible, unknowable discomforts of the grass tufts and stones, the nagging, gnawing uncertainty, the doors opening in my head, unlocked by Markus's half confession, so that I thought of my own sins, submerged for so long.

On a grassy bank opposite a small-boat harbour, in the middle of the night, I remembered Cassie.

Casper. Eighteen years ago. Ten months before I met Frans. A year before I fell pregnant. Casper, the music student, the cellist, taking the same extra class as me. Cassie the vulnerable, Cassie the ugly, Cassie of the crooked teeth and small protruding ears, who made advances like a whipped dog. Cassie the annoying, with his nervous chat without context, his abrupt silences, yet I didn't have the courage to drive him away. It made me feel good, there was something sacrificial, something noble and altruistic in allowing Cassie his conversations, the development of the appearance of a friendship.

Cassie, who wanted more and more, who phoned, who followed me around, who asked for me at the hostel reception, until it all became too much, saturation point, the night of craziness. I stormed down the stairs, grabbed him by the hand, marched him off to his little flat. I closed the door behind us, and standing there in front of him, I took off all my clothes. Bare in front of him, naked, on display. I watched Cassie, his eyes flickering from my breasts to my pubis, the slackness of his mouth, his disbelief, his gratitude, his sudden lust, his transformation from lapdog to guard dog. Like my mother, I had given expression to an impulse, a compulsion, a liberation, and like her, I found pleasure in it. It was a moment of light and darkness. And truth.

I would not let him touch me.

She saw the blue bakkie first, dark blue, battered. It drove slowly past the gate twice, then went away. Towards the Waterfront. Turned back. Two people in the front.

A quarter to one.

At five to, they were back again. They stopped beside the fence, got out. Surveyed everything carefully. One had a cellphone to his ear.

Milla tracked his every move.

At one o'clock the second wave arrived. A panel van stopped in front of the gate. The passenger door opened, a man got out, disappeared in front of the vehicle. Appeared again as he opened the gates, first the right, then the left. He remained standing as the panel van drove in, waited until the dark blue bakkie reappeared, then he also passed through the gateway. He closed them again, but did not lock them.

The rear door of the panel van opened. Six, seven, eight men climbed out, each holding a weapon. She recognised the shape: AK-47s like the one that lay in front of her.

A big man stood and pointed, gave orders, the others walked to the bakkie, offloaded some equipment, cylindrical, big and bulky.

They moved purposefully, everyone seemed to know what to do. Two of them walked left around the bay to the breakwater, two to the right. The rest disappeared behind the building.

God, Lukas, they will see you.

The lights of the vehicles turned off.

Silence. Nothing happened.

Seventeen minutes past one.

Mentz came into the coordination office. Both men saw the smugness. 'I'm sure you've worked it out by now, Bruno. The bad news was that Osman's laptop was severely damaged. The good news, I am happy to report, is that the hard disk is in pretty good shape. We should have data access within the next half an hour. So the question is, how are you doing, with your satellites and stuff?'

The waiting, the endless waiting. She felt hot in the jacket, she wished she could take it off, but dared not move. Her hands perspired against the wooden butt of the AK, her eyes kept searching down below, but nothing moved. She looked again and again at her watch, at the eternity of minutes passing. Her mind asked, 'What if . . .' threatening to let loose the anxiety over strange possibilities. Her lips formed the words, over and over, silently: *just stay awake, stick to the plan.*

At twenty-seven minutes past one she felt as if she was levitating out of her body. She could see herself lying on the slope, the forty-year-old woman with short, black hair, the mother of Barend Lombard, the ex-wife of Christo, her life and *this* moment unreal, belonging to someone else, she wanted to get up and go and find her own. She wanted to stand up and scream, wave her arms. She wanted to stand up and hold the AK aloft and pull the trigger, watch the trajectory of the bullets, pretty bows, fireworks, celebrations.

Her heartbeat brought her back, beating too quickly, too hard inside, so that it felt as though the ground was rising up to swallow her. She knew it was the stress, two long days of stress, and she looked at her watch, sixteen minutes to two, and she almost leaped with fright, a shock wave rippling through her body, where had the time gone? *Just stick to the plan, forget about everything else, stay awake, and just stick to the plan.*

This was not her world. She knew that now.

Fourteen minutes to two.

Rajkumar's hands hopped across the keyboard like two fat birds, 'We have the keys, we have the keys, I'm exporting now, start the decryption, somebody call the Director.'

Then: 'Shit.'

The technicians, his hand-picked team, his good-natured colleagues, all looking at him.

'There's email here. We might not need the decryption, motherfucker has it password protected, let's see, you Muslim bastard, gimme what you got . . .'

They laughed.

He looked up fleetingly, said sharply and angrily. 'Call the Director. Now.'

78

At nine minutes to two the other vehicle arrived.

At first Milla didn't believe her eyes: that shape, those markings. She shifted forwards, stared intently.

An ambulance. It had stopped in front of the gate.

Someone emerged from the darkness carrying a gun, and opened the gates.

The ambulance drove through. Stopped in front of the long building. The big man came walking around it, talked to the driver. Then he walked back, out of sight again.

Why an ambulance?

Six minutes to two.

Janina Mentz watched the screen, where the small program window flickered with files scrolling too fast to read, searching for the keyword.

'Three, four minutes,' said Rajkumar. 'We're almost there.'

The telephone rang.

Rajkumar answered, listened. He held his hand over the instrument, looked at Janina and said, deeply impressed: 'The Director of the CIA wants to speak to you. From Langley. On the secure line.'

She must remember to check her watch when Lukas fired, she must remember, she must concentrate. Movement down below.

The ambulance doors opened, a weak beam of yellow light shining out. Someone moved in the interior. It was the figure of a man, bent over a low stretcher. He was busy. Then he sat on the bench next to it.

An ambulance. Camouflage. They were going to put the missiles in there. Nobody stopped an ambulance.

Relief, she felt relieved, a riddle solved.

'Please hold for the Director of the CIA,' said a woman's voice.

Before Mentz could react, his voice came over the line. 'Madam Director?'

'Yes.'

'I would have preferred our first meeting to be face to face, and under different circumstances, please accept my apology. As a fellow servant of the State, I am hoping for your understanding. Sometimes, we have to follow orders.'

'I understand, and your apology is accepted.'

'Thank you, madam. I have to tell you about the cargo being brought to your shores, but first, I want to ask a favour I have no right to. Would you please consider allowing AIC Burzynski to accompany you when you intercept? It would mean a lot to us, and to our government. And, in a minute, you will understand why.'

'We will gladly include Bruno.'

'Thank you very much. Now, allow me to tell you . . .'

The darkness below melted away, unexpectedly, in slow motion, so that she thought she was imagining it at first.

Four lights, a soft glow. It was the cylinders they had been carrying, two down at the quay, two further away at the end of each breakwater, where Lukas was. Her heart lurched, paralysing her, her body, her arms, her hands were as heavy as lead, her eyes were transfixed.

Light that made the small bay visible, surreal, since the sounds of the night had not altered, there was no additional movement, only the light.

Minutes dragged.

Then she heard the shout, faint and far away against the white noise of the city and the sea. She saw two small, dark figures leaping between the dolosse, impossibly long shadows fragmenting against the hundreds of facets. She knew before she saw, before her brain could decode the movements, knew it was Lukas, he had been seen, their dance was towards him, weapons in their arms, aimed urgently.

Two stick figures became three: Lukas with his hands on his head, the rucksack a small bulge at this distance. Milla was turned to stone, everything flowed out of her, only her eyes followed them, to the right, rifle barrels poking and prodding him like an animal, a lamb to the slaughter.

Rajkumar uttered a shrill sound of triumph. He opened the email program, a long list of messages in the inbox, the subject indecipherable. He chose one halfway down the list, speed read, saw references to the ship, nothing of use. Picked another one, scanned it, another:

Shipment arrives Monday 23 Shawwal 1430 A.H. at 02.00 (GMT +2).

'Shit,' he said and looked up. Janina Mentz wasn't back yet.

He read the next email.

We agree with your assessment. Arrival of The Madeleine and Haidar . . .

'Haidar?' he said aloud. 'Two ships?'

. . . now 24 hours earlier at 02.00 (GMT +2) on Sunday 22 Shawwal 1430 A.H.

'Fuck,' said Rajhev Rajkumar, looked at the wall clock. 'Where? Tell me where?'

He rose from behind the computer, he must go and get Mentz, he moved towards the door. He saw her approaching.

On the concrete slipway they made Lukas kneel, his hands behind his bowed head, two firearms aimed at him.

Four people came out of the building, walked quickly to the ambulance, took out the stretcher and pushed it around the corner.

The boat came through the gap, an illusion unfurling from the darkness, white, sleek and lovely, with the lines of a bird of prey. The deep, dull throb of the engines suddenly ceased.

Her eyes went back to Lukas, her whole body paralysed.

A few of the men ran to the wooden pier.

The big man appeared from behind the building, walked up to Lukas with his hands at his sides.

The boat cut slowly through the quiet water of the harbour, men on deck, ropes were thrown and caught. The vessel bumped gently against the pier, the prow slid against it, ropes were tightened, it came to a halt.

They all turned and looked to where Lukas knelt.

Milla stood up, gravity seemed almost too strong.

The big man in front of Lukas looked down, said something to him.

Walked slowly around behind Lukas. Stopped. Took a step back, stretched out his arm, to the back of Lukas's head.

She saw the extension of his arm, a weapon. Long and thin.

The outstretched arm jerked.

Lukas toppled forward.

The sound washed past her, dull. Lukas collapsed, dropped into a little bundle.

She must go and lift him up.

Keeping her eyes on him, her hands searched and found the pistol. Grabbed the rifle. Stood erect, so difficult, so slow. She shuffled down the slope. She saw them leave Lukas there and all walk over to the quay. There was activity on the deck, but her eyes were fixed on Lukas.

She walked across the pavement, across the tarmac of Strand Road. She pushed the pistol down the front of her jeans, not feeling the scrape of metal against the skin of her belly. She held the AK in both hands, walked down the road to the gate, across the gravel, her trainers almost soundless.

She pushed the gate open with her hip.

The ambulance was in front of her, that yellow light from the interior, the man busy with something, head down. The boat and the others were out of sight behind the building.

She cocked the AK as Lukas had showed her, left hand under, pull the bolt back, let go. Pressed the long safety catch with her right thumb, from top to bottom. In the ambulance the man heard the metallic clicks, looked up, saw her. He was coloured, middle-aged. He had a black fringe. Long. A dark mole on his forehead, above the left eye, big and unsightly. His jaw dropped.

She pointed the AK at him. He put his hands up. 'No. *Asseblief*.' Pleading.

She stopped. She could see Lukas. He lay tipped forward, still half kneeling, his head on the concrete, turned to her as though resting. The blood shone in the light, a wide dark red puddle. One eye was open, white and staring. The other eye was destroyed, horrifying.

Something tore inside her, a world fell away.

Rajkumar sweated, dark stains on his back and under his arms, clicked on the *Sent Items* folder, Mentz stood behind him.

There were messages.

'Thank God,' he said, and opened them one after the other.

She heard them coming, the noise of something moving on the concrete.

The wheels of the stretcher.

She took two steps to the ambulance and got in. The man with the long fringe stared at her in fear, hands raised defensively. 'I'm just the doctor.'

She moved right to the back corner, beside the sliding window to the driver's cab. She poked the doctor in the ribs with the barrel, so that he had to shift forward on the bench.

Then they were there, five of them, guns slung over their shoulders. One held a drip high, four handled the stretcher. A shape lay on it under blankets, beard, hair peppered with grey.

The carriers saw her. Shock like shadows crossed their faces.

The patient followed their frozen stares, to her. He turned his head slowly. And looked at her. Pale, sunken, black eyes, lined, contoured features, beard, face, an eternity before it sank in.

She knew him.

Fragments tumbled through her mind: bits, pieces, words, a splintered mirror that became whole. She saw, she rejected, she tried again, she understood, dizzy, synapses flashed and fired and crackled, an impossible reality that eventually made sense.

The doctor's whispers, respectful, pleading. 'Please don't shoot.'

Brought to her senses, Milla took a deep breath. 'Put him in,' she said.

No one moved.

Milla moved the barrel of the gun to the side panel. Pulled the trigger. The noise inside deafening.

They jumped. Someone bellowed outside. The smell of cordite in her nostrils. She leaned forward, pressed the weapon to the patient's head.

'Put him in.' She didn't know her own voice.

They picked up the stretcher, and pushed it slowly in.

The big man appeared at the ambulance door, pistol and silencer in his hand.

79

Rajkumar and Mentz stood at the back of the Ops Room listening. Over the radio, the racket of the Super Lynx 300 turbo engines. Mazibuko's voice: 'On our way, ETA seven minutes.'

Quinn's voice was calm, every word clear. 'Major, I have a new directive, repeat, I have a new directive. Shipment may be human cargo, of extreme value, order is to intercept and protect, protect at all costs, please confirm.'

'Roger, Ops, target is possible human cargo, extreme value, intercept and protect at all costs.'

Rajkumar looked hopefully at Mentz, wishing she would share the secret with him. She said nothing, her expression grim.

'Roger, Major. Be aware of a black BMW X5, Advocate Tau Masilo and a member of the CIA are en route, five or six minutes away, unarmed, they will wait for visual confirmation of your arrival, at the corner of Portswood and Beach Roads, and approach drop zone from the east, down Beach, please confirm.'

'Roger, Ops, black BMW X5, their ETA five minutes, coming down Beach Road from the east after our arrival.'

Silence.

Rajkumar couldn't keep it in any more. He whispered to the Director: 'Haidar means "lion", that's all I could find.'

'Try "lion sheikh",' she said provokingly, the suspense a mask.

At first he stood processing the clue of a phonetic 'lion's cheek' to the context of 'sheikh'. He walked quickly to one of the vacant computers, set the web browser to a search engine, and typed in the words.

The third link was the one that made his eyes pop. He clicked on it. Arabic script, a simple web page. He had to scroll down before he saw the photo, the familiar face, and the English translation. *From The Lion Sheikh Usama Ibnu Laden May Allah Preserve Him.*

'Shit,' said Rajhev Rajkumar, the sibilant long and drawn-out.

The big man outside the ambulance, the one who had shot Lukas, had a heavy face, as if carved from granite, thick bushy eyebrows above eyes filled with hate, as he lowered the pistol.

Milla, right at the back, stared back with contempt.

The doctor took the drip and hung it from a hook, folded his hands on his lap. The bearers retreated.

'Lukas's money,' said Milla.

No one responded.

She lifted the AK, brought it down on the patient's face, on his nose and mouth, a convulsive movement, the doctor gasped, the big man roared, her voice above everything, screaming, rage verging on hysteria, 'Bring Lukas's money!'

More hesitation. Then the big man shouted at someone out of sight: 'Bring the silver case.'

'And his rucksack,' she said with more control this time.

'Take the rucksack off him,' the big one ordered.

Blood from the patient's nose soaked into the grey-black

moustache. The doctor looked at it, looked at her in question. She shook her head.

A case was passed to the big man, another pair of astounded eyes peered at her, then disappeared.

'Open it.'

He took a step up to the ambulance, put the shiny aluminium case down on the floor, unclipped it, turned it around, lifted the lid.

Dollars, tightly packed.

She nodded.

The rucksack arrived. He took it, put it beside the case.

She saw the blood spatters on Lukas's bag, the flecks of tissue. A sound slipped from her throat. She looked up, saw the contemptuous eyes under the bushy eyebrows. She lifted the AK, leaned forward as she had been taught, and shot the big man, three cracking staccato shots, jerking him back and away, staggering, falling. The doctor called to Heaven, the patient tried to lift his arms from under the blanket, and she turned the weapon, pressed it against him, and said: 'Drive now. Drive.'

The bearers outside the open doors didn't move.

Again she hit the patient with the muzzle of the gun, against the cheekbone. The doctor shouted, in desperation: 'Get someone, please, someone to drive.'

One of the bearers came to his senses, a young man, he disappeared, she felt the springs of the vehicle budge, the front door slam shut, the window behind her slide open.

'Where to?' he asked.

In the distance, the sound of helicopters.

The parking lot of the Tyger Valley shopping centre was dark and deserted.

She gestured to the driver to drive to the Renault. The patient's eyes were on her, intense. Filled with hatred.

They stopped beside her car.

'Open up,' she said to the doctor.

He hesitated.

'I want to get out,' she said. 'Then you can go.'

BOOK 4: MAT JOUBERT
(Form 92)

February 2010

Reporting found persons must be cancelled by personally notifying the police station where the person was reported as missing of his/her return, or by the investigation official investigating the missing person's case. A SAPS 92 is used to effect the cancellation on the relevant Circulation System.

South African Police Services Directive, 2008 (verbatim)

80

He loved to watch her.

Margaret stood on the other side of the breakfast counter, ten to seven in the morning, already showered and dressed. Her long, reddish-brown hair in a plait, pale pink lipstick, an almost invisible sprinkling of freckles on her cheeks. A head shorter than he was, but tall for a woman. And full-bodied. With the slender forearms and delicate hands that now constructed the sandwiches with so much practised skill: a lick of mayonnaise, lettuce leaves, half peppadews, fine rounds of sweet cucumber and, finally, the slivers of roast chicken, before she sliced her creation cleanly with the knife, straight across, precisely in half.

He sat and ate his yoghurt and muesli.

She placed each sandwich in its own transparent bag and looked up at him with her oddly-coloured eyes, the one bright blue, the other brown, flecked with speckles of gold dust.

'So how does it feel?'

'Strange,' said Mat Joubert. 'A bit nervous.'

'I can believe it.' Her English accent was careful, the way her tongue worked the Afrikaans charming. 'Everything will be fine. Ready for your coffee?'

'Please.'

She turned towards the coffee machine. He admired her curves in denim jeans, the white heels. Forty-eight, and easy on his eye. 'You look sexy,' he said.

'You too.'

He smiled, because it was good to hear her say it. She poured coffee into a mug, walked around the counter, right up against him, kissed him on the cheek. 'Jacket and tie have always suited you.' She had picked it all out, Saturday at Canal Walk, because he was never good with clothes. The scale of the search was always so discouraging – it was a constant struggle to find something that fitted his unusually large frame. But this time he *had* to, because at Jack Fischer and Associates the dress code was a little different from what he'd been accustomed to over the last few years.

She pulled the milk and artificial sweetener closer. 'Mat Joubert, Private Eye. It's got a certain ring to it.'

'Senior Security Consultant,' he added. 'Sounds like some guy sitting at a gate with a clipboard.' He shook one sweetener pill into his coffee, added milk and stirred.

She walked across to the sink with his yoghurt bowl. 'I have to go to Stellenbosch. Michelle's washing . . .' Her daughter, third-year drama student, absent-minded and eccentric. 'I have to be back by twelve, for the buyers.'

'Do you think they're serious?' He stood up, picked up the sandwiches. Wallet, cellphone and new briefcase, he ticked off the reminders to himself.

'I hope so. But call me when you can. I'm very curious.'

He walked over to her, kissed her on the forehead, breathed in her subtle feminine scent appreciatively. 'I will.'

'You're going to be early.'

'The roadworks . . . I don't know what the traffic will be like. And better early than late.'

'Love you,' she said. 'My PI.'

He smiled. 'You too.'

When he opened the front door she called out: 'Have you got the briefcase?'

He turned back to fetch it.

'She's a fifty-five,' was how Jack Fischer briefed him in the passageway, police lingo, a reference to the SAPS missing persons form.

In the conference room he could see that the loss was recent. Her narrow shoulders drooped dejectedly, her eyes stared absently down at St George's Mall, the pedestrian area three storeys below. She clutched a cellphone against her chest, as if hoping it might ring.

Jack Fischer let him walk ahead, then said: 'Mrs Vlok?'

She jumped, startled. 'Pardon me . . .' she said, putting down the phone and holding her hand out. 'Tanya Flint.' The smile was forced, the eyes weary.

'Flint,' said Jack Fischer, as if memorising the name.

She was in her thirties, Joubert guessed. Short, dark brown hair. A determination in the line of her jaw, the set of her mouth, now softened by anxiety. And loss. The black jacket, white blouse and black skirt were professional, but somewhat loose, as if she'd recently lost weight.

'Mrs Flint, I am Jack Fischer, and this is Senior Consultant Mat Joubert.'

She shook each one's hand quickly, intimidated by the bulk of the two middle-aged men against her slight frame.

'Sit, do sit.' It sounded almost like an order to Joubert, though Fischer was trying to be gallant.

'Thank you.' With a brave smile. She slid the handbag off her shoulder and moved towards a chair.

They sat around the big dark wood table, Fischer at the head, Joubert and Tanya Flint on either side.

'Madam, firstly, a warm welcome to Jack Fischer and Associates . . .' The big ring on Jack's finger flashed with the genial wave of his hand. He was in his sixties, but his thick black hair showed little grey, the side parting was precise, his moustache bushy.

'Thank you.'

'Has Mildred asked if you'd like something to drink?'

'She did, thank you, but I'm fine.' Her hand wrapped around the cellphone again, thumb rubbing the back.

'Excellent, excellent. I just want to give you the assurance that although I don't handle all the cases personally, I am nevertheless kept up-to-date on everything every day. But with S.C. Joubert, you are getting one of the best in the country. He has recently left the South African Police Services after thirty-two years of service – he was Senior Superintendent, and Head of the Serious and Violent Crimes Unit here in the Cape. He's an old hand, madam, with incredible experience, a brilliant investigator. Now, before I leave you in his very capable hands, just a few admin matters. You understand that, should we accept your case, there is a deposit payable?'

'Yes, I saw . . .'

'Excellent, excellent.' Broad smile below the extravagant moustache. 'We work on an hourly rate of 600 rand, excluding travel costs, naturally also any fees for lab work, external consultants, that sort of thing, but we check everything with you first. We're not the cheapest, but we're the best. And the biggest. And our system ensures that you don't spend more than you want to. We'll tell you within two days if your case can be resolved. When the work reaches eighty per cent of your deposit, we give you a ring. When it reaches a hundred per cent, we ask for a further deposit.'

'I understand . . .'

'That way there are no surprises, you understand?'

She nodded.

'Any questions?'

'I . . . No, not at the moment.'

'Excellent, excellent. Well, good, Mrs Flint, now tell us what we can do for you.'

She set the cellphone down carefully on the table in front of her, drew in a deep breath. 'It's my husband, Danie. He disappeared on November twenty-fifth last year.' As the tears welled up in her eyes, she shifted her gaze to Mat Joubert and said: 'I won't cry. I made a decision that I wouldn't come here today, and cry.'

81

She went off to pay the 30,000 rand deposit to senior financial controller Fanus Delport while Joubert waited for her in his new office. He experienced a measure of tension within himself. For the first time in his career someone had to pay directly for his services. And it was six, seven years since he'd last done investigative work himself, in the front line. 'It's like riding a bicycle,' Jack Fischer had said two months ago during the recruitment interview, 'you just get back on again.'

He hoped it was true.

Tanya Flint appeared in the doorway. 'May I come in?'

'Of course,' he said, standing up, waiting for her to sit down. He saw her look around, take in her surroundings. The room was still bare, the dark wood wall units empty. The only personal items were the leather folder for his notepad, his briefcase with two sandwiches in it, and the framed photo on the desk.

'It's my first day,' he said, by way of explanation.

'Oh. Then I'm lucky.'

He wasn't sure what she meant.

She pointed at the photo. 'Your family?'

'My wife and my . . . stepchildren.' He'd never liked the word.

'She's very pretty.'

'I think so too.'

An uncomfortable silence. He flipped open the leather folder in front of him. Inside it was a pen and an A4 writing pad. At the top of each page, in silver letters, stood *Jack Fischer and Associates*, pale, like a watermark. He slid the pen from its loop and clicked the nib out, at the ready.

She unclasped her handbag, on her lap, and took out a photo and a notebook. She handed him the photo. Postcard size, in full colour, of a man in his thirties. The sandy hair trimmed in a short brush cut, *braai* tongs in one hand, bare chested, outside, laughing. An open, boyish face. There was a certain carefree air about him, someone who had managed to dodge most of life's blows. 'This is Danie,' she said.

She wanted to start on the day that he'd vanished, but Joubert asked her to begin right from the beginning. 'I need all the background I can get.'

She nodded, resolute. 'I understand.'

And she told him. With a note of barely-suppressed nostalgia in her voice.

She had met Danie Flint seven years ago, when she was twenty-six and he was twenty-eight, at a gathering of mutual friends in Bellville. Not love at first sight, but there was a connection, a natural ease with each other. She liked his sense of humour, the way he laughed, his respectfulness towards her, from the beginning. 'He was so considerate.' And, with a small longing laugh: 'His shirt was always hanging out, even though he tucked it in a hundred times a day.' Joubert noted the past tense and thought it was better that way. It meant that she was realistic, she had already weighed up all the possibilities in a country where disappearance and death generally went hand in hand.

Flint was a route planner for the Atlantic Bus Company, the giant firm whose buses, with their bright yellow ABC against a navy blue background, were such a common and irritating presence on roads of the Cape Peninsula. He was doing a part-time diploma in Passenger Transport at the University of Johannesburg – hard-working, enthusiastic, ambitious.

Back then she'd been marketing solar heating systems for swimming pools, knowing that it was temporary, a training ground before she began her own business.

A suburban love affair, unremarkable, unsensational. Thirteen months after their first meeting, he asked her to marry him. She had said 'yes' with complete certainty.

After the wedding they'd bought a townhouse in Table View. Later, with Danie's promotion to area manager at ABC, they'd chosen a small three-bedroom house in Parklands. Children, they agreed, would have to wait for now. He wanted to study, she had her dream of running her own business. 'I set up eighteen months ago in Montague Gardens. We manufacture plastic pool covers and leaf catchers,' she said, fishing a business card out of her handbag and passing it to Joubert. The black silhouette of a spy-like figure in a large hat superimposed over a kidney-shaped swimming pool icon. Undercover was the company name.

'My business was just starting to get off the ground when the economic crisis hit. But Danie carried us, with his salary. We worked so hard . . . And then, on the twenty-fifth of November, Danie disappeared. He was at work the whole day. We spoke on the telephone, must have been about half past three. Then he said he was going to the gym when he left work at five. He'd usually be home by half past six after that, he'd try to go to the gym four times a week. I found his car at the gym, eleven o'clock that night, but he was just gone . . .'

'Mrs Flint, I have . . .'

'Tanya,' she said.

Joubert nodded. 'I need as much detail about that day as you can give me.'

She opened the notebook in front of her. 'I wrote everything down . . .'

'That's good,' Joubert encouraged her.

She looked at her notes. 'I only got away from work at a quarter to six, then I stopped at the Spar for bread and milk and salad. I was probably at home by quarter past and wanted to get the food ready in time, because on Wednesdays we watched *Boston Legal*, it was Danie's favourite, it starts at half past seven. Supper was ready around seven, but he wasn't at home yet. But with Danie . . . Sometimes he'd get talking to someone, he's just so spontaneous, so now and then he'd be late. But then I called him, ten past seven, and his cellphone just rang. I didn't leave a message, because maybe he was still in the gym. But at twenty-five past I started to get worried, because he never misses *Boston Legal*, he was crazy about it, he always said, "Danie Flint", you know, like "Denny Crane". Then I called again, but he still didn't answer. So I left a message. I just said, call me, I'll tape the show for you, because perhaps his phone was on silent, perhaps he'd forgotten to switch it on. Eight o'clock I called again. You know how a cellphone rings for a shorter time when you've had a missed call or a voicemail you haven't listened to yet? Then I thought maybe he'd had a call-out, if one of the buses had been in an accident, or something like that, then they'd call him, then he'd have to go. So I called Neville Philander who works with him, and Neville said no, Danie left work at five, he doesn't know about any call-out, he'll try to find out. Then I started calling Danie's friends, and his mother, she lives in Panorama, but no one had seen him. Then I called his cellphone again and I got in my car and I drove to the gym to look for him, but . . .' She made a shrugging gesture that said he wasn't there.

'The police station is right next to the gym in Table View. So I went in and I said my husband is missing and the guy said to me since when and I said he should have been at home at half past six, and he said, "Ma'am, it's nine o'clock now," and I said he hadn't let me know. Then he asked, "Did you have a fight?" And I said no, and he said, "Ma'am, you know men," and I said not *my* man. And then he said, "He's probably with his girlfriend." That's when I started crying.'

Joubert's first instinct was to defend the charge officers, who had to deal with every imaginable kind of domestic trouble every day. But he just shook his head and asked, gently: 'And then?'

'Then I went home again, because I was afraid that Danie was already there and wouldn't know where I was, maybe someone had stolen his cellphone, I thought it was something like that, I shouldn't worry too much, I must just stay calm, it's probably just something silly. But he wasn't at home and he still didn't answer his phone. Neville from his work called back and said there wasn't any call-out. Then I phoned his mother again, because I wanted to be sure I wasn't being paranoid, but she also said Danie isn't like that. Then I got in my car and I drove and looked at all the places where he might be, maybe he'd gone to have a beer with his friends at Cubana or the Sports Pub, but he was nowhere. And then I drove to the gym again at eleven o'clock and then the parking lot was almost empty and there was his Audi, and I got out and looked through the window and his gym bag was in the back. And I tried the door and it wasn't locked, and then I knew something really bad had happened to him. I walked from there back to the police station. They sent this young chap in a uniform with me, and he came to look and then we walked back and the guy behind the counter took out two forms and said I must fill them in. The one was an indemnity. Since when have the police needed an indemnity?'

Joubert didn't respond. The indemnity was to protect the SAPS in cases where the missing persons report was malicious or false. Which happened quite often.

'And then he said if Danie hadn't turned up by the next day, then I must bring a photo, they'll put it up on the website and they'll see what they can do. But they didn't do anything.'

Joubert looked up from his notepad. 'What type of Audi is it?'

'An A3, a red one. He bought it second-hand. Here's the registration number . . .'

He wrote it down. 'Did they check the car for fingerprints?'

'No. I took the photo the next day and asked if I could take the car home, and they said yes. I called once a day, every day, and went once myself to ask, but they just said, "There's nothing". How does that work? How can they not care? We pay their salaries, their job is to help us. But they do nothing. I made fliers and put them under people's windscreen wipers at the gym. I had to do that, myself.'

'The Audi is at your house now?'

'Yes.'

'Did they get a detective to handle the case?'

'A week later, yes. He came to my work and asked me all the things I'd already written on the form and he didn't listen, he just kept fussing with his fringe all the time. I never heard from him again.'

82

There were two possibilities when it came to missing persons cases. Foul play. Or someone wanted to disappear. For the loved ones who stay behind, both are equally hard to accept. So Joubert asked the easy questions first.

Were his wallet and cellphone in the car?

No, they were gone.

Were his bank card and credit card normally in his wallet?

Yes.

Were there any transactions on those cards after his disappearance?

No, she stopped the cards after three days.

What was in the sports bag?

Only Danie's gym kit.

Any clothes taken from his wardrobe?

Pain moving shadow-like across her face. No, she said.

Any of his possessions missing from the house?

No.

Anything else missing from the Audi?

Not that she was aware of.

No sign of the car keys?

No, she had to go and fetch the spare keys from the house, from Danie's cupboard.

Any strange calls in the week before the disappearance?

No.

Were there any big arguments Danie might have had with someone during that time?

Not that she knew of.

Conflict at work?

Nothing out of the ordinary. He worked hard, sometimes there was stress . . .

What kind of stress?

There was a strike, last year. There's always staff stuff. The bus drivers . . . Sometimes they don't turn up for work, sometimes they're late, sometimes they crash into someone. Sometimes Danie had to fire people.

There wasn't any specific case that he spoke about more than others?

Danie didn't actually ever bring his work home. He hid his stress well, he was always so cheerful. So, no, she couldn't remember him mentioning anything in particular.

And then he said, gently, respectful: 'You must please understand, there are certain questions I have to ask, even if they're difficult . . .'

She nodded her head, but her eyes showed she knew what was coming.

'Were you happy?'

'We were!' For the first time with emotion, like someone trying to convince herself. She straightened her shoulders. 'We had our arguments, but only now and then, like any married couple. The usual stuff, but we always talked it through. Always. We had a rule, never go to bed angry.'

'The usual stuff?'

'You know . . . I wanted a new lounge suite, he wanted a built-in bar area. He wanted to go to cricket at Newlands, I wanted to go to the movies . . .'

'And he never came home late?'

'With his work he did sometimes. But then he would call, twice, three times. He was so considerate, always.'

'You said you looked for him at Cubana and the Sports Pub. Did he often hang out there?'

'Last year . . . In July and August I worked very hard at Undercover, then I would call him and say I was going to be late, then he would say, "Don't worry, babe, I'll just grab something at the pub with the boys." Then I would meet up with him there and we'd have a few drinks together. He never went without telling me. He was the most considerate person . . .'

'He didn't act differently in any way in the month or two before he vanished?'

'Not at all. Danie is Danie. Always the same. I . . . All this stuff, I wondered, could there be something I'd missed? In those first three weeks after he vanished . . . I couldn't sleep, I went through his stuff, through his jacket and trouser pockets, through his wardrobe, through the bedside cupboard, through his car, through all the receipts and paperwork and there was nothing, absolutely nothing.'

'How were your finances?'

'My business . . . We knew that it would be tough, but we believed that it would make a big difference one day. So we struggled a bit last year, but we always discussed it, we never, ever argued about it, he just always said, "We'll get through it, babe, you'll see". But now . . . I don't know how long ABC will keep paying his salary . . .'

'Does he have a computer?'

'He has one at work, at home we shared my laptop, we shared an email address for personal stuff.'

'Do you have his cellphone records?'

'I have. There was nothing. His last call was about quarter past three on the afternoon of the twenty-fifth, to Hennie Marx, one of our friends. Hennie said it was just Danie calling him back about plans for the weekend, we wanted to go out for sushi with him and his wife.'

'Did you list the cellphone?'

'No. What do you mean?'

'Did you report it as stolen or missing at all?'

'No, I . . . Not before I could find out what happened.'

'That's fine,' he said, reassuring. 'Can you give me the cell number and the IMEI number?'

'The aye-mee-aye number?'

'International Mobile Equipment Identity. Every phone has its own, it's usually on the box the phone comes in, or somewhere in the documentation. Every time a phone registers on the network, the IMEI is tested to see if the phone is on the grey- or blacklist.'

He saw her look of incomprehension. 'When a phone is stolen, the owner has the choice of putting it on the grey- or blacklist. The greylist is when the phone can still be used, so you can plot it. The blacklist means the phone is cancelled and no one can use it.'

'Oh. What do you mean "plot"?'

'You can find out where the phone is, within an eighty-metre range.'

'How?' Hopeful.

'Through the cellphone provider. If it's your own phone, you can just request it. If it's someone else's phone, you need an Article Two-Zero-Five subpoena. There are other options too, freelance people who can track the phone.'

'Can we do it?'

'When last did you ring Danie's cellphone?'

'I call every day.'

'What happens when you call it?'

'It just says, "The number you have dialled is not available."'

That could mean one of several things. 'If the phone still has Danie's SIM card in . . .' he said. 'You have to understand, if the phone is off, we can't plot it. But we can find out if it's still being used.'

'Can we try?'

'If we have the IMEI number.'

She stood up. 'I'll look for it.'

'Tanya . . . I have to tell you, there are extra costs. A court order . . . Using the freelance guys.'

She sat down again, slowly. 'How much?'

'I'm not sure. With the police we didn't have to pay for the subpoena. I will have to get you a quote.'

Her shoulders sagged again. 'The 30,000,' she said with despair in her voice. 'It's all I have, Mr Joubert. It's on overdraft, it's all they'd give me.'

'Mat,' he said. 'Everyone calls me Mat.'

She nodded.

'Tanya,' he said, with all the tenderness he felt towards her, 'you understand, it's three months already now . . .'

'I know.' Her voice a whisper. 'I just . . . want . . . certainty.'

83

'What is justice worth to you, Mr Bell? Can you put a price on that?' asked Jack Fischer on the telephone, with his heavy Afrikaans accent, as he waved at Joubert to come and sit down.

Joubert looked at the pictures on Fischer's office wall, landscape oil paintings of the Bosveld and the Boland. Against the opposite wall was a bookshelf that covered the whole wall, filled from end to end with thick legal tomes. Which Jack himself admitted he only displayed for the impression they created. 'Perception, Mat, everything is perception,' he'd said when Joubert had sat here for the first time. 'You must understand they've just come from Green Point police station where it's total chaos, they're looking for order, they're looking for reassurance, they're looking for success. And that is what we give them.'

He hadn't changed at all, still the same old Jack who'd been Joubert's senior at Murder and Robbery, back in the day. Already a legend, a flamboyant success story. The suits were tailored now, the lines in the long face deeper, but the self-confidence, the extravagant verbosity, the emphasis on appearance, were unchanged.

'Of course the police are useless. That's our bread and butter,' said Jack into the phone. 'Look, you know what Jack Wells said?'

Clearly the person on the other end of the line didn't know who this was, because Fischer added: 'You know, Jack Wells from General Electric . . .'

Then: 'That's what I said, Jack Welch. Anyway, he said, "Face reality as it is, not as it was or as you wish it to be". The SAPS is our reality. But Jack Fischer and Associates is part of that reality. It's your chance to get justice, Mr Bell . . .'

Fischer listened, then rolled his eyes at Joubert. 'I ask you again, Mr Bell, put a price on justice. What's it worth? OK. Well, think about it . . . Thank you, yes, we hope to hear from you soon.'

He put the phone down. 'Stingy bastard. The Nigerians stung him for one point four million, but now he says 40,000 is too much to catch them.'

'A four-one-nine?' asked Joubert, referring to the scam ironically named after Article 4.1.9 of Nigerian fraud law.

'A clever one. Rang him and said he's the primary heir of a man with the same name in England . . . In any case, how's it going with our Mrs Vlok?'

'Flint.'

'Fanus says she's paid the deposit.'

'She has. That's why I'm here. Jack, the woman says that's all she has. We will have to cover other expenses out of that.'

'Oh.' Disappointed. 'Not ideal . . . What kind of expenses are we talking about?'

'I want to plot the cellphone.'

'Has she got the IMEI?'

'She thinks so.'

'*Ja* . . . You can ask Dave Fiedler for a discount, but I doubt it . . .'

'Is he the guy you . . . we use?'

Fischer nodded. 'He's here in Sea Point, usually charges one five for a plot if you can provide the IMEI, but we are one of his biggest clients, so you can try. Are you going to pull Vlok's bank statements?'

'I'm going to fetch them from her house this afternoon. Want to look around a bit.'

'Listen, ask her if she can get them electronically off Internet banking, then you give them to Fanus, he puts it all in a spreadsheet, can build you almost any kind of graph, great overview for spotting any funny business. And it costs us nothing, but it's double time, yours and Fanus's. Oh, and your laptop arrives this afternoon, should have been here yesterday. We have a central database with all the contact numbers and stuff. And ask Mildred to give the interior decorator a call, let her come and take a look, we have to tart up that office of yours a bit, you're in the major league now, my man.'

'I was thinking I'd ask Margaret . . .'

'No, man, use the decorator, we get it all off tax.'

The Atlantic Bus Company's Woodstock depot was in Bromwell Street, opposite the industrial area, next to the Metro railway line. Joubert had to stop at the gate and sign in with the security guard before he could drive in. The low office building was in the middle of the big, fenced area. Row upon row of blue buses, a workshop and giant fuel tanks behind them. A train rumbled towards Muizenberg as Joubert got out. Heat rose from the tar, the smell of diesel and oil heavy in the air.

There was no reception. He walked all the way to the end of the corridor before he found an office with *Neville Philander, Depot Manager* on the door. He knocked.

'Come in,' a voice called out.

Joubert opened the door. Philander held a hand over a telephone mouthpiece and said: 'I'll be with you in a minute,' and then, into the receiver: 'Recovery are on their way, Jimmy, just hang in there . . . No, I've got people here, I have to go. OK, bye . . .' He put the phone down, stood up, offered his hand and said: 'You're the private eye?'

He would have to get used to this. He walked into the air-conditioned office and shook the tall coloured man's hand. 'I am. Mat Joubert.'

'Neville Philander. Please sit, it's all a bit crazy here at the moment . . .'

The telephone rang again. Philander stood up, walked to the door, shouted down the corridor: 'Santasha, hold the calls, I've got someone here.'

'OK, lovey,' a woman's voice called back. Philander sat down again. 'Madhouse, I tell you. Where were we? You probably want to know about Danie . . .'

'If you can tell me.'

'HQ says it's OK. Tanya put in an official request.'

'I don't want to waste your time. Just two things really: did Danie Flint have any trouble at work, and did he, in the month before his disappearance, behave strangely in any way, any differently?'

'There's always trouble here at work. Are you ex SAPS?'

'I am.'

'Thought so. You've got that look. *Ja*, well, Danie was area manager, there's usually four of them, it's a tough job . . .'

The phone on his desk began to ring again. 'Jesus,' he said, jumping up, and shouting down the corridor again: 'Santasha, please!'

'Sorry, Neville, my mistake, lovey . . .'

He came back to his chair. 'Look here, the area manager's job is to manage his drivers, and his routes. Danie was Atlantic North, so everything from here to Atlantis, including Milnerton, Montague Gardens, Killarney, Du Noon, Richwood, Table View, Blouberg, Melkbos, not your biggest area, but with all the work on the N1 and the interchanges, it's also a fuck-up, I'm telling you. Anyway, the main problem is the drivers, because one half cause trouble and the other half complain, and your area manager fires at least three or four every month, so if you come ask me if he had conflict at work, then I'm gonna tell you "for sure", there's conflict here, but Danie could handle it. He was good with people, he's a communicator, he had respect, he never played whitey or threw his weight around, if you know what I mean. Between you and me, he was the most popular of the four, so I don't think . . .'

The telephone rang again. Philander looked at it, then at the open door. It stopped.

'Sorry, Neville, sorry, lovey . . .'

'*Jirre*,' said Philander, 'I'm telling you, ABC stands for Asylum By the Cape, you gotta be crazy to work here. I'm one man short and management doesn't want to take on any more, in case Danie pops out of the woodwork, you know? What else can I tell you?'

'His wife said there was a strike here last year.'

'*Ja*, that's another story, went on for two weeks, company-wide . . .'

'About pay?'

'No. Our Driver Risk Management Programme. But Danie was on the sidelines, it was managed by Mr Eckhardt and those guys.'

'Mr Eckhardt?'

'Mr Francois Eckhardt, Chief Operations Officer. Anyway, the strike was bad for us, but there wasn't any conflict here, we just sat and waited every day.'

'Danie's behaviour before he vanished? Did you spot anything . . . abnormal?'

'You tell me what's normal, there's no such thing here, you see for yourself how it is. Anyway, it's hard to say. The area managers are on the road most of the time, especially in the morning and the afternoon, checking out the routes, the rest of the time it's admin in their offices, there's no time to socialise, so I wouldn't have noticed really. And I didn't. Ol' Danie is always full of smiles, his work is right, he's a go-getter. I always say to him, the next thing you wanna go get is my job.'

'So they have a pretty fixed routine?'

'Very fixed. Out early, back by eleven, check email, the DRMP logs, scheduling, time sheets, personnel matters, then they're out again . . .'

'And he stuck to it in October and November?'

'As far as I know . . .'

'Neville!' the woman's voice sounded from the corridor.

'What?'

'Head Office on the line.'

'OK. Put it through.' Then to Joubert. 'This normally means trouble, you'll have to excuse me.'

Joubert stood up. 'His marriage?'

The phone began to ring. 'How would I know?' and he shook Joubert's hand.

'Neville, are you going to pick up or what?'

'*Jirre*,' said Neville. He put his hand on the phone.

'Off the record?'

Joubert nodded.

'She's a bit of a nissen, that Tanya . . .'

'Neville!'

Before Joubert could ask what a 'nissen' was, Philander picked up the phone.

84

He walked across the tarmac to his car and opened the Honda's doors to let the dammed up heat escape. It was the only drawback of a black vehicle, but he didn't mind, it gave him so much pleasure. One night, thirteen months ago, Margaret had looked up from her accounts and said: 'It's time you got a new car.' His Opel Corsa was already six years old then, but it had more than 200,000 on the clock, and left an ominous oil leak on the garage floor. It didn't take much to convince him, their finances were looking good thanks to her speculation on houses, and Jeremy, her eldest, had completed his studies and was on his way to America for his 'gap year'.

So he went looking for a car, in his thorough, considered way. Did his research, collecting catalogues, comparing prices, only to walk into the Honda dealer on Buitengracht, and there was the Type R with the red logo and the lean, low, black lines, and he was in love. Back home he had said to Margaret, in his inescapably Afrikaans accent: 'It must be the Goodwood in me,' and she'd smiled at his joking mention of the Cape Town suburb where he'd grown up, and hugged him close, whispering, 'A little bit of a mid-life crisis too', into his ear. Which was probably closer to the truth, because over the last few years he'd begun to hanker after the Datsun Triple-Ss of his twenties. Then Margaret said, 'Go buy the car. You deserve it.'

And it gave him pure, unalloyed pleasure. Maybe the suspension was a bit hard, seats not the most comfortable in the world, but the handling was incredible. And the power . . .

He leaned against the Honda, took out his cellphone and called

Superintendent Johnny October, former colleague, now head of the Mitchells Plain detective squad.

'Sup!' said October. 'What a *lekker* surprise!'

'I'm not "Sup" any more, Johnny.'

'Sup will always be my "Sup" to me. Howzit going in the private sector?'

'Still too early to tell. And with you?'

'Rough, Sup. With Tweetybird out of the country . . . This power struggle's hotting up.'

'I can imagine.' Tweetybird de la Cruz, leader of the Restless Ravens, had left the country four months ago after a warrant was issued for his arrest. His business and turf were now fair game for factions within the Ravens, and for the other criminal gangs on the Cape Flats.

'Four murders this last week, three of them drive-bys . . . You wouldn't want the old days back, Sup, but things have changed.'

'That's true, Johnny. But I don't want to hassle you, just ask you something quickly: when someone says a woman is a "nissen", what do they mean?'

October chuckled down the phone. '*Ja*, Sup, actually, you know, all women are Nissans.'

'Nissans?'

'You know, Sup, like the cars. Nissan. You remember their old slogan, "We are driven"? If you say someone is a Nissan, then you mean she's intense. Driven.'

'Aaah . . .'

'They say you should rather marry a Toyota.'

'Everything keeps going right?'

'Exactly, Sup. Exactly.'

Albert Street in Woodstock was a termites' nest of big trucks, little trucks, minibuses, cars, people.

Joubert was caught up in the traffic jam and drove without seeing, thinking of his conversation with Johnny October. The two of them so out of step with the times. Anachronisms. Because Nissan's slogan was no longer *We Are Driven* and Toyota had long replaced *Everything Keeps Going Right* with something else that made no impact on anyone. Probably knew they'd be recalling millions of cars for faults.

And what did it say about him and Johnny that they lived with one foot in the past, as if the world began to overtake you at a certain age? Brand names, slogans, fashions, technology, all the in-things, the red-hot conversation topics, the deafening chorus of got-to-have-it-now that faded to a white noise you were only dimly aware of. He was fifty. October was ten years older, when did this happen? Somewhere in your late forties? When all of a sudden you realise you've heard all the day's news before. All the advertising jingles. And all the stories of people's struggle and striving, their victories and scandals, the way groups and countries and regions and continents went through the same cyclical processes, again and again. Everything changes, everything stays the same, and you lose your sense of wide-eyed wonder, that was the pity of it all.

Joubert became aware of the world outside again, saw the traffic, the buildings. Memories stirred in him, this Woodstock made him think of the Goodwood of his youth – the somewhat dilapidated one- and two-storey buildings with corrugated iron roofs, gables and pillars, the entrepreneurial spirit of the corner shops, which sold a little bit of everything, from halal meat to cheap cigarettes, lawnmowers, fish and chips, second-hand furniture, upholstery services, trailer hitches. People on the pavements – jogging, walking, standing, talking, doing business, looking for a gap. Muslims with fezzes on their heads, fishermen with woollen hats, the headscarfed Xhosas, bare-headed whites, this place just as colour-blind as Voortrekker Street in the sixties, before all the trouble began.

But even here it wouldn't last. Between the old dilapidated facades, the charming pastels peeling off, here and there, the Engine of Progress roared: recent restoration, in lurid colours, new boutique shops, *CQINZ Fashion*, *Mannequins Unlimited*. Further down, the old Biscuit Mill, newly slicked with white and ugly turd-brown paint, festooned with signs for *Imiso Clay*, *Exposure Gallery*, *Lime Grove*, *Shout*, *Third World Interiors*, so that the gracious old building lost all its charm.

Loss.

Since Tanya Flint had told her story this morning, it had lurked inside him, this awareness. And his conversation with Johnny hadn't helped. *I'm not 'Sup' any more, Johnny.* It had been a long time coming, now said out loud for the first time. Not in the Service any more.

Thirty-one years of being a policeman, part of the family, the brotherhood, the exclusive club, and now the bond was broken. He was outside. The 'private sector', like Johnny said.

But when he was inside, the last two, three years, another kind of loss had slowly overcome him – a disillusionment, a disappointment, a powerlessness, a realisation of potential leaking away, possibilities lost. He, who had been so positive to begin with, who believed the police service could get better, could adapt to the new challenges, new realities. He had supported the ideal wholeheartedly and enthusiastically, the ideal of a SAPS that reflected the population demographic, which deployed affirmative action to cancel out old injustices, which transformed to a proud, effective, modern instrument of government. Only to see how it was slowly poisoned by politics and good intentions and haste and stupidity. And, in the end, by greed and corruption. And when he spoke up, when he warned and advised and pleaded, they marginalised him, pushed him out of the pack, made it clear that they no longer had any use for him.

A lifetime's work. For nothing.

No, no, he mustn't think like that. If he said it to Margaret, she would give him that loving smile of hers again and say: 'My melancholy policeman,' because this was a tendency of his. He had to think positively, make a new start, be grateful for this opportunity, this chance to draw on his experience, to be able still to serve. Jack Fischer said it was an international trend, a worldwide wave: the rise of the private law-enforcer. 'And we have to ride that wave, Mat, according to Thomas L. Freeman.'

Fanus Delport corrected Jack: 'Thomas L. Friedman.' But Mat still didn't know who he meant.

This feeling inside him, maybe it was because he was an investigator again, no longer the manager, the pen-pusher he'd become over the last few years. And if you worked at this level, as detective, then you had to deal with loss. At best just the loss of property, or dignity. At worst, The Great Loss.

I just want certainty, Tanya Flint had said.

He could see it in her, in her eyes and her shoulders, her hands and her way of talking, that battle between hope and *knowing*, with knowing gaining the upper hand.

Neville Philander said she was driven. He could see that too: the strong lines of her face, the determined set to her mouth. A woman who wanted to run her own business, who was prepared to make sacrifices, to suffer. *We knew it would be tough.*

And just how tough had it been? In his photo, Danie Flint looked like a man without a care in the world, a man who wanted to laugh and enjoy life. Who wanted to hang out with his mates in the Sports Pub. C*heerful,* Tanya had called him. Had the money worries got too much for him?

Leave the Audi there, take your wallet and phone, just walk away. To an easier life.

One possibility. Among many. Too soon to speculate, he told himself.

Mildred, the middle-aged coloured receptionist, held a sheaf of documents out to him. 'This is our PC manual, the technician is busy installing your laptop, sir.' She was serious, focused.

'Thank you. You don't need to say "sir" to me.'

The corners of her mouth lifted, the semblance of a smile, humourless. 'And here are your business cards.'

A package wrapped in brown paper. On it was taped a card with *Jack Fischer & Associates* in elegant silver lettering. Below, in black, *M.A.T Joubert, Senior Consultant: Forensic Investigation.* With his office and cellphone numbers, and a new email address.

'Thank you.'

He walked to his office. The technician was sitting at his desk, moving the mouse around on the pad, looking intently at the screen. To his surprise she was a young woman, in grey overalls, short blonde hair, glasses. She looked up, suddenly shy. Grey eyes behind the lenses. 'Sorry,' she said quietly, 'I'm just finishing up.'

'Take your time,' he said and introduced himself.

'I'm Bella van Breda,' she said, her hand soft in his. There was a logo on her top pocket, and the words *The Nerd Herd.* 'I'm just importing the address database into Outlook, MS Project is already loaded. Are you familiar with the program?'

'No.'

'You've got Project 2007, so it's very straightforward, you just use the Project Guide and the JF template. It's all in the manual,' she waved at the documents in his hands.

'Thanks a lot,' he said, but his tone betrayed him.

'Do you know much about computers?' she asked, sympathy in her voice.

He nodded uncertainly. 'I worked with the police's BI system.'

'BI is a proprietary application, it's usually a lot more complicated than something like MS Project. If you have trouble with the manual, just call us, the number is in the database. Oh, and your user ID, your password, and your email address are at the front of the manual.'

She stood up, looked at him, hesitated for a moment as though she wanted to ask him something, then picked up her equipment case.

'Can you just show me how to find a telephone number in the database?'

'Of course. Come sit down.'

She stood beside him, took control of the mouse. 'You just open Outlook, here . . . Now you select Contacts, and here in the navigation pane you see your contact groups. Personal Contacts is what you'll input yourself, JF Contacts is on the database. Who are you looking for?'

'Dave Fiedler.'

'You just click on the "F" and then you scroll down . . . There he is. You can also change the view, Business Cards or Address Cards . . . like so.'

It was all too fast for him, too much to absorb, but he said, 'Yes, I see, thank you very much . . .'

'Pleasure.' She picked up the case again, walked towards the door, then stopped. 'Do you know Benny Griessel?' she asked, and for some inexplicable reason, flushed to a deep red.

'Yes,' he said, surprised at the mention of his ex-colleague and old friend.

'He . . . We live in the same apartment building,' she said, suddenly flustered. 'Bye,' as she walked quickly out of the door.

'Say hello to Benny for me,' he called after her, a bit bemused. Then he looked at the laptop screen, clicked on Dave Fiedler's address details, pulled the phone closer, and dialed.

Only when he heard the ring tone did he smile to himself. Captain Benny Griessel, rehabilitating alcoholic, newly divorced, and a blushing blonde. What would the story be behind *that*?

85

Dave Fiedler spoke Afrikaans and called Joubert '*Boetie*'. 'Discount, *Boetie*?' he asked, with astonishment.

'Jack says you owe us.'

'No, *Boetie*, I only owe the Receiver of Revenue, my price is my price. Ask Jack Fischer if he gives discount.'

'What does it cost?'

'A thousand five hundred for an IMEI profile, 600 for a trace.'

'So that's 2,100 in total?'

'If there is only one number in the profile. It's 600 for each number.'

Joubert made notes. 'How long will it take?'

'I can run the trace for you today. A guy in Bloemfontein does the profile for us, I'm not geared for that. Takes about a day and a half.'

'I'll have to talk to my client first.'

'That's fine, *Boetie*, you know where to find me.'

His appointment with Tanya Flint was only for three o'clock. That gave him time to look at the program manual, but first he wanted a cup of tea to have with his sandwiches.

He stood up and walked to the kitchen. As he pushed the door open, Mildred's stern voice sounded from reception: 'Mr Joubert!'

He stopped abruptly in his tracks.

'Would you like something to drink, sir?'

'Tea, yes, but I'll just make some myself.'

'No, sir, I'll have it brought to you,' in a tone that brooked no dissent.

He went across to her. 'Thank you. And please don't call me "sir".'

He got no response.

In his office he picked up the manual and started to read. A black woman brought his tea on a tray, and hurried away again. He took his sandwiches from the briefcase, poured the tea, thought about how he would have been chatting with the detectives in the tearoom of the

Provincial Task Team, enduring teasing comments about his 'gourmet sarmies'.

He followed the instructions in the manual. Fanus Delport, the financial controller, had already opened a project file for Tanya Flint. It had a number, JF/Flint/02/10 and the first debit (*Admin expenses: R600*). Joubert did a quick calculation. His two hours, plus the possible expense of R2,100 for the cellphone profile and trace brought the total to nearly R4,000. And he had barely begun. Add the three or four more hours that he would work on it today and it came to over 6,000.

He felt that anxiety again. At this rate her money would run out long before he solved the case.

He would have to get moving.

To start with he drove to Virgin Active in Table View, stopped in the parking lot. He got out, walked around his Honda and leaned against the bonnet, arms folded. The parking area stretched out in front of him, half full now, with the gym behind it. To the right was the public library. Here and there people were walking to their cars. A car guard in a luminous green vest wandered between the vehicles.

Danie Flint left the ABC depot in Woodstock at about five o'clock on 25 November. Considering the traffic at that time of the afternoon, he would have arrived here by six o'clock at best, still in broad daylight – the sun only set at around eight o'clock in late November. Flint had parked his Audi somewhere in the parking lot. According to Tanya he hadn't gone to exercise. His sports bag was still on the back seat. Had he left it there deliberately, just taken his keys, cellphone and wallet, got out and walked away? Climbed into another car? Was he robbed before he could pick up his bag? Because the Audi wasn't locked. Had he got out, been attacked, someone grabbing cellphone, wallet and keys and running away?

Then where was Danie Flint's body?

It made no sense.

So close to the police station.

Why would he leave his car here if he wanted to disappear?

The only other alternative was kidnapping, but why here, so close to the long arm of the law?

Had he been involved in a fight? Pulled the keys out of the ignition, picked up his wallet and cellphone. Got out, banged his car door against someone else's car . . . Or saw something, an argument. What if some aggressive, steroid-driven muscle man had beaten him up, seriously injuring him. Then Muscle Man panics, stows the body quickly in the boot of his car.

At six o'clock in the afternoon, bright sunshine, people coming and going?

No. Surely someone would have seen it.

The gym bag on the seat was the thing that bothered him. It meant something. If Danie Flint wanted to disappear, if he did so on purpose, he would have had a use for the bag.

He sighed, because he knew there was only one way for him to eat this elephant. Piece by piece. Long hours of footwork. Slow, methodical, systematic. Thorough. That was always his style, because he didn't have the intuition, the instinct, the natural flair of a Benny Griessel. That was why he had asked Tanya Flint this morning to tell him everything from the very beginning. That was why he would have to go to the library and into the gym, to see if there were CCTV cameras, to find out what Virgin Active looked like.

There were no cameras outside.

A woman came walking past, bag over her shoulder, and went into the gymnasium. Joubert followed her, through the automatic sliding doors. Inside, he saw her stop at a revolving gate, take out a card and slide it through an electronic laser device. That must be how they knew Danie Flint hadn't gone in that evening – a computer system that recorded everything.

He stopped. Looked around. Modern. Chrome, steel and glass. No smell of sweat or resin. On the right was a counter, a young woman on duty. She smiled at him. He grinned back, his brain busy. The computer system. It would be off sometimes, like all technology, not infallible.

'Good afternoon sir. Can I help you?' asked the young woman.

'Good afternoon . . .' and then he hesitated, because he no longer had the power of a SAPS identification card. 'This gate is connected to a computer?' he said, pointing at the card reader.

'Yes, sir . . .' with the little frown that said 'here's an interesting one', but the smile did not waver.

'Does the system ever go down?'

'As long as you can show your Virgin Active card you can always get in, sir. Are you a member?'

'No,' he said. 'How often is the system down?'

The frown intensified and he realised his approach was too direct perhaps. 'Why do you ask, sir?'

'I was just wondering.'

She didn't answer immediately, first looked him up and down. 'Can I call a consultant to talk to you?'

'No, thanks,' he said. 'Thank you . . .' He suddenly felt self-conscious and stupid. He should have followed another tack, pretended he wanted to join, or something. But it was too late now. He turned and walked out.

No SAPS force behind him to rely on any more. He would have to learn to lie.

But at least he knew now: the gymnasium's computer system did not always work. Danie Flint might have come to exercise on the twenty-fifth after all. The time of his disappearance could have been at least an hour later.

For what that was worth.

He battled to find the Flint house in Parklands' maze of crescents, so that he was ten minutes late. It was a young neighbourhood, property speculation houses squeezed together, three bedrooms and a double garage on a small plot, leaving space only for a tiny lawn in front.

He parked on the pavement, got out, carrying his leather-bound writing pad, and knocked on the door. She opened almost immediately, inviting him in with her weary half-smile. She had taken off the jacket she had worn that morning. In the short-sleeved blouse, her arms seemed exceptionally thin. He wondered how much weight she had lost since November.

The living space was open plan – kitchen, dining and sitting room with TV, chain store furniture, but in good taste. Her laptop was on the dining-room table, next to the three folders arranged neatly and precisely beside each other.

'Shall we sit at the table?' she asked.

He nodded.

'Something to drink?' She moved towards the kitchen.

'No, thank you, I'm fine . . .'

For a second she was undecided, as though she had not foreseen the possibility that he would say 'no'. She gathered her thoughts. 'Please, sit down. I've got all the documents organised . . .'

He recognised a self-consciousness about her, an unease, as though she was not used to a strange man in her house. He sat down at the table, a combination of cane and wood. The chair was uncomfortable, too small for his body.

Tanya Flint took her place opposite him, picked up the first folder, bright yellow.

'These are Danie's cellphone accounts . . .' She opened the file, took out a document and pushed it over the table to Joubert. 'I found the IMEI number, it's at the top here. And I wrote beside each number who it was that he phoned.'

Joubert looked at it. Written in a neat delicate handwriting and blue ink, a name beside each number. It must have taken her hours.

As though Tanya Flint could read his mind: 'I did it in December. There was nothing else . . . Here's a spreadsheet that I made, the numbers, and how many times he phoned each one. He phoned me the most. And his drivers. There's nothing odd.'

He was impressed, and relieved, because it would save him time, and her money. 'This is very useful,' he said.

'I had to do it. I looked . . . I looked for anything. In any case, you can take the whole file, if I can just get it back when . . .'

He filled the awkward pause with a hasty 'Of course.'

'This file is our finances. We used *Moneydance* . . .'

'*Moneydance*?'

'It's software for personal finance. You download your bank statements from the Internet, then you can do all sorts of things: draw graphs, reminders of payments, budget . . . It gives you a very good picture . . .'

'I understand.'

She held out a stapled document to him. 'These were our expenses, it's in chronological order. Oh, it's for the whole of last year, up to November. I arranged it according to category, the trouble is, the American software, their categories are sometimes . . . you know . . . It's for all our accounts, we each have our own cheque account and credit card, but you can put it all together.'

'This will help a lot . . .' He scanned the documents quickly. 'This is for both of you?'

'Yes.'

'Could you give me Danie's separately?'

'Of course. I . . . it will take a while. Do you want graphs as well?'

'No, thanks, this is perfect. If I could just get Danie's separately. His cheque account and credit card . . .'

'OK.' She got up, sat down at the head of the table, behind the laptop. 'But I can tell you now already, there's nothing out of the ordinary.'

'Oh?'

'I mean, there are no expenses that I don't know about. And even if there were . . . I would have picked it up. We sat down with our statements every two weeks. We had to, last year, with the business . . . It was a difficult time. We were entirely dependent on Danie's salary. His biggest expense was petrol, on his garage card, which ABC paid. I did most of the shopping.'

She manipulated the mouse, then got up. 'I have to fetch the printer in the bedroom . . .'

'Sorry for all the trouble.'

'It's no trouble.'

She disappeared down the passage.

He sat staring at the statements in his hands. All this work she had put into it, all the detail, the tables, the tracking of numbers. *I mean, there are no expenses that I don't know about.* That meant that she had considered the possibility that her husband had disappeared of his own volition.

Which begged the question: why?

What was it that she wasn't telling him?

86

The third folder contained photos of Danie, and a list of contacts that Joubert 'might possibly need', she said. 'People at work, his mother, our friends, the detective, everyone I could think of. And here's the flyer that I put under everyone's car wipers at the gym.'

An A4 colour printout, with a large photo of Danie, the same one that she had showed him that morning, and a caption: '*Have you seen Danie?*' Underneath in smaller print was a short paragraph about his disappearance on November twenty-fifth, and her cellphone number.

'And nobody phoned about it?'

'Lots of people phoned. But nobody who'd seen anything.'

He nodded, because he could imagine the strange calls she must have got. Then he told her about the tracking of the cellphone: 'If Danie's SIM card is still in the phone . . . If a cellphone is stolen, the suspect usually uses all the available airtime on the card, and then takes it out. We have two choices now. We can track the phone on Danie's number to find out where the phone is now. But it's been three months, the chances that the SIM card is still in the phone are slim. That means we could be wasting 600 rand. The alternative is to get a profile on the IMEI number. That means they determine what SIM cards have been in the phone since November, and particularly what card is in it now. Once we know that, we can trace the new number, and try to track the phone down. Unfortunately the profile is a bit more expensive. It's 1,500, plus 600 for the details of every SIM card that the profile gives us.'

She listened attentively, thought about it before she asked: 'Do you think it's worth the trouble?'

It was all they had at this stage, but he didn't say that. 'An investigation like this . . . in fact, any investigation, is as much about the elimination of possibilities as the collection of information . . .'

'What are the possibilities?' she asked, with sudden intensity.

Joubert shifted on the uncomfortable chair. 'Do you mind if I take my jacket off?' to gain more time, because he didn't know how honest he should be with her.

'Of course not.' While he stood up, she said solemnly: 'Mr Joubert, I read the statistics on the Internet – 1,500 children disappear every year . . .'

'Eighty per cent of those are found by the police,' he countered instinctively.

'And that is exactly the problem. The police and media focus on the children, but what about the adults? Last year more than 2,000 were abducted . . .'

He shook his head as he sat down again, because it was a misrepresentation of the figures, but she got in first, her voice full of emotion. 'All I'm trying to say is that I realise Danie could . . . I mean . . . there were 18,000 murders in the country last year. You . . . just be straight with me, that's all I ask. I've already been through every possibility.' Her hands were tightly interlaced, the veins on her skinny arms standing out with the effort.

He saw the brave attempt she made to keep control. In her thin body and passionate expression he saw the loneliness and suspense and the uncertainty of three consuming months, the exhaustion she was fighting against now. He remembered how hard it was for him, when he was still doing detective work, to be the messenger, the bringer of bad news, he never could distance himself. The past five or six years he had been insulated from that. Now he wanted to reach out to Tanya Flint to help her bear it somehow.

He took a deep breath. 'I want you to know that I understand what you've been through and what you're still going through . . .'

'I'm OK,' she said, but without conviction.

'I don't think Danie . . . disappeared willingly,' he said, with a fleeting worry that he was talking too soon.

'Do you really think so?' Her eyes fixed on him, hungry to believe.

'It's . . . unlikely. It doesn't fit.'

'Thank you,' she said, and her hands relaxed and her shoulders drooped, as though a great weight were lifted off them. And then the tears began to flow.

She fetched a box of tissues from her bedroom, came back, and told him all her fears. That she was afraid she had driven her husband away with her perfectionism, with her urge to control, to make a success of her business. Because it had been a very difficult year, she had worked so hard, such long hours, she had neglected him sometimes, she was often spiritually and physically absent, and too careful with the finances. Since his disappearance she had wished a thousand times she had let him put in his little bar, the sound system in his Audi, because with his job he lived in that car. All the while the tears ran down her cheeks and she sniffled and blew and crumpled up tissue after tissue, laying them all in a neat row beside the laptop.

He told her again he understood, but he didn't think she need worry about that.

Then he described other possibilities, as he had tried to figure them out in the parking lot. Just a theory, he said, she must please understand that. He suspected something had happened outside Virgin Active, just after Danie had got out of the car, and before he could pick up his bag. Or, after he had finished exercising and had just put the bag back, because he suspected the card system was sometimes faulty.

There were a few things that suggested it wasn't robbery in the parking lot – Danie's disappearance, the car and the bag were still there, the constant presence of people, car guards, and the proximity of the police station. It left them with two possibilities. The first was that Danie might have walked to the shopping centre to draw money, or something. And in the process was lured away, or drawn into something.

The other possibility was that someone had been waiting for him, someone who, for some reason, meant to do him harm. Perhaps someone who knew him, someone he trusted enough to get into another car.

She shook her head at this suggestion.

'You don't agree?' he asked.

'Danie had no enemies,' she said with absolute assurance.

'He had to fire some bus drivers . . .'

'Have you been to see Neville?'

'Yes. And he says Danie was very popular. But it's a strange world. It only takes one unstable person . . .'

She thought about it. 'Maybe,' she said.

'I want to request access to ABC records. I want to search Danie's office. They might not like that.'

'Let me phone Mr Eckhardt,' she said. 'He's been very sympathetic all along.'

'Then I would like to take a look at the Audi.'

He saw her glance at her watch. 'I . . . can I show you how the garage door works? I have to get back to work. There are a few orders . . .'

'Of course. Have you used the car since . . .'

'Not at all. It's just the way it was when I fetched it. I'll get the keys for you.'

* * *

Before she left, they agreed that she would phone Mr Eckhardt, the head of ABC, to get permission, and he would go ahead with the profile of the cellphone. She took him to the garage, showed him where the automatic door mechanism was. Then she stood stock still for a moment, turned to him, put a hand on his arm and said earnestly, 'Thank you so, so much,' before her heels click-clacked quickly across the concrete floor to her Citi Golf.

Deep in thought, he watched the car reverse out, head down the road. Then he came back to the present, went over to the small workbench right at the back of the garage, and stood a while studying the space. Danie Flint was not a handyman. The garage was storage space, not a workshop. Cardboard boxes against one wall, steel shelves against the other, old paint tins, yellowed Sunday newspapers, a broken kettle, half a bag of old *braai* briquettes, a few tools, the wheel of a racing bike.

Joubert took out his cellphone, unzipped his writing pad to find the number, and phoned Dave Fiedler.

'Dave, it's Mat Joubert, from Jack Fischer.'

'*Yip, Boetie?*'

'We want to do a profile on a IMEI.'

'Hit me with your rhythm stick.'

Joubert read the number slowly.

'Gotcha. I'll call you, hopefully by tomorrow, late afternoon.'

He zipped the writing pad closed, turned and studied the Audi.

It took him a few moments to realise he was not prepared. He would have to find his murder kit at home, the one with rubber gloves, plastic evidence bags, tweezers, scrapers, cotton wool, sticky tape, the black and white fingerprint powder. Margaret would know where it had been stored for the last five years. For now, he would have to make another plan.

He walked around the car, carefully inspecting the outside, looking for fresh scrapes or dents. And blood spatters.

He found nothing, just an awareness of something that eluded him. He stopped, thought deeply, couldn't pin it down.

He took out a handkerchief, carefully lifted the door handle, so as not to disturb fingerprints.

He bent down and took a look inside.

The interior was reasonably clean. Sand and gravel in front on the driver's rubber mat, nothing out of the ordinary. The inside of the door had no recent scuff or scratch marks that could indicate a struggle, someone being dragged out against his will.

He looked under the driver's seat. There was nothing, only dust.

He slid in, sat down on the seat, keeping his feet outside, touching nothing.

Black leather upholstery, satellite navigation, electric windows, cruise control . . . *Full house*, a car salesman would have called it.

Then it came to him, the thing that had eluded him earlier – this car, compared to Tanya's. Two-litre, blood red Audi Sportback with the works, compared to the blue simplicity of the 1400 Citi. Earlier she had said that Danie had bought his car second hand, but even then this Audi wasn't cheap, around two hundred and fifty thousand, compared to what? You could buy the Volkswagen Citi for around seventy thousand.

A big difference. He weighed this information against what he knew about their marriage, but it gave him no more insight. Then he used the handkerchief and unclipped the glove compartment, leaned over to see what was in it. A plastic envelope with the manual and service book. He took it out. A spectacle case. Inside were sporty dark glasses. Adidas Xephyr. He put them on the passenger seat, beside the manual. An HTC phone charger with a springy cable and a plug for the cigarette lighter. A cheap ballpoint pen, two yellowed petrol slips a year old, and half a pack of chewing gum.

He put everything back carefully, closed it and got out. Then he walked around the car, opened the other door and peered under the seat.

The boot didn't produce anything either.

Joubert fetched his writing pad from the workbench, put the keys there as he had arranged with Tanya, pressed the switch that opened the door and jogged out quickly.

87

He drove back to Virgin Active, because it was on his way home to Milnerton. There was no sense in going back to the city in the rush-hour traffic. And it was half past four – he wanted to get the feel of how busy the place was in the late afternoon, at the time Flint disappeared.

There were a great deal fewer parking spaces. He found one and stopped, sat a while watching. Then he opened Tanya's file with the contact numbers and went through the list of people. One name caught his eye: *Inspector Keyter, SAPS, Tableview.* In her thorough way, Tanya Flint had written down the case number beside it.

Could it be Jamie, the detective constable who had joined the Serious and Violent Crimes Unit before that was also disbanded? Most likely, since if he recalled correctly Keyter had been promoted from Table View. And Tanya Flint had talked about a detective who fiddled with his fringe.

He took the file along with him, got out, locked the Honda and walked to the police station. The south-easter was well under way, blowing up his jacket flaps and forcing him to hold the folder tightly to his chest.

Table View had never been one of his favourite police stations. He and Margaret had lived nearby in Frere Street after they were married, before she began buying up old houses and renovating them. From time to time he had to pick up faxes or forms at the police station, or go in for computer access. Even then there were already too many cowboys, too much attitude.

The charge office was hot, and fairly busy. He waited his turn, asked if Jamie Keyter was available. Not *Jay-mie*, if he remembered correctly, but *Jaa-mie*. The black constable said he would go and check. A little while later he came back and said: 'The inspector is coming.'

Joubert waited to one side, out of the way. He wished he could loosen his tie, that he'd left his jacket in the car. For five minutes he stood and listened, at the border post where two worlds met, the public and the police. Every police station had its own rhythms, its own atmosphere and sounds. The complainants' voices, some angry, others defeated. Out of an office somewhere came the loud words of an argument. Telephones ringing, the patient footsteps of the three uniforms manning the counter, generally soothing and reassuring, bending over to help fill in statements, probably on their feet for six hours, their movements slow, going through the routine motions.

Then Keyter arrived with a scowl on his face for whoever had come to bother him, until he saw Joubert. His body language changed in an instant. 'Sup?' he said, like a man with a guilty conscience.

'Jamie,' said Joubert and put out his hand. 'I'm not with the Service any more.'

Keyter shook his hand, taken aback. 'Sup?' he said, the information too unexpected to process. Joubert could see that he hadn't changed much. Still wearing tight golf shirts, sleeves stretched over bulging biceps. Today's was black with the silver Nike logo on the chest, to go with black jeans and black Nike trainers.

'Friday was my last day. I'm with Jack Fischer and Associates now.'

'Oh. Oka-a-ay,' Something in his tone that made Joubert's hackles rise.

'I'm working on a fifty-five. One Danie Flint who disappeared last year. His wife said it was your case.'

'Danie Flint?' He scratched his head.

'Last year, late November. His car was abandoned here at Virgin Active.'

A light went on. 'Oh, right. That one.' He looked at Joubert expectantly.

'I just wanted to ask you if you had any insights to share, Jamie.'

'Insights, Sup?'

'I'm not a Sup any more, Jamie.'

'OK . . . I'll have to get the dockets, but if I remember correctly . . . There was nothing. The guy was just gone.'

Joubert suppressed a sigh. 'Yes, apparently that was the original problem. Did you speak to anyone at his work?'

'I . . . No, I mean, the guy . . . There wasn't . . . Sup, you know how things are, the guys go fishing with their pals, they don't tell the old lady . . . I mean, his car was here . . .'

Joubert nodded, put his hand in the inside pocket of his jacket. Keyter's eyes followed the movement with wary eyes. Joubert took out his wallet, extracted a business card and gave it to the detective. 'If you remember something, or find something, Jamie . . .'

'OK, Sup, I'll call you right away.'

'I'm not Sup any more . . .'

He sat in the Honda and watched his theory being systematically confirmed.

The parking lot filled up, people walked to the gym with sports bags, or to the library, with books in their arms. There were short periods when it was quiet, two or three minutes where something could have happened to Danie Flint if the attacker was very confident and efficient. But a struggle here, a fight that went unnoticed, seemed increasingly improbable.

He sat there till after six, and thought of Jamie Keyter and the Flint dossier. He knew the way things were with detectives at stations, even the lazy ones like Keyter – too many cases, too little time, so there was always something that fell through the cracks. Tanya was right, missing adults were not always a priority, unless there was obvious proof of a crime. Otherwise they fell in the category of domestic conflict, he had dealt with countless numbers as a uniformed policeman. Thirty years ago.

Lord, how time flies.

He drove to Milnerton, to Tulbach Street where he and Margaret had been living for the last six months, their fifth house in five years, but he didn't mind, because she took so much pleasure in her 'projects'. She would go looking for a real bargain, a solid house in a good neighbourhood that had fallen into disrepair, 'worst house in a good neighbourhood' was her motto. Then she renovated it with her keen insight and good taste, smartened it up, and when she was done, they would move in. A house sold more easily if there were people living in it, activity, aromas from the kitchen, tasteful furniture in the rooms. When she was expecting potential buyers, she would put vanilla in the oven, or bake a cake, and put on some cheerful music at a low volume, make sure the house was cool in summer, or warm in winter, with a fire in the grate. She was already in the process of buying the next one, in lower Constantia, she could get it for next to nothing in this slow market.

* * *

He sat with her in the kitchen while she made supper and told her about his day.

'Is she pretty?' was the first thing she asked, unashamedly jealous, always had been, thanks to the heartbreak of her first marriage.

'No,' he said. 'But she's brave. And a Nissan.'

He had to explain that.

'And what am I?'

'My Mercedes.' That made her laugh.

'And how was the office?'

He shrugged his big shoulders. 'It's very different. Jack is . . . serious about money. But I suppose he has to be. And it's all very formal.'

'You'll get used to it.'

'I will. What about your buyers? How did it go?'

'They want to think about it.'

He exercised for forty minutes on the rowing machine on the back verandah beside the swimming pool, showered and poured them each a glass of red wine for dinner – pasta with Cajun chicken pieces, feta and sun-dried tomatoes. She told him about her visit to her daughter Michele, her plans to spend most of tomorrow in Constantia.

He took Tanya Flint's files and sat next to Margaret in the television room while she watched *Antiques Roadshow* and *Master Chef Goes Large* on the BBC Lifestyle channel. She put her hand on his leg. He worked through the financial and cellphone records.

Later she turned off the television and asked: 'Anything?'

He put the papers down on the couch beside him. 'No . . . I don't know. There is some sort of a pattern here, but nothing that will tell us what happened to him . . . The trouble is, there is nothing typical in his disappearance. The vast majority of adult men who disappear between work and home, do so as a result of robbery. His car is hijacked, he is forced to reveal his PIN number, they take his bank card, steal what they can, let him go, or kill him. His body is found, the car a day or two later, somewhere . . . But this one. He had a credit card in his wallet, but there are no transactions after his disappearance. The gym bag, just left there. And the car, neatly parked . . .'

'Mmm,' she said.

'The other possibility is that he wanted to disappear. But then there is always a trail. Either calls to another woman, preparations made, money spent. Unless he is very clever, and I don't think Danie . . . And why would he just leave his bag? And his car, his biggest asset . . .'

'What sort of pattern did you find?'

'They . . . It's not a big thing. You have to look closely, but . . . He drives an Audi that cost a quarter of a million, she drives a little Citi Golf. And the bank statements . . . If you ignore the usual stuff, the water and lights, the groceries, clothes, CDs . . . I get the impression that she spoiled him. Or tried to keep him happy . . .'

He sat deep in thought and then realised Margaret was watching him with a gentle smile and her unmatched eyes shining.

'What?' he asked.

'I can actually hear the gears humming,' she said, and squeezed his leg gently. 'I love it when you go into detective mode.'

'Those are not gears humming, those are gears seizing.'

'Nonsense. You'll figure it out. You always do.'

'The gears are rusty.'

Her hand slid up higher on his leg. 'Is that all that's rusty?' She rolled the 'r'. It sounded sexy.

He put his arm around his wife's shoulders. 'Mrs Joubert, I could arrest you for indecency.'

'But you're a Private Eye . . .'

'Oh, no, I am a licensed Senior Consultant: Forensic Investigations. With a business card.'

'Oh, my goodness . . . And if I resist arrest?'

'Then I will have to get physical,' and he pulled her closer.

'Take out your big trungeon?' she whispered.

'Truncheon,' he corrected her.

'It's not how you spell it, it's how you use it . . .'

'Madam,' he said sternly, 'you leave me no choice . . .'

'I know,' she said in a whisper and leaned softly against him, her mouth ready.

Then he kissed her.

At half past eleven that night, with her body lying soft and warm against his, breathing deep, the gears in his head did indeed slowly begin to turn.

It wasn't in the parking lot of Virgin Active. Whatever happened to

Danie Flint happened somewhere else. And then they parked his car there.

Which meant they knew his routine. They knew him.

Which meant he would have to check the Audi for fingerprints.

Which meant he would have to dig out his murder kit. He'd clean forgotten, in the heat of his arrest of Mrs Margaret Joubert.

88

The meeting wasn't what he expected.

'Sir, remember, it's Morning Parade,' Mildred said when Joubert came in. He expected a recreation of the tradition of the old Murder and Robbery Squad, when that word meant a brainstorming session, detectives sharing their dossiers with the commanding officer and colleagues, looking for guidance, constructive criticism, and new ideas.

Now he sat around the table with the firm's five other investigators, while senior financial controller Fanus Delport ran the agenda, and Jack listened attentively. Each investigator reported in turn about the number of hours he had 'booked' the previous week, and gave projections of potential earnings in the coming week.

Joubert knew three of them as former colleagues. Willem Erlank worked with him a year ago on the Provincial Task Team. The other two, Fromer and Jonck, came from the Northwest and Gauteng respectively, but they were unmistakably former Members of the Service, middle-aged, big, weather-beaten, slightly overweight. He would have been like that too, if it weren't for Margaret's care.

They were well prepared, each made broad detailed projections, with deep voices and solemn faces.

He made some hurried sums while the others spoke, added up his hours, decided to leave out his time studying the documents last night, so he could save Tanya Flint some money. She had done that work herself, after all. Then he considered his options for the next few days, made a rough estimate, wondering to himself how it was possible to say how many hours you were going to need to solve a case.

'Matt, how do things stand with the Flint dossier?' Delport asked him finally.

'Five hours yesterday,' he said. 'Plus the IMEI profile, which we expect this afternoon, then we will decide whether to plot the cell numbers.'

'I see you haven't logged your kilometres on the system yet.'

He had forgotten travelling expenses. 'I will do it this morning,' he said, embarrassed.

'No problem, we all had to learn the ropes. How many hours do you think there are in this case?'

Joubert referred to his notes. 'It's hard to say . . . Maybe another thirty-six.'

Delport and Fischer nodded happily.

'I want to test her husband's car for fingerprints,' Joubert said. 'Do we have a contact for identification, if I find something?'

'Excellent, excellent,' said Jack Fischer. 'But we use a private guy to lift the prints. He was with Forensics' lab, but now he works freelance, offers the whole package. He has a pipeline to the SAPS, will get the result within twenty-four hours. Nortier . . .'

'Cordier,' Fanus Delport corrected him. 'He's on the database.'

He could have done it himself, Joubert thought, he might have asked Bennie Griessel if he could put the prints in the system, it would have saved money. 'Jack, Tanya Flint only has 30,000 . . .'

Fischer rubbed a hand across his moustache and smiled. 'His first case,' he said, and the others laughed good-naturedly.

'Mat, that's what they all say. It's a *game*. If she needs more, she will find it . . . Right, gentlemen, I have a Mr Benn . . .'

'Bell,' Delport set him straight again.

'That's him. Bell, Nigerians took him for one point four million with a four-one-nine scam. Who feels like boosting his bonus a bit?'

As he recorded his kilometres on the computer system, he thought how it wasn't a game to Tanya Flint. He'd seen her financial position. This extreme focus on money made him uncomfortable. He would have to sit down with Jack and tell him how he felt. But first he must attend to his responsibilities.

He phoned Tanya. She sounded tired. 'I talked to Mr Eckhardt, he said you can go through Danie's office any time, they'll do everything they can to help, we have full access. You must just arrange it with Neville.'

Joubert thanked her, then told her of his plan to test the Audi for fingerprints.

'How much will it cost?'

'I'll find out and get back to you.'

'Do you think it's necessary? Shouldn't we wait for the cellphone's plot?'

'That might be a good idea.'

After he had rung off, he phoned Jannie Cordier, the forensic technician, explaining who he was and what he wanted.

'I'm full today, but I can fit you in this evening.' A high, excitable voice.

'What will it cost?' Joubert asked.

'Do you want the car done inside and out?'

'Please.'

'One five, plus 600 for every set of prints you want identified.'

'I'll let you know.'

Then he made an appointment for 12.00 with Neville Philander at the Atlantic Bus Company depot, reached for the list of phone numbers that Tanya Flint had compiled, and began phoning her husband's friends. He asked the same questions, over and over: did Danie behave strangely in the weeks before he disappeared? Did he mention any problems, in his work, his marriage? Did he have enemies? Was he involved in any arguments or fights? Did he have any reason to disappear? And the answers, offered enthusiastically and helpfully, were consistent. Danie was 'a lovely person'. Danie was happy, cheerful, always the same. Loyal, everyone's friend. Danie was a 'party animal', 'the life of the party', he lived for his wife and his work and to party, party, party.

When he had dealt with the last call, he leaned back in his chair and pondered the phenomenon of the sanctification of the victim. It was a common syndrome, driven by the guilt of surviving, and the universal never-speak-ill-of-the-dead piety that so bedevilled a policeman's work, as it papered over all the cracks. And there always were cracks.

At eleven he phoned Mrs Gusti Flint, Danie's mother, to ask whether he could talk to her. 'You are very welcome,' she said. 'I'm here all day,' and she gave him an address in Panorama.

* * *

In Neville Philander's office, with a telephone ringing and the air conditioner going full blast, Mat Joubert asked if he could see the records of all the bus drivers that Danie Flint had fired between 1 September and 25 November.

'*Jirre*,' said Philander, standing beside his desk.

'Sorry to bother you,' said Joubert.

'Neville,' shouted the woman's voice down the corridor.

'Just a minute,' Philander shouted back, looking at his phone as though it were a snake. He said to Joubert: 'Do me a favour: personnel records are at head office, if I start *sukkeling* to get it now, my day will be buggered. Don't you wanna go have a look, while you've got Mr Eckhard's blessing?'

'Of course. Where is the head office?'

'Neville!'

'Santasha, please! It's in Epping Industria, Hewett Street, thanks man. Come on, I'll show you where Danie's cubicle was.'

Santasha's voice, impatient: 'Neville, lovey, are you going to answer that phone today?'

Joubert followed Philander down the corridor. 'Not if you take that tone with me.'

He disappeared through a door, Joubert went in behind him, Santasha shouted: 'I'm not taking a tone, lovey, I'm motivating you a little.'

The room was divided into four office spaces by chest-high partitions, cach with a desk and a credenza, all in the same light wood colour. The two visible desks were untidy, a few piles of papers and files, no one sitting there.

'So motivate the caller to hang on a little,' Philander shouted, and walked around a partition, up to a window and pointed. 'That's Danie's cubicle,' he said. 'Pretty much as he left it.'

'Thank you,' said Joubert.

'Have a ball,' he said, then turned on his heel and jogged to the door.

Joubert surveyed the desk, credenza, office chair. Simple, on a grey carpet. The desk had three drawers on the left. Under the desk was the computer case, on top, the mouse, keyboard and screen. One pile of papers and a clipboard, a mug with a Porsche logo, coffee dregs in the bottom, dried up now. Photos and notes were stuck on the faded blue fabric of the partition.

He sat down on the chair and looked at the photos. In the middle was one that had been taken in front of the depot building, probably of the whole administration staff, six men, three women. Philander was in the middle. Danie stood second from the right, at the back, big smile. Joubert wondered which one of the three coloured women was the diplomatically insistent Santasha.

Next to it was a photo of Danie and Tanya Flint, taken at a work party. Her face was fuller then, she was looking in amusement at Danie, in a funny little hat with a beer in his hand, laughing uproariously. Another photo of Danie on a boat, somewhere on a river, arms draped around the shoulders of two friends. Three magazine cuttings of sports cars, an Audi R8, a Ferrari F430 Spider and a Lamborghini Murciélago LP640. Yellow Post-it notes with scribbled names and telephone numbers, reminders of meetings and deadlines for reports, the number of exclamation marks denoting the urgency of each.

He pulled the stack of papers closer and worked through them. Official ABC forms, with figures and references, apparently to buses. One light brown folder with the ABC logo on it, and the word 'Applications' below it, 'Please return to HR, Mrs Heese!!!' in angry red letters. Inside were job applications for bus drivers, each with a photo, a short CV and a report from the HR department.

He pushed that aside, tried the top drawer of the desk. It was locked.

He opened the second drawer. A metal basket for writing materials, with various sized compartments. Cheap ballpoint pens, two pencils, a stapler, blue box of staples, an unused eraser, a roll of Sellotape, scissors, a post code guide, three packs of Post-it notes, a Nokia cellphone charger, paper clips, a Bic cigarette lighter missing its roller wheel, a Ferrari keyholder, and two white electric two-point plugs.

The bottom drawer didn't offer much either – the original disk for the computers; Windows XP, a handbook for an ink-jet printer, two old *FHM* magazines and a *Sports Illustrated Swimsuit Edition*, an *Auto Trader*, and two *Car* magazines.

Joubert moved the chair so he could slide open the door of the credenza. It was full of light brown files, arranged according to date, from 2004 to 2006, and two telephone directories. He took out one of the files and riffled through it. Indecipherable ABC documents. He put it back, and slid the door closed.

Where would the key to the drawer be? On the Audi's keyring, which had disappeared along with Flint?

Only one more thing he could check: the computer. He peered under the desk, found the button and pressed it. The computer switched on. He watched the screen, waited until all the icons had appeared. Outlook. Word. Excel. Explorer. DRMP.

He sat staring at the screen. Would it be a problem if he opened the email program? If he had still been in the police he would have sent for a computer expert, and someone to unlock the drawer, within half an hour he would have had access and insight. But now every hurdle meant further expense, the weighing of potential results against the cost.

This was no way to run an investigation.

89

Mat Joubert sat in front of Danie Flint's computer with his head in his hands, and considered doing things his way. He knew it had implications. He knew it went against the grain, against his better judgement. Three decades of experience had taught him it was wiser to work according to the rules, because doing otherwise always came back to bite you.

What he should do was go to Jack Fischer and say no, he didn't agree with this policy of milking clients. Honest and straight, that was the only way he knew.

But he also knew he wasn't the fastest detective in the world, he was slow and methodical, worrying too much about detail. What would he say if Jack said, 'Then you must work faster'? He couldn't deny his weaknesses.

Then he remembered Jack Fischer saying he must pressure Dave Fiedler, the cellphone plotter, for a discount. That implied at least the right to control costs, and he took out Bella van Breda's business card, the young woman with the glasses and the blush. Bennie Griessel's neighbour. He called her, first had to explain who he was before he could describe his problem.

'I can try,' she said.

'The problem is, my client's budget . . . What will it cost?'

'That depends. If you wait until I've finished this afternoon, I won't charge anything.'

'No, no, you can't do it for free . . .'

'Let's see if I can find anything first . . .'

'What time do you finish?'

'About six o'clock.'

'Can I pick you up?'

'Please.'

He wrote down her work address, rang off and walked to Neville Philander to ask if he could come back in the late afternoon.

He bought a can of Tab at a little café in Woodstock, studied the map that he kept under the seat to see how to get to Gusti Flint's house, and ate his sandwiches in the car on the way to Panorama. Margaret had made his favourite: avocado, grated biltong and thinly sliced parmesan, the flavour and texture were just right, like all her food.

He put the new pieces of the Danie Flint jigsaw together, the photos on the wall, the cuttings of sports cars, the use of yellow Post-it notes as reminders, the magazines in the drawer. A completely normal young man, a fast life and impossible dreams. Extrovert, cheerful, always laughing, but a hard worker, ambitious, reliable. The polar opposite to his wife's serious nature, less concerned about money, living for today, tomorrow would take care of itself. Like most people of that age, they all believed things would simply work out.

Where were the cracks?

There had to be. His disappearance was not random, that was the thing that bothered Joubert the most. The Audi parked at the gym excluded chance, he wasn't the victim of a random robbery.

The only potential source of conflict was the bus drivers he fired. And it was going to take time to work through every personnel file, then cross-reference the possible suspects for previous convictions, since he knew that violence always had a history.

And time was money.

He sighed, drank the last of the Tab out of the can, and put on his indicator for the Panorama off-ramp.

* * *

Mrs Gusti Flint told Mat Joubert, in a controlled and modulated way, how hopeless the South African Police Service was since 'they' had taken over. 'But I'm not a racist.'

She was a very attractive woman, looked in her late forties, but must be ten years older. Tastefully groomed, hair short, expensively cut and dyed blonde, the make-up light and skilfully applied across the wide face, the prominent, regular features. Her bosom surged above the neckline of a short-sleeved lavender mohair sweater. Around her neck was a single string of pearls. Two chihuahuas sat on her lap, their bulging eyes fixed on Joubert in suspicion. Her large hands repeatedly stroked one of the animals when it coughed accusingly in his direction. She had a single ring on her right hand, a complex knot of gold and diamonds. The nails were long and painted a light shade of purple, and below, above one of her high-heeled sandals, a fine gold chain encircled her ankle.

He listened patiently to her objections to the SAPS, which eventually pointed specifically at their handling of her son's disappearance, and how they should accept responsibility for that. 'He went missing right next to them. Right next to them. And now poor Tanya has to hire a private firm and the poor child doesn't have that kind of money, her business is barely on its feet,' and Joubert wondered why Gusti Flint didn't help her daughter-in-law financially, since her house was large and luxurious, the furniture expensive, the air conditioning whispering effectively.

When she had finished, he said, 'Mrs Flint, how often . . .' and the chihuahuas started to bark.

'Fred! Ginger! Quiet! Please, call me Gusti.'

The little dogs turned their eyes on her and wagged their tails.

'How often did you see Danie . . .'

The dogs barked.

'Wait,' she said. 'Let me put them away first.' She picked up the animals, leaned forward and put them down on the thick carpet, displaying her cleavage. Then she looked up quickly at him, saw that he had noticed, her gaze lingering a moment before she got up and called the dogs, 'Come on . . .'

The chihuahuas looked reproachfully at Joubert before reluctantly trotting after her.

He watched her walk away, the sway of her hips, her bottom possibly a fraction too large for the tight white slacks.

Not quite what he had been expecting.

Her high heels clicked back. 'What about something to drink?'

'No, thank you.'

She sat down, crossed her legs, and smoothed her long fingers over the slacks. 'They can be a nuisance sometimes,' she said, 'but they are all I have.'

'Danie's father . . . ?'

'Gerber passed on nine years ago. At sixty. That Sunday he had cycled the Cape Argus, the Monday he collapsed in his office. Massive heart attack, so unexpected, he was fit, always very fit,' recounted with the fluency of oft-repeated facts. 'Most dreadful time of my life, my husband snatched away, my son already out of the house, suddenly I was a woman alone. But you adjust, you rebuild your life. That's what I tell Tanya, time heals all things, you come through on the other side. And now my son has gone as well, and the most awful thing is that we don't *know*. I could say goodbye to Gerber, however hard it was, at least there was a funeral, a letting go. It was hard enough for me, but his poor, poor wife, I wish I could take her pain away, or take it on me, she's so intense.'

'Mrs Flint, do you still have . . .'

'Gusti, please. "Mrs" makes me sound like a *tannie*. We are just as young as we feel.'

'Did you still have regular contact with Danie?'

'I have the most wonderful son. He phoned me twice a week, popped in once a week, I know everything that happens in his life. Let me tell you, this thing is part of the terrible crime in this country, senseless crime; he never had an enemy in the world. He was just like his father. The whole world loved Gerber, that's why he was on the City Council for nearly twenty years. But those days are gone, we're not safe in our own country any more, they're busy ruining everything, I'm not saying we should go back to Apartheid, but there are those of them who say, themselves, things were better then . . .'

She stood too close to him when he said goodbye, held his hand too long. 'Are you married, Mat?' despite the thin gold ring on his finger.

'I am.'

'Come and see me again. Any time.' Her perfume was strong, her eyes full of meaning.

His head was spinning when he drove away. He considered the influence of a mother like Gusti Flint on her son. And how he was going to tell Margaret about this encounter, as that was the one thing that made his wife furious: another woman, knowing he was married, yet giving him the come-on.

Only once he was beyond the Canal Walk off-ramp did he focus his attention on the problems of the investigation. How was he going to get the top drawer of Danie Flint's desk open without paying a few hundred rand for a locksmith? And then he began weighing up the possibilities, and when he thought of Vaatjie de Waal, he turned around at the Otto du Plessis interchange and drove all the way back to Parow.

90

Vaatjie de Waal lay half inside a Subaru Outback, only his short, fat lower body visible in a grubby blue overall, his head and torso under the instrument panel.

'Vaatjie,' Joubert said.

'What?' Irascible, impatient.

'Can we talk?'

De Waal moved so that he could see. He recognised Mat Joubert, shut his eyes, shook his head and sighed. 'No, oh, *Jissis*.'

'Social visit,' said Joubert.

'Like hell,' said de Waal, scrabbling around on the seat till his fingers closed around a small pair of pliers and he disappeared behind the instrument panel again. Joubert guessed the boss of Decible Demons must be installing a radio or taking one out. On the window fronting Voortrekker Street was the promise: *Mad About Car Audio, Crazy Prices, Insane Sound.* That must be Mrs de Waal's clever marketing. Vaatjie's talents lay elsewhere.

'I don't know anything.'

'I want your skill, not your information.'

'What for?'

'I have a drawer that needs opening.'

'Get Kallie van fucking Deventer.'

'I'm not in the Service any more, Vaatjie.'

That stopped him. He dived out from under the panel, extricated himself from the interior with surprising speed and stood up. He was half Joubert's height, but broader. His head was as round as a ball, the frown just a single crease in the high forehead. 'Why?' he asked, and wiped his hands on his overalls.

'Retired.'

'But why?' Hands at his sides, just as much a cartoon character as he had been when Joubert knew him at high school.

'It was time to go.'

'And now?'

'Now I'm in the private sector.'

The eyes flicked from Joubert to the reception desk where Vaatjie's wife was sitting out of earshot behind a computer.

'I'm not in that line any more.' Meaning housebreaking, his first career.

'But you still know how to work a lock. And I don't see customers lining up outside here.'

'Times are tough, friends are few.'

'Two hundred rand for five minutes' work.'

'You're fucking crazy. I don't work for peanuts.'

'What's your price, Vaatjie?'

'Five hundred.'

'It was good seeing you again,' Joubert said, and turned to go. 'At that price I can get a locksmith.'

He was nearly at the door when Vaatjie called: 'Three hundred.'

'Two-fifty,' said Joubert over his shoulder.

A moment of silence. 'OK. Fucking OK.'

As he walked into the office, his cellphone rang.

'*Boetie*, I've got bad news,' said Dave Fiedler. 'Your IMEI profile, there's nothing. Last SIM card was your subject's, last phone call was 25 November, he's been off the air since that day, not a peep since. Sorry, *Boetie*, I wish I could help more.'

He thanked Fiedler, sat down behind his desk. He felt disappointment, and for the first time concern, a deeper unease. That had been their best chance of a breakthrough, to find something to grab hold of in the darkness. More than that, it said something about the disappearance. Your opportunistic thief, your vengeful ex-bus driver would have used the phone, or sold or pawned it. Even thrown it away somewhere, for someone else to sell.

That was 3,500 down the drain. Now they would have to spend more money on the fingerprints, another shot in the dark.

Tanya Flint didn't take the news well. Joubert could hear the despair in her voice, the exhaustion.

'What now?' she asked over the phone.

'Now we'll have fingerprints done. And I'm not finished with ABC, I want to work through the personnel records.'

She was quiet for a long time before she asked: 'Tell me honestly: Is there any hope?'

'There's always hope,' he said, too quickly maybe. Then, 'When I finish tonight, we can reconsider. We ought to have a better idea by then.'

'Thanks,' she said, but without enthusiasm.

He phoned Jannie Cordier, the forensic technician, and asked him to go and take the fingerprints, *after* half past six, when Tanya would be at home. Then he saw to it that his admin on the project programme was up-to-date before he went to pick up Bella van Breda. Less than two days' work and the expenses were over 10,000 already. And there was nothing that he could do about it.

'So, you know Bennie Griessel,' he said to Bella, in his car on the way to the ABC depot.

'We have talked,' she said, and when he glanced at her, he saw the blood-red blush again.

'How is he?' It had been a month since Joubert had last talked to him. His former colleague was, like most SAPS members, very unhappy about his move to Jack Fischer and Associates. And Joubert could only speculate about the reasons. There was the usual antipathy to the private security business, the feeling that someone who left the Service was somehow a traitor. Also a touch of envy. And Jack's outspoken opinions about the police in the media hadn't helped.

'Fine, as far as I know. Bennie is very busy. Been practising his bass guitar a lot. And he's started a band. I think he has a new girlfriend.'

'Oh?'

'Some or other old singer.' Then she changed the topic, very deliberately. 'Tell me, what do you want me to do tonight?'

He filled her in on the background, and said he was on a fishing expedition. He was looking for anything that could throw light on Danie Flint's disappearance.

'OK,' she said. 'I'll give it a go.'

It took Vaatjie de Waal just over forty seconds to open the drawer.

Joubert reported to a weary Neville Philander, who, with a wave of his arm said to them: 'Go ahead, have a ball, Santasha will stay until you're finished, I'm going home.'

They walked to Danie Flint's cubicle. De Waal unrolled a leather bag on the desk, chose a thin, L-shaped tool that looked like an Allen key, fiddled in the keyhole, tried a slightly thicker one, kept his ear close to the drawer and nodded once, before he straightened up and pulled the drawer open.

'Two hundred and fifty,' he held his palm out to Joubert. 'I should have charged you petrol money as well.'

Joubert took his wallet out of his jacket pocket and counted out the notes. 'Thanks, Vaatjie.' He nodded in the direction of the bag that Vaatjie had already folded up and tied with a ribbon. 'I thought you weren't in that line any more?'

'You're not in the SAPS any more,' said de Waal and took the money. 'Tell me, where is Kallie van fucking Deventer nowadays?'

'Kallie took a golden handshake, four years ago. He and his wife run a guest house somewhere. Gansbaai?'

'A guest house?' he asked, as though that were beneath anyone's dignity.

'As far as I know.'

Vaatjie nodded. 'OK. Cheers,' and his short, round figure walked around the corner of the partition.

Bella watched him go, then looked questioningly at Joubert.

'We were at school together,' he said. 'His father, Oom Balie, was a locksmith in Goodwood. Vaatjie learned all about locks. Then he went burgling. For seven years. Tokai, Bishops Court, Constantia, a one-man housebreaking epidemic. Until Kallie van Deventer caught him. Vaatjie went to jail and got very fat. And when he came out, Kallie caught him again within a week, stuck in a kitchen window in Rondebosch, half in, half out . . .'

While she laughed, Joubert pulled the top drawer fully open, had a look inside and saw only three items. He took out a Vodacom Starter Pack for a mobile phone, the packaging cut open, and put it on top of the desk. Then a key holder with two keys and a metal disc on it. On the disc was a design with the letters 'SS' in the middle. Below, the logo '97B' was punched into the metal. The last item in the drawer was a sheet of A4 paper torn in half. On one side four rows of letters and numbers were written in blue pen, neatly and precisely.

2044 677 277

9371

L66pns8t9o

speedster430

Joubert turned the paper over. It was one of the bus company forms, with columns and headings, unused, unmarked. He looked at the writing on the other side again. Was the first one a telephone number? Couldn't be, all local numbers begin with a '0'.

Then he realised Bella was standing beside him. 'Excuse me. If you would like to sit down . . .' and he gestured at the chair and the computer. 'Go ahead, please . . .'

'OK.' But first she bent down and kneeled, pulled the computer drive closer and had a look behind. Then she switched the machine on and sat down in the chair.

Joubert put the page down on the desk, looked closely at the two keys again. On one there was a Yale logo, on the other only six numbers. His fingers turned the metal disc on the keyring. The SS logo. It looked vaguely familiar. And the 97B? What could that mean. A flat number? Could be. A hotel room?

SS.

He rubbed his finger over the punched characters, in search of ideas. He came up with nothing.

He put the keys aside, opened the Vodacom package. There was a small manual, an empty plastic container where the SIM card had been, and the cardboard card with the SIM card and cellphone's PIN number.

His brain made a connection, to something he had seen here earlier. He opened the middle drawer and stared into it. Between the writing materials, its cord neatly rolled up, lay the Nokia phone charger. But in the glove compartment of the Audi there was another charger, another brand, he couldn't remember what, he should have written it down.

'He had another phone,' he said.

'What?' asked Bella, but Joubert didn't answer. He took his own cellphone out of his pocket and called Tanya.

'Danie's cellphone, what kind was it again?'

'A Diamond,' she said. 'An HTC Diamond.'

91

He asked her how long her husband had had the HTC.

'I think he had an upgrade in April last year.'

'What phone did he have before that?'

'Oh, also an HTC, I think it was the TyTN, the one that slides open. Why?' Hope in her voice.

He was afraid of getting her hopes up. 'I'm just making sure. We're in his office, I've found a page with a bunch of numbers on it. Can I read them to you?'

'OK.'

He read the first series and asked her if it meant anything to her.

'No.'

After the third series she said: 'It sounds like a password. For his computer maybe.'

'Maybe,' he said. 'And Speedster four three zero . . . ?'

'I don't know . . . No.'

'Thanks. I'll see you when we've finished.'

'Please, phone me if you find anything.'

When he had rung off, he put the symbols where Bella could see them. 'Could it have something to do with his computer? A password?'

'Maybe . . .' she clicked the mouse, opened a window that said 'Network Connections', then another. 'No,' she said. 'It's not his network password . . . Do you want to see his mail?'

'Please.'

'There's a lot . . .' and she showed him the Outlook panel. 'Two hundred and sixty-five new messages.'

He bent down and looked at the screen.

'Most of them are DRMP notifications, I'm not certain what that is. There's a DRMP icon on his desktop too,' she said.

Joubert tried to remember what the acronym stood for.

'It's something to do with how they manage the company. I'm looking at more personal stuff rather. Just a second . . .' He went around the divider, found a chair next door, dragged it alongside her and sat down.

'The rest are just ABC HR. Bulletins. A couple of junk mails. The rest are ABC email addresses, look,' and she let the list scroll under the cursor. 'I don't see anything funny . . .'

'Can you print out the whole list for me?'

'Just the headers?'

She could see he didn't understand. 'It gives you the sender and the subject.'

'Please.'

'OK. You just use Page Setup and Table Style . . .' The mouse moved with impressive speed. 'I don't know where the printer is.'

'We'll find it later. What else is there?'

'Just give me a minute.'

'I'll go and look for the printer.'

He picked up the sheet of symbols and walked down the passage until he came to an office where a young coloured woman was sitting at a switchboard.

'Santasha?'

'Yup, you must be the Private Eye.' She giggled and put out her hand. She was plump, with large mischievous eyes that laughed along with her mouth. 'This is a first for me.'

He shook her hand. 'Pleased to meet you . . .'

'Is it you people printing?' she said, holding out a sheaf of paper.

'We are. Thank you.'

'Found something?'

'I don't know. We'll be as quick as we can.'

'No rush, I get overtime . . .'

He showed her the symbols. 'Would you know what this is?'

She studied it carefully. 'Absolutely no idea.'

He sat with Bella, staring at the rows of numbers and letters.

Why did the first one look like a telephone number? He remembered the telephone directories in the credenza, took one out and studied the local dialling codes. The Oudtshoorn area was 044, but then the first number '2' made no sense. He ran his finger down the list of international codes, but none of them matched either.

Bella made a humming sound.

'Did you find something?'

'His browser history . . . Can I have a look at those passwords?'

He passed it to her, looked at the screen. She had the Internet Explorer web browser open to a page with the heading 'Yahoo! Mail'. 'His history shows that he used *this* webmail . . .' She looked at the four rows of symbols, typed 'Speedster430' in one box, then something else in the box for the password, but he could only see asterisks.

'Bingo,' she said, as the web browser opened a new page. 'He had a Yahoo mail account. It's his address – speedster430@yahoo.com. And that L66 series is his password.'

'Aah . . . ?' He still didn't know how she could have worked that all out, but then the page loaded fully and there was nothing – no emails.

'Looks like he deleted everything. Let's see if there is anything in the Sent Folder . . .'

She clicked again. The folder was empty.

'That's weird,' she said.

'Why?'

'Look at his Outlook. Look at his Documents folder on the hard drive. He wasn't great on maintenance. But his Yahoo account . . .'

'It's clean.'

'Very clean.' She hesitated a moment. 'But there's another thing . . .' She moved the mouse, scanning the browser again. 'His history shows that he was often on his bank's website . . .' Absa's Internet Banking page appeared on the screen.

'No, they bank at Nedbank,' he said. That had been clear from the statements Tanya Flint had given him.

'Maybe,' said Bella. 'Let's try the first number . . .' The one he had thought was a telephone number.

'And the shorter one may be his PIN.'

A new page loaded.

Your chosen SurePhrase™ is: FLINT D. Your PIN has been successfully verified.
The last time you logged on to Absa Internet or Cellphone Banking service was 25 November.
Type in only the characters of your password that fall in the RED blocks.

'Twenty-fifth of November,' whispered Mat Joubert. 'The day he disappeared.'

Bella van Breda typed in the third row of numbers and letters in the boxes.

The screen changed.

'How did you know?' he asked.

'That's how people are. They use the same things, the same passwords. It's easier to remember.'

They looked at the screen.

Balances
Click on an account name or number to view transaction history.
Warning: the available balance on your account may include cheque deposits that are not yet fully paid over to the bank, and that could still be reversed.

Account name	Account number	Current balance (R)	Available Balance (R)	Uncleared amount (R)
SAVINGS ACCOUNT	2044 677 277	134 155.18	134 155.18	0.00

Joubert whistled through his teeth. A hundred and thirty thousand rand. That changed everything. 'Can you print that out?' he asked urgently.

'It won't disappear,' said Bella calmly. 'Let's see what's going on in the account . . .'

She clicked on the account number and a statement appeared on the screen.

Mat Joubert sank back into his chair. 'Can you believe it,' he said. 'Can you believe it.'

'Four hundred thousand rand?' asked Tanya Flint, her face tight with shock.

'It looks like two cash deposits,' said Joubert. They were in her living room, he on the couch, she on a chair, the coffee table between them. 'On the seventeenth of October, 250,000, and on twenty-ninth of October, another 150,000, which adds up to the grand total of 400,000 rand. Then he made a payment of just under 250,000 rand on the twenty-seventh of October, a direct transfer to an M. Marshall, and another on the twelfth of November, to HelderbergUp, for just over 11,000 rand. The rest is made up of cash withdrawals, interest and bank charges.'

Tanya sat on the edge of her chair and raised her hands to her face, her eyes never leaving the printed statement. Her body heaved. 'Oh, God,' she said.

92

She told Mat Joubert she didn't know where the money came from. She had never heard of an M. Marshall or HelderbergUp.

He asked if there was anything Danie Flint could have sold. He asked whether Gusti Flint could have given or lent her son money, or if there was any source she could think of, however odd, such as the Lotto, anything. And each time she gave the same desperately certain, 'No.' Then: 'How could he have hidden it from me?', pain and betrayal distorting her face.

Before Joubert could try to answer the question, someone called from the kitchen 'Hallo-o-o-o . . .'

When he had arrived, Tanya Flint had told him the forensic technician was at work in the garage, but she was too anxious about the news, so there had been no time to say hello. He got to his feet.

'Jannie Cordier?'

Cordier looked like an Edgars advertisement, in dark blue chinos, yellow and blue checked shirt, neat brown belt around the narrow hips. He stood, aluminium case in hand, looking at Tanya's tear-streaked face.

'Excuse me . . .' he said.

'I'm Mat Joubert. Did you find anything?'

'That car has been wiped,' he said. 'Only one set of prints, on the door and the steering wheel. I will have to take Mrs Flint's to cross-check,' his high-pitched voice matching the boyish face.

'What do you mean, wiped?' Tanya asked.

'From top to bottom. The boot is clean, the radio, the cubbyhole, the whole thing. Someone did a very good job.'

Tanya Flint looked stunned by the news. 'What does it mean?'

Joubert sat down slowly, because he would have to explain the implications to her with a great deal of diplomacy.

'If you ask me: bad news, Mrs Flint,' said Cordier. 'Very bad news.'

She looked at Joubert. He shook his head, unhappy with Cordier's tactlessness. Then he agreed with a sigh: 'It isn't good.'

Cordier waited patiently for Tanya Flint to calm down before he took her fingerprints. When she went to wash her hands, Joubert walked the technician to the door. 'Tact isn't your strong point,' he said to the man.

'What? I'm just honest.'

Joubert just looked at him.

'Someone would have had to tell her sooner or later.'

'Later might have been better.'

Cordier bristled and turned on his heel, barking, 'I'll send my bill!' over his shoulder as he walked angrily to his van. Joubert shut the door and went slowly back to the couch.

Now he had to deal with the other cellphone and the keys. It was going to be a difficult night.

Her hands were shaking when she came back and sat down. The lines on her face seemed deeper, the rings around her eyes darker.

'Tanya . . .' he said.

'There's something else,' she said, already certain of it.

'Yes.'

'Tell me. Let's just get on.'

'He had another cellphone.' He told her about the Vodacom Starter Pack, the Nokia charger. She sat motionless and stared at the carpet. At last she said, 'What else?'

He took the keys out of his pocket, and put them down in front of her. She looked at them reluctantly.

'Do they also come out of the drawer?'

'Yes.'

She picked them up. The keys jangled as she trembled.

'Do you know what this is, here?' she asked and held up the SS logo between her fingers.

'No, but I . . .'

'Self Storage,' she said.

That lit up an image in his head, a big advertising board somewhere at the side of one of the roads he occasionally took: the blue SS logo, the advertisement for storage space. 'Do you know about it?'

'I know the logo. They have a warehouse in Montagu Gardens, close to my business.'

'Then I'll have to go and find out.'

She didn't give him the key. She closed her fist around it, as though it were something precious, a treasure.

'I'm coming too,' she said.

There was a high wire fence around the Self Storage warehouse, a double gate on the right-hand corner, a caretaker in his hut nearby. He stood in the headlights of his Honda, trying both keys in the huge lock, without success. His shoes crunched in the gravel as he walked to the caretaker's window. A black man with flecks of grey in his hair sat there with a tabloid paper spread out in front of him.

'Can I help you?'

'The key doesn't seem to fit,' said Joubert.

'Let me see.'

He took the keys and had a look. 'This is not our depot. Where did you find them?' he asked, his tone one of long-suffering courtesy.

'They belong to that lady's husband. He's gone missing.'

'Very bad,' said the man. 'Very sad. It might be for one of the other two depots.'

'Where are they?'

'There's one in Kenilworth, and one in Salt River.'

Salt River. Near Danie Flint's ABC job. He knew that would be the one.

'Thank you very much.'

'I hope you find him,' said the man, and handed back the keys.

In Otto du Plessis Drive, just beyond Woodbridge Island, Tanya said, 'It has to be for someone else.'

'What do you mean?'

'Danie . . . I know Danie. I *know* him. The money . . . He's helping someone else. He's protecting someone else. That's how he is. He cares about people.'

'Maybe it is,' he said. It was the best he could do for now.

She stood with her hand to her mouth while Joubert unlocked the roll-up door of number 97B, bent down and pulled it up and open.

There was something inside in the dark, in the space slightly bigger than a single garage. The front of a car.

Joubert spotted a light switch on the wall, turned it on.

Tanya was still outside, staring silently at the red-grey car that was parked with its nose to them, the two single headlamps like staring eyes. He recognised it straight away, but went up to it first, looked through the closed doors to see if there was something inside.

Only the keys in the ignition.

'Is there anything?' she asked.

'No.'

She came in, her hand stretched out to the car.

'Porsche,' she read the name of the yellow, red and black logo on the nose.

'It's a nine-double-one Carrera. Please don't touch it. I'll fetch some gloves.' He walked back to the car, to fetch the murder kit he had put in the boot this morning.

She stood at the driver's door and stared, a strange expression on her face, amazement and loss.

'Danie,' she said. 'Danie, what have you done?'

93

At twenty to twelve he was sitting with Margaret in the kitchen as she braised a sirloin steak in the pan. He told her about his strange day, a glass of red wine in his hand.

'He bought the Porsche from a Mark Marshall of Sweet Valley Street in Bergvliet – his name was in the service book in the cubby-hole. The Nokia phone was there too, with three SMSs from Absa that said he had logged on to Internet banking. I think that's why he had the extra cellphone. For the bank account.'

'And she knew nothing about it?'

'Nothing.' He ate some of the salad on his plate with his fingers, his hunger taunted by the aroma of the steak. It was a tradition that they had begun when the children were still at home. When he came home late from work, the steak 'because you deserve it', and the chat in the kitchen so they could have an hour or two together.

'And how did she take it?'

'Not well. She . . . I think she went through the mourning phase in December already. And now she has to do it all over again. Tonight she went through denial, then guilt, then anger. And I didn't know how to . . . The trouble is, there's an unwritten law in the police, you keep your distance from the next of kin, you don't get emotionally involved. As detective you are always one step removed, you can pass on the bad news and get in your car and go and do your job. But it's all different now. She's paying, so she has the right to come with you . . .'

'And now you have to be a kind of comforter as well,' she added as she took the heated plate out of the stove with an oven cloth.

'I find that hard.'

She slid the steak onto the plate, put it in front of him. 'It's because you care.'

'I'll have to find a way to handle it.'

She drew up a chair and sat down opposite him, pushed the salt and black pepper closer to him. 'So he got the money from somewhere, and bought a Porsche . . .'

'It's a 1984 model, over 200,000 kilometres on the clock. Reasonable condition. The upholstery has been redone. Probably the best he could buy with the money he had. Selfish, but it fits.'

'Oh?'

He ate a mouthful of steak first. 'This is delicious, thank you. If you see how Tanya spent most of their money on him. He was . . . "carefree" is probably the best word. An only child. Maybe his mother spoiled him a bit. I saw her today . . . I don't know, I just get the idea she . . . there is something superficial, materialistic . . . You know, one of those houses where everything is used to point out that "we have money". And . . . let me tell you my theory: I think the mother was a bit manipulative. I think she was one of those women who pushed her husband to buy a bigger house and a more expensive car, so people would look up to them. Status. It must have an influence on a child, to see his father working hard, his mother spending. Maybe that's why Danie kept the money for himself, even though he knew their finances . . . How can you buy a Porsche when you know your wife is struggling? That says something about him. It says something about the origin of the money. I just don't yet know what.'

'Eat up first,' said Margaret, and put her hand gently on his arm. 'That steak is getting cold.'

He hadn't smoked for ten years, but as he pushed his plate away and swallowed the last of his red wine, the desire came back, clear and strong. He knew it was the stress and fatigue.

He carried his plate and cutlery to the dishwasher and thanked Margaret for the steak, and the sandwiches at lunch.

'Hunger is the best sauce,' she said. 'Tomorrow I'm going to try something new. Chicken, mature cheddar and a special peach chutney I got from Bizerca. Tell me if you like it.'

'You spoil me.'

She smiled. 'As long as there's not a Porsche in a garage somewhere.' She picked up the pan from the stove and walked over to the sink. 'So now, what's next?'

'Now, I follow the money.'

She came back to him, her face suddenly sombre. 'You won't find him alive, will you?'

'No,' he said. 'I don't think there is any chance of that. She knows it too. Now. Even though she said she had accepted the possibility. She kept hoping. Until tonight.'

'Is she going to be OK?'

They had driven back from Self Storage in Salt River to her house in Parklands in total silence. She sat there curled in on herself, broken, her hands on her lap, mute. In front of her house he asked Tanya Flint whether it would be better if he took her to her mother-in-law.

She shook her head, emphatically, despite the weariness.

'You can stay with me and Margaret, tonight.'

She sat and stared at her hands, eventually drew a deep breath, turned her exhausted eyes to him and said: 'I'll have to learn to be alone.'

She opened the car door. When he did the same, meaning to walk her to her front door, she said: 'No, don't.'

He watched her go. She walked halfway up the paved pathway, paused for a second, then squared her shoulders and lifted up her chin.

'Yes, I think so,' he said to Margaret.

94

Just after eight in the morning, before he totted up his kilometres or recorded his hours, he phoned Mrs Gusti Flint.

'Sorry to bother you so early,' he said. In the background he heard her dogs barking.

'You're very welcome. I'm sure you can hear why I can't sleep late.'

'Mrs Flint, I understand it could be a confidential arrangement between you and your son, but it is very important that you tell me: did Danie borrow money from you in the past year?'

For a second, only the yapping of the chihuahuas could be heard. Then she said: 'Why? What's happened?'

He had been expecting the question, but he wasn't going to tell her. 'Nothing has happened. I'm just trying to be as thorough as possible.'

'No. Absolutely not,' she said with a barely suppressed indignation. 'Danie knew I'm a widow.'

Who lives in luxury, Joubert thought. 'So he definitely didn't ask you for a loan?' His cellphone began ringing. He took it out of his pocket.

'No. But I still have the feeling there's a reason you're asking me.'

'Mrs Flint, I have another call, thank you very much.'

'I have the right to know . . .'

He ended the call, because he recognised the number on his cellphone. It was Tanya Flint. He answered.

'Tanya?'

'You had better come and look at this,' she said. There was something in her voice, an urgency.

'Where are you? What's happened?'

'I'm at work. Someone has . . . Please, it's better if you see for yourself.'

'Are you safe?'

'Yes,' she said. 'The police are here.'

Her company was in a complex of small businesses in Stella Street, Montagu Gardens. He saw the metre-long signboard with the silhouette spy figure, the blue kidney-shaped swimming pool icon, and the words *Undercover. Protect Your Pool.* Two SAPS patrol vehicles stood in front of the door.

When he walked in he saw her standing in the workshop area with two uniformed policemen. Blue and black PVC material in broad rolls, a swimming pool cover that was nearly all cut out, tool boards against the wall. Tanya saw him approaching, pointed at the high white wall to his right.

In huge, spray-painted red letters was: DROP IT.

He went over to her.

'They broke stuff up there,' she said. He was puzzled by her tone. It was calm. Almost satisfied.

He looked where she had pointed. Concrete steps leading to a wooden deck. He could see the legs of a desk that had been overturned, standing upside down.

'Is this the investigator?' one of the uniforms asked, a black sergeant.

'I am,' said Joubert, and took a business card out of his pocket, held it out.

'You must wait for Inspector Butshingi. He is coming.'

Then Tanya Flint spoke, with happiness in her voice, 'I knew it was someone else. I knew . . .'

Joubert did not respond. He stood and looked at the passive infra-red detectors on both side walls. 'Why didn't the alarm go off?'

'I don't know,' said Tanya Flint, as though it was of no importance.

'But did you switch on the alarm last night?' asked a patient Inspector Fizile Butshingi. He stood with Joubert and Tanya Flint at the small bathroom window, its glass smashed, the burglar bars ripped out.

'I can't remember.' Her euphoria a thing of the past, the adrenaline drained from her system.

Butshingi raised his eyebrows.

'Last night . . . Mr Joubert called just as I was locking up, about my husband's cellphone. I . . . Maybe I forgot . . .'

The inspector sighed. 'And you are sure nothing was stolen?'

'Not as far as I can see. They just broke all the PC monitors. And threw the files around.'

Butshingi pointed at the big red letters on the wall. 'And you know what this is about, Sup?' he said, because he knew who Joubert was.

Joubert had been in two minds about how he would answer this question when it came. Putting his cards on the table held many implications. Long hours of making statements, the Porsche, Audi, cellphone, financial records that might be seized, the momentum of his investigation broken. Tanya's 30,000 seeping away as the hours ticked by. But he didn't want to lie either.

'Well, Mrs Flint employed us to try and find her missing husband. There's a docket at the Table View Station . . .'

'Table View,' sighed Butshingi, who operated from the Milnerton station.

'It's Inspector Jamie Keyter's case. He would know more than me.'

'Ay, ay,' said Butshingi. 'I know him. But those words . . .' He pointed at the wall. 'Someone wants you to stop. You must have found something, Sup.'

'I've gone through his cars, his financial statements, his office . . .' Joubert shrugged.

'And nothing?'

'I still can't find him.'

'Who knew? About your investigation?'

That was a question he also wanted answered. 'Obviously, Mrs Flint, her mother-in-law, his colleagues, and Jamie Keyter.'

Butshingi looked at Tanya. 'And your employees, here?'

'No, they knew nothing.'

The inspector stared at the graffiti. 'Sup,' he said slowly and carefully, 'are you sure there's nothing you're not telling me?'

'Inspector, if you want to, we can give you access to everything. Maybe you will see something I missed.'

The detective shook his head. 'Let me talk to Keyter first.'

When they were alone, Tanya Flint asked him what he thought.

'You talked to nobody else about the investigation?'

'Our friends know. And you, and his work.'

Joubert thought about it, shook his head. 'There are too many variables. Someone could have been watching Self Storage. Or asked the caretaker to call if someone went in there. I'll try to find out.'

'It's the people who harmed Danie. Now they are trying to stop us.' But without the sense of conviction she had shown earlier.

He told her the money was key. They would have to talk to Absa, as soon as possible. They needed more detail about the transactions, about the account itself. Anything. Everything. If she took the SAPS case number, their marriage certificate and identity book along, the bank should help.

'Let me just sort out this chaos,' waving her hand around the trashed office. 'Get the insurance guys in, see if I can get new computers.'

'I'll be back at the office.' He made a move to go, turned back. 'I don't think you should be alone. We must make a plan.'

At the office he found a telephone directory, opened it at 'H', ran his finger down the columns, until he found it.

Helderberg Upholstery.

He called the number, asked the woman who answered if they could replace the leatherwork of his Porsche.

'That is our speciality, sir,' she said.

'I'll bring it in for a quote,' he lied.

Another riddle solved. Despite the break-in at Tanya Flint's business and the warning on the wall, he felt a certain satisfaction. He had made progress. Despite the rusty gears. He had climbed on the detective bicycle and ridden again. And now it seemed he could solve this thing after all, before the money ran out.

95

He found Mark Marshall's home number in the telephone directory and phoned him. A woman's voice answered cheerfully. 'This is Helen.'

He asked if he could talk to Mr Marshall.

'Hold on. He's outside having a clandestine smoke. I'm not supposed to know . . .'

He heard the woman calling, then footsteps before a man picked up and said: 'Mark Marshall.'

Joubert asked him if he had sold a 1984 Porsche Carrera nine-double-one to a Danie Flint in October.

'Yes. That's me. Why? Is he selling again?'

'No. He has been reported as missing, and I'm working the case. We're just trying to get a profile of his spending this last year.'

'The car has gone missing?'

'No, sir, Mr Flint was reported missing by his wife.'

'Good grief. Is he all right?'

'We don't know, sir.'

'Good grief. Such a fine young fellow. It was a real pleasure to . . . When did he disappear?'

'Last year in November. According to our records, he bought the car from you.'

'He did. Cash, on the nose.'

Joubert asked him how Flint had heard about the Porsche.

'I advertised it. In *Auto Trader*, last year September.'

'And when did he contact you?'

'I'll have to . . . It happened pretty quickly, just a couple of days before he bought it, must have been . . . That's the problem with getting old, you can't remember the details any more, I'll have to go check.'

'He made the payment to you on October twenty-seventh . . .'

'That's about right. Then it must have been around the twenty-fifth when he called. In the morning, asked some questions. And no haggling, which was a nice change, all the other chancers were making these ridiculous offers. Anyway, then he came around at lunchtime to take a look. Knew his stuff, too. Said he was also interested in a 1981 Ferrari 308 GTSi, and he would let me know . . .'

Joubert made some notes on his notebook. 'The Ferrari. Did he mention the price?'

'No. But it was also advertised in the *Auto Trader*, and I went and had a look. Can't remember exactly, but it was more than 400,000. Anyway, two days later, he called, said he was taking the Porsche, and he asked for my banking details. He made an Internet transfer. And then he came with a taxi to fetch the car the following day. Really nice guy, good manners . . .'

'That would be the twenty-eighth?'

'It was one day after he made the payment.'

'Did he say anything about how he got the money?' A shot in the dark.

'Well . . . Not really. I asked him what he does, and he said he was in business for himself. So I asked what kind of business, because I used to be an entrepreneur myself. He said something about being a dealmaker.'

'A dealmaker.'

'He was sort of vague, but, you know, nowadays you get all kinds of brokers and businesses, I don't understand half of it. And it wasn't my place to be nosy.'

'Mr Marshall, was there anything else you can remember. Anything he said?'

'Well . . . not really. I mean, when two petrolheads get together, they talk about cars. And he knew his stuff, knew the history of the nine-eleven, how the French objected in the early sixties to the original name, the nine-oh-one, so Porsche had to change it, that sort of thing. I remember he said the 1967 S coupé model was the most beautiful, but I like the Carrera better, so we had this little argument going, all in good spirits. He had a great sense of humour, very likeable guy. So do you have any idea what happened to him?'

'Not yet.'

'And the car?'

'We found the car last night.'

'Well, then he won't be far away . . .'

He tore out his notes, put them beside the writing pad and began building up a timeline:

17 October: Deposit of R250,000.

25 October: Phoned about Porsche. Went to look at it.

27 October: Paid R248,995 for the Porsche. (Internet bank)

28 October: Collected the Porsche.

29 October: Deposit of R147,000.

3 November: Cash withdrawal of R1,000.

9 November: Cash withdrawal of R1,500.

12 November: Paid Helderberg Upholstery R11,000 (Internet bank)

25 November: Disappeared.

He sat staring at it, read his notes again. Eight days between the first deposit and Danie Flint's enquiry about the Porsche. He'd had a look at what was on the market first. And why would he have been interested in a Ferrari of more than R400,000 if he only had R250,000 in the bank? Or was it merely to give Mark Marshall the opportunity to drop his price? But Marshall had said *no haggling . . .*

Joubert wrote at the bottom of his timeline. *Ferrari? Over R400,000??? Try to trace seller. Get September's Auto Trader.* There had been a magazine in Danie Flint's drawer. Maybe that was the one.

Then he wrote: *Date bank account opened? What kind of deposits?*

And: *Self Storage – date of lease? Costs?* There had only been two cash withdrawals, made five days after he had collected the Porsche. Where had the car been in the interim?

He thought again before writing down the word *dealmaker*, with three question marks behind it. And finally, in large capital letters: WHERE DID THE MONEY COME FROM?

Tanya Flint phoned him when he stopped at the Self Storage depot in Salt River. She said she had an appointment at the bank for half past two, the Heerengracht branch, since that was where the account had been opened.

He arranged to meet her five minutes before the appointment at Absa. Then he took his writing pad, climbed out and walked to the office of the depot, which had been locked and empty last night.

A coloured woman in her thirties sat behind the counter paging through *You* magazine. When she saw him she pushed it aside and asked if she could help. He put his business card on the counter and told his story.

When he mentioned Danie Flint's name, she asked, 'Ninety-seven B?' as though a light had switched on.

'That's right,' and he took the keys out of his pocket.

'Mary,' the woman called over her shoulder. 'The mystery of ninety-seven B has been solved.'

Mary appeared from behind a partition. She was coloured, older, plump and indignant.

'Where have you been, sir?' She looked him up and down.

'It's not his contract, it's Flint's, and he's gone,' said the magazine reader.

'Gone?' asked Mary.

'Missing person,' the other one said.

'So who will pay what's owing?'

Joubert said he was sure the overdue amount would be paid.

'We would have had to sell that fancy car at the end of next month, because the third warning is due.'

'Did you send notices out?'

'We tried to phone him, since December already, when he went into arrears. But he'd given us the wrong number, the woman said she had never heard of him. And the contract says, three months, then we auction.'

'What address did you send the notices to?'

'The one on his contract.'

'May I see it?'

'That's private information,' said Mary, but without great conviction.

'That's the only way the outstanding money will be paid,' he said persuasively. 'If you help me.'

The older woman thought it through before nodding slowly, turning around and going to fetch the information. She came back with the folder already open. '179 Green Park Road in Monte Vista,' she said. 'And there is his cellphone number.' She put the documents down on the counter, so that he could see them.

He wrote down the details. 'Is that the date he signed the contract?'

'That's right.'

October twenty-eighth. The day Danie Flint had gone to collect his new, second-hand Porsche.

'Did he arrive here with the Porsche?'

'He parked it just in front there.' The younger woman pointed a finger at where Joubert's car was, right in front of the office. 'I remember him well, because of the fancy car. A boy's face, wouldn't hurt a fly, full of jokes. He stood there and told me his garage at home was too full now, he would have to add more space. Could take six months.'

'And the rent is 3,000 rand?' Joubert pointed at the amount at the bottom of the account.

'No. It's 1,500 deposit , and 1,500 per month.'

'How did he pay?'

'It must have been cash, because there isn't a credit card slip stapled to this.'

He looked at his timeline. Flint had only begun making cash withdrawals from his secret account on the third of November, and according to Tanya's financial tables he couldn't have done that from their ordinary account. Then his eye fell on the entry for 29 October. *Deposit of R147,000.*

Add 3,000 and you have a round R150,000.

96

He took his Cape Town map book to the office, laid his briefcase flat on the desk, clipped it open and took out the sandwiches. While he ate, he checked the map index for Green Park Road in Monte Vista.

The new sandwich filling was very tasty. He ate slowly, making it last longer.

He couldn't find a Green Park Street or Road anywhere. Nowhere in the Cape Peninsula. There was a Green Street, Greenfield Crescent, Green Valley Close, Greenside Close, a long list of other names with

'Green' in them, but Green Park or Greenpark did not exist in any shape or form as a street address.

Deliberately false. Had to be.

He opened his notepad and filled in his timeline. Between *28 October: Collected the Porsche* and *29 October: Deposit of R147,000* he made a new entry: *28 October: Paid R3,000 cash deposit to Self Storage.*

The last thing to do was to call the cell number that Danie had given Self Storage, just make sure. Something about the number bothered him.

A woman answered. He asked if he could speak to Danie Flint.

'Ag, no,' she said, her tone resigned. 'Not another one.'

'You don't know Danie?'

'Not from Adam.'

'And other people have also called this number?'

'Just the storage people.'

'Ma'am, if you don't mind me asking, where do you live?'

'Paulpietersburg. In KwaZulu.'

When he'd put the phone down, he looked at the number again. Why did it look vaguely familiar?

It took him several minutes of intense concentration to put two and two together. He paged back in the notepad, to where he'd written down Tanya Flint's cellphone details. Her number was almost identical. Only the last four numbers were jumbled in the number her husband had given to Self Storage.

They sat waiting in silence while the woman at the Absa Bank enquiries counter went to get permission from her superiors, before she could give them information about the account. She was away for a long time.

Joubert wondered what Tanya was thinking about as she stared at the wall. He knew he would have to tell her soon that her husband had been a liar and a cheat. And a slick one too. False addresses and cellphone numbers, stories about overflowing garages and fictional phone calls. And he knew that it was a trail that would lead to even greater trouble. Deceit was always part of a wider pattern of behaviour. He was going to unearth other things. After last night's break-in, Tanya believed that someone else lay behind the whole affair. But he didn't think so. He couldn't explain the burglary, didn't understand exactly how it fitted in, but he had his suspicions.

It was about the money. Four hundred thousand rand. Find out where that came from, and you'd find the burglars, the graffiti painters. Danie Flint was part of something. The money was dirty, stolen from somewhere, and Danie wasn't the only one involved.

Had he been too free with his ill-gotten gains, making his buddies nervous? Did they begin to think he posed too great a risk?

Wouldn't be the first time.

Was the original amount bigger, divided between accomplices, the 400,000 only Danie's share?

Then it would be easier to trace the source.

But how did he break all this to Tanya? Because she had no idea about this side of her husband.

The bank clerk came back, the good news beaming across her face. She called up the savings account details on the computer. Danie Flint had opened it on 15 October, with a deposit of R200. He had fulfilled all the identification requirements. The email address he gave was speedster430@yahoo.com. The cellphone number was for the phone they had found in the Porsche.

And the two deposits for R250,000 and R147,000 were in cash, information that made Tanya Flint shake her head in disbelief.

'Can I see the photocopy of the ID?' she asked. And turned to Joubert to say: 'It can't have been Danie.'

He had no idea how she could make that assumption.

'It should be on the system,' the woman said, and called it up from the database, swivelling the screen so that Tanya could see.

Danie's face on the ID photo.

Tanya frowned.

'Is that his ID number?' the bank clerk asked.

Tanya nodded.

'What about his proof of address?' asked Joubert, because according to FICA legislation an ID alone was not enough. Anyone who wanted to open an account also had to supply a utilities or phone bill.

'Let's take a look,' said the woman, clicking through tabs on the computer.

She found something, turned the screen again. A scanned electricity bill, clearly from a photocopy. It was addressed to D. Flint, Green Park Street 179, Monte Vista.

'That's not our address,' Tanya said with obvious relief.

'That address does not exist,' said Mat Joubert. 'The account is forged.'

In the shade of a street café's umbrella on Tulbagh Square he spoke gently to her. He knew that he could be physically intimidating, so he leaned back, and kept his voice low. He asked her how she felt after all the events of the past few days.

She said she was OK, but he could see that she was suffering.

He asked if she was getting any sleep.

'Not much.'

'Have you thought about seeing a doctor? To get something for the stress?'

'No.' A determined shake of the head.

He gave her a moment to think it over.

'I have to face up to the truth some time.'

'It doesn't have to be now.'

That shake of her head again.

When he began to speak again, he chose his words with care. 'Years ago I was married to someone else,' he began, 'someone who worked with me in the police force. I loved her very much. She was . . . in so many ways . . . the person I wanted to be. Like Danie. An extrovert. Funny and smart and . . . sunny. She shone. Brightly. Everyone loved her. And every day I gave thanks that I'd found her. And then I discovered a different side to her. By accident. And it was . . . painful. I felt betrayed. Deceived. As if she had deliberately set out to harm me. Me. Personally . . .'

Tanya Flint looked away from him. She didn't want to hear this.

'It took me many years to realise that I was wrong,' he said. 'It was just part of who she was. One of the aspects, the facets of the greater whole. Perhaps her conscience bothered her, perhaps she didn't want to be that way, but I don't think she could do anything about it. We are all programmed in one way or another.'

Her eyes were focused somewhere else, her body language a shield.

He pressed on. 'We've got a whole lot of new information since yesterday. And all of it points to the fact that Danie wasn't the man you thought he was. That's going to hurt you. On many levels. But the one thing you have to try to remember is that this was just one facet of him. There were many others . . .' And it all seemed to him so pointless, so that he didn't know how to carry on.

Her eyes turned slowly back to him. 'Thank you,' she said.

They sat in silence, the world rushing by. Then, eventually, she said: 'What else have you found?'

97

Back at the office there were two messages from Inspector Fizile Butshingi, Milnerton Station, asking Joubert to call back urgently, but first he sat down at his computer to update the project programme. He wanted to know exactly how much money Tanya Flint had left.

The account stood at just over 21,000 rand, if you included Cordier's fingerprint bill and his latest hours and travel expenses. Nine thousand left. He wouldn't test the Porsche for fingerprints then. He deliberated over the new cellphone's profile and call record, and decided to see what a trip to ABC's headquarters threw up first. He had a strong hunch that the money had something to do with Danie's work.

He called to make an appointment with Mrs Heese, the bus company's head of Human Resources. She said she could see him in the late afternoon, round four o'clock. Then he called Margaret.

'How's my new recipe?' she asked.

'Fantastic.'

'Good. And the investigation?'

'Very good. Great progress. But I'm worried about Tanya. Someone broke into her office last night and painted a message on the wall: 'Drop it'. If I invited her to come and stay with us, for a night or two . . .?'

'Of course. But what about her mother-in-law? Doesn't she live in Panorama?'

'I got the impression that Tanya wasn't crazy about her mother-in-law. And that would still be two women on their own . . .'

'She's very welcome. I'll get Jeremy's room ready.'

'I don't know if she'll want to come. I'll let you know.'

He called Tanya, phrased the offer diplomatically.

'Thank you, but I'm not going to let them intimidate me.'

'Think about it,' he said, but he knew what her answer would be.

'There was a message for me from the detective from Table View. He wants me to call him.'

'Keyter?'

'Yes.'

The SAPS was in uproar since Inspector Butshingi had gone to the break-in this morning. 'Make him wait,' said Joubert. 'If he calls again, say he must talk to me.'

Last of all he called Milnerton police station and asked for Butshingi.

'The case was neglected at Table View,' the detective said. 'I've spoken to the SC, and he will light a fire. But I need to talk to you urgently.'

Not now. It would break his momentum.

'I'm pretty busy at the moment . . .'

'When can we meet?'

'Tomorrow? Around lunchtime?'

'You live in Milnerton, don't you?'

Joubert's heart sank. 'Yes.'

'How about tonight, after work?'

'I'm not sure when I'll finish,' he parried.

'I'll be at the office until late. Please call me. Let me give you my cell.'

On the way out he ran into Jack Fischer and financial controller Fanus Delport in the passage.

'You're a busy man,' said Jack, looking pleased.

'I'm making progress.'

'Oh?'

Joubert gave them a quick summary.

Fischer whistled softly through his moustache. 'That means that Vlok is fucked. You don't leave your Porsche just to take a dump.'

'Flint,' said Joubert. 'And I will have to give the SAPS our information. After this morning, there's an official request.'

'Jesus,' said Fischer. 'Listen, the law says that we have to give them "information which has relevance to an investigation". It's impossible to say exactly how much is "relevant".'

'I'm going to lay my cards on the table here, Jack.'

Fischer brushed back his abundant hair. '*Ja, ja* . . . They'll be able to do sweet blow all with it anyway. Who's the detective?'

'Inspector Fizile Butshingi. Milnerton.'

'Well, there you go.'

As Joubert turned on his heel, Fanus Delport called after him: 'Now don't you go making too much progress . . .'

At the major roadworks on the N1's Table Bay Boulevard, he felt his rising impatience with the heavy traffic, the slow pace. As though his brain had shifted into a higher gear.

He could see the whole thing now, he didn't need his notes and his timeline. All the pieces were there, in focus, thoughts dancing back and forth, his hypotheses strong, his deductions logical, as though he were standing on a hilltop, seeing further than before, even though he didn't know what was on the horizon.

He recognised it, this sense of urgency, clarity, this barely-suppressed euphoria. He'd struggled to find the signs, sniffing around, scratching here and there, but he had it all now, now he was running alongside the trail, he had the spoor, the scent of blood in his nostrils, the fever of the hunt in his head.

It had been five, six years since he'd last felt this way.

He'd expected a much older woman. Perhaps it was the name that had misled him, but Bessie Heese was in her thirties. And attractive with it. Short, brown, curly hair, fine features, rimless silver glasses that gave her a faintly professorial air. Elegant. Grey pencil skirt and a white blouse with lace detail.

She invited him to the 'meeting room'. Round table, four chairs, no windows. She called him 'inspector'. He let it go.

'You must understand, inspector, under normal circumstances ABC would supply confidential information only to the police. But because Mrs Flint is the wife of an employee, and has made an official written request, I'm authorised to answer certain questions.' Her voice was even, professional. She made no movement as she spoke, sat up straight and still. In complete control.

'I appreciate that,' he said.

'So, how may I help you?'

He zipped open his writing pad, found a clean sheet, slid the pen out. 'Was there ever any suspicion that Danie Flint was involved in anything criminal?'

She hid it well, but he could see the question surprised her. 'Criminal? No, absolutely not.'

'No large sums of money going missing at ABC?'

'Area managers don't handle money, inspector. It . . . no, it's not possible.'

'None of his people handle any money?'

'His bus drivers, but then we're not talking large sums. A few hundred rand a day at most.'

'Ma'am, did any significant amount of money vanish from ABC last year? Cash in particular.'

'I . . . I have to say, these are not the questions I expected.'

'It would help me a great deal if you answered them.'

'Inspector, the nature of an area manager's work . . . The way we collect money – it's worlds away from Danie Flint's job description.'

'Can you tell me how it works?'

She thought for a moment, nodded, then went through it for him. Bus passengers could basically buy tickets in three ways: on the bus itself, from the driver. Or from the ticket sellers working at any of the fifty or so sales kiosks dotted about at strategic spots around the Cape Peninsula. Or at one of the bigger ticket offices, where bus drivers and ticket sellers also had to hand their cash in every day.

'So,' she explained, 'the area manager is just not in that loop.'

'I understand,' said Joubert. 'But he knows people in that loop. Every day he works with people who are part of that loop.'

'Then he could only be indirectly involved.'

'In this case that's very likely. Was there any major theft of cash last year? September, October?'

She sat dead still, her eyes blinking twice behind the glasses. 'Inspector, am I to understand that Danie Flint was involved in a crime?'

Joubert realised that this would seriously affect ABC's loyalty to Flint – and their cooperation with him. 'No,' he said. 'We just have an inexplicable sum of money to account for here. I don't yet know how he came by it, but crime is one of the possibilities.'

She digested the information, with a slight, controlled frown. 'But why do you think this money has something to do with ABC?'

'Statistics.'

'Oh?'

'When a white-collar worker without any history of criminal activity is involved in fraud, the chances are more than eighty per cent that his employer or place of work is in the picture.'

'I see.'

He asked the question again: 'Was there any major theft of cash from the company last year?'

Bessie Heese considered the question. 'Will you excuse mc a minute?'

'Of course.'

She stood up and walked out of the room.

He stared after her, dimly aware of her shapely calves and ankles, his thoughts overwhelmed by the possibility that she was going to ask permission to share a secret with him that might blow this whole thing wide open.

98

He was mistaken.

It was ten minutes before she returned, tucking her skirt carefully underneath her as she sat down opposite him again and said: 'Inspector, you must understand, as manager of human resources I only get involved when a staff member has to face a disciplinary hearing due to misconduct. If money goes missing without anyone being implicated, I would not necessarily know about it. So I had to ascertain the facts from our Managing Director first. And get his permission to share them with you. Because this is highly confidential information.'

Joubert nodded. He knew that if the stolen sum was large enough, most big companies would handle it internally. And keep their lips sealed about it, for fear of damage to their corporate image.

'Our Managing Director has authorised me to share the information with you. But with the proviso that you inform us immediately if Danie Flint is involved in a crime.'

'Very well.' He would have to give something in order to get something.

'The fact of the matter is that our largest single financial loss due to theft last year was just under 60,000 rand. At one of our ticket offices, in June. We realised it within twenty-four hours of the theft, identified the guilty parties, and the case was dealt with within two weeks. Flint was not involved at all.'

'Sixty thousand,' said Joubert. He couldn't keep the disappointment out of his voice.

'Inspector, you must realise, our systems are highly sophisticated. I know one doesn't always associate it with a bus company, but we use the best technology available, especially regarding the finances. We do a daily reconciliation, we can identify anomalies immediately. Even relatively small amounts.'

He was still battling to accept the bad news. 'Are you absolutely sure there were no other amounts? Four hundred thousand or more?'

Her eyes widened a bit at hearing the amount, but she recovered quickly. 'I give you my word.'

Joubert sat there, his whole theory destroyed.

'Four hundred thousand? Danie Flint stole four hundred thousand?' Bessie Heese asked, some expression in her voice for the first time.

He parked the Honda at work, but he didn't walk to the office. He left via the basement, walked around to the St Georges Mall, then up towards the cathedral. He didn't notice the street hawkers, the stalls, the tourists, the diners and drinkers at the tables outside restaurants. He was oblivious to the way the stream of home-bound office workers parted for his tall, broad figure as he moved against the flow, his brain occupied with the big question: where had the money come from?

Statistics were on his side, the general rule: a white man in his thirties, with a good job and no previous criminal record, steals first from his place of work. It all rested on the universal principle of Predisposition + Environment + Current Circumstances that is drilled into detectives in every criminology course. In other words, the suspect's inherent tendency to resort to crime, plus his formative environment, plus opportunity. And it was the latter that was under consideration here. Opportunity.

Danie Flint's psyche made him capable, allowed him to grasp the Big Opportunity. And the profile said the opportunity was usually in the work environment, because that was where he spent most of his time. That was where his knowledge was, his experience, his insight into systems, procedures, security, so that he could assess possibilities, make judgements about the likelihood of getting away with the crime.

But Bessie Heese of ABC said they'd never lost 400,000 rand.

And he had absolutely no idea where another opportunity might have come from.

He put aside everything he knew. He walked past the cathedral, up the footpath through the Company Gardens, to Government Avenue. He went back to the beginning, and tried to construct a new theory. He thought about the money. A considerable amount. Cash. The key factor was cash. White collar crime was about cheques, falsified accounts, doctored tenders, Internet transfers, cooked books. Not cash.

Bank robbery was cash of 400,000. Or cash-in-transit heists, casino robbery, pension pay points. The rest was small change. Even the robbery of supermarkets, restaurants, shops. Ten, twenty, thirty thousand rand if they were lucky.

But banks, cash-in-transit vehicles, casinos were not Danie Flint's world. In this country that was largely the territory of organised township crime gangs. Far removed from the bus milieu.

He considered Flint's other activities and environments. Gym. Circle of friends. Residential neighbourhood. The only potential was the neighbourhood, he had heard people refer to Parklands as 'Darklands', with reference to the number of Nigerians who had moved in there in recent years. But the majority of them were good citizens, working in legal jobs.

Anything was possible. What if Danie Flint had struck up a conversation with someone in a sports bar, someone with a plan?

Unlikely. What could he have offered them? Nigerian cartels specialised in drugs, credit card and four-one-nine fraud. And given

Flint's age, his job, the circles he moved in, he couldn't have been of much assistance.

Unless . . .

He would have to ask Tanya about it, even though it was a wild guess.

Two amounts, two deposits, twelve days apart. Two-fifty, and one-fifty.

Why two separate amounts? Caution? Not wanting to attract too much attention? Or was there a more practical reason?

He stood on the pavement in Annandale Street, with the entrance to the Mount Nelson Hotel across the road from him, and he knew he would have to delve into it again, deeper and more thoroughly. Somewhere there was a piece of information that would answer all the questions.

The only problem was, he had no idea where to look. And Tanya Flint's money was running out.

A quarter to six, and Jack Fischer was still in his office, papers spread out in front of him, head bowed in concentration.

Joubert hesitated at the threshold, fighting thirty years of SAPS conditioning not to disturb a senior officer when he was busy. He shook it off. This was not the service.

'A moment, Jack?'

Fischer looked up. 'Of course, of course. Take a chair.'

When he had settled himself in one of the large chairs opposite Jack, he said: 'Jack, there's something here that worries me.'

'Tell me.'

'What do we do if Tanya Flint doesn't have more than 30,000 rand?'

'I thought you were nearly finished with the case?'

'It might take a couple more days. Maybe more. She has fourteen hours left, if I don't book any travelling expenses. What do we do if it is not enough?'

Fischer leaned back, smiled at Joubert in a fatherly manner. 'I told you, they always find the money.'

'And if she really can't?'

The smile disappeared. 'Of course she can. How much money is in the account you discovered?'

'You know it could be months before she has access to that money. If it isn't connected to a crime.'

'But it's security. And she has the house, the cars . . . Doesn't she have some sort of business too? What about policies? If they have a mortgage bond, there must be a life insurance policy on the husband. Come on, Mat, you know she'll make a plan.'

He considered Fischer's point of view. 'I want to clarify the principle,' he said. 'Let's say she tries everything, but still can't raise the money. Or she can only get it in a month's time . . .'

'She'll get it, Mat.'

'Jack, theoretically. Let's just say.'

Fischer's patience was wearing thin. 'We don't work with theories. We select clients, we don't accept them if they can't pay.'

'Has there ever been a single client who said "I just can't carry on"?'

'I won't say there was never . . .'

'What was the policy?'

'We handle each case on merit.'

'Jack, you're evading the question.'

Fischer threw his hands in the air, his face reddening. 'You keep harping on this. What for?'

Mat Joubert leaned forward, his shoulders loomed. But he kept his voice even. 'Because before I left here this afternoon, Fanus Delport said, "Now don't you go making too much progress". Because at morning parade . . .'

'He was joking, fuck, Mat, where's your sense of humour?'

'It's the context, Jack. You're the one who wanted me to get her bank statements electronically so we could book Fanus's hours too. "Double time", so we could milk her. It's the norm here. At morning parade no one asked how any cases were progressing. It was all "how much money did you make?" "Did you book your kilometres?" . . .'

'How the fuck do you think you run a business?' Aggressive. 'This isn't a charity here. There are salaries and infrastructure. Do you know how much the office rent is every month? And our telephone account? You tell me, how do we pay for that if we just start working for people for nothing, a bloody free-for-all? You tell me.'

'Free-for-all? Who said anything about free-for-all?' Joubert felt his own temper rising. He took a deep breath, shook his head and said: 'That's not the point.'

'Well if you're so fucking smart, tell me what the point *is*.'

It took him a while to regain control: 'The point is, if I'm *this* close to a solution after two days, and she doesn't have the money, I want you to tell me to carry on. Finish the job.'

'You know as well as I do, "this close" means nothing. What if the case takes another week or so? Or a month? Where do you draw the line?'

'Jack, we're not fools. We know how long something will take, we know how far or how close we are to a breakthrough. And I'm telling you now, I need another three days for this. Four, maximum. To either solve it, or to know it can't be solved. She can pay for two days. Surely we can afford to give her two days free. Or on credit. Or something.'

'Have you got a thing on with her? Is that what this is about?'

Mat Joubert rose out of his chair, ready to smack Fischer with the back of his hand.

What saved him was Jack's reaction, suddenly rolling his chair backwards, raising his arm defensively, the cowardliness of it.

It made Joubert stop, fight for control, get it into his head that his whole future hung in the balance.

He stood there for a long time, then turned and walked to the door.

Jack said nothing.

He was out of the office and halfway down the passage when he stopped and went back. Fischer's hand reached out for the telephone. Joubert ignored it. 'I left the Service because I didn't count any more, Jack,' he said, his voice very quiet now. 'I felt it was unjust. Because I believe we do count. All of us. Tanya Flint as well. Especially Tanya Flint. Because she borrowed 30,000 rand to hire us. Not to enrich herself. Not to go and buy some or other meaningless thing. But to do her duty by her husband. And now it's turning out to be a hell of a painful process, but she has more guts than you and I together, Jack. *She* wants to get this done. And I'm telling you tonight, if Tanya Flint says she's tried everything and she can't raise more money, then I will finish her case. For all I care, you can subtract the cost from my salary.'

99

The first thing he did when he got into his Honda was to phone Tanya Flint to find out if she was already at home.

'Our pistol is gone,' was the first thing she said to him.

He asked what pistol.

'Danie's. I wanted to take it out of the safe, after the break-in and the . . . message. But it's not in the safe.'

'When did you last see it?'

'About a month or two before Danie disappeared.'

'I'll be there in twenty minutes.'

He drove to Parklands. Tried to concentrate on the meaning of the missing pistol. Had Flint taken it? Why?

But the thing with Jack occupied his attention. In Otto du Plessis Drive he found he was handling the car roughly. Angry. With himself. With Jack Fischer. With the whole fucking situation he found himself in.

He should have known, because he knew Jack. Granted that was fifteen years ago, before Fischer had been promoted to Johannesburg, but the signs were there, and it didn't help saying time heals everything. He should have listened to his police colleagues, Benny Griessel and Leon Petersen, who both had the same reaction when he broke the news to them. *Jissis. Isn't Jack Fischer a bastard?* those had been Griessel's words.

He was right.

Because when he had told Jack how he felt, told him the Flint case could be subtracted from his salary, Jack had sat back in his chair and smirked at him and said, 'Well, then that's what we will do,' and he had gathered up the papers on his desk and began reading again as though Mat Joubert was no longer standing there.

No 'Sit down and let's talk it out'. No reconsideration of his viewpoint, no measured, adult discussion of the case. Just ignored him.

As though he didn't count.

And now?

Three days on the new job, fifty-one years old, white, Afrikaner, what did he do now? He wasn't going to stay with Fischer, and he couldn't afford to resign. There was no other work that paid nearly as well, and he couldn't face shopping centre, or corporate, or neighbourhood watch security, he would die before fifty-five. And with the housing market so slow, and Margaret already having made an offer on the Constantia house, they would need his income.

What did he do now?

He asked Tanya what kind of pistol it was.

A small Taurus, she said, Danie bought it so that she could use it too.

Could she shoot with it?

She had. At the shooting range.

Had Danie said anything about the firearm, in the month or two before he disappeared?

Not a word.

Was it definitely in the safe?

Always.

So Danie must have taken it?

Yes. Her expression said she knew it was confirmation of his opinion that Danie was involved in something.

He talked with Tanya again about the money. He asked her about Danie's friends in particular, the possibility that he might have met someone at the gym, in the neighbourhood, at a restaurant or a bar, with whom he could have done business of any kind.

She insisted that she would have known. All their friends were married, all the women loyal, if there had been something, she would have heard about it. And besides, he almost never partied without her. Sometimes, the exception, but mostly they were together, side by side.

Now what, she asked.

He had to find the source of the money.

How?

He would keep digging.

She just nodded.

He invited her again to stay over with him and Margaret.

She thanked him, but said no thank you again. Although the pistol was gone she had the house alarm, the panic button, the armed response would react to that. She wasn't going to be intimidated.

'I've been thinking about the break-in,' he said. 'There are many ways to pass this message on to you. They chose a specific modus operandi. A careful one. Almost half-hearted. That says something. I'm not yet sure what . . .'

He met with Inspector Fizile Butshingi at Milnerton Police Station. Butshingi made them tea in the kitchen, which they drank sitting on either side of the battered government-issue desk, piled high with dossiers.

Joubert told him about the investigation, from beginning to end. He left nothing out. When he was finished, he said, 'If you could look at cash-in-transit robberies, August, September, October. Four hundred thousand rand, probably more. Something out of the ordinary.'

'Let me try,' said Butshingi.

'And if you could help get Table View to keep an eye on Tanya Flint's house tonight. I would appreciate it very much.'

'OK. And maybe have our people patrol her business.'

'Thank you very much.'

Then he looked at Joubert and shook his head. 'Weird world, Sup . . .'

'Yes,' said Joubert. 'And getting weirder by the day.'

Margaret had always been sensitive to his depression, read the signs easily.

'What happened?' she asked straight away.

They walked through to the kitchen. He told her about the dead end in the investigation. And his falling out with Jack Fischer.

She did what she always did. Talked to him, about inconsequential things. Asked him to pour them each a glass of wine. While she applied her skills in the kitchen and made them *bobotie*, yellow rice and sweet potato, one of his favourites.

In front of the TV she looked for something to watch that he enjoyed, found a rerun of *Everybody Loves Raymond* on a satellite channel. Leaned against him, head on his shoulder, both of her hands wrapped around his.

* * *

In the night he lay thinking about Danie Flint. Tried to follow the spoor as he had found it. Cheerful extrovert, party animal, ambitious area manager with sports car pictures on the wall, lost a father, somewhat self-obsessed, materialistic mother, married to a serious, dedicated, driven woman.

Received a large amount of cash. Spent it on himself. Sly. Selfish.

Then, overnight, gone.

No new insights. The signs all pointing in the same direction. Until he finally dozed off, well after two a.m.

In the morning Margaret was cheerful. As he ate his yoghurt and muesli, she said: 'You know, I've been thinking. All this moving around, all the trouble with the building contractors, the property market, buyers in and out of the house, any time of the day. Maybe it's time for a change.'

'What do you mean?'

'I was out in Constantia yesterday, and I was standing there, looking at this tired old house, thinking what it was going to take to fix it all up, going through it all again, and I asked myself, why? Do I really want to? Do we really need to? Maybe I'm getting old. Maybe I need something entirely new, but I just couldn't work up much enthusiasm for it.'

'No,' he said. 'You're not getting old.'

She kissed his cheek. 'There's money in the bank. And I like this house. It's perfect for us. And I like Milnerton. It's . . . central, we're close to everything, the neighbours are nice . . . I'm happy . . .'

He nodded, not sure where she was going.

'Start your own agency,' she said.

'My own?'

'Mat, these last few days . . . It was like the old days again. You were so immersed. Despite Jack Fischer, you were enjoying it.'

'That's true.'

'So, start your own agency. You're a detective. It's what you do. Do it for yourself. I know, it will take a while to generate the income, but we're comfortable, financially.'

'Margaret,' he said seriously. 'You're not just saying that because I'm a bit down?'

'You know me better than that.'

It was true. He nodded.

'I can help. Do the books, answer the phone, decorate the office.'

'I . . .'

'And besides, I've always wanted to be a PI's babe.'

'You are . . .'

'A private dick's dame. A gum-shoe's gun moll. A sleuth's skirt . . .'

He smiled.

'A shamus's broad, or dame, or chippy . . .'

She kept on. Until he laughed.

100

Back at the office you could cut the atmosphere with a knife. The silence hung oppressively. Fischer and Delport were in consultation, behind closed doors. Mildred, the receptionist, scarcely greeted him.

He sat down at his computer, brought the project up-to-date, made sure everything was correct so that Jack couldn't point an accusing finger at anything. Then he walked out, to Greenmarket Square, went and sat in a coffee shop, so he could think things through.

He knew where the gaps in his knowledge lay, but he wasn't sure how to fill them.

Danie Flint had spent the greatest part of his day at work. He operated his secret life from there, the bank account and the Yahoo email. And it was in his working hours that he had found the financial opportunity. Had to, Tanya was dead sure she would have known if it came from somewhere in their social circle.

But how? What was it that he didn't know about Flint's daily tasks, his routine?

Hard to say. Because Neville Philander, the overworked, frenetic, telephone-answering Operational Manager, never had the time to give him the detail. And Philander sat with all the information, the personal contacts, the first-hand experience. How would he get him to share that calmly?

He outlined his plan as he drank the coffee, then he took out his cellphone and made the call.

Bessie Heese was in a meeting. He asked her to phone him back urgently. He couldn't drink *more* coffee, he'd had two cups at home as well, but he didn't want to go back to the office. He paid his bill and left, thought of lingering in Clarke's Bookshop, there was nothing else to do.

Heese phoned before he reached Long Street.

He described the situation with Neville Philander.

She was businesslike, faintly irritated. 'Didn't we ascertain that the money didn't come from us?'

'We only ascertained that it wasn't your money. I can't remove his work environment from my list yet. I'm only asking for an hour or two of Philander's time. Away from the office.'

She countered. 'That is the nature of Mr Philander's job. He has a central managerial role.'

'I know. But he's the one who can help.'

He deduced from her silence that she was weighing things up. 'Very well,' was the reluctant response. 'Can he come to your office?'

They met at the Wimpy on St George's. Joubert drank tea, Philander a cappuccino, and exclaimed to Heaven when Joubert told him about the money. 'No way, he couldn't have stolen it from us.' Then, dumbfounded, he wiped the milky foam from his upper lip.

'I know. But the chances are good that in some or other way in the course of his duties he spotted the opportunity.'

'He only works the bus routes,' said Philander, shaking his head. 'Tell me where he could scratch out that kind of money.'

'Tell me exactly how he worked.'

'I *did* tell you.'

'I want detail.'

'Like in every hour of the day?'

'Please.'

'It's not gonna help you.'

'Then I can rule it out.'

Philander stared out of the window, in no mood for this conversation. He shrugged. 'If Aunt Bessie says talk to the PI, I suppose a man's got to do it.'

'She's a bit of a Nissan,' said Joubert.

Philander laughed. 'That's the truth.' He sipped at his cappuccino, took a deep breath, and said, 'OK. Danie Flint. Typical working day. Leave home, half past six, seven o'clock, doesn't go to the office, goes directly to his areas, drives along his routes. Every day a different routine, to keep the drivers on their toes. Milnerton, Montagu Gardens, Killarney, Du Noon, Richwood, Table View, Blouberg, Melkbos, Atlantis, in no specific order. Too much to cover in one day, so the idea is to cover your whole area in two or three days.'

'In his Audi?' He wanted to see it in his mind's eye, exactly how it was.

'That's right.'

'Sticking exactly to the bus routes.'

'That's it. The routes of choice, for that day.'

'Can you give me the routes?'

'Do you want to drive them?'

'Yes, I do.'

'Sure.'

'Why must he drive the routes every day?'

'To check if the driver is keeping to schedule. Are they on time? How they drive, how full the buses are. He's there if a bus breaks down, or is in an accident. He scouts new routes, where there are people standing waiting for taxis, and he looks for opportunities, he checks how the routes can be improved.

'Then around eleven the area managers come back to the office. To do the admin. Write up the notes from the morning, record and process accidents and mechanical problems. Handle driver infringements. Check fuel figures, new drivers trained and started on the job, answer emails, fine-comb DRMP logistics, read bulletins, attend meetings, it's mostly the same, every day.

'Then, around three o'clock, it's back on the routes, exactly the same story, for precisely the same reasons. There's no time to snooze, no time to make big bucks, it's just not possible.'

'He got the money somewhere,' said Joubert.

'Maybe he inherited. And he didn't want to tell Tanya.'

'Inherited money doesn't come in cash.'

'Fair enough.'

'Were you ever an area manager?'

'I was,' said Philander.

'Imagine you needed a lot of money. Cash. Urgently. You have to get it, even if you have to steal, let's say your wife is in hospital . . .'

'You mean, where would I steal it at work?'

'Or in the work environment.'

Philander drank the last of his cappuccino while he pondered.

'There's only one place. The big ticket office. But you would need two or three other men, walk in there with guns and masks, and rob the place.'

'No other possibilities?'

'Not for big bucks.'

Joubert hid his disappointment. 'Another cappuccino?'

'Aren't we just about finished?'

He wasn't sure if there was anything else. He thought back over everything Philander had said. One thing stood out. 'The DRMP, tell me what that stands for again?'

'Driver Risk Management Programme.'

'Is that the thing that caused the strike?'

'Just so.'

'But it's a computer program. Why would they strike over that?'

'It's much more than a computer system.'

'Oh?'

'It's a long story.'

Joubert nodded. He had the time.

Philander sighed. 'Maybe we better order more coffee.'

101

'It's all about the DriveCam.'

'The DriveCam?'

'In 2007, we were the first depot where Mr Eckhardt and them experimented with the new system, because we are the smallest. And the best, even if I have to say so myself. The thing works like this: every bus gets a video camera up front, here by the rear-view mirror. The DriveCam. One eye looks forward, and one eye looks back, and there's a hard drive inside. Now, obviously the camera doesn't put everything from morning to night on the hard drive. It's on all the time, and it records everything, but it's got like a motion detector and a little computer thingy inside, if the bus jerks, then it saves image and audio, ten to fifteen seconds before the event, and ten to fifteen seconds after, depending on the severity. Are you with me?'

Joubert said he thought so. But didn't a bus jerk a lot?

'Look, I say "jerk" for explanatory purposes. The motion sensor works with what they call "inertia". You know about G-forces? Now, *that's* the thing. If the driver *donners* into something, then it's negative G-force, negative inertia, then your DriveCam records. If he brakes helluva sharply, or accelerates too quick. Even if your driver goes around the corner too fast, then the sensor registers, and it saves the video . . .'

'Why include cornering?'

'Why? When do you go around the corner too fast, my bro'? When?'

'Tell me.'

'When you run a red robot, that's when.'

'Aah . . .'

'Now we come to the mind-blowing part. When that bus comes back to the depot tonight, then all those bits of video of the jerks automatically download wirelessly onto our server. Just like that, when the bus drives in the gate, you see? And that server is connected to the Internet, it sends all those clips to America, because that's where the system was developed. The Americans have software that analyses it all, and they email those video clips of trouble back to the area manager. The serious stuff, like accidents, are cc-ed to me and Mr Eckhardt.'

'Let me just make sure I understand,' said Joubert. 'If the bus accelerates or brakes too fast, the camera records it . . .'

Philander nodded. 'With a back and front view. You can see what the driver is doing, and you can see what is happening in the road.'

'And at your gate it sends it via a radio signal to a computer, that mails it to America.' In disbelief.

'More like a wireless transmission, like a cellphone. It's high tech, my brother, you've got to open your mind to understand it. But it's not just people looking at it in America, it's software that first detects if it was an ugly thing, then the analysers look at it . . .'

'And have you received any videos like that?'

'Lots. Last month a driver hit a pedestrian, and when we looked at the video, we saw the driver bend down and take his cellphone out to make a call. *Then* he hit the pedestrian. We fired his *gat*, in twenty-four hours, because what could he say? There was the evidence. In Technicolor.'

Insight: 'That's why the drivers went on strike.'

'Right. The union said it was unconstitutional, invasion of privacy. But the fact of the matter is, it actually protects them. Because there are a lot of accidents when those cunts with their expensive German cars cut in front of the bus, that class of thing, because everybody hates a bus, never mind that it's taking the poor people to work, the fat cats don't think that way. Anyway, we use the videos for training, your drivers get better and better. And the big thing is, collision damage is down sixty per cent, my bro', sixty per cent! And traffic fines also. You don't just save money, you save time, you've sixty per cent less grief too, that's the thing. And you can reward the drivers who have a clean record, because there's more money for a pay rise.'

'So Danie got the videos every afternoon?' A possible source for the 400,000 rand stirred in the back of his head.

'He checked them in the afternoon, but they come in the morning already. Tonight the server sends it to America, tomorrow eleven o'clock when Danie clocks in at his PC, the emails are waiting for him. If there was big shit, Mr Eckhardt would have phoned me already, and I would have phoned Danie next, so the stuff he checked in the afternoon was run-of-the-mill stuff, stuff that he would have to take up with his drivers. You know, careless driving, doing stupid things. That's the stuff he would talk through with his drivers in the afternoon.'

'It's a lot of power to have . . .'

'I'm not following you.'

'The videos. Danie Flint had the power every day to fire drivers. Because he had proof. Like you say. In Technicolor.'

'So?'

'How many drivers did he supervise?'

'About eighty.'

'And what does a bus driver earn?'

'Depending on the overtime, between four and six a month.'

'Six thousand?' while he did the calculations in his head.

'That's it.'

'Very well. Let's say Flint begins to say to the drivers, I've got the evidence, I'm going to fire you, but if you give me a thousand, I'll drop it.'

Philander thought about it, but soon shook his head. 'No, it wouldn't work.'

'Why not?'

'A thousand rand? A week's pay? Most of the drivers couldn't afford that, that guy would run to the union to complain so fast you would just see a blur.'

'Make it less. Five hundred. Two-fifty.'

'With all due respect, you're thinking about two-fifty with a Whitey brain. These are people with a wife and a bunch of kids, payments on the house and the car, school fees . . .'

'But if you lose your job, you have nothing.'

Still the head shake. 'Let's do the sums. Maybe three or four serious incidents a week. At two-fifty a pop, you're getting a thousand rand a month with your extortion. Now it would take you . . . about 400 months to get to 400,000 rand. Let's double the income, then it's 200 months . . .'

His theory collapsed. 'That's true.'

'I'm telling you, that money isn't coming from ABC. There's no way.'

Joubert wasn't ready to give up, he grasped at a straw. 'May I look at his material? The actual videos?'

Philander looked sceptical. 'That's union trouble. Confidential stuff. I'll have to phone Mr Eckhardt . . .'

'I'd appreciate that very much.'

'Are we finished now?'

'We're finished now.'

He knew he would have to return to the office some time or other, but he hoped Philander would soon get permission for him to go through the DRMP statistics, so that he had an excuse.

He walked to Long Street, went and stood in front of the science fiction shelves at Clarke's, but found nothing he wanted to read. Fantasy was all the rage these days, and he had tried it, but to no avail.

Inspector Fizile Butshingi phoned him after eleven. 'Nothing that will help us. I've checked everything. Cash-in-transit heists are the only possibilities. And they don't fit.'

Joubert thanked him.

'Anything new on your side?' Butshingi asked.

'Not really. I'll let you know.' And then a light went on and he said quickly before the detective rang off: 'Inspector, could you tell me, were there any in-transit robberies in the area north of the N1?' Reconsidered, made the area larger: 'And west of the N7. Or on the N7. Montagu Gardens, Milnerton, Richwood, all the way up to Atlantis . . .'

'Why there?'

'That's where Flint's bus routes ran.'

'It's a stretch,' said Butshingi.

Maybe not. But Joubert just said: 'I want to cover all the bases.'

'I'll get back to you.'

Seven minutes, and his cellphone rang again. It looked like Bessie Heese's number. He answered.

'Mr Joubert, my name is Francois Eckhardt. I am the Managing Director of ABC. Do you have a moment?'

'Of course.'

'Mr Joubert, you will excuse me, but I'm going to be frank with you. Up to now we have done everything in our power to accommodate you. For the sake of Mrs Flint. But I am at the point now where I must begin putting the interests of the company, and all its other employees, first. Especially when it comes to the DRMP records, I have to protect the confidentiality of the bus drivers' performance information, and be very careful not to violate our agreement with the union. We can't afford another strike. I hope you understand . . .'

'I understand,' he said, but his heart sank.

'We can grant you access to the system, but you will have to sign a confidentiality agreement with the company. No records may leave our premises, no information may be made public. Unless you have my written permission. And now I must say that I think you will be wasting your time, that system misses nothing – but if you identify any indication of misconduct by ABC employees, however insignificant, you must immediately and personally bring it to my notice. I will make my cellphone number available to you.'

He weighed up the implications. 'Even if I sign it . . . If there is evidence of a crime, we will have to hand it over to the police. That's the law.'

'Mr Joubert, all crimes that have been demonstrated by the system have already been communicated to the police. That is not a factor. Are you prepared to sign?'

He wondered if it was worth the trouble, aware that he was desperate. Perhaps he was holding too tightly onto his theory that the money and Flint's job were somehow connected. But he owed it to Tanya to be thorough, to follow the statistics and a vague notion to the bitter end.

'I am.'

Before he reached the ABC depot, Butshingi let him know there was one in-transit robbery in the broader Flint area. 'But does Century City count?'

'I'm not sure. Do you have details?'

'Nineteen September, ten o'clock in the morning, on Century Boulevard . . .'

Joubert felt the small injection of adrenaline. It fitted his timeline perfectly.

'. . . between Waterford and Waterhouse Boulevards. Seven men, two vehicles. More than 800,000 in cash taken. The transit driver was killed.'

'Thanks, Inspector. I will see if I can find anything.'

'But how can Flint be associated? It was a black gang.'

'I don't know. But I have nothing else.'

'OK.'

He signed the faxed confidentiality document in Philander's office. And went to sit with him at Danie Flint's computer.

'I'll show you how to run the DRMP system. But please, I only have fifteen minutes.'

'Thank you very much. Can I ask you: was Century City part of Danie's routes?'

'Absolutely. Why?'

Joubert had to hide his new optimism. 'I just want the complete picture . . .'

They got Flint's computer going, opened the DRMP program. Philander explained the basic principles. 'All the videos are on the server. They are cross-linked with the route, the bus, the driver, and the action taken. You can view it according to the bus, the driver, the route, or according to the date and time. With this menu you can sort, if you only want the videos where there was further action.'

'What "further action"?'

'Disciplinary, accident reports, third party claims, legal action. Take your pick. You can watch the forward view and the backward view at the same time, or you can select here to see only one of the two . . .'

'Can we begin at the nineteenth of September?'

'That's easy. Here's your calendar, so you choose the month here, then this window opens up. Now click on the nineteen, and there's your list. Four videos. You can refine your search with this menu, if you just want to check a certain driver or route.'

'Which route is Century City on?'

'I don't know Danie's codes off by heart, let me see . . .'

It took him a while to get the information and apply it. 'There are no videos on the nineteenth of September for that route.'

'Can I see the four videos for that date?'

'You just click on the icon every time . . . the video will play automatically . . .'

They watched the videos together. Fifteen seconds of forward and backward view, the images side by side. Philander turned the sound down, so they wouldn't bother the other route managers in the office.

Not one of the four videos had anything to do with a cash-in-transit robbery.

Philander noticed Joubert's disappointment. 'What did you hope to find?'

'I haven't the faintest idea.' But he would have to do the footwork. Or in this case, the finger work. Until he ran out of options.

102

Alone in front of the computer he struggled so much that he forgot about his sandwiches. The system was complicated, with so many choices to activate. It was some time before he realised he had activated the option for disciplinary hearings, and was only seeing videos relevant to that. He had to go back, to his initial limit of 1 August, and watch them all again.

It was twenty to three when hunger overcame him and he went in search of tea. Santasha showed him where the kitchen was, asked if he was making progress.

'No,' he said.

The sandwiches were *bobotie* and chutney, and a packet of cashew nuts, with a note from Margaret pinned to it. 'Nuts about you.'

He smiled, ate with gusto, drank his tea while he scanned every video, concentrating on the forward view from the bus. A small percentage were serious accidents, where pedestrians or other vehicles were involved. The majority were insignificant, bus drivers braking sharply and too late for traffic, cyclists, cattle or sheep on the N7 at Du Noon, or dogs in the residential areas.

August produced nothing.

September gave the same result. His eyes grew weary. His concentration lapsed. He began to suspect his search was fruitless.

He nearly missed it.

The twenty-ninth of September. Time stamp of 11.48. Open road, no buildings, just veld. Too narrow a following distance between the front of the bus and a black Mercedes sedan, looked like an E-series. The car braked suddenly and inexplicably, the bus bumped the rear, the boot sprang open. Another ten seconds where the bus and Mercedes pulled off the road, nearly came to a stop.

He clicked to end the video, just another one, useless. Somewhere in the back of his mind there was an exclamation mark.

He started the next video, but his subconscious said, go back to the previous one, there was something. Watch it again.

A moment of indecision. Just another minor accident.

No, there had been something.

So he sighed, shut down the new video, clicked back to the previous one.

What was that in the boot?

His brain recalled the image. He suspected he was imagining it.

He clicked again, it played, he watched intently.

The boot jumped open. There. Inside. A hand. Fleeting, in the strip of sunlight that shone in on that single moment when the boot was fully open, just before it came down again, then it was gone, the gap between the Mercedes and the bus widened, the lid of the boot swung down again. He didn't know how to freeze the image, looked anxiously at the screen, but the video had already stopped.

He clicked on it again, quickly studied the icons, experimented with a few of them. Found the one that froze the image, but he was too late. Joubert grunted with annoyance. He began again, the mouse pointer poised, ready, waited for the moment. Stopped the video at exactly the right time.

No doubt about it. A hand. Lifeless. A delicate white hand resting on a torso. In the boot.

There were three figures in the Mercedes, two in the front seat, one at the back. All men. The one in the back seat turning his head after the jolt of the collision. Massive shoulders, a peculiar face, twisted, as though there was no nose. Maybe it was just the resolution of the video.

Joubert looked carefully, he could see the series number of the car. E 350. The registration number was much easier to read.

He looked at the rear-facing video image. The bus driver, the empty seats looking forlorn behind him, his body jerking at the impact. 'Fuck,' the driver said, the word clearly audible. Then a hand gesture of frustration, rage. He turned the steering wheel to pull off the road. 'Fucking cunt.'

Back to the forward view, freezing it again on the moment when the boot was open wide.

A hand. A person, inside. Dead still.

He stared at the image, his brain racing.

Had Danie Flint seen that?

Had it anything to do with his disappearance?

A person in the boot of the car. And something about the way the hand lay, how it responded to the jolt of the collision, told him it was unconscious. Or dead.

Should he search for more, up to about 15 October?

And how would he handle it? It was powerful evidence of a crime. Abduction at the very least. He would have to call the SAPS, after he had phoned Eckhardt.

But he wanted to retain control.

Don't be hasty. Take it step by step. He reached for his writing pad, clicked on the screen. He wrote down the date and time. Looked for a reference to the exact spot it had occurred, found only the bus and route number. He wrote down the bus driver's name. Jerome Apollis. Then the details of the Mercedes. Zipped his notebook closed, so no one could see the notes. His insurance policy.

He took out his cellphone and called the Operational Manager of ABC. 'I think you had better have a look at this.'

Eckhardt was in his forties, fashionable glasses, tall, lean, professional. He wore the sort of tasteful suit, shirt and tie combination that made Joubert sigh over his own non-existent sense of style. The Operational Manager stood with Philander, and they both watched the video before he said: 'Neville, see if you can get hold of Apollis. As quickly as possible. If he's on duty, get a relief driver.' Then he turned to Joubert, 'Let's get the police involved.'

'There's an inspector in Milnerton I'm working with . . .'

'Call him.'

'I'm going to give him the registration number of the Mercedes in the meantime.'

'Do what you think is necessary. You have our full cooperation.'

Joubert called Fizile Butshingi. 'I think I've found something . . .'

'What?' Sharp and serious.

'Evidence of a serious crime. Could be kidnapping, could be worse . . .'

'Ay, ay. Where are you?'

Joubert gave him the address of the ABC depot. 'There's a vehicle involved, and we will need the name and address of the owner. If you could run it in the meantime.'

'Give it to me.'

His euphoria was tempered with disappointment, because he knew what to expect.

This was the other big difference between private investigator and policeman, he thought while he waited. You had to come to terms with the fact that sooner or later you had to hand over control.

There had been a moment, a minute ago, when he had considered another course. The option to keep quiet – make an electronic copy of the video, use Jack's contacts to find out who the Mercedes belonged to, follow it up . . .

But that implied that he would have to be dishonest, break the ABC agreement, break the law, because here was clear evidence of a crime. And he couldn't do all that.

Now Butshingi was going to take it and run with it. He seemed like a good detective. As long as it shone light on Danie Flint's fate, it didn't matter.

He sighed.

At eight minutes past four his phone rang. Mildred, receptionist at Jack Fischer and Associates: 'Mr Fischer would like to know if you are coming back to the office today?'

'I don't know.'

'Please hold on.'

She put him on hold, elevator music tinkling in the background. Then Jack was on the phone, his voice jovial. 'Mat, looks like you're hot on the trail?' As though nothing had happened last night.

'I am, Jack. There's good progress . . .'

'Excellent, excellent, happy to hear that. Mat, Fanie and I have been talking this morning. We discussed the whole thing. From all angles. Financial. Human aspect, that's important to us, Mat. Very important. We would like to meet Mrs Vlok halfway . . .'

Joubert choked back the impulse to correct Fischer.

'. . . so we thought, we'll give her one day free. Under the circumstances. Right thing to do. In this particular instance.'

'Thanks, Jack. If all goes well, it may not be necessary. But thank you.'

'Excellent, excellent. I thought I would let you know . . .'

Inspector Fizile Butshingi's face was sombre when he arrived. 'This is a big thing, Sup. A very big thing.'

'Why?'

'Show me what you have.'

Joubert invited him to take a seat, then played the video, froze it, pointed at the hand in the boot.

'*Hau*,' said the Inspector. 'This is bad.'

'Who does the car belong to?'

'That's the big trouble. First, I went on the Natis system, it told me the Mercedes belongs to a Terrence Richard Baadjies, vehicle registration is a residential address in Rosebank. So I thought, let's see who this man is. And I put him through the database. And I found a bad man, Sup. Terrence Richard Baadjies, aka Terry, aka Terror, aka The Terrorist. Juvenile delinquent when he was fifteen years old, sentenced to a facility for stabbing and killing another child at school. Released after three years, then followed sixteen cases, seven charges of murder, but only five convictions, three for dealing drugs, one assault with intent, one for manslaughter while he was in Pollsmoor. Did fourteen years.'

'Gang member,' said Joubert.

'Not just any gang member. He's number two of the Restless Ravens.'

'*Bliksem*,' said Mat Joubert, because that changed everything.

'Yes.'

It took him a while to appreciate the possibilities fully. 'We will have to call Superintendent Johnny October.' The Cape Flats were October's turf. But far more important was the fact that Johnny was his good friend. Johnny wouldn't cut him out.

103

Superintendent Johnny October, with his tall, sinewy body, short grey hair, the narrow moustache that he had trimmed the same way for thirty years, one of the few Cape detectives who still wore a suit to work every day, always in a shade of brown. He was the most decent person that Joubert knew, soft of heart, soft of speech. Too modest for his own good at times. His courtesy, even towards criminals, was unshakeable.

'*Jinne*,' said October, once he had seen the video, since he never swore.

'*Umdali*,' said Butshingi. 'Very bad.'

'Can you see whether it is Terror?' Joubert asked.

'It could be him, Sup, in front beside the driver. But this is the one we must concentrate on,' said October, and pointed at the broad figure on the back seat of the Mercedes. The one with the deformed nose.

'Why?' Butshingi asked.

'It's KD Snyders . . .'

Butshingi made notes and asked: 'How do you spell Kaydee?'

'KD It's an abbreviation. For Knuckle Duster. That's his thing. His real name is Willem, but they call him KD. To his face, and "King Kong" behind his back. Because of his nose, and his size. He's a tragic figure. Comes from the Sabie Street courts, in Manenberg, very bad circumstances. And then a dog attacked him when he was eleven, one of those pit bulls at the Friday night dog fights. KD sneaked in the back past the dog pens, they say, and this mad animal grabbed him by the face, and by the time they pulled the dog off, it was very bad. The doctors' work didn't take so well, the wounds began to fester, most likely because the parents didn't do a good job of the treatment and things. Drink, Sup, the evils of drink. There's not much mercy to be had in Manenberg. The children mocked him. And KD only knew one answer to that. Violence. They say around fourteen he once wound a bicycle chain around his fist, that's when the knuckles began. Of course, when he began to gain a reputation and grow big, the Ravens saw his value. Terror Baadjies was the one who initiated KD. From then on they've been like this,' and Johnny October crossed his index and middle finger. 'He's Terror's bodyguard and hit man.'

'*Yoh-Yoh*,' said Inspector Butshingi.

'But the main reason we must concentrate on him is that right now KD is in Pollsmoor. Awaiting trial. For assault with intent, and attempted murder. And this time we have a witness. It's not going well with KD, he's in solitary. Barely a day in chookie and they tried to stab him. There's a war on between the two factions of the Ravens, now that Tweetybird has left the country. It's a power struggle . . .'

'Wait, wait,' said Butshingi, and looked up from his notes, worried. 'Tweetybird is the gang boss?'

'Was. He's gone.'

'Where did he go to?'

'The grapevine says he's in South America. And now there's a power vacuum, and it's Terror Baadjies against Moegamat Perkins for the crown. War. Four months now, and there's still no winner, and we can't keep up . . .'

'And KD Snyders is inside because of this war?'

'Yes. We have him for attempted murder. And if he stays in Pollsmoor, Moegamat Perkins's men will kill him. So we have a bit of room to negotiate.'

Mat Joubert thought. About Danie Flint and Cape Flats gangs. A very strange combination.

How did it all fit together?

Johnny October asked, 'Sup, how did you get this far?'

Joubert gave him the whole story. In detail.

Jerome Apollis, the bus driver, was forty-three years old. He had fat cheeks and a beer belly, and he was frightened. The proximity of the detectives, the looming presence of Mat Joubert, and the serious circumstances made him look with great anxiety from Bessie Heese to Butshingi, October and eventually at Joubert, where his gaze stayed fixed.

They sat in Neville Philander's office, the room too small for comfort. 'Don't worry,' said Bessie Heese. She looked just as professional as the previous day. And fresh, though it was nearly six o'clock. 'The police just want to ask you what you can remember about the twenty-ninth of September,' and she pointed at Philander's computer, where they had shown him the video. Without freezing the image.

'I remember well.'

'Can you tell us about it?' Johnny October asked, his voice respectful and caring. 'It would be a big help to us.'

Apollis licked his lips repeatedly, lifted his hands in innocence. 'Mr Flint said it was not an issue. When he saw the video. He said it wasn't my fault.'

'I understand,' said October. 'We're not saying it was your fault. But we really want to know what happened that day.'

'And where,' said Joubert.

Apollis just stared at him.

'Mr Apollis . . .' October urged.

Apollis dragged his eyes from Joubert, focused on Bessie Heese, a safe haven. 'It was between Atlantis and the R27. Just after the turn-off.' He wiped perspiration from his brow.

'Which turn-off?'

'The road to the shooting range. There was a sign, but it's gone now a long time.'

'In which direction were you driving?' Joubert asked.

'Towards the sea. To the R27.' And then he stopped.

'Go on, Jerome.'

'The Mercedes. They were driving slowly. I wanted to pass. I had my flicker on already. That's why I was so close. I had to wait for the oncoming traffic. Then they stopped suddenly. For nothing. So I bumped him. At the back. On the boot. Behind. We both stopped. I got out, and they . . .'

'Did you see anything strange?' asked October.

'No, sir,' he answered, a little bewildered.

'Then you got out.'

'We all got out. Then the one who had been sitting in front . . . No, the one with the nose, who had been sitting in the back, he came towards me. Then the other one said no, wait, wait, wait. Then they first looked at the damage. I told them, right then. I said, you just stopped, for no reason. The one man said, don't worry, it wasn't my fault, everything was fine. So I said no, I have to make a report. Then he looked at the bus and said no, there's no damage to the bus, and they wouldn't make a fuss, don't worry . . .'

'Where were they standing? Where did each of you stand while this conversation was going on?' asked Butshingi, head down, writing frantically.

'We stood between the car and the bus.'

'Did any one of them touch the boot?'

'It was four months ago,' said Apollis.

'Jerome, if you can't remember, we won't blame you,' said Bessie Heese, soothingly.

'I . . . I think . . . the big one with the face. Maybe he stood with his hand on the boot like this.'

'And then?'

'Then they said I must go. I said no, I have to get names and telephone numbers, because Mr Flint will want a report. Then that one got sort of angry, and he said . . .'

'Which one?'

'The one sitting in front.'

'Which side in front?'

'Passenger side.'

'And he said . . . ?'

'He said, I better not mess around, he said he would fix it, but I better go then. Then I said no, they don't understand, it's not that easy with the DRMP. Then he got angry, he threatened me, he would tell the big one to hit me *moer toe*, get in my effing bus, sorry madam, but he said eff off. Now. So I got in the bus and as I drove away, I phoned Mr Flint and told him the whole story. He said, Jerome, don't worry, if they don't want to make a case and there's nothing wrong with the bus, I know your record is clean. Then, the next afternoon, when I was finished, Mr Flint came to me and said he had watched the video, and he could see what happened, my record would stay clean. And that's the whole story, madam, on my word of honour.'

'I know, Jerome. You have nothing to worry about.'

'But then why are all the police here, madam?'

104

While Johnny October phoned Pollsmoor to arrange for them to question KD Snyders, Joubert considered what the involvement of the Restless Ravens meant. It was they who had broken into Tanya Flint's business premises.

The danger was greater than he had suspected.

He asked Inspector Fizile Butshingi if the SAPS could send a police patrol vehicle to Tanya's house in Parklands. 'If they could just park down the street,' he added, not wanting to upset her more than she was already.

Butshingi was quick on the uptake. 'Good idea.'

Then Joubert called Margaret.

'I'm going to be late.'

'Is that good news?'

'Looks like it.'

'I'll wait up. Be careful.' A policeman's wife.

He debated over whether to phone Tanya as well, but decided against it. There were still too many questions, too many uncertainties.

They drove in Johnny's car to the prison at the other end of Tokai. Joubert sat in the back.

'Sup, the bus driver . . .' Johnny said. 'The law clearly says, it's always the fault of the one driving behind. He was too close to the Mercedes.'

'Flint must have seen that clearly on the video, Johnny.'

'And he ignored the offence. Because he saw the hand in the boot. And the opportunity.'

'And from then on it was easy. Track down Terror Baadjies with the registration number of the Mercedes. Phone the home number with your new cellphone, so they can't trace you.'

'Blackmail,' said Butshingi.

'But would Flint have known who he was dealing with?'

Joubert shook his head. 'I doubt it. I think he saw the expensive car, that Mercedes costs around 700,000 rand . . .'

'And said, pay up or I'll give the video to the police.'

'Something like that. The Ravens tracked Flint down, Johnny, he slipped up somewhere. But what bothers me is why the break-in at Tanya's workshop was so . . . half-hearted. A few tables overturned, a weak message on the wall . . . You would expect more from a gang from the Cape Flats.'

'You must see it in context, Sup. The faction war. KD Snyders, the hit man, is sitting in jail, Terror Baadjies needs all his troops, so he sends two or three foot soldiers, inexperienced, a little scared.'

'What I can't understand,' said Butshingi. 'These guys . . . I mean, why did they pay at all?'

'What do you mean?'

'The video. It doesn't prove much. I mean, let's say Flint called Terror Baadjies, and tried to blackmail him. So Terror torches the Benz. Or he has it chemically cleaned, or steam-cleaned, or whatever. He makes sure there's no forensic evidence in the boot, and he cooks up a story, should the police come asking questions. He can say, no, it was my niece, she drank too much, so we put her in the boot, didn't want her to throw up on my nice upholstery. And he gets his niece to corroborate . . .'

Joubert and October said nothing, because they knew the point was valid. An awkward one.

'Is he clever enough, this Terror Baadjies?' asked Butshingi.

'He is,' said October. 'Definitely.'

'So why did they pay? Twice?'

Willem 'KD' Snyders, heavily shackled hand and foot, didn't say a word. Just sat there at the steel table, staring at the wall.

Johnny October talked politely to him. Sketched his position in detail. Said he wouldn't survive in jail, Moegamat Perkins' Ravens faction would get him. The second he was transferred out of solitary back to the general prison. Only a question of time.

'You are a dead man walking,' said Butshingi.

'We can help you,' said October.

No response. The face, so terribly damaged, remained expressionless. The scar tissue deformed the lips in a permanent grimace as though he scorned the whole world.

'Right now someone is sharpening a *shiv* just for you, King Kong,' Butshingi began to play his pre-planned role.

'No, we can hide you. Witness programme. Protection. A new life, Willem. A new beginning. With a bit of help, a few thousand rand in your pocket. Anywhere in the country, just where you want.'

But all that, they knew, was just the prelude, to get his attention.

'Just think. Never to have to look over your shoulder again. Never.'

KD Snyders sat as if made of stone.

'You're wasting your time, Johnny,' said Butshingi.

'Maybe not. Maybe Willem can see the opportunity.'

'Judge is going to put you away for a long time, Mr Kong. Murderer like you.'

'Slow down, partner, we can help him.'

'Maybe he doesn't want to be helped. Maybe he's ugly *and* stupid.'

'I know you're not afraid of anything, Willem. I know. But just think a moment about the alternatives. Think for a moment what it *could* be like . . .'

And so they played the game, one of them his friend, offering the olive branch of peace and understanding, the other his enemy, cursing and insulting him. Snyders said nothing, did nothing. He didn't react, wouldn't look at them, even when Butshingi held his face only centimetres from the twisted mask, and screamed in rage. Willem 'KD' Snyders was a statue, and Joubert sat silently watching, wondering if their plan would work.

Eventually, Johnny October said, no, Fizile, enough. Leave us. Both of you, whiteys and darkies don't understand what it means to be a coloured. I will talk to Willem.

Butshingi and Joubert pretended to get up reluctantly, and walked out.

In the next room they watched through the one-way mirror. They saw how October sat down beside Snyders, his expression one of compassion, his hands clasped together on the table in empathy and sympathy. Then he began to play his trump card.

'Willem, I come from Bishop Lavis. I know what it's like. I know the hardship and I know the pain. I know, yours was much greater, with the accident. I can't even begin to think how hard it was for you. And I can't blame you, I'm telling you now, no one can blame you. You've been through hell. And as life goes on, it just gets worse . . .'

'He's good,' said Butshingi.

'Yes,' said Joubert.

'Willem, I know, somewhere there inside you there is still that child. Somewhere in there is someone who asks, why couldn't it be different? Why couldn't I have a good life. A normal life. Now, Willem, I'm telling you, you can. If you help us tonight, I will get the government to pay the medical expenses. We'll take you to the best place in the country, doctors who can fix anything. And we will give you your life back, Willem. Your life back.'

Johnny October let that sink in, before he said, 'A new face, Willem. New and handsome.'

KD Snyders didn't react immediately. It took him a while before he started to turn his head for the first time. Until he was looking right at October. The corners of his mouth moved, slowly, into a grin.

Then he spat in contempt, on October's hand.

105

They regrouped, sent for coffee, sat in the room next to the interview room, analysing their strategy. In the background the sounds of a prison at night, now and then the dull clang of a metal door slamming, a stern order over the loudspeaker, the voices of inmates, like night animals calling to each other in the dark.

Between the three of them, there was more than eight decades of law enforcement, and the shared knowledge that patience was the only way. Their most effective weapon was time.

'Blind loyalty,' said Butshingi.

October: 'That's the way they are. Unto death.'

'And he's not scared to die.'

'Sometimes I wonder if they want to die, my friend. Seems like they're looking for it.'

Joubert sat with his elbows on the table, head bent, working through the information.

'Johnny, what were they doing on that road. Near Atlantis?'

'That's the question, Sup.'

'Is that traditionally part of the Ravens' territory?'

'You know how it's been the past ten years, Sup. After PAGAD and POCA. The leaders live in the white areas, recruit members in the coloured townships. And sell *Tik* there. Tweetybird used to live in Rondebosch, Terror and Moegamat Perkins live in Rosebank, they never showed their faces at a place like Atlantis.'

'And yet he was there.'

'With someone in the boot of his car . . .'

'On his way back from Atlantis?'

'Maybe not. Maybe they were just looking for a place to get rid of the body. Far away from where they live. Or maybe they were going to shoot someone. At a place where gunshots wouldn't attract attention.'

'Which shooting range are we talking about?' asked Joubert.

'The army has a shooting range out there,' said October. 'It's massive. They might have been looking for it, turned back. The bus driver said the sign board isn't there any more.'

'And that's a sandy area,' said Joubert. 'Easy to dig a hole. Quick.'

'Could be, Sup. But it's just as easy anywhere on the Flats. Sand everywhere . . .'

'So they go looking for a place far from the traditional hunting grounds to dispose of a body. Terror Baadjies, his strongman, KD Snyders, and a driver. They don't know the area very well, want to turn off somewhere away from the main road . . .'

'That's why they were driving so slowly. All three were looking out for a spot, they didn't realise the bus was on their tail. They missed the shooting range turn-off. Someone says "we should have turned off there". The driver hits the brakes.'

'Bang! The bus rams into them.'

'They get rid of the bus, go on and do their thing.'

A long silence while they pondered.

Joubert scratched his head: 'Twenty-ninth of September. Flint only opened his bank account on the fifteenth of October. Let's say he took a week or two to get hold of Terror's phone number, and to call him personally. "I've got you on video, out at Atlantis. I know what you were doing." Lies a bit, but vaguely, just enough to let Terror know the evidence is damning.'

'And they pay up.'

'But not straight away. They take their time. Nearly a week.'

'While they try to find him?'

'But why did they pay?' Johnny October asked. 'Like Fizile said, get rid of the forensic evidence in the Mercedes, make up a story. Then you don't have to worry about the police . . .'

Silence, more thinking.

Butshingi wiped his hand over his face. Then raised it slowly. 'Maybe . . .'

The other two looked at him.

'Maybe,' Butshingi repeated, 'that's it. Maybe they were not worried about the police.'

'What do you mean, my friend?' October asked.

'When did this faction fight start?'

October rubbed his moustache. 'Our intelligence says it began last year in August already, late August. That's when *Die Burger* wrote about the plans of the Democratic Alliance to appoint a special prosecutor to try and get Tweetybird de la Cruz on tax evasion charges. That's just about the only thing they *can* prove. Then Tweetybird sent for The Accountant, Moegamat Perkins, and Perkins said this is trouble, because the Tax Man is a bulldog, where he bites, he won't let go. No matter how they cooked the books, Revenue Services would clearly see there was something fishy.'

'So that's when it started?'

'The story goes, that's when they decided Tweetybird should leave the country. And Terror Baadjies blamed Perkins, because he's the one who does the books. Tweetybird tried to keep the peace, but if your people know you're soon leaving for Uruguay, you don't have much authority. Why do you ask?'

'Terror Baadjies. If he wasn't worried about the police, if he could cover up. Why did he pay? Maybe because he was worried about his own people finding out.'

'Aah,' said Johnny October.

'I'm not sure I understand,' said Joubert.

'Sup, where's that timeline of yours?' October was suddenly invigorated, Butshingi shifted closer.

Joubert opened his notebook and thumbed through to the right place.

'We focus on everything *after* the incident with the bus. We think this thing began on the twenty-ninth of September,' said October. 'But Terror Baadjies already knew at the end of August that trouble was brewing. There would be an opportunity to become leader of the Ravens.'

'Yes,' said Butshingi. 'So he started planning his coup.'

'And that's what Fizile is talking about, Sup. Terror and KD Snyders and the Mercedes. We've been thinking all along they were busy with their usual crime on the twenty-ninth of September. But maybe they were busy with the coup. Maybe the one in the boot was a Raven, a member of the rival faction . . .'

A light went on in Joubert's head. 'That's why they drove all the way to Atlantis. To get out of the Ravens' territory.'

'Exactly,' said Butshingi.

'And that's why they paid Flint. Not because they were afraid of the police finding out . . .'

'But because they feared some of their own people would find out. Maybe the other lieutenant . . . the money man . . .'

'Moegamat Perkins.'

'That's right.'

'Or Tweetybird himself,' said Johnny October. 'If Tweetybird found out before he left the country that Terror Baadjies was planning to usurp his throne, he would have had Terror shot so fast . . .'

'Because they expect blind loyalty.'

Joubert, with suddenly insight, pressed his finger on the table. 'That is what we must use, Johnny.'

'Sup?'

'KD's loyalty. We have to turn it around.'

'Now I'm not with you.'

'What would happen if the Ravens found out that a month or so before Tweetybird fled, Terror had been murdering his own gang members in order to seize power?'

'His own faction would turn against him.'

'Exactly. And that's the secret KD has to keep. Terror brought KD into the Ravens. Initiated him . . .'

'That's right, Sup. Terror is like a father to KD.'

'Exactly, Johnny. KD won't talk because he is loyal to the death to *Terror*.'

'Absolutely.'

'That's what we have to use. The one thing that KD is afraid of, is rejection of his Ravens father.'

'Aah . . .' said Johnny October.

'Devious,' said Fizile Butshingi. 'I like it already.'

Joubert sat right next to KD Snyders, October and Butshingi opposite them.

He leaned in close, so that his face was only centimetres from Snyders. He bluffed in a big way. He said: 'We know everything, KD. Everything that happened over there at Atlantis. We know how Terror stabbed the Ravens in the back, we know what's lying under the sand.' He listened very carefully to Snyders' breathing, he knew the disfigured face would reveal nothing.

He heard the man's breath stop for one second, as though his heart skipped a beat.

That gave him courage.

'We know about Flint and the video. We know how you got rid of him. We don't know where you put him, yet, but we'll get there. KD, your problem is that only we three know who betrayed you. No one else. But I tell you what we're going to do: we're going to get up from here and tell the warders you sang. You sold out. You gave Terror to us, you handed us his head on a platter. Superintendent Johnny October is going to broadcast that all over the Cape Flats, that it was you who helped us get Terror. You betrayed your own blood, and Terror betrayed the Ravens . . .'

He stopped and listened. The breathing was shallow now. Rapid.

'You stabbed Terror in the back. That's what he will believe. And he can forget about becoming the new boss . . .'

The chains joining the hand and foot shackles trembled slightly, tap-tapping against the metal edge of the steel table.

'Then you will have nothing, KD. Nothing and nobody.'

At last, the face twisted. Then KD Snyders lunged at Mat Joubert with a bellow of rage and despair erupting from the depths of his great body.

Joubert jerked back, out of reach. But he knew. They *had* him.

Johnny October waited for KD to calm down. Then he said, with his unshakeable courtesy. 'There's a way out KD. Terror doesn't ever have to know. But you have to help us.'

106

In his hoarse voice and with the speech defect that prevented the deformed lips from forming plosives, KD Snyders reluctantly answered a few questions. Curtly, with the fewest words possible, his eyes glistening with hatred and fury, his hands trembling slightly.

Johnny October asked him: 'Who was the one driving the Mercedes when the bus bumped into you?'

'Mannas Vinck.'

'Terror's chauffeur.'

KD nodded.

'Now you must tell us where we have to dig, KD.'

Snyders looked away.

'You have one chance, KD.'

'Montagu's Gift. In Philippi.'

'The farms? Next to Mitchell's Plain?'

He received only a nod as answer.

'Where on the farm?'

'Next to the Olieboom dune. On the Morgenster side.'

October nodded, as though he knew where it was. 'And the body you buried near Atlantis?'

'At the gate of the shooting range. In the corner. Behind the 900-metre.'

'The 900-metre?'

Another nod.

'What does that mean?'

Snyders signalled the limit of his betrayal with a shake of the head. He would answer no more.

'Who's buried there, KD? At the shooting range?'

Silence.

'What happened? How did you kill Flint?'

The gangster turned his face away, stared at the wall.

'Who left his car at Virgin Active?'

Nothing.

Until October said: 'I'll keep my side of the bargain, KD. But if you're lying to us . . .'

They stood up then. October phoned his station, told them to get manpower, there was digging to be done. Mat Joubert phoned his wife and told her not to stay up for him.

It was going to be a long night.

The first place they looked was on the farm in Philippi. They woke up the farmer, drove in convoy to the spot where October showed them to dig.

Past two in the morning, in the lights of the SAPS patrol cars and the Forensics minibus, spooky shadows of police dogs barking, wagging their tails, sniffing and searching, the spades of the constables rising and falling. The houses of Westridge and Woodlands were only two kilometres away, Mitchells Plain was asleep. A dairy cow mooed in the distance.

The cry came at seven minutes past three. Everyone put down their tools, and gathered at the spot. Torches and searchlights, while two men uncovered the bundle in the sand. A corpse, wrapped in what was once a black bedspread with a faded orange floral pattern.

There was enough of the remains for Joubert to look at the face with the bullet hole between the eyes and say, 'That's him. That's Danie Flint.'

Underneath the cocoon, a firearm. Johnny October had it carefully stowed in a plastic evidence bag.

Joubert knew he should phone Tanya Flint. She had the right to know. But he allowed her a few more hours of sleep before turning her life upside down one more time.

The search near Atlantis only began at a quarter past five, as the eastern horizon changed colour and the south-easter picked up, a bleak wind gusting small plumes of sand off the shovels.

'The gate' in KD Snyders' minimalistic description was the main gate of the South African National Defence Force's Good Hope shooting range, permanently wide open, the only deterrent yellow warning signs with *Ongemagtige toegang verbode, No unauthorised entry*.

And just inside the gate, on the left, the place where marksmen at 900 metres could fire at targets far to the right. It was a platform of concrete blocks, sand and gravel as high as Joubert's head. It stretched for easily twenty paces, and behind it, the 'corner' in KD's description, where two boundary fences and the platform made a triangle. A hundred and fifty square metres of grass-covered sand. It was a good place to bury a body, for when the SADF was not there, one person could easily keep an eye on the single access road, while two more prepared the soft sand out of sight behind the high platform.

The uniforms from Atlantis and Table View, under direction of Thick and Thin, the Laurel and Hardy duo of Forensics, began to dig carefully at the northern boundary.

Six o'clock came and went without success.

At half past six, Joubert could postpone the phone call no longer.

He went and sat in his car to get out of the wind, and phoned.

She answered quickly, as though she had been up for ages.

'Tanya, it's not good news.'

The sound she made told him that, despite everything, she had still hoped.

'I'm so sorry,' said Joubert, and he knew it was inadequate.

'How did he die?'

'He was shot.'

There was silence over the phone. Eventually she asked: 'Who did it?'

He played for time, said they didn't know enough yet, but before the day was over they should have the full picture.

'I want to know,' she said.

At ten past six they found the first body.

It was a shallow grave, in the middle of the triangle, scarcely a metre below the fine sand.

Joubert knelt beside October and Butshingi, watching the forensics team in the soft morning light carefully scrape away the sand from the body with their hand-brooms and brushes. Others were busy widening the hole, taking buckets of sand away to pour carefully in a heap.

'A woman,' said October in surprise. Recognised by the sandals on her feet, the shape of her body. The grey-white sand clung to her. Forensics brushed it solemnly and carefully from her face. The features were unrecognisable, thanks to three bullet wounds. Only the long, black hair in a plait, undamaged.

'They didn't even cover her.'

A minute later a constable pulled the yellow bag out of the sand. October, wearing rubber gloves, opened it, found a woman's purse, and inside it, a driver's licence.

'Cornelia Johanna van Jaarsveld,' October read out quietly.

The surprise was the second body. It lay barely a metre from the woman, at the same depth, but with a black plastic bag wound tightly around his upper body. Only when forensics had cut it away, did October recognise him.

'*Jinne*,' he said, astounded. 'It's Tweetybird.'

Johnny October asked the SAPS Task Force to arrest Terrence Richard Baadjies and his chauffeur, Mannas Vinck, at Baadjies' house in Wynberg with a big show of force. And to bring them in in separate vehicles.

In the Wynberg Police Station, at nine minutes past eleven, they kept the two of them apart. An imperious Terror Baadjies in one of the cells, where every now and then he shouted: 'I have the right to an attorney, you fucking Nazi cunts,' and then grinned smugly.

They kept Vinck in the tea room, the only place they could question him.

'I'm just the driver,' he kept saying. He was short, fast-talking, punctuating his speech with animated hand gestures. The face under the yellowish-white Panama hat was deeply lined. Tattoos on the sinewy arms.

Butshingi and Joubert sat and listened. Quietly and politely, October sketched the situation. 'You're in trouble now, Mannas, you're in a really deep hole.'

'I'm just the driver.'

'You're an accomplice, Mannas, to three murders. We have a video that links you. You know, the one Danie Flint was using to blackmail Terror? You're in it, large as life.'

'I don't know Flint.'

'You helped to bury him, Mannas, down at Montagu's Gift. But that's not even your biggest problem. You helped to murder Tweetybird. You won't last an hour in Pollsmoor. And that's where I'm going to send you now.'

'I'm just the driver.' But the eyes were flitting back and forth now.

'I'm taking you to Pollsmoor, and I'm going to show the video to all the inmates, Mannas. In slow motion.'

'*Jirre.*' The hands were suddenly still.

'But we can help each other, Mannas.'

107

'It was a buy,' said Mannas Vinck. 'But the whole thing was a fuck-up from the start.'

He and Terror, KD Snyders and Tweetybird de la Cruz had driven out, past Atlantis, about ten kilometres beyond Mamre. It might have been the twenty-ninth of September, he couldn't remember. Terror and Tweetybird had argued over the 'partners', but they had deliberately never mentioned the partners' names, it was none of Vinck and KD's business.

What partners, asked Johnny October.

He didn't know, there were partners in the whole diamond deal, the Ravens were the middlemen, he was just the driver, he didn't want to know everything.

And then?

Then they went to do the buy, ten kilometres past Mamre, amongst the Port Jackson bushes. Buying *klippies* from a whitey bitch with a fucking gun in her hand and some fucking attitude, talking to The Bird like he was shit.

The words bubbled out of Vinck, a slippery stream. He said Tweetybird had a bag with four million rand, the bitch wanted to see it, holding the fucking notes up to the sun as though she would know what counterfeit looked like. Then she showed the stones, a shit-house full.

Then Terror hit her, right on the mouth with his fist. He took the gun away from her and he shot her between the fucking eyes and The Bird said what the fuck are you doing now and Terror turned around and shot The Bird in the heart with the bitch's gun, three shots, and he, Mannas, and KD Snyders stood there and they had no words, Terror had just shot Tweetybird, the fucking Boss of the Ravens. But then Terror said, don't look so fucking scared, load them in the fucking boot, what did you think was going to happen when *he* was sitting in Bolivia? Are we going to take orders from Moegamat Perkins? Is that what you want, from that cunt who got The Bird into *this* shit in the first place?

Then we loaded up and drove away, the bitch's car is probably still there, if the fucking thing hasn't been stolen a long time ago. And then the bus buggered into us, just past the shooting range.

Vinck said Terror first thought it was the bus driver who was blackmailing them.

Then they found out who it was, someone knew a *chlora* at ABC, Santasha Somebody, but when KD Snyders confronted the driver with his brass knuckles, they saw, it wasn't him, it was the fucking supervisor with the red Audi. Then Terror said they must handle this thing very carefully because if it came out that they had shot The Bird, it would be total war. And Mannas Vinck thought, what shit is this, *he* hadn't shot anyone, but what could he do? Then Terror said, pay the supervisor, we don't need the attention of a whitey murder. So Mannas had to take the plastic bag of money and put it in the shit-house tank of the Atlantic Sports Pub in Table View, like the whitey said.

But then it was a fuck-up when the whitey phoned and said he wanted more.

Then Terror paid again, but he knew, the whitey wasn't going to stop. So they tailed him, three weeks, and made their plans. So somewhere late October, KD Snyders hijacked the whitey in his red Audi at the stop street where Bramwell joined Railway Street in Woodstock. They dragged him out and put him in Terror's Mercedes. Vinck drove the Audi to Virgin Active in Table View himself. Then he wiped it clean and took four fucking taxis to get back to Rosebank.

Then they shot the whitey with the bitch's gun and buried him there beside the dune.

Mat Joubert sat in Tanya Flint's home, at the dining-room table. Fatigue weighed him down. He wanted to shower, eat, sleep, it was nearly three in the afternoon.

She came back from the kitchen with the coffee mugs on a tray, her movements slow and mechanical, put it down in front of him. Sat down opposite him, her hands on the table. Silent. There was weariness in her eyes, far greater than his.

And loss.

POSTSCRIPT

108

WOMAN'S BODY AT ATLANTIS:

Mystery over tracker deepens.

CAPE TOWN. – SAPS detectives are still baffled by the involvement of Cornelia Johanna van Jaarsveld (28), a professional tracker from Nelspruit, with crime gangs from the Cape Flats and an alleged illegal diamond transaction.

Van Jaarsveld's body was found last week beside that of the murdered gang boss Willem 'Tweetybird' de la Cruz in a shallow grave at the SADF shooting range near Atlantis.

Supt. Johnny October, leader of the investigation team, admitted to *Die Burger* that 'we are still looking for a great many pieces of the jigsaw puzzle' . . .

Die Burger, 19 February 2010

1 March 2010. Monday.

He hung his degree on the wall of his new office in the Centre Point building in Milnerton, the MA in Police Science that he had earned ten years earlier. He wondered if that wasn't bragging too much.

Then he took a step back. Margaret had made the place look really nice. An old, used red and blue Persian carpet, the antique desk she had sniffed out in a shop in Plumstead. Along with the stylish pair of mahogany and leather chairs for visitors.

On the desk was a laptop. Beside it lay his writing pad, bought at CNA. An Oregon pine bookshelf against the wall with his Police Science textbooks, and a photo of him, Margaret and the children.

And on the glass door, just:

Mat Joubert
Investigations

He shifted the framed certificate so that it hung level, heard a knock on the door. Probably Telkom, coming to connect the phone.

'Come in.'

A man opened the door, medium height, almost colourless hair, cut short.

'Mat Joubert?' he asked.

'That's right.'

He closed the door behind him, came closer, put out his hand. 'I am Lemmer.' The grip was strong.

Not Telkom's man, Joubert thought. There was something about the sinewy, physical ease, the watchfulness of the cool eyes that reminded him of a predator. He knew this sort. Mostly trouble. He had worked with them, he had arrested some, usually with difficulty.

The man reached for his pocket, took out a piece of paper and unfolded it – a newspaper clipping, which he held out. Joubert took it and looked at it.

Mystery over tracker deepens, the heading read. He recognised it, his name was also in it, more than a week ago.

'I have information,' Lemmer said.

Joubert looked up. 'You'll have to give that to the police.'

Lemmer shook his head. 'No.'

Joubert folded the clipping up again, gave it back to the man, walked to his chair. 'Then you'd better sit down.'

On the other side of the desk he took something else out of his pocket, put it down and pushed it closer to Joubert. 'Is that her?'

On semi-glossy paper, a photo of a young girl, torn out of a black-and-white publication, maybe a school yearbook because she was in uniform. The long black hair was held back with an Alice band, pretty face. The small smile betrayed a rebelliousness, a challenge.

Joubert picked it up in his big fingers, studied the features. Tried to compare it to the disfigured face he had seen at the shooting range in Atlantis. There was a strong resemblance.

'Maybe.'

'Did she have a small red birthmark, just behind her left ear?'

'I don't know.'

'Can you find out?'

Joubert nodded. 'I can. Did you know her?'

'No.'

Joubert looked up from the photo, querying.

'Her name is Helena Delfosse. She has the birthmark. She was last seen on the twenty-first of September in Nelspruit, at the clothing boutique where she works. In the presence of her cousin, Cornelia Johanna van Jaarsveld, also known as Flea. And I suspect Delfosse was in Loxton in the Bo Karoo some time during the night of September twenty-sixth to pick up Flea.'

Joubert studied the man again. 'How are you involved?'

The grey-green eyes drifted to the degree certificate on the wall. Then Lemmer got to his feet. 'You can keep the photo. Her parents' address is on the back.' He turned and walked to the door. With his hand on the knob he looked back. 'The newspaper didn't say what firearm was involved . . .'

Joubert did not react, just folded his arms.

He saw the glimmer of a suppressed smile on Lemmer's face, then the man came back slowly, put his hands on the back of the mahogany chair. 'I was in a truck with Flea van Jaarsveld for eighteen hours. Coincidence, chance circumstances. It was long enough for her to lie, cheat and steal from me. I went looking for her, to get my stuff back.'

Joubert folded his arms. 'And did you?'

'No.'

'What was her driver's licence doing in Delfosse's bag?

Lemmer deliberated before he answered. 'In Nelspruit they say Helena Delfosse was the tamer version of Flea – a little wild, a little rebellious, but never overboard. Just enough to be the favourite grandchild of her grandpa, big Frik Redelinghuys. The same grandfather who refused to recognise Flea. The cousins had no contact with each other the last ten years. Until August last year. When Flea walked into the boutique.'

'What are you saying?'

'I'm saying the driver's licence was no accident. With Flea nothing is accidental.'

Joubert digested that. Then he said: 'The firearm in the Atlantis case has been ballistically connected to the one that was found under the body of Mr Danie Flint near Mitchells Plain. It was a Beretta 92 Vertec.'

A shadow crossed Lemmer's face, unfathomable.

'Thank you.' And he walked back to the door.

Joubert began to understand. 'You're going to stay on her trail.'

'If I can find it.'

'You're looking for trouble.'

Lemmer opened the door. 'I don't look for it.' And just before he left: 'It finds me.'

BEST-SELLER'S SUCCESS BUILT ON RUMOURS OF TRUTH

Did Osama Bin Laden get medical treatment in South Africa?

'Nonsense,' says the publisher. 'It's pure fiction.' But the author refuses to comment, and expert opinion maintains that the success of the thriller, *A Theory of Chaos*, can be ascribed to the persistent rumours that writer Milla Strachan based it on the truth. The book recently became the number one best-seller in South Africa.

A photo of Strachan, a former housewife from Durbanville, appeared in the Sunday papers in October 2009, along with that of the missing former navy diver and anthropologist Lukas Becker. Becker was wanted at the time by the SAPS in connection with unspecified, serious crimes, and was described as 'armed and dangerous'. The authorities published a statement shortly afterwards, admitting that Strachan's supposed involvement was 'an administrative error', and offered her a public apology.

The book's main male character, Markus Blom, is an ex-soldier and archaeologist. The story is told from the perspective of a housewife from the Northern suburbs (Irma Prinsloo) who accepts a position at the now-disbanded Presidential Intelligence Agency – and is involved in an international terrorist plot where Osama Bin Laden is smuggled into South Africa for emergency medical treatment.